SHADOW TRAPPED—

Shadith woke to the smell of leather and herbs. She was kneeling on a rough plank floor, held there by men standing close to her. A light came on over her head. Blinding. A hand grabbed her hair, jerked her head up.

Someone came round a tall pile of crates. He bent over h_____ _____ _lid down the side of her face, the si__ _____ _____ ____ e hawk acid-etchec _____ ____ ____ ____ e murmured. ''Y___ ____ ____ ____ to me. Where is y___ ____

''I don't ____

''I said don't lie.'' Without str_____ _g from his semi-crouch, he turned his head, spoke to someone in the darkness. ''Get the probe, Kasedoc.''

''It's not a lie, it's not. He's somewhere around, but I don't know where. That's his gift. People don't see him. Or if they do, they forget what they saw. He doesn't trust anyone any more. Not us. Not anyone.''

He heard the terror in her voice, felt her desperate trembling, and believed her. He took his hand from her neck and stood erect. ''Then there is nothing more I need from you.'' He stepped into the darkness beyond the cone of light. ''Keep her here until sundown. If I haven't countermanded the order by then, shoot her. . . .''

JO CLAYTON
in DAW Books:

A BAIT OF DREAMS
SHADOW OF THE WARMASTER

SHADITH'S QUEST
SHADOWPLAY
SHADOWSPEER

THE DIADEM SERIES
DIADEM FROM THE STARS
LAMARCHOS
IRSUD
MAEVE
STAR HUNTERS
THE NOWHERE HUNT
GHOSTHUNT
THE SNARES OF IBEX
QUESTER'S ENDGAME

THE DUEL OF SORCERY TRILOGY
MOONGATHER
MOONSCATTER
CHANGER'S MOON

THE SOUL DRINKER TRILOGY
DRINKER OF SOULS
BLUE MAGIC
A GATHERING OF STONES

THE SKEEN TRILOGY
SKEEN'S LEAP
SKEEN'S RETURN
SKEEN'S SEARCH

JO CLAYTON
SHADOWSPEER

DAW BOOKS, INC.
DONALD A. WOLLHEIM, PUBLISHER
375 Hudson Street, New York, NY 10014

DAW Book Collectors No. 827.

First Printing, September 1990

1 2 3 4 5 6 7 8 9

PRINTED IN THE U.S.A.

SPEER: TO TRACE, TO ASK ABOUT,
TO MAKE TRACKS

I. OPENING MOVES
(Ginny wins on points)

TARGET VOALLTS KORLATCH

TZAYL 7
Capture crew on ground—Vivalyn the Zadys
(Capture Chief)
Capture ship in orbit—Rosshyn the Szajes
(Ship's Captain)

1

The camp was set up in scrub and red dust on an oval undulant plain, half a dozen matte-surfaced shelterdomes huddled together, raised alongside a brown and bleached local village, stick-and-mud domes inside a dessicated brush-and-stick fence connected to other fence circles where the local livestock slept off the tag end of night. In the distance, faded and abraded purple-brown hills gummed at a sky that during the day was red with continually circling dust clouds. The dawn wind was beginning to rise as it did every morning at this season, sweeping across the scrub plain, lifting more of the dust into traveling devils dancing in staggers across the flats.

A sled hummed from the mountains, cut a jigging devil in half and nosed through a dustpeller screen into an enclosed berth in the side of the workdome.

Yawning and scratching at her sleek silver-gray head-fur, Vivalyn the Zadys strolled into the comcenter. "Servoos, Maskay."

The young Dyslaerin tilted the swivel chair back, bending her neck until she was looking upside down at the newcomer. "Servoos, Viv. How's it go?"

"It stinks. Nothing in those hills worth putting psalt

1

on its tail. Unless the other team comes up with a poss, I say we undust and try the next system on the list.''

Maskay let the chair squeak upright. "Rosshyn up in the Hajautka, she'd agree, she's been paitshing at me the past hour, she thinks this world's on a par with toxic waste, she says why don't you find somewhere with pretty beaches. Just once, huh?''

"Never satisfied, is she? I gave her beaches last time.''

Maskay giggled. "Yeh, I remember. Very nice they were, with sandworms all mouth and carnivorous crabs the size of young houses.''

Vivalyn strolled over and scanned the instrumentation. "Report time again. Ondue. I see you've set the line for us.''

"Right. Two hours on. I thought I'd lay in a hiatus for a confa.''

"Practicing for your own team, huh?''

"Why not? I notice you came up comside, cousin.''

Vivalyn slicked her hand over the girl's hot-copper headfur. "Why not, indeed.'' She stepped back. "Put me through to Sotarys, May. Likely she's in by now since she's working daylight, should be near sunset that side the world.''

2

The red sun crept up and the whine of the wind grew louder.

The village woke and the locals began moving through their day lives; they were a sullen stolid lot, built for endurance rather than beauty, stubbornly peaceful and self-enclosed, not so much tolerating the offworlders as ignoring them.

Inside the workdome Vivalyn the Zadys comtalked with Rosshyn the Szajes, setting up the outline of the next day's departure while she waited for the Calltime to Spotchals. ". . . to zeta Hyronix, then that stargroup in the Aradica Arm, then over to Shavonari Pit where we transfer cargo, if any—let's hope Luck won't be quite so stingy on our next dips—and treat ourselves to a few days

R&R, sorry Ross, no beaches at a Pit unless you count the sensi shows.''

The monitor showed Rosshyn the Szajes pulling an inverted grin and twitching her ears. "We'll make do, Viv. I got a inventive crew. When do you want. . . .''

The monitor went blank, the speaker crackled with a sudden burst of noise.

"What. . . . May?''

"I don't know. . . .'' Maskay swore. "Incoming some. . . .'' she stabbed her hand at the domeshield activator, but it was too little, too late.

3

After they buried their own dead, the locals gathered to stare into the blackened glassy crater where the strangers' camp had been.

TARGET VOALLTS KORLATCH

PILLACARIODA PIT
Capture Crew at R&R
Nightcrawler Cobben from Helvetia

1

To the Coryfe, Cobben Nerlkyss/HIT LIST
1. Capture Chief: Dyslaeror, has a weakness for sensi, dangerous at other times. Wait until he is under; take first if possible.
2. Capture Specialist: this particular Crew has three—A Dyslaeror too good at his job to be trapped easily. ?Sniper? If so, take last to avoid alarming the others.—Two Grydeggins, these being lanky canids, six limbed, highly developed noses, taste. Unpredictable and dangerous, hard to drug but susceptible to alcohol. Minimum of two operatives—if necessary to work through surrogates, remove surrogates before departure.
3. Xenobiologist: From one of the cousin races, standard type, reticent about the world of his origin, physiology unknown, poison therefore uncertain, mechanical means necessary, what is known about him suggests considerable care in approach. ?Net-and-electrocute?
4. Ecologist: Spotchallix, should offer little difficulty, known to like variety and change in female companionship during R&R.
5. Logistics Specialist: This Crew has a Master (Javitand) and four Apprentices (Hallgats), all young Dyslaeror.
   The Javitand is a cranky ancient, an adoptee from the Foglala clan of Csilldys 4/Dysstrael; take care around him, word is he is a bloody old monster capable of ripping the guts out of anyone foolish enough to get

4

close when he is smoking geezert which he starts the minute he hits a Pit. Since he won't let anyone near him, you'll have to work at a distance.

?Sniper? If so, you will have to make the hit at the same time as the one on the Capture Specialist, otherwise there will be too much Noise for safe Work.

2

SEVENTH DAY IN THE DEKADIURNE OF PILLA-CARIODA, (LUCK DAY to the superstitious):

Vanassorn the Zadant lay sprawled across the water mattress, his eyes closed, the sensi-net fitting like a second skin over his head and his broad hard-muscled body. His ears twitched, twitches moved in waves along that body as he dreamed: *running across a hot yellow plain, the scent of the yrz herd like musk in his nostrils.*

The cell door opened, a small wiry man dressed as an attendant slipped in. He crossed to the bed, took a needlenose popper from a slit in his sleeve. Working carefully, he eased its fine glass tube through the net field until he had the end resting on the Dyslaeror's inner elbow, then he triggered the poisonshot and watched for results.

The sleeper shuddered, his breath caught in his throat, then he started a rapid panting.

The assassin smiled with satisfaction, slid the popper back in its sheath and went quietly out.

3

She was small and sleek, dark hair, dark eyes, dusky skin, quietly sensual. She touched Tenekiloff's wrist, her fingertips caressing, soft, leaving small warm spots as she took her hand away. The Ecologist blinked at her, smiled foolishly, then followed her into the twilight of a privacy alcove.

When he reached for the drink pad, she stopped him, flattened his hand on the table, moved her fingertips around and around his palm. So suddenly he hadn't time to react, she sank her fingernails into his flesh; they were razor sharp, there was no pain, only four small cuts. She slid from the banc and vanished into the murk of the bar before he recovered enough to protest.

He sat staring at the tiny curved cuts beaded with blood, finally decided he'd better get something done about them. He tried to stand; he couldn't. His tongue swelled and went numb. His eyes blurred, then he couldn't see anything.

Sometime later, annoyed at the man for hogging the alcove, a bar patron shook him, then gagged, jumped back and yelled for the manager.

4

The net came out of nowhere, whipped around Perdo the Xenobiologist's top half. He dropped backward, twisted as he fell, nearly escaped the trap, but the pair holding the leashes sent a massive charge through the web strands and fried his head.

5

Argao and Kutyoh chased each other through the miniature hills of the Chassedrome, giggling like fools, so drunk they kept losing track of their legs, a serious lapse in a hexapod, and went tumbling in knots down the grassy slopes. It was very late in the Pit's arbitrary Night cycle so there were few patrons in the Drome, even the Grydeggins weren't so much hunting as playing.

After a long night of chasing each other and sparring with other patrons, their energy levels were low and their flasks were almost empty. With triplestrength a'hiwai purpling their tongues and wiping away any alertness they might still have possessed, they lay in a cosy dell, sucking at the drink tubes and watching without much interest as a pair of slight wiry figures in black hunt fatigues and leather vizards came trotting along the path.

Moving with a quickness that was too easy on the eye to register as such, the newcomers split apart, dropped beside the recumbent Grydeggins and flipped Menaviddan nooses over their heads.

6

In their fourbed restroom, the Dyslaeror apprentices were sleeping with the fervor of healthy youth, having exhausted their purses and their imaginations during the past seven days.

Dressed in the veils and glittersilk of Kantella courtesans, two small dusky females wiped the lock without triggering the crude alarm and slipped inside the room. They worked silently, efficiently, were out, relocking the door, five minutes later.

7

Borszastag the Javitand came out of his restroom, banged loudly on the next door over, then went down the slidestair without waiting for an answer from his apprentices. As was his custom, he lowered himself into a chair on the terrace of the hostel's eating place and lit a stib of geezert as he sat watching the official arrival of morning, a rainbow flow of color like the play of light across a diffraction grating as the polarity of the Shell shifted to its Day setting.

He blinked suddenly, stiffened, then plopped over, his face in the fruit slices, a sniperdart sticking like a small stub from the back of his head.

Half the Pit away, Capture Specialist Udvarorrn came from the Vervhus limp and sore from his night's exertions; he stretched, yawned. The yawn sagged into a witless gape, his eyes opened wide, went blank. He sprawled on the walkway, a sniperdart sticking like a small stub from the back of his head.

LIST CLOSED.
SATISFACTORY.
COBBEN RETURNED BASE (The City/Helvetia)

QUERY: NEXT OPERATION?

TARGET VOALLTS KORLATCH

SPOTCHALS (Jorbar 14). SPOTCH HELSPAR:
world capitol
Meeting: Transfer Station, synchronous orbit
above Spotch Helspar
Miralys, Rohant, Lissorn,
Dyslaerin Zimaryn (eldest aunt to Miralys, chief
aide)
Dyslaror Sotabaern (uncle/cousin in third
degree, Miralys' chief bodyguard)
Shadith, Kikun

1

Miralys tapped her claws seriatim on the brushed steel of
the lokcase. The small ticks fell like hail into the tense
silence. "Tzayl 7," she said tightly. "Report Ondue.
Line cleared. Vivalyn. Experienced Zadys, one of the
best at opening new worlds. Time came, nothing. We
couldn't even raise an echo. I sent out a scoutrat, zapped
it over tripletime. There's a hole in the ground where the
camp was and a ring of dust instead of a ship. That was
the first one. In spite of being warned to watch for trouble, next three months two more Crews missed Ondue. I
sent scoutrats each time. No Crew. No ship. Sometimes
there was debris, sometimes not. This morning another
Ondue failed. I imagine the rat reports are waiting for
me downbelow. Someone is getting into our files or listening to our transmissions to Field. Or both. I have
checked security and checked it again and I have ordered
another look this morning. I expect the same nothing!"
She slapped her hands on the table, gazed at the inverted
vees of fine bronze hair on their backs. "Last month the
Hoddj of Pillacarioda Pit informed us we had eleven bodies in his freezer. Come get them, he said, and if you

9

ered. Half a dozen different ways. MO suggests it was a
Nightcrawler cobben from Helvetia. Paid a bonus to go
offworld. Which is an appalling indication of the funding
back of these attacks. Worst of all. One week ago. A
shipment coming in. Voallts Korlatch Transport. The
Nyaralo Ous. The Szejant being one Halevant.'' Her hot
gold eyes went from Shadith to Kikun to the others sitting
round the table. ''My halfsib. Not brilliant, but steady.
Careful. Dependable. Spite of that, someone got to Foltsorn the cargo chief. A cousin. Ours. Someone must have
dangled a moon of gold in front of his twitchy nose, even
he wasn't fool enough to sell his honor for slop. He let
someone put bombs in two of the transport cages. He
rode the Shuttle down with them, then he ran. We have
declared him Unmate and Cursed. Kinkiller. I sent word
home to Dysstrael and the Council. No argument from
them. Five adults, ten children . . .'' her voice broke,
but she quickly regained control and went on, ''ten children dead, seven children badly maimed, they'll need
treatment on a meatfarm and mindwork so they can deal
with what they saw, what happened to them. Sixty percent of the resident beasts killed outright or so badly
maimed they had to be destroyed. A number of others
escaped and caused damage to twenty-three citizens and
several properties which we will have to pay for. It could
have been worse; we might have been completely wiped
out, but one of the bombs didn't go off. Faulty chip in
the detonator. Preliminary indications, detonators and
other materiel associated with several merc supply
houses. There's no Tradewar registered with Spotchals
Business Bureau, so we don't have to escrow an indem-
nity fund, but the Bureaucrats are annoyed and talking
seriously about rescinding our License to Trade if we
can't assure them that such a disaster won't happen again.
Someone is intruding and attacking us. It's reasonably
clear who that someone is.'' Her claws ticked on the
table's hardwood, small angry sounds. ''Ginbiryol Seyirshi. Who else could buy teams of assassins and two or
more merc attack forces, who else would have reason for
such free-handed scattering of funds? When I got your

call, Rohant, I set Digby the Tracer pulling in whatever
he could find on Seyirshi.'' She opened the lokcase, took
out several folders of faxsheets and three flakereaders,
gave them to Zimaryn who distributed them to Rohant,
Kikun and Shadith. ''Lissorn has already been through
these. I'll summarize. One. There are rumors of a new
Limited Edition soon available. *Revenge of the Avatars.*''

Shadith looked at the folder and felt sick.

''Two. An extended explanation for the attacks on us,
including a history of similar actions. It seems Seyirshi
has a reputation for creative vindictiveness. Anyone
crossing our Ginny, she ends up dead or wishing she was.
According to the report Rohant ratted ahead to me, the
three of you managed to thwart him in at least part of his
plans for Kiskai; he wouldn't love you for that. And
Voallts Korlatch refused to deal with his agent over the
Ri-tors and the worldlist. Digby thinks he took the refusal
as an insult. I concur.''

Rohant pushed back from the table and began prowling
about the room, his dreadlocks bushed out, anger musk
boiling off him.

Miralys waited a moment for him to comment; when
he said nothing, she went on. ''Three. Digby has compiled a tentative list of Seyirshi's customers. Not for the
ordinary snuff shows, too many of them, too many out-
lets. Digby went for the buyers of the Limited Editions.
So far he can't guarantee any of the names—except one.
He got confirmation this morning. I don't have details of
how it was done, but Digby's always reliable on this sort
of thing so I didn't push him, he doesn't like to uncover
his sources. The Confirmed Buyer is one Wargun
Muk'hasta dan Fevkindadam, Head of the Family Fevkinda. Chissoku Bogmak. Seventh planet, Yildakeser
System. Digby promises more names certified by the end
of the week, but it's going to be a slow operation and a
costly one. Lives and money. He's already lost two operatives. The Buyers are protecting their reputations. A
taste for death's about as savory as pond scum and snuff
flakes are sordid. Nothing more vicious than the respect-
able saving face.'' She mimed fastidious distaste, ears

flicking, corners of her mouth pulled down. "They're a powerful covey of mokhas, you'll see that when you read the names, they can afford a lot of whitewash. Talking about what's affordable and not, we need to decide how much of our resources are expended where, Ciocan. We can't opt out so we can't waste credit; it's a fight to the death and we have to make every florint count. There's no way we can match Seyirshi's backstash." She shut the folder, dropped it on the table. "That's it. Simple enough, isn't it. We get him or he gets us."

Rohant pulled his chair out, sat down. "Four ships gone, maybe five, maybe more by now. That's not a drain, that's a hemorrhage. Exactly how bad is the damage from the bomb?"

2

The edgy abrasion between the two alpha Dyslaera was scraping at Shadith's nerves. Both of them were angry and upset and there was an added stressor, Miralys was moving into her season; the pull on Rohant was tidal and growing. They were a lifepair, mated near to thirty years, in storm and calm, half a dozen kits, the bond between them as much memory as passion, both memory and passion operating powerfully at this moment. They'd been separated for more than a year with Rohant in serious danger and Miralys frantically trying to locate him and this was their first meeting, a public greeting, restrained to the point of absurdity—all business on the outside, but underneath the efficient surface a mess of churning emotion that tended to peak every few minutes and break through the barriers Aleytys had been teaching Shadith to put up on the long trip from Kishkai to Spotchals, barriers between her growing Talent and the chaotic world outside.

She felt like baggage again and played with the notion that she'd made a mistake allying herself to the Dyslaera, not a real quarrel with the situation, only a venting of her irritation at sitting silent for so long. When Rohant was one Dyslaera as Kikun was one dinhast and she was one whatever she was, she was a partner with considerable say in what they did.

Now that Rohant was back among his kind, she was shut out.

The Dyslaera weren't doing it deliberately, there were just too many of them here.

She thought about Kikun, caught hold of the tail of that thought before it slipped away under the influence of his peculiar Talent, looked around at the dinhast.

He smiled at her, the corners of his mouth curling up, the soft folds of gray-green skin that hung from prominent cheekbones lifting and squeezing together, his eyes narrowing to orange slits. His long thin hands were folded over his diaphragm and he was leaning back, enjoying the show. His smile invited her to relax and enjoy with him. She sighed.

3

A lull.

Rohant smoothed a thumbclaw along his mustache; he looked congested about the eyes, his hair was bushed out as if he'd put starch in his dreadlocks. Miralys' ears were pressed flat against her head; her nostrils were flaring; there were patches of red over her cheekbones; her breathing was a series of snorts.

Shadith lost patience. She sat up straight, slapped her hand on the table, breaking into the taut contest between the two alphas.

They started, turned to stare at her, Rohant raising a brow, Miralys looking affronted.

"This is wasting my time. Maybe not yours, but mine for sure. And Kikun's." Shadith flicked the report with her forefinger. "You told us all we needed to know an hour ago when you gave us the Buyer's name. The rest of this is your business, Ro, not ours."

Rohant held his hand up, silencing Miralys for the moment—and with her, the others. "All right, Shadow." He smiled affectionately at her, his tearing teeth carefully covered. He hadn't changed, so he didn't see that every-

thing else had. "Don't blow out your backtrail. What are
you on at?"

Shadith took a deep breath, let it out slowly. "We've
got some wiggle room, Ro. We're fools if we waste it.
Ginny probably still thinks we're dead, but that won't last
long. We could play dead, but it's not worth the effort.
Anyway, we can't out-labyrinth him. You know that.
Waste of energy trying it. He's got more kinks in his
thoughtpath than a worm on Acid. Only time we got anywhere was when we smashed ahead as hard and as fast
as we could." She closed her eyes for a moment, irritated
by the blank Dyslaera faces, the gold Dyslaera eyes staring at her. "He's busy now," she said, claws in her voice
if she didn't have any on her fingers, "working on his
production, putting it together, leaving the hits to surrogates. I want to lay a line on him before he wakes up
enough to know he's being got at."

"I see."

"Caught the habit from Aste, eh? I see. I see. I see.
Hah!"

"Stop fooling, Shadow. Talk about wasting time."

"Step by step, then." She waggled her forefinger.
"University first." I've got connections there. I'll pick
up the langue and whatever else I can get on . . . what
was that world?" She flipped through the fax sheets.
"Chissoku Bogmak." Two fingers. "Next, jump in. See
what I can find there. Lee left me a bag of tricks which
should be useful once I can get at . . . um . . . Wargun."
She remembered the dinhast again, touched his arm.
"Kikun, come along if you want."

His eyes went suddenly wide, his hands beat softly at
the tabletop, drumming a quick heart-rhythm. "It is the
road. It is the road. Yes." He winked at her. "Can't keep
me out, Twiceborn."

Rohant dug in his mustache with his thumbclaw; the
corners of his mouth twitched up. "To coin a phrase, I
see. Right as usual, Shadow." He exchanged a long hot
stare with Miralys who was getting restless as this cross-
talk proceeded; she subsided once more, but her patience

talk proceeded; she subsided once more, but her patience
had visible limits and he acknowledged them by getting
to the point. "I'll be coming with you, me and Sassa."

Shadith managed a smile. "So it's hey-ho and Ginny
watch your ass. Sure, come along."

Myralis' claws cut grooves in the wood. "Ciocan!"

"We'll talk in private, Toerfeles." Another eyeclash.
"Give us a minute more, it's almost finished. Tell us the
rest, Shadow."

"All right, I'll throw my florint in." She set the reader
on the folder, aligned them with the table's edge. "Your
mindset's wrong. Even yours, Rohant, and you should
know better. You're thinking business, all of you Voallts.
Assets and liabilities. Efficiency and optimums. Sar!"
She paused, raised a brow as Miralys started to protest.
The Toerfeles settled for a glare.

"I've spent the last half hour listening to you argue.
You haven't got it, any of you. Ginny's going to kill you
all. This isn't business, it's survival. Forget about efficiency and the rest of that gunge. When you're scrambling to stay alive nothing counts but that, staying alive."
She cleared her throat, fingered the fax sheets. "You need
money. That's a weapon, you've got that right at least.
The Tracer Digby seems good value, except you're wasting him. What does it matter if those names are confirmed or not? Obviously, you've got to keep some of
your teams out, working. Call in the rest, all you can
spare. They've got skills that should transfer to capturing
people. Use Digby's ops to do what you're not so good
at. If he'll play. Set up new teams, three, four of your
people on each, them doing the slogwork with one of the
Tracer's operatives directing them. Pick the likeliest
names from that list—no, the closest to hand, that's better—and go after them, as many as you have teams to
cover. If a team hits a dry hole, pull them out and try
another. Uh-mm . . . another point to consider: the auction almost certainly won't be down any gravity well, but
it will be someplace solidly established with more than
one back door. You know our Ginny, Ro."

"Um . . ." She chewed her lip, stared past Rohant's

head at the expensively paneled wall, madura wood from
Telffer—which reminded her of the woman she'd met at
Quale's place. "I suggest you get Adelaris Security in to
go over your systems. They're expensive but not so expensive as paying damages and losing assets. I'll give
you a note to Aici Arash; she's usually booked for years
ahead, but she owes me a favor and I think she'll make
time. Um . . . have Digby send someone down the merc
market. I'll give you the names of three mercs who've
worked for Ginny. They might or might not be alive . . .
it doesn't matter, you could backtrack them anyway, locate people they talked to, that sort of thing. That
amounts to . . . what? about half a dozen lines at him.
Think survival and work them all." She sat back and
sketched a smile. "I'm betting us Three, we'll get there
first." It was a heavy-handed attempt to dissipate the
prickly heat in the air around her and fell as flat as it
deserved. She shrugged and shut up.

Miralys stood. "Ciocan, I must remind you. . . ."
She broke off, struggling to subdue her temper so she
wouldn't embarrass herself in front of outsiders. She
turned to face Shadith and Kikun. "If you will wait in
the anteroom, please? Lissorn, Zimaryn, Sotabaern, you
also, I'll speak to you later. Ciocan, we have to talk."

Kikun blinked. Laughter like warm water filled him
and spilled over into Shadith, though she didn't understand what he found so amusing in this confusion. She
got to her feet and circled round to Rohant. "Ciocan."
She closed her hand on his forearm, felt the tension in
his muscles. "There's not much point in Kikun and me
hanging around, but you've got things to do here so why
don't you meet us on University? Don't say anything now.
Think about it. I'll be at the ottotel booking passage on
the first ship I can find going there nonstop. Coming,
Kikun?

II. WHITESIDE IN PLAY
(Ginny in abeyance)

CHISSOKU BOGMAK, KARINTEPE (the world
    capitol)
local time: 63-Kirar (63rd month in the reign
                of the Kralodate Kirar)
             Sorizakre (Name of the Great
             Year—84.3 years standard—taken
                from the House reigning for this
                particular Great year)
             day 14 (of a 30 day month)
             hour 15 (of a 26 hour day), early
                        afternoon
Pikka Machletta and the Razor T'gurtt

1

Pikka Machletta walked into Old Town, elbows out,
shoulders swinging.

An ivory-handled cutthroat razor, folded shut at the
moment, dangled from a snapclamp on chains triple studded into her left ear. Fann beside her and the other four
t'gurtsas weaving through side streets in prowling pairs
wore razors like that though hers was the only ivory one.

There was a wide leather band about her neck, stiff
and black with pointed studs hammered into it and a
leather arm-and-knuckle guard on her left arm, also black
and stiff and studded.

Her right arm was bare to the shoulder; slivers of
brushed steel were bonded to her fingernails.

She wore a tubetop with one sleeve, black and shiny,
hugging a torso like an adolescent boy's; her trousers
were loose, fold on fold of black wool hanging from nar-

17

row hips, tucked casually into the tops of limber black
boots zipped tight to her calves.

Her straight black hair was waxed into quills, held out
of her eyes by leather thongs slip-knotted over her right
ear, the four ends passing through lead line-weights.

Her eyes were an astonishing blue in a face with bold
but elegant bones and a matte olive skin, a rigid face
trained to resolute immobility. She gave nothing for free
not even a smile. Fifteen years standard surviving in Old
Town had taught her that, though her mother lived long
enough to protect her through Winter's End and Thaw,
the first nine of that fifteen. The next three or so she was
a child whore; at puberty she was thrown out and left to
find her own living.

Her eyes moving constantly, flickers of blue and fugi-
tive gleams of wet white in the yellow incandescence of
the Old Town bulbs, Pikka Machletta walked along the
Raba Katir, elbows out, shoulders swinging. Fann walked
beside her, smaller and wilder, two years older.

The t'gurtsa Second had thick black hair, straight and
fine; it hung to her knees when she let it loose. Most
times she wore it braided into a club which she would
either leave hanging down or pin on top her head with
forked pins whose knobs were set with pseudo diamonds,
whose razor tips were cased in flimsy sheaths that came
off instantly if she jerked the pins loose; the knobs were
on the left because she was left-handed. The T'gurtt
totem-razor, redwood handle, swung from her right ear;
she wore heavy rings on her fingers with barbed and
pepper-painted bezels (the better to mess up anyone she
hit) and a chain wound around her right arm, weapon
and defense in one.

Her trousers were three-way stretch, clinging to her
long slim legs, one leg green the other crimson, and she
wore a loose, blousy tunic with narrow green and gold
stripes; jewel colors head to toe shimmered in the shifting light while the pdiamond knobs threw off sharp white
sparks.

She had delicate, lovely features that no one ever noticed because dark purple splotches were spattered across

her pale pale skin and a white, puckered scar cut through one eye and jagged past her mouth.

Pikka Machletta and Fann her Second bopped along the Raba Katir, whistling a song called *Perfumed Nights,* that month's favorite, Fann elaborating on the melody and Pikka doing harmony.

Ingra and Mem moved parallel to them on a street to the left, flashing T'gurtt signs with hand mirrors as they moved past cross streets and were momentarily visible; Kynsil and Hari moved parallel to them on a street to the right, the T'gurtt guarding itself as always.

Letting Fann whistle alone, Pikka Machletta counted side streets aloud: "Teggil, Eggel, Unagatyl." She stopped at the corner of Trinagil to drop a guim in the bowl of the round little monk begging there. " 'Roi, Kaoyurz. What do tha' night?"

"Bless, O sister." Kaoyurz sang the shidduah with a grace-smile in his fluent tenor voice, giving the syllables full value despite the meager status of the donor; he had a fondness for the Razor T'gurtt, they'd done him more favors than one. " 'Roa, Razoort, Starstreet be full and runnin ov-ar. Lot of hoshyid t' Fair tha' night, ready fer drunk and dip. And Bouni Vissin's *Steam Coaster* come in with a load o' fancies and a heavy thirst. And word is Goyo mean to slum tha Fair so watch thy backs, young sh'kiz."

"Nara, Kaoy." She dropped another coin in the bowl, made an awkwardly graceful yayyay that sent the razor swaying and the lead weights on her head thongs tunking against each other. "May Guintayo She-Who-Burns grow you three for one." She looked both ways along Trinagit, whistled and waited until her sisters-in-T'gur came drifting toward the Raba Katir, then she and Fann her second went swaggering on, talking idly, minding their own business, threading through the thickening crowd of strollers and shoppers.

As they passed by one of the teahouses, a man came elbowing up to them, a tall thin type with a shaved head and blue tattoos, a starman wandering off Starstreet, arrogant in his assurance of superiority and his skill in

negotiation. Ignoring Fann, he dropped his hand on Pikka
Machletta's arm, jerked a thumb at the teahouse. "Come
Upper, Pretty. Let's party."

She snatched her arm free, whipped around to face
him.

Fann stepped away from her, ready to mind back if
minding were needed, her eyes skittering about, searching for City Police who'd haul them to jail and forced
labor mostly for being a T'gurtt and handy to blame for
any trouble with visitors.

The locals faded away despite the congestion, leaving
a wide opening around the stranger and the two t'gurtsas.
The rest of the T'gurtt clustered on the walkway, ready
to move if needed.

Pikka's face froze, her voice shook with anger and
scorn. "How tha Hell you got the nerve to come up to
me thinking I gonna let you jogga me ov-ah how you
want?"

"Cumma cumma, pig, how much?" He rubbed thumb
against fingers, grinning at her, treating her words like
windbreaking.

"Sssaaa!" She swept the razor loose, flicked it open
and leaped at him.

"Hey!" He jumped back, clutched at a hand spurting
blood where his thumb had been. "What? What?"

"Cumma cumma, mamajogga. Say't again. You think
you sooo bad. Say't again." She shook the blood off the
razor and bared her teeth at him. "Cumma cumma ov-
ah here, jigjog. You wantta party, les party."

"Up your ass, you whore," he shrieked. "A doctor.
Where's a doctor? I want a doctor."

"You a big man, whyn't you come ov-ah here, I stick
it up yours. Party, party."

He wouldn't look at her; blundering into tables, followed by curses and fist shaking as he crunched down on
feet in his way, knocked over pots and bowls, he plunged
into the teahouse, still shouting for a doctor.

Pikka Machletta wiped the razor on her trousers, swung
it shut and squeezed it into the snapclamps, took a step
after him.

Fann slapped her arm. "Hari flashing Police round corner, coming this way. Some kanch whistle on us."

2

The T'gurtt slid hastily down a side street and into a tenement, climbing to the fourth floor where an electronics factory was squealing and fuming along in a half-floor apartment. They eased behind some crates piled outside the factory, crouched in a dusty doorless closet.

Pikka clapped hands with the others; Fann sat back, contented and silent, listening to her sisters-in-T'gur giggle and joke over the starman.

Sobering, Pikka said, "What y' get, Ing?"

Ingra dragged open the drawstrings of her dittabag and thrust a hand inside. "We cleaned the Goomoo, Pikk. Look." She pulled out an energy gun. "Goom won't report this gone, he get his skin peeled they knew he brought it off Starstreet." She giggled. "Look, he got a vibraknife, too." She laid the black rod beside the gun. "Thought he king a tha world with all this. Wah!"

"What he have in his cre-belt, Mem?"

"Not much." Mem was tall and thin, so colorless she might have been albino though her eyes were ice-gray, not pink. She was thirteen and still growing, afraid she'd never stop; in her more extravagant flights of fancy she stalked across the Land on seven-league legs. Apt to trip over shadows and bang her head on any projection around, she was awkward in every way except with her hands; she'd studied brush painting from the moment she could hold a handle. Before he was killed in a pressgang sweep, her offworld father taught her how to grind ink and set her to interminable exercises which she did with the enthusiasm of first love. She was ten when he died and would have died herself—he was her only kin and an offworlder besides—so there was no one obliged to care for her and no one willing until she stumbled into Pikka's notice, joined the T'gurtt and put her improbable deftness of finger to work picking pockets. She upended her dittabag and sent coin rolling everywhere. Fann tutted,

Pikka and Ingra grinned, Kynsil and Hari scrambled after
the errant cash.

Ingra at sixteen was the laughing one, chunky and
freckled, with fine brown hair she kept cut short and
greenish-brown eyes in a round, pretty face; she was the
second best dip, deft in her movements and strong despite the birth defects that left her with multiply jointed
arms and two-fingered hands with stubby thumbs, a pa-
riah who whistle-baited ill-wishers and went her cheerful
way.

Kynsil and Hari were eleven, half sisters though they
might have been twins they were so alike—their mothers
had been the mistresses of some nameless Goyo (they
never saw him, had no idea who he was). They were
small and dark and quiet except when they were giggling.
Kynsil used her face instead of her voice and was elo-
quent in her silent way. Hari was her shadow, doing everything she did as if strings tied their limbs together.
They piled up the coins beside the vibraknife, then sat
on their heels and waited for Pikka to tell them what next.

Pikka Machletta frowned at the unsteady piles. "Not
much. Fann, count 'em and give us each some to blow
tha night. Mem, he have a cre-card?"

Mem nodded, scraped back the white-blonde hair falling across her eyes. "I dropped that down cinerator next
the shop." Her rare smile lit her face. "I really did,
Pikk-luv. It really did go in and down, no one's tracking
us with that."

"Good." She took the coins Fann held out to her,
flipped a guim to Mem who got to her feet and set it on
a high shelf as a grat for the worker who had dibs on the
space, pushed the rest into the hidabelt behind her
trouserband. "Fann, y' bring these," she tapped a nail-
sliver on the gun hilt, "we'll go see Tuck the Tick. I
don't care if that Goomoo can't raise a stink, I wanna
shuck this trouble. Ing, you'n the others, y' go on to the
Fair, see what y' can spot. Don't touch till Fann 'n me
we get there wi' the futaks. Y' hear me?" She waited as
they wiggled and made faces but finally nodded; they
knew the rules and the risks. "Hit the Mirror Court every

twenty minutes or so, Fann and me, we'll pick y' up there soonest.'' She waved Hari and Kynsil out first as troublescouts, followed with the others when the Half-twins whistled the all-clear.

3

day 14, hour 19

Pikka Machletta, Fann beside her, stopped beside the Blurdslang Alley, jigged from foot to foot and watched the moon Myara slide through wispy clouds so she wouldn't have to look at Herv and Bugeye and Prettybutt of Dragon Torkkus while she waited for their boss Kidork and his Second Mordo to buy their futaks off the Blurdslang.

The NightFair started at sundown and ended at Mompri-set. This was month 63-Kirar, the 14th day, so moon Mompri wouldn't be setting until hour 6 tomorrow morning. There was plenty of time for prospecting the Fair, but she didn't much like waiting. She clicked her tongue and snapped her fingers in counterpoint to the ti-tunk of her bootheels on the pavement, shifted her scowl from the moon to the dark mouth of the alley, ignoring the jinsbek standing there like a doorbeast totem carved out of stone, ignoring, too, the comments Bugeye was passing to Herv. She didn't like them, she didn't like Kidork, she didn't like anything about Dragon Torkkus.

Back in month 91-Atsui (Atsui the Soused to the folk in Old Town), the very same month when Atsui was killed in the duel with his stepson Kirar the present Kralodate, Kidork and his toady that slimesac Mordo and the rest of that turdy lot cornered a pair of six year olds with some gangrape in mind. Pikka, Fann, and Ingra happened on the scene. Bugeye lost a hunk of his butt to Fann's razor and Pretty walked round with chainmarks on his face for a month after, couldn't party like he wanted to celebrate the Change. Kidork was missing a thumb and two fingers from that fight, though Pikka'd gone for his throat; when she thought about it, which was almost never, she regretted her foot slipping right then. No matter, the Razor

T'gurtt got two new members, Hari and Kynsil. It was a
good mark for a new Kralodache, made her think she had
some Luck coming under Kirar. The 91 months under
Atsui's rule had been disaster for her family and her.

Pikka Machletta watched warily as Kidork and Mordo
came out with their futaks pinned to their sleeves, but
the Dragons ignored her and Fann. They handed around
the rest of the metal squares and went off trailing boasts
and laughter.

Pikka flipped a finger at them, bounced a sass-spiced
yayyay at the jinsbek, walked past him, elbows out,
shoulders swinging. She knocked at the wicket at the end
of the alley, losing her swagger as it slid open and the
Blurdslang looked moistly out at her. "A'sat'hroi, Oow-
alu Toop," she said, her voice subdued, respectful. "I
bring Roush and the workfee for tonight." She yayyayed
again, produced the pouch with the Roush (one sixth of
the cash she'd gotten for the two weapons, the Sirshak-
kai's cut) and piled beside it the six guims for the futaks
that let them work the NightFair without being tossed out
by any jinsbek that took a notion to do it.

An oozing spotted tentacle wrapped around the pouch,
suckers squishing wetly as they sealed onto the shiny
leather surface, another looped around the guims and
dragged them into the darkness. The wicket closed.

Pikka waited, sliding the fingers of her right hand along
and along her waistband.

Fann stood silent beside her, facing back along the
alley, watching the Fairgoers move past. She stiffened,
swallowed a gasp.

"What?" Pikka muttered.

"Later."

The wicket opened again. A tentacle tip pushed six
futaks at Pikka.

She yayyayed with care and took them, suppressing as
she always did her disgust at the cold slick surfaces. They
weren't slimy, not really, but she could feel slime anyway. She tacked one to her sleeve, handed the others to
Fann. Then she pulled her swagger back on like a jacket
she'd dropped and sauntered down the alley. " 'Nara,

Zassh.'' She flicked her fingers at the jinsbek, grinned into his scowl and strutted into the Raba Katir.

Fann pushed her into the shadows near the wall of Shiintap Tenement. ''Headdown time. Y' want to know what bit me?''

''Dragons come back?''

''Na. The Goomoo, the one you cut.''

''Huh?''

''Him and three maybe four friends, they go jiggin past, I figure he lookin for you. Goin to get him back some face.'' She giggled. ''He thiiink.''

''Koyohk!''

''Ay-yeh. Gonna be one of 'em watching the Gate. Least one.''

Pikka chewed at a hangnail and watched the foot traffic flood past. ''You think he fool enough to ignore this?'' The metal fauxnail on her right forefinger clinked as she tapped the futak tacked to her sleeve.

''Stargoo, an't he? He probably don' know.''

''Whatcha think, we whistle a jinsbek?''

''Could.''

''Na. I got 'n idea. Just come to me.'' She blinked, giggled. ''Look a that, Fann, that rush of marks coming, what a mishmash, you could even lose ol' Blurdslang in that lot. Les go, we pass the Gate in the middle of them and if the Goo he sees us, he can't do nothin. Ri'? Ri'.''

ON THE WORLDSHIP KEZZEDVA DINNYEE IN PASSAGE FROM UNIVERSITY TO CHISSOKU BOGMAK
Shadith, Rohant, Kikun

1

Rohant dropped three coins on the table, a Chissoku guim, a Spotchallix zurst, a copper florint.

She looked at them, cocked a brow at him. "Got it all thought out, huh?"

"Don't want to spend the next three days arguing. Pick one." After Kikun set a fingertip on the silver guim and Shadith took the zurst (feeling momentarily sentimental, zursts being mixed up in the beginning of this business), Rohant slid the florint off the table, balanced it on his retracted thumbclaw. "Odd one goes down first," he said and snapped the florint into the air.

The coins wheeled up, clattered down on the table: heads heads heads.

Kikun smiled lazily. "Luck says we go together."

Shadith snorted. "Then Luck's a dork. Let's go again."

This time Rohant's florint was odd out. He tucked it in his belt and leaned back while the others called for second, dragging his claws through his mustache, his eyes slits of satisfaction, irids gone red in the glow of the artificial light.

Shadith inspected the zurst. "Looks like I'm the tail on this dog." She wiggled her nose. "Hmh!"

2

The worldship *Kezzedva Dinnyee* surfaced and swept insystem like a moon on the loose, slowed and slowed again and drifted past world after world until, in a balancing act more delicate than any performed by the acrobats on board, it slipped sweetly into orbit about one of the seventeen worlds, *Yildakeser 7* on the charts, *Chissoku Bogmak* to the Goyothinaroi who opened and owned it.

3

A muted, musical chime sounded, followed by the pleasant, androgynous voice of the kephalos. "Passenger six-aught-four-three, passenger six-aught-four-three. If you are present, please respond by touching the green light." In a thousand other rooms, a thousand dorms it was calling other numbers, calling with the same message, speaking in the same voice.

Shadith straightened her back, shook herself. "It begins," she murmured. The finger she stretched to touch the light was trembling and her stomach felt as if someone were stirring it with a slotted spoon.

"The next tier of departures will occur in thirty-two minutes. Six-aught-four-three, you are assigned seat 9 on shuttle 27. Please confirm your reservation by touching the green light. Thank you. The glide chair will be at your cabin door in approximately seven minutes. All impedimenta except one carry item should have been dispatched to the baggage transfer system. If you disregard this warning, the extra items will be taken from you at the loading chute. Although we will do our utmost to reunite you with your possessions, in such circumstances we cannot guarantee delivery. Five minutes to arrival of the glide chair. Four minutes. Three. . . . ."

Shadith lifted her shoulderbag onto her lap and sat stroking the soft wrinkled leather.

Passenger 6043, one out of 7000 plus. Who cares who 6043 is? Lovely privacy, sweet neglect. It's what I like about cities. And worldships. Who cares who you are or what you're doing? I couldn't live on Wolff, there's . . . what . . . less than a hundred thousand Wolfflan on the whole miserable planet

*. . . everybody KNOWS everybody . . . well, al-
most . . . got a thousand noses hanging over your
shoulder whatever you do . . . Ginny times a thousand . . . not so malevolent, of course . . . that's a
good word . . . I like that word . . . malevolent . . .
it even SMELLS evil . . . malevolent . . . red-eyed
spider squinting from his web . . . why the hell am
I here anyway . . . should have cut my losses, done
what Lee wanted me to do, settled down at University cultivating contacts . . . sheesh! and one day
not too far off some jerk walks in and blows my head
off, present from Ginny . . . University . . . Aslan,
Aslan, keep on Hoban's tail, see my sun moths are
built and ready to fly. We'll be needing them on a
moment's notice, I hope, I hope . . . give you one
blinding beautiful surprise, Ginny you creep . . . I
hope, I hope. . . .*

She twitched when the announcer bonged, got to her
feet, and went out.

4

Shadith watched the world come up at them, blotches
of color and cloud that spread and spread, then they were
in the clouds, dropping through level after level of poufs
like swatches of spun glass, the details of the land alter-
nately visible and veiled as the shuttle plunged down.

Ferries moved slowly across bright brittle water stiff
with whitecaps, carrying people and goods back and forth
from the Landing Field to Karintepe, a city built on a
spatter of islands on the east side of the Jinssi (an immense bay like a mushroom cap on a crooked stem) and
spread along Jinssi Eastshore, its parts connected by a
tracery of suspension bridges like fine black spiderwebs.

The shuttleport lay on flat land west of the Jinssi, where
the southern grasslands met ancient forest that stretched
like a blue-green smudge across the curve of the world.
The Field was a square of metacrete a mile on a side with
a cluster of oversize structures on the eastern end. It was

enclosed in a triple barrier of chainlink and barbed wire, with an electrified mesh on the outside of the innermost and tallest of the fences.

More important, to her, if not the Bogmakkers, there was a smaller enclave a short distance north of the field, Starstreet, encysted and separate from the rest of Chissoku.

The shuttle set down with a faint jar, then rolled along for what seemed hours until it reached the disembarking tube assigned to it. There was a click, a subaudible sigh. The chair turned Shadith loose, she stood and walked out.

1

The arrival hall was an immense space, a barrel roof
perched on walls three stories high, a double array of
tall, narrow, stained glass windows marching along the
side walls; the sections of glass surrounding the monu-
mental Goyo figures in them constantly changed polarization, generating a play of sunrays that crossed and
crisscrossed the echoing interior in subtly shifting, gently
jagged patterns. It was a megalomaniac's cozy menage,
meant to intimidate the incomers, an effect it didn't quite
manage, having gone over the top into the absurd, an
absurdity underscored by a horde of bored hirelings of
assorted species and subspecies seated at haphazardly
scattered counters tap-tapping into their terminals endless lists of answers to endless questions.

Shadith glanced at her form, made her way to the
counter with the form number painted on a tatty sign at
the end of a skinny aluminum pole.

She laid the form on the counter and waited for the
pale little being to notice her. He was a stripped twig,
white and shiny, with hair like a tangle of crinkled root-
lets gathered in twin bushes over convoluted little ear
nubbins.

He blinked at her out of colorless red-rimmed eyes,
scanned the form, looked up again, frowning. "You
travel alone?"

"Yes." Shadith kept her voice quiet, colorless. It was
a matter of getting through this interrogation without irritating the functionary. He couldn't turn her back, but

30

he could make her life a hell if he decided he didn't like her.

"You're very young and female. What is your family thinking, letting you go about like this?"

"I am older than I seem."

What's this? Damn that Kephalos shunting me over to this little creep. Sounds like he's got a problem and I'm it.

He looked at the fax sheet again, turned it over and scanned the backside. "You have not indicated your planet-of-origin or your species."

"I believe that is not required, only requested. My folk have a religious objection to breaching privacy. I will provide such information only under duress. Do you compel me?"

The lies begin again. How many is this world going to need?

He started to speak, then stared past her.

Before she thought about it or considered whether it was a wise thing to do, she turned her head to see what he was looking at.

A Goyo stood a few paces off, a tall thin yellowish man with a lot of heavy copper ornaments and chains. As if to accentuate his height and leanness, he wore a black bodysuit like a shiny second skin and draped a heavy crimson robe around this, a kind of thick toga arranged in careful folds. He moved his hand slowly back under the robe and his eyes went blank.

The twig cleared his throat. "Purpose of visit."

Shadith pulled herself together. "Mostly sightseeing, some gambling."

He pressed his mouth into a line so thin it nearly vanished. He didn't like that answer, but he swallowed it after another glance at the Goyo. "You must show that you have sufficient discretionary funds."

She pressed the credit bracelet to the sensor he pushed across the counter.

He glanced at the report, thinned his lips again. She began to wonder why the Goyo had hired him, he certainly wasn't apt at ingratiating himself with visitors. She thought about her number status on the worldship and sighed. The cubicle she'd occupied was just a hair above the dorms in respectability, probably why she got this jerk. Well, better a little obscurity given the circumstances. "Duration of visit," he said.

"Until the next ship comes by going my way. Preferably but not necessarily a worldship."

"Age?"

"That is a private matter."

"It is necessary, despina. If you are below the age of consent as determined by local standards, you must be provided with a chaperone during your stay here. If you are below the age of responsibility as determined by local standards, a warning will be incorporated in your ID bracelet. There are limitations on the activities of children here."

Shadith closed her eyes, searched memory. . . .

Age of consent, 12 std. Age of responsibility for non-Goyo femmes and hommes, 26 std. Never for Goyo femmes. Gods be blessed I wasn't born here. Ridiculous. I could have sex in the city square with fifty Goyo, but I couldn't see sex shows. Hunh! What can I get this creep to believe. . . .

"I yield to your coercion," she said aloud, arrogance in the lift of her chin and anger in her voice. "29 years standard, plus 52 days standard. I am adult. I will not welcome any doubt of that."

"Of course, despina." He looked nervously past her shoulder.

That Goyo again. Must be. Why is he . . . interfering . . . Ah, gods, don't tell me it's happening again. If he's a veal hound looking for meat, I swear. . . .

"Despina." The nervous scratchy voice broke into her unpleasant speculations. "If you please, place your wrist in the receptacle."

She tensed her muscles and pushed her arm a thumb-width farther into the bracelet machine than he would have allowed if he hadn't been preoccupied with the Goyo. When the machine finished its complicated clashing about her arm, she withdrew it quickly and held it against her bag so he wouldn't notice how loose the bracelet was.

The functionary ran the form through a duplex, attached a second sheet, pushed them across the counter to her. "The bracelet will be removed when you leave Chissoku Bogmak. Do not attempt to remove or otherwise tamper with it before then. If you do, it will blow your hand off. You have the freedom of the city for the space of one year standard. At the end of that time, if you are still here, you must leave on the first ship available no matter where it is going. This information plus such rules and limitations as apply to you are listed on the second sheet. You are required to be familiar with these. Breaching any of them will bring severe penalties and ignorance is not acceptable as a defense. The most serious infractions could bring terms of servitude in the mines or on the factory farms. Welcome to Chissoku Bogmak."

2

Welcome to Chissoku Bogmak. Hmp.

Shadith glanced over her shoulder as she left the Hall. The Goyo was following her, his eyes blank, his body loose, almost shambling. He wasn't hurrying, but he didn't need to. She shivered, shifted the strap of her shoulderbag, stepped outside into the grit-laden wind sweeping east across the field and joined the crowd of other worldship transfers waiting with varying degrees of patience for the jits that would take them to the ottotels on Jinssi Westshore or the ferries to Karintepe Proper.

There were groups of Goyothinaroi standing like stat-

ues in a concrete garden, posing for the admiration of
the incomers and each other; tall lean young males with
gaunt eagle faces, grayish-yellow skin, and long coarse
black hair either hanging loose or braided into complicated plaits with fine copper and silver wires twisted
through the strands. They wore skintight black bodysuits
and dark red wool togas like the one following her,
though they were younger, with fewer copper chains and
armlets, smaller earrings and brooches. Some just stood
about with as much majesty as they could contrive, others stalked along portentously, a kind of dance where
each maintained a set distance from all others, using their
extravagant length and young vigor like cocks parading
before dull undistinguished hens whose admiration they
yet desired. It was, in its way, a remarkable display of
wealth, the only wealth that had real meaning to travelers
and landbound alike. Leisure. Limitless, boundless leisure. The time to cultivate totally useless activity, the
space to be spectacularly nonproductive, even wasteful.

Their wealth was the first thing she learned about the
Goyo when she talked with Aslan's mentor, Tseewaxlin,
the old man who'd spent half an ordinary lifetime studying them. Wealth, he said, and the power it gives. It
colors everything on Chissoku Bogmak. The Goyothinaroi own Chissoku. They own the air you breathe. If
they decide you should stop breathing, they have that right
by local law. Remember this, child. Keep it in mind at
all times. Have value to the Goyothinaroi and you live.
Cease to have value and you can cease to live.

A roving Goyo, older than the others, stepped onto the
shadow of a stationary poser.

It was deliberate, a silent provocation.

The poser screamed, a sudden wild shriek that cut
through the muted noise of the assorted conversations
among the travelers and the rattle of the approaching jits.
"Odumeydo shi-olum, A-apta!" he cried. "Odou,
odou."

Shadith frowned. Those words weren't in the vocabu-
lary she'd learned on University.

*Special langue for ritual acts? Plenty of precedent.
That going to be a problem? No indeed. If I have to
fight Goyo, I'm going to find a handy building to
hide behind.*

The challenger tore a chain off his neck, one heavy
with round medallions, and swung it hard against the arm
of the man who stepped on his shadow.

The provoker swung round, caught at the chain, pulled
it from the challenger's hand and flung it aside. "Shish-
shi," he cried. "Sholoom."

The jit drivers and the tour guides were busily pushing
the incomers into seats on the jits, carefully ignoring the
two Goyo whanging away at each other with heavy
copper-coated swords; when one of the offworlders
seemed about to comment, a guide interrupted ruth-
lessly, cutting her off in mid-word. That only happened
once, mostly because not many of the incomers even
bothered to look at the fighters. They were traders and
gamblers, experienced travelers quick to pick up on local
nuance, with no interest in getting involved in local quar-
rels.

Shadith maneuvered so she was one of the last to get
in. She wanted to see the end of this.

The duel went on, the duelers stepping through stately
patterns as they beat at each other with those improbable
swords. Despite the stagy look of the contest, it had a
vicious intensity; both Goyo were very quick and stronger
than they looked, constrained by the prescribed forms but
going at each other with murderous determination.

She took the end seat in the jit, ignored the tacit dis-
approval of the driver and the other riders and sat half-
turned, watching the duel to its end. The challenger was
outclassed from the first exchange; the Goyo who'd pro-
voked this slaughter blocked and struck with daunting
precision and speed and high-nosed contempt for his opponent.

*That bastard knew he'd win. So this is Goyo honor.
Ah-me ah-my, times don't change though the millen-*

nia slide past and away. Driver's sweating rivers, he'd be chewing me out if he wasn't afraid some other Goyo'd hear him. You're not being very nice, Shadow. It isn't his fault, you know what the old man said. This is how things are here. Huh. I don't feel nice.

The young one fell, blood spurting in twin fountains from his arm and neck. The older ignored the blood, bent over the youth and stripped off his neck chains. He straightened, left the dead Goyo sprawled on the grit as he walked off with the chains and their pendant charms swinging from his hand, his bloodied sword held before him like a staff.

Then the jit was round the corner and she couldn't see him any more.

Well. Lovely, lovely. And that's what we're going after, only older. And worse. He didn't only survive, he came out top dog. Head of the House of Fevkinda. Richest Goyo on Chissoku. Able to afford Ginny's price. Limited Edition. One year's World Income per version . . . I like that . . . perversion . . . Gods, why don't I just say hell with it and go spend the rest of my life on Vrithian with Harskari? Bastard'd never find me there. Ah, well, looks like it's a good thing I did a little double-knotting of my own. Wonder if Arel's here yet? He was eager enough when I called him. . . .

She chuckled softly, settled herself more comfortably in the seat and closed her eyes; it'd been a long day already and it wasn't noon yet down here.

GETTING INTO KARINTEPE 2
Shadith

1

The ottotel's lobby was plastic and impersonal; the plants were real enough, but they looked as if they were vacuumed for dust and rewaxed every day. There weren't any echoes, the tel-engineers had seen to that, but voices had a curious quality in here as if the air wasn't quite sure it was up to transmitting coherent sound. There wasn't less noise, it was simply less intelligible.

Shadith yawned, rubbed at her eyes, spent a few moments wishing futilely that she had earplugs to keep the clamor out of her head. She didn't know any of the *Kazzedva* passengers in line with her so she didn't bother trying to talk; besides, she was tired and cranky, not fit for human discourse. Lines and questions and the tension from not knowing what was going to happen next, it added up—or rather it subtracted, mostly energy. The line shuffled ahead a few steps. She shifted the strap on her shoulderbag and shuffled with it.

Ottotels . . . gods, you'd think a busy place like this they'd have more than one token dispenser . . . I suppose it's only crowded when a worldship's in . . . Rohant and Kikun should be settled by now . . . that Goyo . . . he wasn't putting out lecher vibes . . . I don't know the Goyo . . . reading about them isn't the same as . . . ah, well, time'll take care of that. . . .

The line moved again. The air was gamy with the smell of travelers of assorted species sweaty with excitement

37

or apprehension or plain weariness. Shadith had no doubt
at all she was contributing her share of stench to the fug
that filled the place—which made her even crankier.

Someone touched her arm. She looked round, scowling.

A worn, handsome woman stood half a step behind
her—tall and narrow, maybe a touch of Goyo in her. Her
hair was Goyo blue-black and long, wound into a complicated knot at the back of her head; her skin was the
color of old cream, soft and smooth as velvet drapes with
about as many folds; her eyes were long and narrow, the
irids brown with flecks of orange and a black rim. She
wore a narrow black coat over black trousers caught at
the ankle and narrow black slippers. And no jewelry. Her
ears were large, set close to her head, mostly covered by
her hair; the pendulous lobes hung free, the holes in them
oversized, distended by heavy dangles which she'd left
off for some reason.

> *Discreet and . . . hmm . . . not identifiable. All*
> *right, madam, say your say, I'm not going anywhere*
> *a while yet. . . .*

"I am a licensed Hindor, despina; that is, I bring together who wants to buy with who wants to sell." The
woman's voice was a creamy alto, warm and pleasant to
the ear; it made everything she said sound a touch more
reasonable than it probably was. "This is my card; if you
wish you may run it through the verifier at the desk. I
have an offer to pass to you which could bring you
much. . . ." She rubbed her thumb across her fingertips.
"You understand."

Shadith looked at the card but didn't touch it. The line
moved again and she moved with it, brooding over what
she should do about this. When she looked around, the
woman was quietly following.

"I'll listen," Shadith said. "I'll give you fifteen minutes. Engage a conference room and meet me at the
desk."

"It will be so." The Hindor touched bunched finger-tips to brow, lips and heart, bowing as she did so, the Bogmakker yayyay. She straightened and moved away with an odd gliding gait, as if her feet were wheels.

2

Shadith punched in her room requirements, then fed ottotel tokens into the desk clerk until it burped out a cardkey and a fax sheet of instructions. She slipped them in her bag and turned away.

The Hindor yayyayed gracefully, straightened with a smile, holding out the card. "Do you wish to verify, despina?"

"Not at the moment. I'll listen to the proposal first. Where?"

"Only a step, despina. Across the hall and down a little."

"Go. I'm tired, so don't waste my time or yours."

3

The room was a cube the size of a closet with two comfortable chairs and a table with a sensor panel at one end. The Hindor waited until Shadith was settled, then took the other chair, folded her hands on the table. "There is a man of power in Karintepe who is charmed by you, despina; he wishes a liaison with you for such time as pleases you both. He is a generous patron, a lover of charm and delicacy who will teach you many delights; he will take care of your expenses while you are onworld, even your gambling expenses, within reasonable limits, and will provide a parting gift under terms to be negoti-ated after you accept his proposal."

Shadith caught the tail of her temper. Though it looked like things were starting here exactly as they had on the Transfer Station, there was something wrong with the echo. She frowned. Her Talent told her the Hindor had nothing riding on acceptance, no emotional commitment to the proposition. Odd. Especially on this world. She wasn't exactly lying, but this was not a serious offer, it was a try-on of some kind. . . .

What now . . . what now . . . damn all interfering . . . I'd bet anything Ginny's back of this somehow. Old spider sitting in his web, tying knots where no one else would even see threads. I thought he thought we were dead. Looks like that's wrong. Stop stalling, Shadow, you need an answer now, something that won't make a gift of your head . . . ah! yes, I have it. . . .

"I am desolate, O Hindoro," she murmured, speaking slowly and with a pernickity precision borrowed from Ginbiryol Seyirshi (a private joke that tickled her and distanced the fear and anger she'd brought into the room). "It is my shame that I cannot respond favorably to such a generous and elegantly phrased proposal. Alas, my appearance is misleading. I am not of the cousin races, I am not remotely connected with them. I am a neuter member of a mimetic species; I am neither physically nor emotionally capable of entering into such an agreement." She got to her feet without hurry but also without lingering over it and left the room, more disturbed than ever because her Talent told her the woman was pleased with the refusal and the reason given for it. . . .

Pleased! Because she doesn't like her patron? Or because she does and I'm not the scourge she's waiting for? Ahlahlah, what a mess to be diving blind into. . . .

4

Shadith keyed open the door to her room and went inside.

It was sterile, impersonally pleasant, a bed a chair a table a lamp, all neat and dust free, made from nonwear materials in nondistracting colors. She dropped into the chair and closed her eyes, suddenly depressed as if in looking into that room, she was looking into the rest of her life. And if she was, it wasn't much worth living. Rooms like this, world after world. She brought her hand slapping down on the table beside the chair, then she stared at her reddened palm, shook her head. Foolishness.

Get busy, girl. You've got more important things to do. Bath first. Sar! I'm going to soak till I'm a prune. Idjit, you want clean clothes, don't you? And you'd better check the Bulletin Board, let old lion and Kikun know you're in and ready for company, well, almost . . . bath, bath, bath . . . on your feet, woman, the sooner you do all this, the sooner you get your nap. . . .

She groaned onto her feet, slid her baggage check into the slot in the sensor panel and left it there while she called up the BB and left a message in Dyslaer (Rohant insisted she absorb the langue when they were on University picking up everything they could find about Chissoku Bogmak; he still had the illusion it could serve in a pinch as a secret langue when they wanted to say things they didn't want others to know about), then she strolled into the bathroom and sank herself to her neck in hot soapy water.

5

Shadith scratched at the sole of her foot. She was perched in the middle of the narrow bed, dressed in a toweling robe, her hair a wild tangle of tiny curls that looked completely uncombable, released from the gel that held it flat and smooth and turned the brown to a pale blonde. Rohant had the chair and Kikun was sitting on the carpet with his back against a wall, so still and unblinking he was more like an odd statue than a breathing being.

"She turned out to be a professional pander—or at least

that was what she was pretending to be. I don't quite believe it, I think she was checking up on me, matching me to some kind of description. To sum it up in one word, Ginny. Double-knotting again. I suppose he found out Kiskai didn't go boom after all.''

Looking spacy and idiotic as he usually did when his peculiar ways of knowing were in operation, Kikun began humming a monotonous, irritating tune, rather like a mosquito zeroing in on succulent flesh.

When Shadith was on the verge of screaming, he broke off his humming and said, ''Ginny don't know. Too busy to know. Puk the Lute, he's the one. He thinks we're golems. Can't kill us. He tried and he tried and it didn't work. Sent a description to Ginny's prime clients, us three, didn't dare send phots, said we trouble, don't mess with us, dump us down a deep hole soon's we show our noses.'' He gave his throat-catch giggle, opened his eyes wide. ''Ginny don't know. If he finds out, the Lute gets skinned. Maybe. Balance on the knife point. Maybe he sends the Lute hunting us. Hope he does, oh yes, if he does, I sniff his backtrail to his nest. And Boom goes Ginny.''

''Backtrail, huh?''

Kikun didn't answer; he was back to staring at things no one else could see.

''Right.'' Rohant ran his thumbclaw across his mustache, began teasing at it, winked at Shadith. ''You needn't boast your attractions, Shadow, you weren't the only one to get an offer. A Hindor came eeling up to me with a proposition he said would make me independently wealthy.''

Shadith giggled. ''How much?'' she said, miming extreme interest. ''How much she goin to pay?''

''Don't be a fool, Shadow. Species difference, a real one. Dyslaeror don't fool around outside the Family.''

''Species difference, my foot! You're as much cousin as I am. So tell me, tell me who's the local matron sighing over all that prime meat?'' She waved a hand, the gesture sweeping from his head to the claws coming out the end of his open toed boots.

"Dio, girl . . ." He moved uneasily in the chair, more disturbed by the idea than she'd expected. "I'm pairbond and don't you forget it. No, this was an offer to turn pro. Maul and claw, gladiator if you want it fancy. They don't get many Dyslaeror, he said. I'd be a star, he said." He grinned, threat not humor, showing his tearing teeth. "Maybe even true. I don't know. Haven't got your talent, Shadow. I had Sassa on my wrist. He liked that. Very impressed. Or so he said. Told him I wasn't interested at the moment. Maybe later. He went off without arguing. Didn't think about it much then, just some ten-per boy trying to scam a likely greenhead. Now I'm remembering how easy he went off, and I'm wondering. Hmm. Get you, too, Kikun?"

Kikun let his eyelids droop half-shut. "Didn't notice me."

Rohant gave a shout of laughter and Shadith smiled.

She fiddled with her locator bracelet, squeezed her thumb around and began trying to ease the circlet over her hand. Her wrists were thin, her hands were big for her size, graceful and tapering but definitely big; she started sweating and that helped.

Kikun smiled sleepily at her, constricted his hand, slipped the bracelet off without any effort at all.

"Worm," she said.

He chuckled, three throat-catches and a snort. He turned the white plastic band around and around in his delicate fingers, then slipped it back on and sat watching Shadith's struggles.

Rohant dropped his head on the back of the chair as Shadith got the bracelet over the widest part of her hand and shook it off onto the bed. "Not a hope for me to try that." He held up his arm. His wrists were thick and powerful, but his hands were too well-muscled, his bones too big to let him imitate her. He closed his hand in a fist, turned it back and forth, contemplating it. "Unless I want to gnaw it off."

She poked at the white plastic ring, moving it about the coverlet, organizing the small scratchings into a rudimentary rhythm. "Yeh." She sighed. "You'll be all right if they don't link us together. I think."

Rohant grunted.

"Stupid thing, this." Shadith hooked her finger through the ring, sent it spinning to the ceiling, caught it again. "Same old story, isn't it?"

He looked up. "What?"

"The Goyo way with outsiders. Keep them separate, milk them of everything they got, boot them out."

"It's their world."

She frowned at him, shook her head. "Kikun over there. You ever wonder what he thinks of us cousins?"

The dinhast was in his personal *nevernever*, looking close to braindead.

Rohant clicked his tongue, started scratching at the upholstery on the chair arm with the needle-pointed tip of his right foreclaw. He wasn't interested in this kind of speculation and made it obvious he thought she was wasting time.

Shadith sat rubbing at her knees. "Ahhlahlah, I don't know."

He inspected the claw. "To go back to when you were still making sense, yeh, we do need to keep some space between us so we don't make the wrong kind of picture for the wrong kind of eyes. You go your way, I go mine." He laced his hands over his stomach, flattened his ears, and twitched his nose. "I'm going to give my Hindor a call. Surprise the hell out of him, probably." His lids drooped half shut, his eyes phosphored red. "He mightn't want me, but he's got me."

"Hmm." She picked thoughtfully at a bit of callus on her heel. "I'm going to go sign up for some tours, I think. After lunch. See what I can put together just looking."

"Then you better slide that thing back on."

"Hmp. Makes me feel like a cat with fleas."

"Be glad it's not a collar. You'd play hell trying to get it over your head."

Kikun jumped to his feet, startling both of them. "I'm going now," he said. "I'll be back here come sundown.

We dance together again, ah Shadow Twiceborn.'' He came darting across the room, touched his fingertips to her face, then was out the door before Shadith could close her mouth.

Rohant stood. "What's he mean by that? Twiceborn.''

"You know him better than I do. Ask him.''

"When he explains things, I end up knowing less than when I started. So?''

"It's an idea he has about me.''

"You don't want to talk about it, tell me go to hell.''

"No . . . it's . . . um . . . complicated. Reincarnation of a sort.''

"Not so complicated.''

"The difficulty's in the details, Ro.''

"Isn't it always? Take care this afternoon, kit. Could be twice is all the born you get.''

"No nine lives for me?''

"Remembering Kiskai, you've already used them up. See you when.'' He touched the tip of a claw to the inside of her wrist, drew a line across it. "And don't forget the bracelet.'' He dropped her hand and left.

Shadith scowled at the door, then at the white circlet beside her knee. She poked a finger through it, hooked it up. "Sar,'' she said aloud, "I need you to get on Starstreet and I need you to play tourist. Then you can sit here and rot.''

STARSTREET
63 Kirar Sorizakre, day 14, hour 12
Shadith
Arel the Smuggler and his bodyguard Joran

1

Starstreet was a clutch of plasticrete structures inside a
fence as multiple and formidable as that shutting in the
Landing Field. The street was dead now, gray, dusty,
silent, all the holos turned off, all the holoas silent, ga-
raged until the street woke up enough to call them out.

Shadith caught a monojit at the last in the line of ottotels—not the one where she had a room, not Kikun's
or Rohant's; monojits were supposed to be independent
of the tel-system and fares not traceable, but she wanted
no records left around that could be read later; Ginny
Seyirshi wasn't the only one who could knot his knots.
She tapped in the code for Starstreet and rode the emjit
round to the Flowgate, a creation worthy of a contract
labor camp, all lethal utility and overkill ugliness—as if
what it locked in was more feral, more dangerous than
the worst of the beasts prowling the Dread Green, so
dangerous that local types had to be kept out, forceably
if necessary.

All she had to do to get in was show her locator bracelet to prove she wasn't local.

2

On University she tied the first and most important of
her double-knots; she made a skipcom call.

Tulppanni's, Arel said. Big green Tau. Look for it. I'll
be there.

What's your price, she said.

A story, he said.

Oh? she said.

I've seen you before, he said.

Yes, I know, she said.

Before Kiskai I mean, he said.

Yes, I know, she said.

But I don't know you, he said. You know me, but I
don't know you.

Why? he said. That's what I want to know.

And, he said, this. How do you know a very private
set of hand signals?

That's the story I want, he said. For being there. For
anything else, well, we'll argue that when we meet.

All right, she said. Aleytys tells me trust you.

Good, he said. *Tulppanni's* on Starstreet, ask Panni for
Teyjahn Kuiva. You have that?

I have it, she said, and terminated the skipcom connection.

3

Tulppanni's was near the edge of Starstreet, where its
higher windows could look out across the grass and see
the darkness that was the southern rim of the Dread
Green.

Shadith stopped the emjit at a hotpost in front of a
place called *Hyperion*, plugged it in and slotted a handful
of tokens to keep it waiting for her until she was ready
to leave.

She walked along the dusty flags until she could see
the big green Tau painted on a facade with all the charm
of a cement slab. *Tulppanni's* kept its beauties a secret
from anyone uncouth enough to view it in the daylight.

She pushed open the swinging door, stood blinking at
the darkness until her eyes adjusted enough to let her

move without falling over her own feet, then she threaded
through tables with chairs upended on them and climbed
aboard a stool at the bar.

A woman came through a bead curtain and stared at
Shadith, a large woman in her middle years, long black
hair in braids with beaded rounds pinned over her ears.
She had a square impassive face and square hands, a
crisp clean white blouse with a square yoke and long
sleeves and a long dark skirt. "Bar's not open and the
whores are sleeping. I can make you a sandwich if you're
hungry. That's about all."

"You're Tulppanni?"

"Who's asking?"

"Lee's friend."

"That would tell me more if I knew who Lee was.
Yes, I'm Panni."

"Teyjahn Kuiva said ask for him."

"You're younger than his usual."

"His business, I think."

"Snippy, too. Come round through here. He's upstairs, waiting for you."

3

Joran opened the door; his flat black eyes moved over
Shadith without any sign he'd seen her before. After a
moment he stepped back and waved her in.

Arel got to his feet. He was a small dark man with a
bony sardonic face, fans of fine wrinkles about the outer
corners of his eyes and his mouth. His long dark hair was
pulled through a filigreed silver clasp at the nape of his
neck and hung halfway down his back. "That blonde
doesn't suit you," he said. "Fades you out, makes you
look insipid."

"That's the point of it."

The wrinkles round his eyes and mouth deepened
slightly, a ghost of a smile. He came round the table,
drew out the wooden chair. "Despina. . . ."

When they were both seated, she tapped the black cone
in the center of the table. "Mute?"

"You got it." He touched a sensor. "On full. Takes in the table and the chairs plus a handspan beyond. Closed cylinder configuration, warning light if one of us breaches the limit."

"Joran's looking as lethal as always. Is Vannik still with you?"

"He got himself killed three, four years ago. Interesting, your knowing about him. Tell me a story, Shadow."

"Before I start, thanks again for getting the word to Aleytys. I'd be dead now along with Kiskai if you hadn't. I owe you."

"Kiskai?"

"Ginny had a Boombox counting the minutes when Lee showed up. She shifted it. Was the next world out went boom. You need something I have, it's yours. I'm like Lee, I pay my debts."

"I'll bank that and draw on it later, if you don't mind. Cumma cum, my story, luv."

She laughed, enjoying his enjoyment. "Once upon a time, a long long time ago. . . ."

"And how long is long?"

"Call it twenty thousand years, give or take a millennia or three. Twenty thousand years ago, there was a world called Shayalin and on that world the Shallana lived and among the Shallana were certain families called the Weavers of Shayalin who could dance dreams into being.

This is how the generations went among the Weavers. First there was One. She was fertile and female, a singer who could not dance dreams nor bring them alive for others to see. She mated with an ordinary Shallana male and hatched six daughters who were true Dancers, the Weavers. When they were grown and dancing, she mated a second time and produced a fertile daughter, a singer like herself. And so it went, six and one and six again, generation upon generation until a freetrader happened upon Shayalin and had Dreams danced for him by the Weavers of Shayalin. He stole a family of Weavers and ran with them. He was only the first of the raiders. In a hundred years there very few Weavers left.

"And then there was another raid, more vicious than

most, the raiders stupid and arrogant and above all ignorant. They killed Shallana a hundred at a time until a Weaver family was brought to them. Then they left. They shot the Mother/Singer and tossed her out an air lock because she was old and ugly. When they reached the Marketworld, they sold the Daughter/Singer for a pittance because she could not dance and was young and ugly and then they tried to sell the Weaver/Sisters and found no takers because the Weavers needed the Singer for the Dream. They tried to find the Daughter, but she was gone with her owner no one knew where, so they shot the sisters, too, and went back to Shayalin for another set.

"The Daughter wandered far, moving from master to master, acquiring a name that non-Shallana could pronounce. Shadith. No surprise, I'm sure. It meant Singer in the langue she took it from.

"Her last Master/Teacher died and left her free to move on and she did. In the course of her travels she found work with an expedition of scholars digging in the ruins on a world older than most of the suns around it. She found a thing there, an exquisite thing, a shimmering lacy diadem." She laughed at the sudden interest in his face. "Yes, O captain, THAT diadem.

"Time passed and the time came when her ship crashed on a primitive world and she died the first time.

"She died, yes, but her soul or consciousness or whatever you feel like calling it was encrypted into the diadem and stayed there as the millennia passed.

"The diadem moved. And moved again. Shadith moved with it. Aleytys brought her aboard your ship. You didn't know it, but she was there. Invisible witness, learning whatever Aleytys learned. That's it. Story."

"Hmm. Any Weavers left?"

"Someone told me once in my first go-round that the Weaver sun went nova and Shayalin was a cinder."

"And?"

"I had no way of finding out how true that was, I hadn't the faintest notion how to get there, I was only four when I left."

"You never tried to go home?"

"By the time I was old enough and free enough to go back, no one knew its location."

"What about the raiders?"

"The ones whose names I could find were mostly dead; if they weren't dead, they were out of reach. The Weavers? By that time they were worked to death, most of them. The ones still alive were as ignorant as I was. I put it out of my head and went on scrambling a living. You know how that goes."

"Mmf. Yes. Talking about scrambling a living, what am I doing here?"

"You can bypass Goyo Security, get a lander down unnoticed, and leave again equally unnoticed?"

"Oh, Shadow Shadow, you need to ask that? All right. In a word, yes."

"What do you want to stay here for the next two, three months? I need a back door. Just in case."

"Finance me."

"What precisely does that involve?"

"I'm a smuggler, Shadow. Remember?"

"Let's do it this way." She folded her hands, pursed her lips, then laughed aloud as one of his thin black brows shot up. "I give you a line of credit up to 50,000 Helvetian gelders, you return the principal and say forty percent of the profits, the line good till I'm off-planet one way or another."

"50,000 is adequate. Twenty percent."

"Thirty-five."

"You're keeping me hanging around a long time, you know. That could get dangerous. The Goyo are tricky bastards . . . you're operating against one of the Families, aren't you?" His brow shot up again.

She didn't answer, figuring it was none of his business.

"Avosing, Kiskai, if that's what happens when you kick up your heels, you owe me danger money."

"Sar! Arel, you spend half your time in trickier messes than anything I could possibly think up."

"I see you acquired some of Lee's more irritating habits when you were, what shall we say, co-dwelling? Twenty-five.''

''Thirty-five.''

''Thirty, that's my top offer.''

''Well, it was nice talking to you.'' She got to her feet, pushing the chair back. The Mute-cone blinked red as she broke through the barrier.

''For an ex-ghost, you're a hard woman. Sit down, luv, we can work this out.'' He waited until she moved back inside the barrier and the cone stopped blinking. ''Thirty-five it is. We can do the set-up here, Panni has a comlink with Helvetia. Guaranteed private. You'll want an audit, I suppose.''

''No. If you get funny on me, I'll sic Lee on you.''

''Hard woman.'' He got to his feet, held out his hand. ''Shake?''

''Deal,'' she said, took the hand. ''I'll let you know if things get urgent.''

''You do that.''

1

The afternoon was bright and clear. The wind had dropped a little, but there was still a nip in the air. Shadith buttoned her jacket, pushed her hands into her pockets. She hadn't brought gloves, this north latitude was more than six years standard into the long Chissoku spring and she'd expected the days to be warmer.

She dropped a guim and two dokies in the slot and walked on board the ferry. It was a tidy little steamboat with a paddlewheel in the rear and twin black stacks that spouted gouts of white smoke into the air. Most of the passengers were already inside, away from the smuts flying from the stacks and out of the wind that was still blowing the tops off the waves. Shadith was cold and getting colder, but she was tired so tired of the confinement on that ship, no matter it was a worldship and large as one of the bigger moons; she enjoyed having room to swing her arms, to let her eyes look beyond the immediate, out across the salt blue water that stretched to the horizon on three sides, she liked the fresh salt smell of the air and the brilliant colors of the birds flying in noisy flocks overhead, the blooming trees on this shore—she couldn't see the other from water level, it was too far off, at least three hours away.

The ferries were drawn up like square white waterbugs, one to each of the ottotels; they were big enough to carry in comfort around a hundred passengers bound for the other side, but dainty, with clean white walls and a delicate tracery of wrought iron balustrades like fine

53

black lace. There was a bar inside and a window where
you could buy hot meat pies and other delicacies, padded
benches and a few tables, a lot of counter space and brass
rails for leaning on. She could hear the noise booming
out of there and the salt water sloshing along the sides as
the passengers moved about.

The tailgate slammed shut behind Shadith as soon as
she walked on board, the steamwhistle hooted and the
boat started off with a liquid chuffing from the paddle
wheel, a chugachug from the motors below. She laughed
and grabbed at the rail to steady herself.

> *I could get paranoid about this if I tried hard
> enough. Snare slamming shut? Naa. Don't be silly,
> girl. You know what the notice said, they don't leave
> until they're as close to full as seems likely. You're
> it, you're the lucky number, you rang the bell and
> started the whole mess going. Crazy mix this boat.
> Absurd. Steam age and computer age improbably
> collapsed together. Lean back and enjoy. Till your
> ass starts to freeze off. You don't want to go inside
> yet. Wonder what Kikun's into? Funny little man.
> Wouldn't mind having his Talent. Ro's off to audi-
> tion. Good luck to him. Good luck to me. Wonder
> what Arel's up to? Gods, I'll strangle him if he's
> caught and thrown in the Mines. Well, Shadow, he's
> stayed alive, intact and solvent all these years, I
> doubt he's going to mess up his record now. Slip-
> pery little git. Wonder what he's thinks of me . . .
> I wouldn't mind losing it with him . . . Hah!
> Shadow, keep your mind on business or the only
> thing you'll lose is your skin.*

2

The boat went chug-chugging along, crossing the bay
at a crawl that gave Shadith an itch in her back teeth. She
shivered, warmed her hands in her armpits, and once
again thought about going inside, but the blast of noise
still coming through the thin walls repelled her and she

didn't feel like standing elbow to elbow, smelling the assorted odors of her fellow travelers, with hands on her body fore and aft.

As they got close enough to the East Shore she began to see the black tracery of the bridges and the spikes and spires of the buildings on the island chain. Some were gilded, others were brilliant spirals of crimson and emerald, azure, ivory and topaz, while the upper floors of the towers were faced with black and white stone—or it might have been tiles—in a dizzying variety of patterns, especially on the Goyo island Joggoreyzel Shimda, where the Gotasaray was.

The Gotasaray. It belongs to the Kralodate, the old man said, but the Goyo all have apartments inside those black basalt walls, hereditary holdings passed from father to eldest son, though the passing can be deflected at the will of the Kralodate and sometimes is.

Aslan would kill for a pass in there. I don't share her tastes, I must admit. Take a tour? Wonder how much good a run round the outside would do me. We might have to fetch Wargun out of there. Gods, I hope not.

She stood alone in the bow of the ferry watching Araubin Shimda, the largest island, come gradually closer, white birds flying and crying overhead, black and white gulls, longtailed redbirds and sleek black divers. The thing was starting. It was finally starting. She tasted the familiar excitement of easing into a new world, wriggling and scratching to fit herself into the local life. If it weren't for Ginny . . . out there somewhere . . . sniping at them . . . Wargun would be a kind of afterthought, an excuse for doing something she'd forgotten how much she liked. Ginny . . . out there, watching, sniping. . . .

Enjoy it, Creep, we're coming, riding the lightwinds into your face . . . damn . . . that's just words . . . but true . . . I hope . . . riding the lightwinds and you don't know it . . . I hope, I hope . . .

3

day 14, hour 15

Standing inconspicuously in the shade of a prickly tree, careful not to back onto the murderous thorns that covered every inch of the trunk and lower branches, Shadith inspected the rest of the tour group milling about the plaza beside the Ferry Building. They were a motley lot, most of them daytrippers down from the worldship to take a look at local decadence and pass the time in port by sniffing at new things.

There was a Menaviddan family, the clutch of spiderlings clinging to their mother's stiff black hair, the smaller male fussing around his mate, his bright red hat slipping over one of his several eyes. There was a bonded trio of Katsitois, two men and a woman, tiny elfin beings barely a meter high chattering endlessly in voices that vanished into the bands above the hearing range of the others in the group. There were several anonymous males, business travelers taking a safe way to find entertainment for the evening; a group of players contracted to the worldship looking for new material; a Clovel matriarch with her attendant clones fluttering about her. She was a puzzle. Matriarchs usually insisted on their importance so fiercely that a mere tour shared with what she considered mongrels and less than human critters was close to abomination. Since her silks were worn, darned, and a little dirty, it was possible she was in temporary disgrace and separated from their common fund.

The tour guide was a Goyo mix. He was lanky and bald with an aggressive mustache and a braided beard.

There are a lot of those about, the old man said, mixes are a sign of a Goyo's virility. Helps a young man make a good marriage if he can count healthy bastards by the decades. Their bloodfathers mostly ignore them, though they do much of the House work that keeps those fathers comfortable in their excesses.

Smiling a plastic smile, impersonal and bloodlessly competent, he gathered them up and got them onto a vehicle he called a heyyil, stowed them one behind the other in the surprisingly comfortable seats. The thing was an articulated snake with segments like wingchairs, only wide enough for one, though the Katsitoi triad insisted on squeezing into the same seat; he capitulated with grace, provided an extension to the seatbelt and got them tucked in without much fuss. The Menaviddans were more of a problem for him; this conveyance was not adapted to their form. He suggested as tactfully as possible that they take a special tour but didn't press the point when the little male started to bounce up and down on his hinder pair of legs and whine with a rising anger. He was adept at concealing his distaste for them, though Shadith could smell the sourness of it four seats back. He even managed to soothe the Matriarch, arranging to seat her clone-companions before and behind her and allowing two of them to run beside the conveyance as long as they carried nothing of value. "Take care," he said, "the streets will be congested and a citizen always has right-of-way. If you cause a disturbance, you will be fined."

Shadith had maneuvered for a seat in the middle; her hair was plastered down again, gelled into a smooth blonde cap; she wore an inconspicuous gray shipsuit, nondescript in cut and material and was satisfied she looked bland and uninteresting. She had Arel's endorsement for that.

4

The Mix's pleasant tenor came through the speaker by her left ear.

"I am Jute, your guide through the windings of Karintepe-on-Araubin. We will be going through the heart of the business sector first, then into Old Town. When the Firstship *Kushtori* brought the Goyothinaroi to this system, the landfall was on the ground where the Field is now. They were fortunate enough to arrive at the end of Winter. Our winters here are more than twenty years long, years standard, that is. Hereafter, if I say year I am speaking of the space-standard year. If I mean the local

variety, I will say Great Year. It was a difficult time for
the newcomers, there were many predators out on the
Plains and in the Forest—especially in the Dread Green
to the north of us, powerful and clever beasts who were
very very hungry. Despite their heroic efforts, the settlers
were forced to retreat from the Main and build on this
the largest of the islands in Jinssi Bay. It gave them a
natural moat while they regrouped and got ready to take
back the land. There were, of course, no indigenes; intelligence beyond the beast kind never developed here.''
He paused while the motors hummed and the effect lifted
the heyyil. ''We will begin moving in a moment. Before
we do, I caution you all, keep your appendages inside
the arms of your chair, especially if you are wearing jewelry or electronic items. The thieves of Karintepe are
legend. This is even more true within the Maze of Old
Town.''

Shadith smiled skeptically. She didn't entirely disbe-
lieve him, but a good part of it had to be giving the
tourists a safe thrill.

5

''As you can see from the structures around you, we
start our journey of exploration in the Wharf District.
The Outland Houses send their furs and the other products of their Holdings, with the exception of the ores and
gems from the mines, to these warehouses around us
where they are bought and sold and traded each Spring.
The ores are sent to the smelters north of Jinssi Bay, the
gems come into the Vaults on Jazinedain Shimda, the
small island you can see off there, near the horizon.

''The prime pelts are taken during the sixth through
fifteenth year of Winter. The furs are cured and kept in
stasis until Thaw. You come at an opportune time, despoies; the first flurry of trading with its Closed Auctions
has finished, but there is plenty of value left for you at
prices traders dream of.

''Very few visit us in Winter. Only the mines operate
throughout the Great Year and even they slow to nothing

at High Winter, so there's not much point in it—though we do get our share of hunters during the milder times, coming mainly for the White Hyospars, our most dangerous big game. There is a goodness in Winter, but Spring, ah, Spring is the best, I am Winterborn and I know it. This is my first and only Spring. When I was a boy, I was convinced that nothing existed but snow and cold. Yes, Spring is the best of all.

"But enough of this. As you can see, we have passed into another sector. On both sides of the heyyil you will see large and small fur shops. This is the G'sok Kuraweg. The Street of the Furriers. The garments on display are all hand-made on the premises, work of a quality rare on any world. If you are interested in the preparation of the pelts and the construction of the finished garments, I can set up a tour of one of the Factories.

"If you are resident in any of the Island Hotels, you can arrange for a private showing in your suite or in one of the conference rooms. I must ask your pardon, but it is not possible to show the goods at the ottotels, no Chissoku products are allowed onto the Landing Area without a tax-on-purchase stamp. We are plagued by smugglers seeking to escape the transfer fees."

6

"Smell the air, despoies, how delicious it is. This is the G'sok Koryess ve Baharat. The Street of Perfumes and Spices. In the upper rooms delicate young girls work under the supervision of Master Blenders to produce the odors and flavors that have made Chissoku Bogmak justly famous among the discerning. For the newcomer to our products there are sample kits, some for as little as a dokie, nothing costing more than a guim. They have a selection of Chissoku's best known essences, only a drop or two of course, but how much does one need to appreciate true beauty? These kits will be available for your consideration at the staging area when we have finished the tour.

7

"Here we come to a street that interests everyone. The G'sok Chosovher. The Street of Gems. The finest products of Chissoku's mines come here to be cut and polished and set. All gem quality stones are the common property of the Goyothinaroi and held in trust for them by the Kralodate. Even more than her essences, Chissoku is noted for the variety and quality of her gemstones. See how they gleam and sparkle in the windows as we move past. Sorry, despoies, there are no sample kits from this street. I do recommend another tour, though. You should see the Gem Museum on Jazinedain Shimda; the finest and rarest of gems are displayed there, the ones the Kralodate keeps back and will never sell, of which the best known is the Star of Guintayo. It alone is worth a visit to Jazinedain and the Museum.

8

"We will pause a moment here in the Gate Plaza. Though many of you may find our pride in the antiquity of our city amusing since the Goyothinaroi have been on Chissoku Bogmak a mere millennium, I think you will find Old Town quite interesting. It is a place of remarkable fecundity and—I must remind you—of considerable danger to your person and your possessions, though you will be safe as long as you remain on the heyyil. You will occasionally see heavily armed individuals, large and ugly," carefully contrived laughter in his voice, "very, very ugly. These are the jinsbeks, what you would call enforcers. They belong to the local Sirshak-kai, the crime and vice lords, the secret societies. If you plan to return to these precincts—which we sincerely advise against—you will be responsible for the safety of your person and your possessions. We do suggest you carry a stash of guims in a moneybelt or some other place inaccessible to pickpockets and cutpurses. Why do I say this? So if you run into trouble you can bribe a jinsbek to deal with the situation. The bribe is standardized at three guims, but

the jinsbek may demand more. Do not bargain. Pay him
or he will simply take it all. You do have some recourse
if you think you have been cheated. Report this extortion
to the Blurdslang at Blurdslang Alley. I will point it out
as we move past. You will be quite safe there, it is truce-
ground. Do not expect the return of your money. You
must content yourself with an explanation of the charges
if the Sirshaka of the Night decides the jinsbek was jus-
tified by circumstances. Or with a finger or some other
appendage of the offender if the decision goes against
him. The Sirshak-kai appreciate your patronage and do
not wish a reputation for extortion to scare off future
visitors. Do not approach a jinsbek to recover lost property or avenge a minor jostling. They will take the bribe
to pay for their wasted time, but otherwise ignore you.
Only appeal to them to avoid immediate bodily injury.

9

"As we pass through it, note the design of the Gate.
The flanking pillars are pods off the *Kushtori*'s probes,
while the arch over the top is made from locking rings
welded together. The gate itself disappeared long ago,
no one knows exactly how or why. Much of the wall was
pulled down as the city expanded, though there is still
quite a lot of it about, incorporated into the buildings.
The street we will move along is the G'sok Raba Katir.
The Heart Line. It is called that because it leads to the
most sacred spot on all of Chissoku Bogmak, the Temple
of Guintayo whose Totem is the Sun, Who is Giver of
Life, the Generance of the All." His voice changed from
a heavy pseudo-awe to the brisker tone of commerce.
"The Temple Square is the location of the NightFair
where there are bargains beyond belief and no questions
asked about provenance; if you wish to view the Fair, it
is best to go with a professional guide who can protect
you from counterfeits and other traps. *Caveat Emptor*
should be branded on every brow in there. There is no
prohibition against attending the Fair and indeed you will
be safe enough within the Square itself, but please do not

attempt to go there without a guide unless you are one of
a large group. And I must emphasize one final thing. Do
not go armed. Carrying energy weapons out of the Landing Zone is forbidden. It will bring on your head a ses-
sion in the mines—at a minimum. If by chance you should
injure one of our citizens with a forbidden weapon, you
will vanish down the mines for the rest of your life. There
is no escape from this penalty, it does not matter who
you are or what names you throw at the Goyothinaroi
who judges you.''

The heyyil lifted and hummed forward, the guard con-
tinuing his practiced spiel. Shadith tuned him out and
looked around alertly, focusing on her own points of interest. The noise was constant though not as deafening
as she'd expected; the tonnes of masonry around and over
them must be absorbing a lot of it. No echoes. Feeling
of secrecy and life lying in ambush. Eyes looking down
on her. Everywhere eyes.

The street peddlers crowded around the heyyil waving
their merchandise, shouting prices, even the more sedate
food stalls had shills out shouting their specialities, walking menus giving dish and price, boasting the succulence
of the food.

The whole place throbbed and seethed with life and
more than a little desperation. These people had survived
Winter and still were gaunt with the strains of that time.
The old man had been here for Thaw, Spring and a part
of Summer and then was forced to leave some thirty years
ago, so University had little information about how the
Mixes and other non-Goyo in the several Karintepes
managed to feed themselves and keep warm during Winter. The Old Towners spent the snowtime in these ancient
rotting buildings and lived on . . . what? Credit? Another
way the Goyo wrung wealth from their world?

Old Town buildings were a congealed mass of masonry, all visible surfaces patched and repatched, a pal-
impsest of centuries of paint and playbills. Dark and
oozing tunnels wandered off on either side, daunting pas-
sages the Old Towners misnamed streets. And yet . . .
and yet there was an astonishing ferment of life on every

side, excitement, anger, joy and sorrow, all of it with an intensity that stirred her blood in ways she hadn't experienced for thousands of years. It frightened her, this surge of emotion.

##

This street they were on was supposed to be the widest way inside Old Town, but the heyyil had to creep along, blowing its honking siren to move aside the strollers, the two-wheeled tiltcarts, the delivery flats and the shills that choked the artery to a tricklet flowing down the middle. It was almost ceiled over by projecting third stories and the fourth stories finished the process so there was no sunlight in here, only looped cables studded with bare bulbs (some white, many colored) that crawled over every surface, lights that had a propensity for fusing suddenly and dangerously as frayed insulation fell apart and bared the wires to the moisture condensing on the stone and stony wood.

Around them were strollers and buyers, hawkers, shills and street stalls—a pawnshop, a jeweler's shop—according to the guide, his stock was mostly silver and semi-precious stones, acquiring what value it had from the skill of the contrivers he bought from. You might pick up some pretty memories in these shops, the guide said, inexpensive but attractive. There were cookstalls selling sausage rolls, noodle dishes, tripe, fritteries, soup, meat pies, hot and cold sandwiches, even full meals—all woven into a tapestry of smells that eddied from point to point, lingered in alcoves, sat in pockets to surprise with sudden delight as the heyyil whined past. There were stalls selling wine, paper and incense sticks, a shoemaker—he was sitting out front, finishing a pair of boots as his son shilled for him, calling out the excellence of his work and the minuteness of his prices. There were stalls selling old clothing, piece goods, iron and copper wares, clocks and watches, bedding straw, rice, beans, tubers. There was a teahouse/whorehouse, its murky interior running back into one of the permanent

buildings, its clutch of small square tables scattered
across the walkway, its barkers striding back and forth
among them, playing the crowd to pull in customers,
shouting the virtues of the women and men—and others—installed in the cubicles up the stairs at the back.
The Upper Floors, the notorious Upper Floors. There
was a smokeshop, a clogmaker's, a stall selling baskets
and wickerware, another selling books and stationery.
Another teashop, a coffeehouse/restaurant/betting shop,
a money changer, a cabinet maker. There was a tavern/
whorehouse with a trio whose performance became
measurably more sprightly as the heyyil got closer, and
twin girls singing a local brand of counterpoint. There
were stalls selling toys, tools, springs and screws and
nails and other such small necessities, spare parts used
and new (more used than new), stalls selling music recordings and flakereaders and other electronic items.
There was a gymnasium/whorehouse. There were stalls
selling wires and cables, ropes, plastic pipes, stalls selling used everything, second hand, third and so on. Stalls
crowding one after another, pushing into the street until
there was barely room for the heyyil to glide past them.

The ancient quarter was filled and overflowing with
noise—music, men, women and others talking at a sustained shout, laughter, groans, screams, spiels, the shuf-
fle of countless feet, the creak of the rotting, crumbling
buildings, the moan of wind sucked into the holes and
hollows, the streets and corridors, the scratching and
scraping of the grit and rubble it blew with it, the buzzing
of the naked bulbs, sputters from fusing wires, the thousand thousand unclassifiable noises from the sweatshops
and the factories—a subaudible undercurrent that the old
man said was a mix of all these, the SOUND Shadith had
heard in his recordings, the SOUND he'd dissected and
analyzed at paralyzing length, the characteristic SOUND
of Old Town. No one living here for any length of time,
the old man said, was ever fully comfortable in other
parts of Karintepe because that Sound was in their blood
and bone, written in their synapses. Even I, the old man
said, I spent less than a full Spring studying Old Town;

it still got to me and I was uncomfortable away from it
the rest of the time I was on Chissoku. There were
wealthy men and women in Old Town, he said, not Goyo
wealthy, but well enough before the world, folk who
could afford to live almost anywhere, men and women
who could lead the shiny lives other locals could only
dream of, with space and clean, new things about them,
men and women who moved away a short while, but came
back into the squash and squalor of Old Town; they always came back, they needed that HUM in their bones.

The progress of the heyyil was slow and undulant with
the guide being sprightly and voluble, doing his best to
overcome the heat and smell and noise and general dis-
comfort with a continual flow of comfy chat. . . .

"When we pass through the Sun Gate, observe closely.
It is the gift of the K'marumcek Kralodate in the fifth
Goyo century. The mirror tiles are natural crystal, each
one hand-polished for five years, then backed with films
of purest gold; the priests clean them every morning and
every evening with the softest and purest rumshaka fiber
and distilled water. The matrix they are set in is an amalgam of gold and diamond dust and aromatic resins. Since
you will see it best in the Sun's Ownlight, I suggest you
look back once we have passed through. During the day
the Temple Square is not at all crowded, as you will see;
local custom is a strong hedge against loitering here. Let
me warn you, do not come here before the NightFair
opens. We cannot guarantee your life or well being and
we will take no action against anyone who injures you.
Your presence is Blasphemy and you are fair game for
anyone you offend." His voice was filled with portent,
low and hushed, meant to thrill his charges.

Shadith looked around, unimpressed. The Square was
ten hectares of graystone flagging and graystone walls,
pitilessly sunlit with rapidly passing cloud shadows sliding across the pallid colorless space. The Temple was
reasonably magnificent, a stepped pyramid faced with
mirrors with a court in front set with black and white
paving stone, punctuated by rows of mirror-tiled columns
standing about like dead trees in a sterile orchard. What

their purpose was she hadn't the vaguest notion and she wasn't interested enough to buzz the guide and ask.

He took the heyyil along the side of the court farthest from the temple, giving them a brisk tourist version of the Goyo version of Truth and Holiness: "The Universe is Order, Hierarchical and Cyclical. Change is Illusion, nothing more, a mirror into which the Blind stare futilely. Blessedness is seeking out and conforming to the inner patterns of the Light. The Light is the Birthright of each being, but only that part of it suited to him. For the beast there is Sun and Star and Fire, and these three are one to him because he has not the capacity to look beyond the dazzle in his eyes and the warmth on his skin. To those that see deepest into the Light, responsibility is given for the guidance of those blinder than they. To each is given the Light appropriate to the State of his Soul. Happy is he who knows his Light." He stopped talking as he turned the heyyil and cut back across the Square to the Gate.

Shadith's nose twitched and her lips thinned as she heard this far too familiar gloss on Life and how to live it.

Yes, oh yes. Let us all tug our forelocks and bow before the righteous. Let's hurrah for the compassionate, the benevolent, the all-knowing Goyo, those high-souled heroes of the ringing cash register and the mighty machete. If they don't get you the Devil will . . . or is it God who'll plant his thumb on you and smoosh you to a smear on the stones? Theology in the service of the powerful. Ahlahlah, one thing they have right, the more things change, the more they stay the same. The NightFair. That's more interesting . . . according to the old man, it's my kind of place . . .

NightFair. That's where you fit, Shadow, the old man said, if you can get at the Sirshaka and buy a space. You and that odd little creature, with your harp and your dancing dreams, you'll fit right in.''

The Square turns into a bigger version of the Raba Katir, the old man said.

Bogmakkers come there from the other parts of the city.

Offworlders come from Starstreet and the hotels on the Islands and the Main, looking for the exotic and the depraved, slumming in relative safety with just enough danger to add spice. And hunting for bargains.

Bargains. Oh, yes. Prices are low and you can find almost anything you want there.

Your heart's desire if it's for sale, the old man said, smiling at her, shaking his head. If it's for sale. . . .

It's a thieves' market, the old man said. A smuggler's den—a lot of small items come from starship crewmen who peddle them to local fences for coin to gamble with or buy time in the Upper Floors. The Kralodate tolerates all this as long as he gets his cut.

Oh, yes, the old man said, he owns the world, but he'll stoop to wring a copper from a beggar.

The NightFair. He turned the words over in his mouth as if they were candy bits.

There are tent bordellos tucked into the corners of the Square with gambling tents set up near them. Be careful around those, the old man said, pressgangs hang out there, if you let your guard down, you could find yourself scrubbing matrix in a Dreadlands mine.

There are wine shops selling by the glass and by the bottle and drug dealers in the shadows selling by the pop and by the packet, with a wary eye out for the pressgangs hunting for rogues and vagrants to fill out their quotas.

There are food stalls. The old man sighed. Wonderful food. Seafood fresh from the bay, cooked on the spot to suit the customer's fancy.

There are singers everywhere, standing on crates and stepladders, belting out their repertoire through portable bullhorns. Some of them will try sabotaging you, Shadow, you're too good. You'll take their light away. So watch your back.

There are acrobats and ropewalkers, dancers and fire eaters, jugglers and mimes.

There are silversmiths and goldsmiths ready to work to the buyer's designs. You see this? He showed her a small silver oval with his portrait etched delicately into the metal, the likeness still strong despite the years that had passed. No, I know, he said, it's nothing special, not great art, but I like it.

There are stalls selling watches and rings, clips and moneybelts, ring chrons and flake players, bits and pieces small and expensive, all stolen of course, mostly from tourists passing through; a lot of them add sextoys, revitalizers and aphrodisiacs, nostrums and tonics.

There are fortune booths of all kinds, palmists and diviners, stick casters, fate birds, card and smoke readers, mediums . . . name the charlatan, you'll find him there, or her, or it, the old man said, smiling fondly, his eyes turned inward; it made her wonder what he was remembering. Especially when a worldship is in, he said.

It's noisy and it's dangerous, exciting, frenetic. . . .

The old man sighed again. It's the bright face of poverty, Shadow. It's the perfume on the unwashed body. I loved it and I loathed it. I'll never forget it. That's the NightFair, that is.

10

As the heyyil hummed back along the Raba Katir, there was a sudden rush of locals coming at it.

They faded into buildings and sidetunnels.

The area cleared impossibly fast, considering its congestion a moment before.

A girl stood near the middle of the street, balanced on her toes, her thin body spring-taut with anger and challenge. She wasn't pretty, but given a little effort she could have been beautiful. The man she was facing was tall and skeletal with a shaved head and blue tattoos where his beard might have been if his branch of the cousins had had facial hair; he wore a shipsuit with greasy patches on the sleeves.

Shadith leaned forward, watching intently.

*Connafallen freetrader trolling for whores. I'd say
he's got good taste and lousy judgment . . . like
every other Connafayl . . . got a feeling he's going
to learn . . . sheesh! look at that. Ah lah my lah,
even old Lion'd have to watch himself round her.
Like a goosed snake. You better remember this and
mind your manners, Shadow.*

The starman pushed through a quartet of younger girls
who'd stopped to watch the fight and went running into
a teahouse, yelling for a doctor, cursing and half blind
with the pain in his hand. The girl in the street kicked at
the thumb she'd gotten with that first slash, sending it
bumping into a storm drain. She wiped the blade of her
razor on her trousers, then put it back where she'd
snatched it, swinging from her lobe like a fancy earbob.
She started after him, but another girl stopped her and
the two of them went swaggering off. Shadith watching
them vanish down a sidetunnel (she couldn't think of them
as streets) as local police came running up.

The guide sent the heyyil trundling on, smoothly ex-
plaining what they'd just witnessed and using the incident
to pitch once more the need for an experienced local
guide.

"As you can see, despoies, life in Old Town can be
dangerous. The crewman apparently mistook that girl for
a woman of pleasure and offered her insult. In his ignorance he accosted a t'gurtsa; if he had managed to offer
more than insult, he would have had the others in the
T'gurtt to deal with. A T'gurtt is a girl gang. Mostly
they're thieves with connections to the Sirshak-kai; they
run in packs of four, five or six and like rats are dangerous if interfered with. Those other girls watching were
part of the fighter's T'gurtt. I don't know if you noticed
it, but they stood deliberately in the crewman's path as
he ran. I have no doubt they cleaned his pockets for him
and got everything he had that wasn't tied down. Please
do remember what I'm telling you about Old Town. If
you come in here alone, especially if you come after dark,
your property and your skin are equally at risk."

He went on about the services available from the Guide Bureau, but Shadith tuned him out again. She'd read about T'gurtts—not much, because there wasn't much data on them. The girls were hostile and suspicious of outsiders. With good reason. They were usually dead before they reached their mid twenties and the ones that trusted anyone outside the T'gurtt died off first. Connections to the Sirshak-kai . . . hmm . . . it would be difficult . . . her body age might be an asset for once . . . the right T'gurtt . . . who better for learning what was where and how to trap a Goyo . . . the girl with the razors . . . she reminded Shadith of herself as she'd been once when her first Teacher died and left her stranded on a world not too unlike this one. Tonight, she thought, yes, this is where I go to ground . . . I have to figure a way to . . . she smiled . . . to seduce a T'gurtt . . . with a little Luck . . . hmm, wonder how Rohant is doing? And what Kikun is up to ? Ah, well. . . .

She settled back in the chair, listening more closely than he deserved to the tired spiel of the guide as he tried to sell them package tours of the other islands—specially junkets to Cumarhane Shimda where the casinos were, and the domed arena with its nightly bloodgames.

11

Shadith stood at the end of the Ferry Landing waiting for the next boat to come in, turning over and over in her mind all the things she wanted to do before sundown. Some of the heyyil riders had gone off to hotels on this island or on the Main, the rest were fidgeting around behind her, talking, yawning, belching, coughing, giggling, the spiderlings were whining, the matriarch was complaining at the top of her needle voice, her companion clones soothing her in basso rumbles. The noise made thinking difficult, but she wasn't really thinking, just vegetating.

The noise died suddenly and completely.

She started to turn. The last thing she heard was the whine of a stunner.

GLADIATOR (without sword)
63 Kirar Sorizakre, day 14, hour 15
Rohant

1

The hawk Sassa flying in slow circles over him, Rohant
the Ciocan ambled down G'sok Jimish (Commerce
Street), the street that bisected Dysinnia Shimda, the second largest of the Islands, heading for G'sok Kobsavash
(Gladiator Street)—an inaccurate name for that collection
of gymnasia. Few of the pro fighters used swords. It was
too dangerous, a provocation and a temptation for Goyo
hotshots to take a cut at them. No one profited when that
happened.

G'sok Jimish was busy with foot and flat traffic, buyers
and sellers, workers and managers moving up and down
it, arguing and bargaining at the top of their voices, slapping fingers into palms, stopping by cookstalls to wolf
dripping meatpies or sausage rolls, wash gargantuan
mouthfuls down with tea or something mildly intoxicat-
ing, trading and nosing out other trades with each chew,
every second of every hour, never stopping. Summer was
ahead, only fifteen years before the Heat began,
SlowDown Time when trade was a trickle and walking
uncovered a punishment. And Winter howled on Summer's heels less than forty years away.

G'sok Kobsavash was different.

There was a hush here.

Cathedral hush.

Solemn. Portentous. The kind of hush that make any
self-respecting inconoclast yearn to throw a stone through
the nearest window.

No street stalls, no hawkers.

71

No shill shouting the Blessings on the Upper Floors.

Only the chaste facades of gym after gym with the occasional house of assignation sandwiched between.

Discreet houses whose word-of-mouth advertising was a whisper in the ear, not a shout.

Rohant the Ciocan wasn't showing it, but he was nervous and more than a little uncertain about what he'd jumped himself into. Dyslaera didn't play bloodgames; they went hair and hide to the death or walked away. During prepubescence there was some ritual sparring to determine status within the male cadres and the female cadres, but any time after that, if they fought at all, it was serious business and done for serious reasons though there was one battle game adults indulged in, one whose wounds were trivial, where the only dying was the little death of orgasm.

He was trained, of course, and his physical equipment was more than adequate, but he had no experience in these deathgames and the closer he got to them, the more distasteful he found the prospect of involving himself in them.

Sassa felt his unease and cried out several times as he glided in wide circles above the roof peaks and the pointed cupolas atop the towers.

A Soncher Hunter, scarred and tonsured, came out of one of the gyms. He stopped on the top step and stared at Rohant, a challenge in narrowed eyes and knotted muscles.

Though his dreadlocks stirred at the unvoiced threat, the Ciocan ignored him.

The Soncher hesitated, then shrugged and went back inside.

It was a taste of what he had ahead of him, a taste that left a coppery bitterness on his tongue.

He thought about Miralys, about their children and only grandchild busy that day tending the beasts in the Spotchals compound . . . children and grandchild dead or maimed by Ginny's bombs . . . S'ragis the baby. His eyes teared. He stopped dead still in the middle of the street, wanting to howl his anger and his grief; he wanted Mir-

alys and their children there with him, howling with him,
Jessetty and Grayand and Hegejarn and Lissorn. . . .

Overhead, Sassa cried out, a wild anguished sound that
momentarily filled sky and street.

He drew a long shaky breath and walked on.

He thought about the children Miralys and he had
sponsored in the business, the cousins and the others who
were also dead or maimed . . . about the beasts, dead
and maimed. . . .

He thought about Lissorn, his little girl slaughtered,
grieving and going into danger daily because of Ginny's
spite . . . about the capture teams struggling to keep the
business together under the constant threat of attack . . .
to keep the money flowing. . . .

He thought about all these things, whistled Sassa to his
wrist, and climbed the stairs to the Taiikambar Tay.

2

day 14, hour 12

"Ask for the Rij, the Gym Master," the Hindorek
Gumbaouz said. "He's expecting you."

Rohant waited, saying nothing.

"He's a Goyo," Gumbaouz said, "so be careful how
you answer him. He's also the eldest uncle of the Kralodate which makes him doubly dangerous. Sorizakre,
they're a treacherous bloody lot, all of them. Carrion
Dragon, their eponym, spirit image of their souls. You
can repeat any of this if you feel like it, he'd take it as a
compliment. He'll eat you for breakfast if he takes a notion against you. If he likes you, he'll make you rich."
He stopped talking, scratched his nose, winked his good
eye. "I've an interest in this, you know. The size of my
fee depends on how well you get over. So listen, Dyslaeror. There's only thing he wants. Only one. That's for
his gym to be el supremo, supra-issimo, if you get me.
Number one on the ratings list." He ran his murky eye
over Rohant's body with greedy satisfaction. "Help him
to that and you can just about ask and get. There could
be fortunes bet on you, Dyslaeror. You and that bird. The

bird, that's a big plus. Handsome thing. Almost a totem. Goyo like that. They say you Dyslaerors talk to your animals. Play on that. It's different. But be careful. Be very very careful. It's not easy walking the highwire with the Goyo snapping at your feet. Maybe you and I can do business. Not now. You're too much of a gamble. You'll need someone watching your back and telling you how to keep from getting yourself killed or thrown to the mines. But not now. Not now. Wait till you show what you're worth, then we'll see.''

3

day 14, hour 15

Sassa trembling unhappily on his wrist, anger triggering his scent glands and the erectile tissue on his scalp so his dreadlocks bushed into a formidable mane, Rohant walked up the broad marble steps and pushed open the door with his free hand, grunting at the weight; it was a massive slab of wood four meters high and two wide.

He stepped into an anteroom barely wider than the door but filled with jewel-colored light pouring through narrow, stained-glass windows rising from the floor to a ceiling at least two stories up; there was a sword in a mailed fist to the right of the door and crossed spears over a bloody shield to the left. The anteroom was empty except for a faint smell of old sweat. Murmuring reassurance to the hawk, he moved toward an inconspicuous inner door at the left side in the back.

A hatch in the sidewall crashed open and a seamed and scarred old Goyo leaned out; hazy, rheumy eyes, one of them white with cataract, peered at him through a fringe of coarse gray hair. The Goyo gummed a series of harsh noises that Rohant with some difficulty translated into *who you, whatcha want?*

"Hindorek Gumbaouz sent me to see the Rij." He glanced at his thumbchron. "Five minutes from now."

With a growling gargle that defied interpretation, the ancient dragged the shutter down.

"Ru-ru, Sassa, it's a bad place, but nothing to bother

us, ru ru, my dal, ru ru." Keeping up the flow of gen-
tling nonsense, Rohant headed for the inner door.

There was no handle on it, only a metal-lined slot a
little higher than his shoulders.

He pushed at it.

It didn't move.

He scratched thoughtfully at the back of his neck and
contemplated the situation. Looks like Gumbaouz was
shooting hot air . . . I called him on his play and he sent
me here to get rid of me. Dio, what a fiasco. He turned
to leave.

"Dyslaeror." A boy's voice, as yet unbroken, filled
with arrogance.

Rohant turned slowly. The boy was young, ten, twelve
at most, a Goyo mix, stockier than a fullblood would be
even at that age—and he was beautiful with strong yet
delicate features, silky skin the color of thick dark cream,
shining black curls, rosy lips, and seagreen eyes.

Someone's pet.

Kicked and caressed until he was vicious as a crippled
weasel.

Goyo bastards, Rohant thought.

He remembered Lissorn at eleven, awkward and de-
structive, mischievous, loud, show-off and shy. Trying
everything that popped into his lamentably inventive mind
because whatever happened, he KNEW in his bones that
his Family was there to catch him if he went too far.

Good boy, good man . . . how it was supposed to work
out.

He said nothing to the boy, just waited, staring at him,
Sassa staring at him.

"Are you armed?" The boy twisted the cord at his
waist, plucked at the loose weave of his knee-length robe;
Sassa's fixed gaze was making him nervous. He didn't
like that and showed it in his scowl, in the growing shrill-
ness of his voice and the nervous wandering of his hands.
"You have to pass a scanner. And you can't take that
bird in 'less it's in a cage."

"I have a knife in my boot and Sassa will not be put
in a cage."

"You can't take it in like that."

"Then I bid you good day." Rohant swung round and started for the street door.

"Wait." A sudden urgency in the word, almost panic. Rohant twisted his head around.

There was a sheen of sweat on the boy's face, cold malevolence in his eyes.

"Make up your mind." He checked the chron again. "I'm already late for the appointment."

"Then come. Follow me."

Rohant got Sassa calmed—the hawk loathed low ceilings—then ambled along the featureless corridor, unhurried and unworried, forcing the boy to slow down or lose sight of him.

His reluctance was more empowering than he'd expected, it gave him a sense that he was the one controlling the situation, not the Goyo he was going to see. If he got hassled more than he felt like taking, he could just walk out. There were other ways of getting at Wargun.

Dio, never thought I'd see the day when the best way to get a job is not want it all that much.

Three turns later the boy stopped before a door. He touched an announcer. "The Dyslaeror is here, Rij-Seffyo."

4

The room was large with a high ceiling and the tall, thin windows the Goyo insisted on despite their impracticability, given the extremes of heat and cold the world was subjected to on its trip about its sun. There was one-way glass in those windows with a golden tinge to it that deepened the yellowish tones of the Rij's face and gave him a kind of spurious health; the light caressed the wood, waking golden lights deep in it and there was wood everywhere, uncarpeted floor, paneled walls, the desk the Rij was sitting at, the rest of the furnishings.

There was a sword rack with half a dozen copper plated swords in it, a stand with short tailed spears, their blades copper plated also.

There was a single bookcase with several rows of leatherbound books, no titles visible, only numbers, the leather dyed to match the wood.

In the corner behind the desk there was a groundside com, a flakereader and a tall case with row upon row of small drawers.

A bare room, no frills—with a richness in its materials that quickly contradicted the first impression of austerity.

The man behind the desk had little in common with either aspect of the room he inhabited. The Rij was skeletal. His nose had a high bridge and the nostrils were large but pinched together. There was a black mole on his upper lip half obscured by the deep creases that ran from his nostrils past the corners of a mouth as lipless as a lizard's. The shoulders and front of his black bodysuit were covered with gray flakes of dead skin.

When Rohant strolled in, the Rij was brushing at the polished top of the desk, scattering skin flakes like dessicated confetti; his long bony hands had a faint tremor which he didn't bother trying to disguise. He fixed dull brown eyes on the Dyslaeror, eyes set deep in their sockets, shadowed beneath wrinkled horny lids.

Rohant suppressed a shudder; it felt like being pinned by a merguit in the Heggerregs. He did what he would have done back home, froze and waited to see if the viper would strike.

The minutes stretched out.

Though Sassa was beginning to put a strain on his arm, Rohant stood relaxed, gazing blankfaced at the old man, sullen, stubborn, not giving an inch.

"Sit down. There." The Rij jabbed a finger at a long low bench beside the door. "I am the Rij Tatta Ry dan Sorizakredam. Address me as Rij-Seffyo. Is that bird going to mess on my floor?"

"Might." After a minute, Rohant added, "Rij-Seffyo.

" 'Tayo's C't!" The Rij got to his feet, unfolding it seemed forever until he was stretched to his full height, nearly three meters of thin bone and dessicated flesh in a shiny black skinsuit; his arms and legs looked like wire wrapped in black rubber. He wasn't wearing his toga or any of his copper ornaments; they were displayed on shelves and hooks behind the desk. He limped across the room and slapped a palm against a door in the sidewall, reached through the opening and pulled out a roll of paper toweling. "Shove this under it. It misses, you clean. With your tongue."

5

The Rij leaned back in the swivel chair, let his hands rest on the arms. "Name," he said. "It doesn't have to be the one you own, I don't give a ghibb who you are. If you're good enough to make the team, you can call yourself what you want, if you're not, the question of calling you anything doesn't arise."

"Rozash, Rij-Seffyo," Rohant said. He'd given some thought to this; males called Rohant were common enough among the Dyslaera, but he didn't want to take a chance that Puk had included the name with the description. As Shadow said, it was better not to start the Goyo adding this to that. After a minute he finished it. "Unmate Rozash."

He thought he'd prepared himself, but it was hard, very hard to say that epithet and attach it to himself. Even though it was a necessary lie and only a lie, Unmate was the foulest thing one Dyslaera could call another—male or female, it made no difference. It meant much more than unattached, it meant being thrown out of Family, Clan, and Species. It meant being invisible to all other Dyslaera. To call himself Unmate was to shout to the world: I AM FILTH! He hugged to himself the memory of Miralys and the children and the business Voallts had built with Honor (not S'ragis, he couldn't afford to think of her, not in here). For them, he told himself. Daring the Rij to comment on the Unmate, he stretched his mouth into the Dyslaeror threat-grin, his ripperteeth fitting upper against lower in yellow-white arcs. On the bench beside him Sassa moved uneasily, mantling his wings and treading at the paper toweling.

The Rij watched the bird until he settled, then he

tapped fingertips on the desk top and ran his tongue over thin bluish lips. "We haven't come by a Dyslaera before. What do you think you can do for us?"

Rohant could smell his pleasure. He exuded it like sweat. The old bastard knew enough about Dyslaera to understand he wouldn't face a succession of angry family members coming to avenge any hurt the Unmate Rozash took in the Games.

Unmate. A selling point. How odd.

A touch of fortunate serendipity, if anything about that foulness could be considered fortunate.

He'd decided to use the Unmate to explain his traveling alone, something Dyslaera just didn't do, but the fight circuit . . . it hadn't occurred to him as a possibility. He said as much to the Rij. "I hadn't thought of such work, not before the Hindorek Gumbaouz made the offer. You tell me what you want, I tell you if I can do it. Then we both know."

"The offer. Yes." Another lengthy pause. "The Hindor must have muddled his presentation. It was not an offer of employment, but an opportunity for a try-out."

"You're saying the thing's a sham. Hindor was just trying it on to catch a greenhead for a fee." Rohant shifted his feet, started to rise. "I'm wasting my breath and your time. Might's well go." He thought about sketching a yayyay, decided against it. "Worldship's leaving next week, I'll be on it."

"No, no. You misunderstand." The Rij dredged up a touch of animation. "We are interested, yes, interested. You said it, I tell you what I want, you tell me if you can do it. You know the Games?"

Rohant settled back. "No . . . Rij-Seffyo."

"They are athletic contests of a sort."

"What sort?"

The Rij primmed his mouth, annoyed that Rohant kept forgetting to use the honorific, leaving it off altogether or tacking it on after a perceptible pause. He said nothing, but there was a promise of retribution in the twitch of his nose and that knotted mouth. "Man against beast. That's to death always, beast or man, whoever takes it. Man against man. Take down. First blood. Third blood, Death. You a swordsman?''

"No . . . Rij-Seffyo.'' Rohant leaned forward, spread his fingers, crooked them, extruded his claws. "These. My feet. I fight barefoot. I've got speed on the flat or climbing. Reaction time, average two seconds quicker than the majority of the cousins. A Goyo'd outreach me. I doubt he'd catch me.'' He spoke flatly, no expression on his face, none in his voice to show the bruises his pride was taking. Parading his parts, a yrz haunch hung on a butcher's hook. "The hawk works in tandem with me, he's a weapon or a distraction or both. That's it.''

"I see. What do you say to a man-on-man with the Taiikambar's stickman, takedown, no blood?''

"What am I fighting for?''

"Honor?''

"I say 'nara, Rij-Seffyo, it was interesting.''

"You're a prickly git. Well, we'll work on that. My offer. Take it or leave it, I do not bargain. Lose, you get fifty guims for your trouble. Win, you have a position in the Taiikambar Tay's string of fighters, room and board and a maintenance salary, a share in the purses taken in the Games, your share increasing with each victory you bring in.''

"And it decreases as I lose?''

"No. If you lose, you leave.''

"All right, let's do it.''

6

day 15, hour 16

The Practice Room was an immense echoing cavity in the center of the Tay. There were groups of men standing about the perimeter, some of them there to watch, some there for practice, their practice interrupted by this trial. There were quite a few of the younger Goyo there, seated in comfort in their own boxes or choosing to stand close to fighters they deigned to patronize, whose careers they were following with varying degrees of detachment. Toward the far end of the room, near the Rij's box, a rope had been stretched between temporary stanchions, marking out a square about six meters on a side. Rohant scowled. One of his primary assets was his speed; anything that limited movement would lessen the value of that asset.

There was an audible inhalation when he walked in with Sassa on his wrist. He'd chosen to fight bare except for a cachesexe and his falconer's glove; his body was broad but sleek with well defined muscles, covered by pale golden-brown fur less than a centimeter long, fur that shimmered and shadowed like silk as he moved. His dreadlocks were stirring and he could smell his own rage at the trap he'd gotten himself into.

The Rij walked beside him, leaning heavily on a knotty cane, one leg stiffer than the other, refusing to bend far at the knee. He ignored this difficulty as he ignored the tremor in his hands. Despite these small weaknesses, he was formidable, only a fool would think otherwise.

The Hindor was no fool. He'd laid the warning out.

Rohant wasn't so sure about himself; being here was no testimony to any wisdom he'd acquired.

They walked in the thickening silence to the marked-off area.

Leaning on his cane, the Rij looked around. "Where's Hikisa?"

A small wrinkled man came from a group of five standing stiffly erect by Tatta Ry's box. He yayyayed with oiled and easy movements, light as a dancer and twice as smooth.

Rohant watched with apprehension; if this was the one he was supposed to fight, he didn't fancy his chances.

"In the locker room warming up, Rij-Seffyo. He had no match scheduled today and was elsewhere when your summons came. I offer his apologies. If you wish, Rij-Seffyo, I'll take his place."

The Rij leaned on his cane and thought that over. "No. Get him." He turned to Rohant. "In there." He nodded at the roped-off area. "Wait. The Tinda-rij will bring the stickman."

"I hear, Rij-Seffyo." Rohant launched Sassa.

The hawk circled warily under the rafters, not liking
the dead air up there. No thermals to hitch a ride on.

Rohant whistled. Sassa stooped in a lightning strike
that just missed his head, went sweeping back to land on
one of the crossbeams. "Right," he said aloud. Hand on
one of the cornerposts, he vaulted the rope and stood on
the mat working his claws in and out, flexing his joints, trying to call down the kind of concentration he needed.

Miralys. My Kedi. He smiled fiercely, showing all his
teeth. My Mystka Drygg. if you were here to mind my
back for me, I might even enjoy this. Enjoy! Get your
mind on what you're doing, Ciocan. Takedown, no blood.
Dio, parading about like this, showing my paces in a
bidding war, only thing worse would be getting beat so
bad I crawl out of here tail between my legs.

7

Hikisa was short and stocky. His head wouldn't reach
Rohant's shoulder, but he moved with that quiet ease the
Tinda-rij had. The staff he carried was about a handwidth
taller than he was; it was dark with age, polished smooth
with much handling despite the dents here and there along
its length. Either the man had inherited the thing, or he'd
been at this long enough to make Rohant look a clown
given half a chance.

Hikisa dipped through a respectful yayyay, then jumped
lightly over the rope and landed with his feet a little apart,
the staff held before him parallel to the floor.

Rohant bowed quickly, stiffly. Given the choice, he'd
avoid this preliminary pretty-play, it was gliding on dogshit as far as he was concerned, but he wasn't standing
on his own ground. Steep yourself in any set of rules,
his teacher said, it's only when you know them inside
and out that you can break them to your profit rather than
your cost. It was a teaching he'd proven out more times
than he could remember and he put it in effect now.

The Tinda-rij snapped his fingers and two of the fighters came to take their places at the north and west sides
of the enclosure. He turned to face the Rij, yayyayed. "I

present to you, Seffyo Tatta Ry, Hikisa Sankatar for Taii-kamabar Tay, fighting with staff only, and the Unmate Rozash, fighting with claw and hand and hawk.'' His voice wasn't loud, but his articulation was so precise every word was etched on the ears. He turned again to face the two inside the rope. ''This is an audition bout,'' he said. ''It continues until the first takedown. For the benefit of the stranger, takedown is counted when the shoulders of one fighter both touch the floor. This must be a result of the act of the other fighter; shoulder flips and other such activities do not count unless the opponent seizes the advantage and forces a pin. The two touches need not be simultaneous but must occur within a limit of thirty seconds. The judgment of the Three is final if their verdict is unanimous. If one disagrees, the bout continues. Are there any questions? Then proceed on signal. Wait. Wait. Now!''

Rohant exploded into a low raking dive, intending to hook Hikisa's feet from under him, hoping his speed could counter the other's skill.

Hikisa stepped aside, at the same time striking at a nervepoint on Rohant's shoulder with the end of the staff, intending to disable at least one of the Dyslaeror's arms.

Slapping the staff down into the mat before it touched him, Rohant used it as a pivot, curled around it and struck at Hikisa's ankles, his claws catching a sandal thong—it wasn't quite enough to take the stickman down, but it drove him into a rapid backpedaling, his timing off, his confidence momentarily shaken by how seriously he'd underestimated the Dyslaeror's speed and the length of his reach.

Rohant whipped onto his feet and ran at the stickman. He blocked a thrust of the staff with his padded gauntlet, was a hair short on his attempt to get his claws into the stickman's tunic. Hikisa managed a back-and-side move that got him clear and gave him space for a quick jab at Rohant's mid-section that would have cracked a rib if it had landed with a touch more precision.

Still off balance and out rhythm, Hikisa ran backward,

swinging the staff in figure eights to fend off Rohant's attempts to get inside, up close, where the Dyslaeror's strength and claws would count most.

Jabbing and slashing where he saw opportunity, getting hits when he could, slowly but inexorably, by force of his years of experience, Hikisa moved toward the mastery of the situation.

Rohant saw it happening. He was keeping the stickman on the defensive, but he couldn't get inside and he was taking a pounding. Nothing disabling so far, but it was only a matter of time. . . .

Hikisa sensed his faltering, went for his knee.

Rohant dropped, slapped the staff aside with his gauntlet, pivoted, struck at the stickman's legs with his clawed feet; at the same time, he called Sassa down.

The staff came round in a smooth swift strike, going for his knee again.

He twisted away, whipped his arm out, caught it before Hikisa could snap it back, curled up and began climbing it, struggling to keep the staff immobilized, without letting the stickman flip and pin him.

The hawk dived, struck at the stickman's eyes.

Hikisa flinched.

Rohant loosed the staff, drove inside and got his arms around the stickman's waist, his head into the stickman's ribs. He muscled Hikisa up and over, took him to the canvas and forced his shoulders down.

The Tinda-rij called out, "Takedown, Unmate Rozash." The other two echoed him.

Breathing hard, Rohant got to his feet. He thought about extending his hand to Hikisa, helping him onto his feet with a laugh and a compliment. He got a look at the man's cold black eyes and decided to save his energy for something useful.

The Rij got to his feet. "Not a pretty fight, no. You'll never make the list of classic warriors, Dyslaeror, but you'll kill a lot of them before someone gets you. Tinda-rij, show him his room, give him the Tay futak and bring him to my office at the beginning of the next hour. And get rid of that locator bracelet. Can't have that on a Taii-kambar fighter. Too tempting. Blow his hand off." After a short pause, he added, "Welcome to the Taiikambar Tay, Unmate Rozash."

1

Shadith woke to the smell of leather and herbs. She was kneeling on a rough plank floor, held there by men standing close to her; she could smell them, rancid, sour sweat and body odor worse than Rohant at his maddest. It was dark around her, an echoing darkness—wherever she was, it was big. Warehouse?

A light came on over her head. Blinding. She could see the curve of the front edge of the cone just beyond her knees.

A hand grabbed her hair, jerked her head up.

Someone came round a tall pile of crates. She couldn't see much more than a shadowy bifurcated form, but the height told her he had to be Goyo.

He bent over her. One hand slid down the side of her face, the side with the fauxskin covering the hawk acid-etched into her cheek. "Clever," he murmured. His voice was emotionless, all life squeezed out, no anger, not even any triumph; he was all the more terrifying because he wasn't trying to frighten her. "Not clever enough. You should have diverted the Dyslaeror. I do not believe in coincidence. No." His thumbnail dug into her cheek, drawing blood as he sought the edge of the fauxskin. He found it and jerked it off, touched dry fingertips to the fine brown lines. "Ah, yes. You lie fluently, child. Don't lie to me. Where is the third?"

"I don't know."

"I said don't lie." He didn't move. His hand rested lightly on her neck, cool, dry. Without straightening from

86

his semi-crouch, he turned his head, spoke to someone in the darkness. "Get the probe, Kasedoc."

"It's not a lie, it's not. He's somewhere around, but I don't know where. That's his gift. People don't see him. Or if they do, they forget what they saw. He doesn't trust anyone any more. Not us. Not anyone."

He heard the terror in her voice, felt her desperate trembling, and believed her. He wanted to believe her. She read a consuming, overwhelming distaste for hurting her and didn't understand it; this was the man who'd bought at least five of Ginny's Special Editions. He took his hand from her neck and stood erect. "Then there is nothing more I need from you." He stepped into the darkness beyond the cone of light. "Katil, Sujin, keep her here until sundown. If I haven't countermanded the order by then, shoot her. Take her body out and drop it in Jinssi Hole. The rest of your fee will be waiting at the Shuttle office."

NightFair
63 Kirar Sorizakre, day 14, hour 19
Pikka Machletta and the Razor T'gurtt

1

Pikka Machletta bopped through the Sun Gate, elbows out, shoulders swinging, Fann beside her, the small herd of tourists they'd wiggled into giving them plenty of room and a rain of sidelong stares.

Their involuntary escort began breaking apart as soon as they were past the Gate, the tourists peeling off as one thing or another caught their eyes.

Pikka Machletta eeeped as Fann poked her in the ribs. "What 's?" she said.

"Him. Over there by Hotso Harry. The one with the flat nose and the tattoos. He was one of 'em. I don' see the others."

"Don' matter, they round somewhere, bound to show up. Les do it." She waggled her tongue at the crewman, then went skipping off with Fann close behind.

The offworlder started after them, calling to him the rest of his mates including the git whose thumb Pikka had removed. They were grim-faced and determined and terminal brainwipes. Not the sense they were born with, hitting on a local like this. Served them right, should they end in the mines.

Pikka Machletta skipped behind a tailorbooth. "Sheeh! Goomoo cubed."

"Eh, Pik, when the thumbless wonder brings a uh-uh off Starstreet, y' know his headbone solid clean through. Watcha thinkin? You din' say."

"I'm thinkin they do 't once, they do 't again, got more reason, huh?"

"Maybe so. So?"

"So we find usselves a pressgang, one standin round wishin. Huh?"

"Ooooh, you ev-il, Pik."

##

The colored lights flickering and flowing through the crisp, pungent night air, washing over them, painting them crimson and sapphire and gold, Pikka Machletta and Fann wove in and out of the booths, giggling and switching their behinds at their pursuers, teasing them with more tongue and a play of obscene gesture, calling back insults, provoking them into running harder and faster until they were banging into tourists and locals alike, kicking up a growing fuss.

When Flatnose stepped on an acrobat's hand, he got laid out by a club of a neighboring juggler.

Pikka celebrated by dropping two dokies in a cook-stall's changebowl and snatching up a pair of hot egg-rolls. She tossed one to Fann, juggled the other hand to hand while she darted round the back of the stall.

They jigged past a fire eater who took one look at what was happening and set the lead man's hair on fire.

Clapping and whistling with the drummers, they went skittering past a theater company putting on a dance show, blew twin razzberries at the starmen, then plunged through the middle of a tourgroup listening to a fortune-teller's shill.

As they neared one of the gambling tents, they slowed to a sedate walk, then poked each other and giggled when they saw four men in dull black cowls standing in the shadows. They angled toward them.

There was a sudden burst of shouts and shrieks. Pikka glanced over her shoulder. Two of the pursuers were shoving past a wrinkled old woman with a small herd of servants who looked like they were hatched from the same egg. She was yelling and hitting at the starmen, screaming at the blank-faced servants to kill the blasphemers. At least that's what it sounded like. Pikka

Machletta had enough Interlingue to chat up offworlders
or run a small scam, but much of that crone's noise was
too fast and garbled for her to make sense out of it. The
hashshar were trying to untangle themselves but otherwise ignoring her.

Pikka shivered, suddenly frightened. This wasn't fun
any more.

The front man was soggy and singed and raving. His
eyes were fixed on her. He wanted to tear the meat off
her bones and eat it raw; the second wasn't so bad, but
bad enough. The one who started all this was several
paces behind, looking whitefaced and weary—having
one's thumb sliced off and losing a couple pints of blood
was enough to blunt the sting of a rabid shek, let alone
a braindead Goomoo. No sign of the fourth, he was probably still out, the juggler and the acrobats stripping him
of everything remotely salable. "Fann," she breathed,
"les do it."

They squealed, waved their arms and ran straight at
the pressgang, dodged around behind them and scooted
on hands and knees into the narrow space under the back-
flap of the tent, between the tent and the Square wall.

                              2

"You. Come outta there."

Pikka Machletta started to crawl out, swore under her
breath at her stupidity and tugged the razor loose from
its snapclamps. She tucked it into her hidabelt and
slapped back at Fann's razor. "Off," she muttered, then
went wiggling out.

Two of the starmen were laid on their faces, straps on
their arms and ankles, their clothes torn, cre-belts gone
along with anything else they had worth a dokie at Tuck
the Tick's or one of his scurfy cousins. Thumbless must
still be loose somewhere, but she didn't dare look for
him.

Papa Pressman was holding two energy shooters, tiny
things no bigger than his pointing finger. He slipped them

into a pocket and scowled at Pikka. "What's all this, rat?
You t'gurtsa, an't y'?"

"Uh-huh. Got futak." She tapped at the metal square
shining wetly in the wavering torchlight.

"Don' mean shit you foolin with starshit. What you
playin, huh? An' you say Presser Sef, you talka me."

"My friend 'n me, Presser Sef, we an't whores. Hashshar wanna jogga us ov-ah, we say no, hafta say it strong.
They turn mean, go chasin us. We get away. They come
after us. I say true. Swear it 'fore the Blurdslang." She
flared her nostrils, toed the nearest body. "No 'count
mommajogga, only good for mines."

Pressman cuffed her. "Don' you go smartmouthin,
rat." He grunted, inspected her with insulting slowness,
pushed her aside and looked Fann over. "Tayo's C't, gotta
be numbbrains and blind besides, jumpin you two erf-
erfs for some jig-jag-jogga. Get outta here 'fore I change
my mind and dump y' down with 'em."

Pikka Machletta yayyayed respectfully, then went darting off, Fann following close behind. They danced around
the old woman being expertly soothed by her attendants,
disrupted that soothing with slow warbling sarcastic
whistles, went giggling off as the crone started shrieking
for their blood.

3

The high melted fast. Pikka Machletta walked with her
shoulders down, her heels dragging. She was tired, so
tired, but she couldn't go home and rest; she couldn't
walk back across the bridge to the Main before she and
the T'gurtt had got something for the stash. Summer
slows were coming and Winter snows. They might not
live that long, but if they did there had to be money for
food and fuel. No rest, not now, not ever.

Fann pinched her arm. "They din' get Goomoo."

"Nah-nay." She yawned. "Him or Flatnose. Have to
keep an eye out for 'em." She yawned again. "Les go
find the others. Time we get to work. Koyohk!"

"Huh?"

"Mordo. Talking with Goomoo. Don' bother lookin, they ducked."

"Dragon an't gonna start trouble, not here."

"Ay-yeh, but we gotta go home. Nother thing we gotta do, huh?"

"Stomp some dragon."

"Ay-yeh." Pikka frowned at the sky. "Mompri's up. I guess we can go home light, seein what we got from the Tick. Give it 'n hour, then we slide quiet, leave 'em sucking tit. Huh?"

Fann shrugged. "Maybe so maybe no."

The t'gurtsas strolled across the Square, heading for the Temple Plaza and the Court of Columns; they were quieter now, both of them, shifting back to business, looking about for marks.

The crowd was thickening nicely. The worldship was leaving in a few days so passengers were dropping in droves to hunt for bargains, cupidity excited by the show-and-tell of others who'd already been. There'd be more and more of them as the days passed, green and greedy with cre-belts dripping coin. Doing their part in the ecology of Chissoku, giving sustenance to all the little fleas that bit them.

The futaks would go fast as long as the marks kept coming. There'd be challenge fights all along the line as Torkusses hit on T'gurtts, looking to cut in ahead of them, dead T'gurtsas and Torkksos dumped into the cinerators or down the sewers, the wounded patching themselves up and going back for more.

The Blurdslang didn't care about precedent or rights, he passed out the day-futaks first come first served until they were gone; nor did he make any distinction between male and female—unlike his masters and the ruling Goyo; it wasn't known if he could recognize the difference, it wasn't even certain he was HE and no one had the courage (or was it stupidity?) to ask. He was simply the Blurdslang of Blurdslang Alley, truthreader and incorruptible adjunct to the Sirshak-kai.

Tonight it was still easy, rumors of the Goyo slummers kept a lot of the gangs away, so Razor T'gurtt had gotten

their futaks without a fight. Pikka Machletta thought
about tomorrow and sighed and her feet dragged even
more. She loathed stand-and-slash brawls; her sisters-in-
T'gur got hurt that way. So far Razor had been clever
enough to win by surprising the Torkusses that hit on
them, but there were only so many ways to fight a fight
when you had to stand in line.

4

In the short time it took to traverse the Square, the
noise increased from deafening to nerve deadening.
Singers were trying out their bullhorns, shills were pro-
claiming the excellences of those who hired them, visitors were shouting to each other or to the stallkeepers as
they bargained for this'n that. Theater drums were booming out conflicting rhythms . . . noise piled on noise,
peak reinforcing peak until it was like hammers in the
face. . . .

They ran up the curving walk and stepped into silence.

Pikka Machletta leaned against a mirrored column,
closed her eyes; there were times in this place when she
seemed to touch something beyond and behind the desperate clamor of her life. It was a pleasure she never
sought and could not endure for long. It confused her
and started her questioning everything she believed in;
she had a feeling if she indulged herself, she'd end up
slitting her wrists, unable to face the grinding ambigui-
ties of day-to-day surviving.

Except for such brief, private moments, she refused to
give more than minimum service to the Temple, being
assessed with all the others in Old Town to pay for the
ceremonies, herded like beasts for the ritual blessings,
yayyaying to order and all that, while she transferred the
corrosive hatred she felt for the Goyo and all their works
to Guintayo their god.

Pikka straightened, scrubbed at her eyes with the heels
of her hands. "No. We an't leavin early. We goin to pull
in as much as we can and if any trogg tries jumpin us,
we snap his danga. Huh?"

"Eee-villl, Pik," Fann said absently; she set her hands on her hips and scowled at the shadows drifting about them, dark-rimmed splotches of colors changing with each breath of the wind that rambled among the columns, tilting and turning the movable mirrors. "If they went fishin before we got here, I'm gonna snatch the little sommm-thins bald both ends."

Pikka Machletta dropped her hand on Fann's shoulder. "Give 'em a whistle, maybe somethin chased them farther in."

Being cautious by nature, what Fann whistled was a phrase from a Guintayo hymn; she listened, whistled another phrase.

A second later three of the youngers were fluttering around Pikka Machletta and Fann, hugging them, gabbling at them in hushed voices, looking around, peering into shadows, excited, anxious, triumphant; even the silent Halftwins Kynsil and Hari joined the chorus of voices . . . we saw them waiting at the Gate . . . Pik, Fann . . . we saw them . . . we couldn't come on here . . . we had to watch . . . we had to be there . . . if you needed us . . . we followed . . . we stayed back far enough they din't see us . . . you din't see us . . . pressgang neither . . . ooooh, you eee-vil, Pik . . . that was great . . . ooooh yeh . . . did you see . . . did you see Mordo and the Goomoo . . . Ingra. . . .

"Ingra," Pikka burst out, "where's Ingra? Hush, rest of you. Mem, give it to me."

"Ing can be stubborn, you know that. She went off after Goomoo. The Halftwins and me, we were going to thump her, playing with Dragons alone was stupid, but she said she wasn't going to DO anything, just watch 'em. She said she wouldn't be more than a half hour, she'd be back here then for the futak. Maybe Goomoo won't do anything but hang about, but she thought she ought to have a look."

Pikka Machletta sighed, patted Mem's arm. "An't your fault, Mem. Nothin you could do." She tapped Fann's arm. The Second dug into her hidabelt, took out the futaks, handed them around. "Hari, Kyn, Kaoy says

there'll be Goyo here tonight. I din't see any, but Fann
and me we were a bit busy, you know. You spot any of
'em?''

Kynsil shook her head. A second later Hari followed
her lead.

"Well, you know what to do if you see a Goyo comin.
Say it Kyn. I mean it."

"If we settin a mark, we back off and duck for cover."

"I catch you playin games with Goyo, I'll do like Fann
says and snatch you bald both ends. You hear?''

Kynsil grinned at her, then wiped the smile away and
nodded with careful sobriety. "We not stoo-pid, Pik."

"Not stoo-pid," Hari said.

"Huh." Pikka Machletta flicked a black curl off Kynsil's forehead. "Not stoo-pid, y' jus don' think sometimes. Y' can't not think when Goyo's around. And watch
out for Dragon, but don' back off. Yell for jinsbek if you
gotta. This 's one night we don' count cost, huh? We'll
meet by the Sun Gate just 'fore Mompri-set and go out
with the last push. Y' hear? Huh? Scoot."

She watched them dance away, turned to Fann. "You
go with Mem." She pinched Fann's arm to stop her protest. "I'll fish around, see if I can come up with Ingra.
Mompri-set. Sun Gate. Remember? Go on. Get!"

Mem was the most striking and the most vulnerable in
the T'gurtt. She was clumsy and fragile and no kind of
fighter, though she could throw anything small enough to
pick up and hit what she aimed at hard enough to hurt.
Without making a fuss or even talking it over, all of them
kept an eye on her. shielding her not just from people
who wanted to hurt her, but from disturbing sights (as
much as they could). Mem was special. They all felt it.
Gentle and loving and gifted. And lovely. Terribly lovely.
It was showing more every day. On nights like this when
the Goyo were about, Pikka Machletta was sick with fear
one of them would fancy her.

##

   Pikka Machletta walked slowly from the columns, frowning and chewing her lip. She couldn't see any escape for Mem. She wouldn't stay away from the Fair or let Razor go out without her when they worked othertimes, that would shame her. Besides, the T'gurtt needed every hand earning and she had the cleverest fingers. But if she came out, it was only a matter of time before some Goyo noticed her and sent his guards to fetch her.

   Shaking off her malaise, Pikka plunged into the crowd and began the night's work.

THE LITTLE MAN WHO WASN'T THERE
63 Kirar Sorizakre, day 14, hour 20
Shadith, Kikun

1

Shadith strained at the ropes on her arms. They'd tied her elbows in back and her wrists in front, wrapped more rope about her legs, knotting it at her knees and ankles

Talk about your double-knotters. That pair might've had lessons from Ginny.

She could almost reach the top of her left boot. Almost. She'd tried it again and again and again until her arms were swollen, her wrists cut and bleeding. Half the width of her palm farther and she could touch the hilt of the knife she kept in there. A braincrystal blade sharp enough to cut a thought in half. Saved her life more than once. Didn't look like it was going to do it now.

Katil and Sujin had picked her up, carried her to this room. It was an insulated storage room, a cube two meters on a side with no windows; the door had a rubber seal, air came in through what looked like multiple filters. She couldn't hear a thing in here, not even the long low sighs of the air conditioner. Couldn't hear and wouldn't be heard, no matter how loudly she yelled, so she didn't waste her strength trying.

She leaned against the packing case, closed her eyes. Ironic. That's what it was. When she wanted some creep to try a little rape, he wasn't interested.

Too frightened of that Goyo, won't take a chance on fooling with me. Sar! Just let one of them come

97

*in here and cut this rope off me. . . . Got till sun-
down. Is it darker in here? Gods, I can't tell anything, could be high noon outside and I wouldn't
know. Relax, Shadow. Tenser you get, the less you
can do. Stupid, stupid, stupid . . . we should have
known . . . once Wargun knew there was a Dyslaeror after him, they'd all be suspect and anyone
with them. I don't believe in coincidence he says.
Stupid, stupid staying together. World like this.
Eternal vigilance is the price of tyranny. Poor old
Lion, Wargun knows who you are and why you're
here. Going to let you bleed for his entertainment.
Cage you like a fighting cock . . . gods, I've got to
get out. Got to warn him. Wonder what Kikun's doing? At least he's safe. What are they going to do
about the locator, you don't drop a corpse wearing
a beacon saying here I am. Sheeh! Don't be denser
than you have to be, Shadow. They'll slice your
hand off and the thing drops free. That's if they
haven't noticed already how loose it is . . . aaaah!
this isn't getting me anywhere. . . .*

She wriggled around until she was on her side, brought
her heels up as close to her buttocks as she could, bent
her shoulders around, then twisted. Her fingers brushed
the top of her boot; she strained, trying to reach an extra
inch . . . her fingers, her hands went numb, she couldn't
feel what she was touching . . . she cursed passionately,
kept fumbling at her legs, trying to force her hands to
catch hold of something, anything. . . .

Her legs shook, her arms shook, her torso shook . . .
she couldn't hold that position a second longer . . . she
went limp, came out of the twist and lay shaking on the
smooth wood floor. . . .

She heard a sound at the door. She couldn't move yet,
she couldn't see anything. She lay frozen, waiting.

Brush of the rubber seals against wood, faint creaking
from the hinges. A gray light crept into the room, a
shadow moved across it.

Kikun knelt beside her. "Well, Shadow," he said. "This is a mess, isn't it."

"What happened to Katil and Sujin?" She sucked in her breath as he began easing the rope out of the furrows on her wrists.

"Those two men, their names?"

"Uhhh . . . h' " Her legs came apart as the ropes fell off them; the backs of her boot heels rattled against the floor.

"Stuck them in a freezer, under some packs of fur. Not very good fur, they won't be found for a while. Think you can stand?"

"Let me try sitting first. Give me a hand, will you?"

He helped her up and settled behind her, holding her in the circle of his arms.

They sat like that for ten, maybe fifteen minutes, neither of them speaking.

2

"Rohant," she said. She leaned against the wall as he pushed the door shut, slid the bars in place, and clicked the locks shut. "Wargun knows about him. I don't know what's going to happen."

Kikun eased his shoulder under her arm, helped her to walk away from her ex-prison. "I had a word with the Ciocan a short while ago. He's signed with the Rij of the Taiikambar Tay, who happens to be eldest uncle to the present Kralodate. He should be all right as long as he keeps winning."

"And as long as he keeps away from Wargun. You going to tell him?"

"Oh, no. The Ciocan wouldn't take it well. Oh, no. Through here. The door's a few steps farther."

"Is it dark yet?"

"Just."

"Good timing, Kikun. They were going to shoot me soon's it got dark. Where are we anyway?"

"Fur warehouse quarter of a mile from the Ferry

Landings. I found a place not far from here. You can rest, have a bath. All right?''

She chuckled. ''You're a life saver twice over, god-dancer.''

''Mmmmm. Can you stand by yourself?''

''There's a wall, I can lean against it. Um, wait a minute, let me have a look outside first.'' Shadith settled her shoulders against the stone, it was cool and solid and reassuring. The feeling was back in her hands, her arms, her legs. And the pain. More and more pain with every minute. She ignored it, *reached* for the nearest bird.

She brought the gull swooping down the street outside the warehouse, circled it round and brought it back, spiraling up for an overview. No one about. No one at all. Good. ''Let's get out of here, Kikun. The place stinks.''

NIGHTFAIR 2
63 Kirar Sorizakre, day 14, hour 21
Pikka Machletta at work

1

Pikka Machletta drifted behind a rotund cousin female and bumped her into the display of silver and copper medallions she was inspecting, creating a small confusion as the stallkeeper grabbed for his goods and the woman tottered. Pikka darted a hand under a wobbling arm and plucked a flakereader from the shoulderbag of a man fending off the cousin and trying to maintain his own balance. The reader went down her leg into her dittabag and she harvested a loose ringchron from another tourist, then several other bits and pieces until the stallkeeper howled for a jinsbek to straighten out the mess.

She'd been working toward the edge of the knot of visitors, now she slid away, whistling descants atop the song Beba Firehair was belting out at her stand a few paces off. She grinned up at Beba, snapped the fingers of both hands in a pantomime of applause and tossed a guim into the changebowl. It started a rain of coins, as if the tourists gaping at the singer needed some kind of validation before they admitted they liked the song. Beba winked at her, made an *O-U* sign and threw herself into the music, body as well as voice, producing undulations that looked impossible in a woman her size.

Ingra pushed out of the crowd, jerked a thumb at the Temple, and faded.

Anger rising in her, Pikka went charging toward the Temple Plaza.

2

When the silence hit Pikka Machletta this time, she
barely noticed it. And she forgot prudence completely,
yelled: "Ing, get over here. Where are you?"

"Hey, tune it down, Pik, you wan t' get naged to a
penty cell?"

"Haah!" Pikka Machletta pulled her hand down her
face, wiping away the anger with the sweat. She didn't
speak again until she had her mask pulled back in place.
"You left Mem and the Halftwins. You left them, Ing."

"I left them." Ingra wrapped her misshapen arms
across her chunky torso and glared at Pikka Machletta.

Pikka closed her eyes and set her shoulders against a
column. "Ah ri'," she said. "Why?"

"Got my futak?"

"Here." Pikka fished in the hidabelt, brought it out.
"Catch. Why?"

"You could ask 'fore you yell." Ingra tacked the futak
high on her shoulder. "I left 'em in here. 'S a sanctuary,
an't it?'Sides, Kyn and Hari can take care of themselves
and Mem, too, comes to that. And nothin's gonna happen
in the Square. Not any more. Even Goomoo an't THAT
crank. 'S worth a takin a little chance to see what him
and Dragon's up to."

Pikka Machletta straightened up, stood rubbing slowly
at the small of her back. "Did y'?"

"I got close enough to hear a snatch now 'n then.
Pressgang got him that Jaggarix conked. Goomoo sorta
moaned when he hear that. Mordo look like he'd died
and faked into heaven, he know he got ol' Goomoo by
the oogas, can name his price. He whistle up Bugeye,
send him off for Kidork, he buys some *X-ta-cee* off Germ
the Pusher and feeds it to Goomoo who looks like he
don' know what t' hell's goin on, then he hustle Goomoo
into the *Filigree Hole* behind Weststage, I can't go in
there, I don' know what I should do, wait or get back.
I'm thinkin maybe I can find someone I know and sike
out what Goomoo's at in there, maybe just the usual, but
the Hole's doin too much business, none of the workin

girls get a breath. I'm about to give up, when Goomoo comes out with Bugeye and they go for the Gate.'' Ingra paused, caught her breath, then plunged back into her story. ''Wan't hard to keep outta sight, problem was followin 'em in that crowd. When I lost 'em, I kept headin for the Gate and after a while, I'd pick 'em up again. Goomoo was floatin out t' nowhere, Bugeye had to keep yankin at him to keep him from wanderin off, so they wan't makin much progress, but they finally did get out the Gate. The Raba Katir was worse 'n the Square, tryin to go 'long there's like fightin The Sluice at Tideturn. They hung out a few minutes in a doorway 'cross from Blurdslang Alley, but a jinsbek chased 'em. Me, I wan't about to fool with the Katir, I got Mama Fubenno to let me in the Shiintap Tenny and went long the inways, lookin out a squint when I get a chance to see if they still goin 'long, last I see 'em, they out the Old Town Gate, goin east 'long G'sok Shikopru. I figure they gonna hole up and wait for rest of Dragon and jump us somewhere on G'sok Shikopru or maybe on Eastbridge itself. So I come back.''

Pikka Machletta stroked the cool ivory handle of the Razor. ''Ah ri','' she said finally. ''Les get working.''

3

day 14, hour 26

The Goyo came when the moon Mompri touched zenith, two men strolling through the Gate as if there was no crowd at all—and of course there wasn't where they were, there was a clear three-meter ring about them and theirs.

Pikka Machletta slipped into shadow, Ingra quick beside her, both of them tense with worry about Mem, hoping Fann had got her into cover soon enough. Then she recognized the older and taller of the two men. The Rij Tatta Ry. She couldn't see enough of the other Goyo to name him, but he almost had to be Tatta Ry's kin-by-law, the Fevkindadam; they usually came together. She relaxed. Once upon a time, Tatta Ry was said to be a horror, look on him and prepare to suffer. That was a long, long time ago; the ages and age itself had sucked the danger out of him. And Wargun's habits required very special talents; the one thing you could say for the man, he didn't run after children; she knew that from personal experience. Pikka Machletta licked her lips, shut her eyes. She wouldn't pay homage to Guintayo or any other god or devil the Goyos tainted, but there was one entity she gave careful reverence. The Lady who beckoned once, then passed on. Sweet Luck. Fickle Luck who so quickly turned sour if you neglected her gifts. She touched her lips, heart, made the *O-U* sign and silently promised a guim for Kaoyurz' begging bowl as a Thank Offering for letting the slummers be these two and keeping Mem safe another night.

The fairgoers circling past her opened up for a moment and she saw why the Rij had come to the Square this night. At the head of the straggle of fighters pacing behind him like a bevy of chicklets following their hatch-mother, there was a new favorite. The Rij wanted to show him off, set rumors running that would reach the ears of the other Tay Rijes. The new fighter was a wide man, not particularly young, who moved with an angry ease that Pikka Machletta found extraordinarily erotic. She couldn't take her eyes off him. And there was the bird he carried on his arm, a raptor, its breast speckled ivory, glints of gold in the dark brown plumage on its back and wings. It looked straight at her as if it could see her . . . kept looking at her until the man's body intervened.

Pikka Machletta straightened, retied her headthongs and patted at her bulging thighs; the dittabags were plumping out nicely, but there was still room for more and a bunch of hours before the Fair shut down. "We got work, les do it."

CONFIRMING THE GETOUT
63 Kirar Sorizakre, day 14, hour 21
Shadith, Kikun
Arel the smuggler

1

Shadith rubbed the ointment in, pulled her mouth down as she inspected her swollen, abraded wrists. "This I didn't need. Good thing this body heals fast." She realized what she'd said, clicked her tongue in exasperation.

When oh when is it going to be MY body? The day I get myself killed, I suppose.

She shook her head, called out, "Kikun, what is this place? For a hidehole it's pretty elaborate."

His voice came back, muffled by the intervening wall. "It's listed on the plan as the caretaker's apartment."

"You don't sound very convinced."

He came back into the room carrying a bowl with hot towels rolled up in it, settled by her feet, and began tending the abrasions about her knees. "From what we know of the Goyo, do you?"

"Generosity is not one of the traits they're noted for." She sucked in a breath as the hot cloth touched her skin, first one knee, then the other.

"Yes. I think this was a home-from-home where somebody could relax without worrying about his reputation."

"What happens if someone wants to use it again?"

"Won't."

"You're very sure of that."

"Am."

"Spirits talking to you again?"

105

He hiccupped a chuckle, took the cloths away and began spreading ointment over the bruises. "No need. The Goyo Family that owns this warehouse has come on hard times. Give me your hand."

Sweat popped out on her face as the heat hit the torn flesh. "H h hard times?"

He worked in more ointment, then began wrapping gauze bandage around her wrist. "There's not much family left," he said, "just one old dodderer. He stays in his apartment on Joggorezel. Other Families rent space from him to store their overflow. Gives him some kind of income. He's too miserly to pay for a caretaker and the others don't bother. How I spent my afternoon, looking for a place like this. Other hand."

"A a and you j just walked in, lifted the key and settled down." She used the back of her released hand to wipe sweat off her face.

"More or less."

"If there's a hard search. . . ."

"There won't be. I had a talk with one of the mercs before I killed him. Wargun paid them to dump you, then go offworld. He'll be thinking you're dead and he's safe. Except for Rohant and he doesn't have to worry about Rohant as long as the Ciocan is shut up in the Tay." He finished with the ointment and began bandaging her other wrist.

"So we might as well go on with it. The singing and the rest."

He dropped her hand, leaned his head against her knee, and went off to *nevernever*.

She sighed, touched his head, was surprised as always at how soft and warm he was. She didn't understand much about him, why he stayed with Rohant and her when he didn't need to. He could go home and Ginny couldn't do a thing about it. His world was one of the Voallts Korlatch capture worlds and the Dyslaera weren't about to give out the location of any of those. He kept coming up with useful hints and assurances, as if he were some kind of computer they turned on when they needed it. And he didn't seem to get tired of that. She would, she knew that, she'd yell and fuss and get the hell out.

He wriggled under her hand, moved away from her. "Go and do it, go and do it, bad and good come from it, but go and do it."

2

day 14, hours 23
at the ottotel on the Westshore

Shadith slid her shoulder through the strap of the harp-case, looked at the rest of her belongings. "Kikun, you mind taking these things and stowing them for me? I've got something I should take care of before I go back otherside."

Kikun pulled up the hood on his cloak. "All right. You're still planning to approach the T'gurtt? Why not wait till tomorrow? You're tired and torn up and I'm wasted enough to sleep on a rock."

"My turn to have vibes, clowndancer. I'll rest better if we get this business done before morning. Anything else?"

"You coming to the warehouse?"

"No, better not. There's a teashop on the Raba Katir. *Amod' Aachana's*. Meet you there in . . . mmm . . . four hours?"

"Mind your feet, Shadow. And watch your back."

"I'll do that."

3

"Call Tulppanni," she told the girl who answered. "Tell her it's Lee's friend." She looked around. The ottotel lobby was empty, silent, there was no one near the bank of coms, no one coming in or going out.

"What is it now?" It was hard to hear the woman through the bursts of noise the speaker was picking up from behind her.

"Tell him I'm coming round to talk to him. Be there within the half hour."

"He's not here."

"Can you find him? It's important."

"See what I can do. How long you got?"

"Not sure. I have to be somewhere asap."

"Right. To save time, come round here, you can wait in his room. If you want."

"Thanks, I'll be there."

"Wait. In the back, there's a door. Knock. I'll have someone waiting to let you in."

"Thanks again."

4

Starstreet was rocking.

The emjit shuddered and twisted as it worked through the crews and visitors moving between the nightspots. Holoas were yelling and flickering like bright colored bats, swarming around her and every other warm body in sight. The dull facades of the blocky buildings had vanished behind holos of women and men and exploding stars and whirling vortices and anything else the owners or franchisers thought might entice a customer.

She found a hotpost around behind *Tulppanni's*, fed the slot, and left the emjit.

The night was bright and clear, but moonlight wasn't much help in finding her way through ragged bushes and along a halfhearted path and the shadow at the back of the building was as murky as day-old kaff. After some fumbling about, she found the door and knocked.

It was tugged open almost before her hand hit the wood. The girl who'd answered the com inspected her, nodded with satisfaction. "This way."

" 'Preciate this," Shadith said.

"Nada."

They went up narrow twisty stairs, not the ones Panni had taken her up before, stopped before a narrow panel. The girl touched it with a tronkey, stepped back as it slid aside. "Back door," she said. "If you'll go inside, I'll lock this behind you."

Arel walked in, scowling, annoyed at having his evening interrupted. "What's this?"

"Thought I'd better warn you. I was picked up by my target."

"He let you go?"

"At the moment, he thinks I'm dead."

"You leaving?"

"No. I'm going after him. You want to cancel the deal?"

"No. Thanks for the offer."

She smiled. "That's Lee's fault. I'd say she's scarred me for life, a wound on my heart so it bleeds for such as you."

He came closer, touched the hawk mark on her cheek, flicked a finger at the exuberant halo of curls. "You look more like I remember you. I like you better this way." He caught her hand, pushed her sleeve back, and inspected the bandage. "Rope?"

"Right."

"Stay here the night?"

"Wish I could." She caught his hand, held it a moment, then got to her feet. "There are too many things I still have to do before I even look at a bed." She grinned. "And when I do, I'm going to sleep like the corpse that Goyo thinks I am."

"Raincheck?"

"It's a long ride home and nothing much to do on a ship."

"I know some pleasant ways of passing the time."

"Oh, yes, I know."

He blinked. "You were watching?"

"What else did I have to do?"

"All three of you? Gods! What an appalling thought."

"Only one at a time these days."

"Take care, Shadow. Remember what you've got to look forward to."

She laughed. "I'll keep it in mind every second."

NIGHTFAIR 3
63 Kirar Sorizakre, day 15, hour 6
Razor T'Gurtt goes home

1

The moon Mompri dipped his lower cusp behind the Shaggar Tower.

The light strings flickered, the Closure Gong boomed and boomed again.

All over the Square futaks went dull and rough.

The NightFair was finished.

Pikka Machletta collected futaks and dumped them into the basket by the Gate. "Anyone see Dragons about? No? Huh. Means they set up waiting for us. Well, les do it."

Clumped into a tight knot, they plunged into the final outsurge of fairgoers and were swept like bits of flotsam along the Raba Katir and out the Old Town Gate into the round Plaza beyond.

Most of the tourists climbed into jits waiting there, provided by the hotels and guide services, and went humming off, safe from wandering predators. Those who'd come on their own coalesced into clumps and walked to the Ferry Landings in large groups, taking seriously the warning posted in their rooms: *When in Karintepe-on-Araubin, go NOWHERE alone after dark.*

The Bogmakkers didn't have to be told; they knew their city. They came in groups to the NightFair and shared the expense of hiring jinsbeks to escort them home. T'gurtsas and torkksos were not welcome anywhere near them, were warned away if they came nearer than the width of a street.

Before the hour was out the Gate Plaza was empty.

110

2

Razor in her right hand, ready to open with a flick of her wrist, Pikka Machletta ghosted through the shadows. Ingra came after her, then Mem, then Kynsil, then Hari. Fann took rearguard. They went quickly, soundlessly, on their toes, not quite running. G'sok Shikopru (Bridge Street) was empty, the lightcones about the lampstandards turning the darkness beyond them inkier; a predawn wind was rising, blowing grit along the asphalt, lifting and dropping litter from the Fair. At each crossstreet Pikka hesitated, listening for a careless scuff or brush against stone; her eyes moved restlessly along the street level and above it, probing the irregularities in the facades for any sign of movement or suspicious bulges. Dragons were old hands at ambushes, but to attack, they had to move and she was going to catch that movement as soon as it happened. She listened, then looked, then whipped across the street and stood watching, listening, guarding, while one by one the others came.

At every corner it was the same: watch, listen, dash, guard.

It was in her mind that Kidork would set the ambush fairly close to the water's edge so he could strip them and drop them in, once he and the Torkkus had killed them, then scat across the bridge and go to ground Mainside, but she wasn't taking any chances he'd do a double bluff and hit her sooner, trying for the extra edge surprise would give him. That wasn't very likely. He was sly and mean rather than clever. And lazy.

G'sok Jikdilki. Two more streets, then the bridge.

Pikka Machletta scrubbed the back of her hand across her brow, wiping away the nervous sweat that was stinging her eyes. She was getting jumpy as a mog in heat. She wondered if she was going a little crazy. There was no one on the street but Razor, no sign of Dragons. She could see the bridge towers ahead, a dark tracery against the River of Stars. Maybe he'd grown him some brains finally and meant to hit them on the Mainside, so close to home they'd be just the least bit off guard. . . .

Let's go, let's go. He's where he is and wishing won't change it.

Pikka Machletta ran across the lighted intersection, slid into shadow and waited for the rest of Razor, her eyes searching, searching, her ears straining. . . .

Ingra came. Mem. Kynsil. Hari. Fann.

A patch of shadow by a narrow flight of stairs suddenly acquired a bulge.

Pikka Machletta stretched her mouth in a feral grin. *Gotcha, trogg.* She flicked the razor open, swung it round, catching light on the blade, a signal to the others to watch and be ready. . . .

A scream.

She flinched, almost cut herself. *That's Mordo. What. . . .*

Dragon Torkkus came cursing into the middle of G'sok Shikopru, dancing ludicrously in the moonlight, dancing with a humping carpet of fur. Bits of fur sprang loose from the mass, leaped on Prettybutt and Bugeye, Herv and Mordo, on Kidork himself—she saw the hand she'd mutilated wave wildly as he stumbled and nearly went down. The street was alive with rats and mice, with four-legged hashshar, with nezbyrks and sheks, with every sort of vermin infesting the walls of Old Town. A stinking, squealing, writhing horde of vermin. They threw themselves at the Dragons, attacking without letup. It was insanity, terrifying.

Pikka Machletta began backing cautiously away. She meant to circle round, hit the bridge, and run like crazy.

Mem screamed, it was a small sound but sharp, more startled than fearful.

Pikka Machletta turned. A ring a meter thick of rats and nezbyrks and so on was drawn up around them. Thousands of the little beasts. They sat on their haunches, silent except for a few scratching and brushing sounds and an occasional chatter of teeth, staring at Razor from eyes phosphoring red in the lamplight. Tiny red eyes filled with ancient malice.

She swung back. Dragons were running for the bridge now, driven by that other horde, that humpy rug.

"Crazy," she said aloud.

"Not really." The speaker stepped into the light. A hoshyid femme with some kind of case on her back. Looked like she wasn't much older than them.

"Who you? What's this?" Pikka swept her left hand in a wide circle.

"A manifestation of sisterhood. No? Then say I'm putting an obligation on you. I'll trade you, favor for favor."

The girl had a singer's voice with a smile in it; she was easy to listen to, but Pikka Machletta wasn't going to trust her one fingerwidth. "Witch," she said, accusation but not much conviction in her own voice.

"Don't try it on, t'gurtsa. You believe in witches about as much as you'd trust a stick reader with your Winter stash."

"So YOU say. You doin us a favor, why them?" She wiggled the fingers of her left hand at the silent beasts.

"It's been a long day, I didn't feel like chasing you."

"Why'd you wan' to?"

"Not here. It's a bit exposed, don't you think?"

"Ah ri', we meet you somewhere come morning, you say the place."

"It's not nice, t'gurtsa, insulting a friendly soul like that. Don't measure me by your former opponents. They'd have to scrape hard to assemble a brain between them."

"Ya true." Pikka Machletta flipped the razor shut and shoved it back into the snapclamps. "There's a teahouse cross the bridge, y' wan'. The *Zatsudedi Oy*. Um. They won' let those hashshar in."

"I wouldn't myself. Hmm. Think about this a minute. Flushing that collection of oinkoids was just part payment for a hearing." She brought out a small sac, held it up so it was clearly visible in the light from the streetlamp. "The rest. Thirty guims for thirty minutes. Catch."

The sac arced through the air and landed at Pikka Machletta's feet with a satisfying chunk chink.

Kynsil squatted, pulled the drawstring loose, and dumped the coins into the street. She stirred them with the tip of her bootknife, counted them. "Thirty ah ri'."

She gathered them, dropped them in the sac, and got to her feet.

"Satisfied?" The offworlder sounded tired, her voice was getting sharper.

Pikka Machletta tapped a metaled fingernail against a stud on her neckleather. "You pay the shot at the *Oy.*"

"Nonsense. Pay for yourself, I'll take care of me."

"Ah ri'. We s'posed to walk on that lot?"

"No problem. Plenty more around if the occasion should arise where I needed them."

Pikka Machletta grinned. "Ya true."

The horde twitched, then seemed to explode it disintegrated so fast. Within a breath or two, the street was empty.

The girl resettled the strap, then strolled over to Razor. She seemed very calm, matter-of-fact, as if she'd played games with street gangs every day of her life.

Pikka Machletta considered that, added it to past events and decided to go very very carefully about this hoshyid. She signaled the T'gurtt to come round her.

"Fann, take point, Ingra, rear. Mem, you be here beside me. Kynsil, Hari, in the middle, keep your eyes open. Les do it."

6

Pikka Machletta waited until they were on the bridge before she spoke again. "You got a name?"

"Shadow."

"Really?"

"Really."

The wind was snatching at them and making the cables sing around them, a multiplicity of notes, chords of whines and groans. The sky was starting to gray in the east and along the shore, fishing boats were lit up like the fair as they unloaded the night's catch.

"You speak the Bogmakker. Most . . . um . . ."

"Hoshyid?"

"You said it, not me; anyway, they don't."

"I learned it on University. From a man called Tsee-waxlin. Old man. You may have heard of him. Or not."

Pikka Machletta clicked her tongue. "You a studier like him?"

"Not exactly like him, but close enough. He's an opener, I'm one who comes later."

A heavy flat pulling a trailer came rumbling past them, both piled high with boxes of fresh produce from the farms beyond the rim of Karintepe-on-Main. The loaders in the trailer stared stolidly down at them. One spat, the wind splattering the gob of mucus against the down-swooping cable, just missing Ingra.

She slapped her hand against her forearm. "Ketch-kang," she yelled. "Kanch. Goomoo. Yossyoss."

Silent Hari patted Ingra's arm, closed her hand about the wrist of her sister-in-T'gur, and tugged her after the others.

Ingra snorted her disgust, but yielded.

Pikka Machletta ignored the whole incident. "How'd you get those hashshar to do what you wanted?"

Shadow did a thing with her mouth, a quick pull back of the corners, a quicker release; she'd done it several times before, it didn't seem to mean much except she was tired of questions. "It's a Talent, that's all. Like singing. Something one's born with."

"Huh." Pikka Machletta brooded over that while produce flats trundled past, then a city bus loaded with factory workers and cleaning staff for the Island hotels, then more flats.

Pale hair whipping wildly about her face, her gray eyes watering, her hands tucked into the pockets of her jacket, Mem circled round Pikka Machletta and walked beside the stranger.

Pikka started to object, but changed her mind. It gave away too much. She shivered. The bridge was empty for the moment; the wind sweeping along it was strong enough to shift the lead weights on her hair thongs, making them chunk dully together, hit against her earlobe, the side of her neck.

The tension was drained out of her; she was tired, tired, tired.

She wouldn't get her edge back until she managed some sleep. If Kidork popped up in front of her right now, she couldn't do a thing about it. Or about the girl, if she went crank on them.

Luck stay sweet, she thought and cast the thought like prayer to whatever ears would hear it. She scowled at Mem.

Her sister-in-T'gur was sneaking sideways looks at the stranger, a muscle working beside her mouth as she fought her shyness, starting to say something and losing it, starting again, losing it again.

Pikka Machletta thought she knew what Mem wanted. Her sister-in-T'gur missed her father terribly. Razor could cherish her and protect her, but they couldn't talk to her like he did, they didn't have the education. Pikka winced, jealousy was a stab near her heart. She steamed along, hating that offworlder, that fairhaired unfairness who had everything Pikka Machletta wanted and could never ever get.

"University," Mem said finally, her throat so tight she squeaked when she spoke. "What's it like?"

Shadow looked thoughtfully out past the vertical cables at the dark irregular skyline of Karintepe-on-Main and walked along for a while without saying anything. When she finally spoke, it was as if she'd forgotten them and was talking to herself. "The ultimate in metaphors," she said. "Unlike items juxtaposed to illustrate an ineffable somewhere in between, a process repeated ad infinitum. An exercise in ordered chaos. A place where you can learn anything in the universe—if you know how to ask. And nothing at all if you don't." She shifted the strap again, rubbed at her shoulder, still looking past them, seeing things they couldn't know.

Pikka Machletta watched Mem struggling to understand what she herself hadn't a hope of translating into terms she knew. It was a cruel joke the stranger was playing on them.

Shadow looked at Men and smiled. "But that's not

what you want. What's University like? Not nearly as pretty as this." She swept her arm in a wide circle. "Kind of bleak, actually. An old world. The mountains are like worn down teeth. It was a mining world once; it's mostly worked out now, honeycombed with caverns. No life on it, not until the miners came. Everything from spores on up was brought there from somewhere else. The Scholars keep adding to the collections, they've been doing that for more than ten millennia now." She looked up, held out her hand. A red bird swooped from one of the towers, landed on her wrist, and sang a moment before she let it go.

Pikka swallowed; it was such a little thing, such a pretty gesture, such quiet power. She noticed for the first time the bandages on the hoshyid's wrists and wondered about them. She didn't ask; the moment felt wrong for that kind of question.

"University gets wilder every year," Shadow said. "Pets get away, you know, go feral. Always experimental subjects escaping. Absentminded types set things down and forget where they put them. You don't know what you're going to come across where." She grinned suddenly. "All in all, it's one of the weirdest places I've ever been."

"And anyone can go there?" Mem said, almost whispering.

"Just about. But it's not a dreamplace, little one." Shadow touched her tongue to her lips, shook her head. "More like a nightmare for some. If you don't have connections who can get you a room and a job, it's one of the best places around to starve to death. Or freeze. Or get tunked on the head, stripped of everything you own."

Ingra laughed; she'd come closer and was listening to Mem and the stranger. With only a little way to go before they were off the bridge and the traffic thicker by the minute, she was getting careless. "Sounds a lot like Old Town," she said. She saw Pikka Machletta scowling at her and dropped back to where she should be.

"Could someone like me go? Someone without papers or . . . or anything?" Mem sighed. "I NEED to know."

"Ay-yeh. Say you get there, there's no one to turn you away. You don't need clearance, you don't need papers, they don't even want to know your credit balance. Long as you don't make too much trouble or bother anyone important, you can stay till you die. Or you can stay a while and move on . . . move on . . . anywhere . . . ships come, go, anywhere, everywhere, always new ones. . . ."

Pikka Machletta closed her hands until the metal slivers on her nails pricked her palms. Move on . . . move on . . . those words woke a yearning in her, the words and the girl who said them . . . she didn't want to feel like this . . . she wanted . . . she didn't know what . . . something . . . there was a smell coming off that girl, a wild smell that made her tremble . . . she felt like she felt when she sniffed the wind blowing down from the Dread Green the first time it had the perfume of Spring on it. Like she wanted to run without stopping, away and away, howling at the moon, like she could jump off the Shaggar Tower and fly with the birds. . . .

The hoshyid shifted the strap once again, worked her shoulders. "Gods, I am tired. How far off is that tea-shop?"

"Two streets past the end of the bridge."

"They rent rooms?"

"For the hour, if y' know what I mean."

Mem touched Shadow's arm. "What does it cost, getting to University?"

Shadow looked blank. It took her a while to make the connection, then she rubbed at her forehead, sighed. "On a worldship, even a dorm bed costs . . . ummm . . . I suppose the equivalent of two, three thousand guims, if you got a favorable exchange which you won't. And you'll need to eat and drink, the trip takes several months. Add another thousand." She stopped talking for a moment as they began moving down the gentle slope off the bridge. Her eyes narrowed.

Pikka Machletta felt a tightening in her diaphragm; the idea of the offworlder communing with some bird or beast made her queasy.

Shadow blinked and was back with them. "The street ahead is clear, except for a few drunks staggering home. Um . . . what was I saying . . . oh. You might find a freetrader to take you for less. If you're lucky, you'll get there eventually. If you're not lucky, he'll take your money and leave you floating in the middle of nothing, a gory little corpsicle."

Her brief hope dead, Mem forced a weak smile. "Bless, O sister," she said, sketched a yayyay and drifted away.

As Pikka Machletta watched Mem slip into place ahead of Kynsil, her shoulders drooping, her eyes on the concrete walkway, she tried hating the hoshyid again, but she couldn't. She'd spoken the truth, that's all. The sorry truth.

Pikka's insides felt like they'd been churned with a spoon, she'd been up and down, angry and placated, her feelings kicked about like a yakkar ball, possibilities had opened up before her, then slammed shut before she had a chance to do more than sniff at them.

As Razor and the offworlder moved off the bridge and turned down the G'sok Sokuna Siska, Pikka glanced at the hoshyid and wondered. She wanted something from Razor. She'd have to pay for it. And maybe, just maybe, she was the answer to saving Mem. Everything depended on what she wanted. Everything. . . .

THE TEAHOUSE PACT
63 Kirar Sorizakre, day 15, hour 7
Shadith and the Razor T'gurtt

1

As she and the T'gurtt turned into a grimy street between rows of bulky warehouses, Shadith yawned for the
umpteenth time, resisted an urge to rub at her wrists.
They were burning. Her arms ached, her legs. Her head
was a rotten melon. And she felt horribly exposed. Doing a wardance under Wargun's nose.

> Gods . . . if I had a brain in all my body, I'd be out
> of here. These girls would sell me for a dokie if the
> chance came up. The albino one . . . she wants
> University worst way, and I can give it to her. That's
> something . . . I can . . . but will I? I don't know.
> Depends. What am I doing! Bloodgames. Bloody
> fool. I'm about to stick my head up and scream here
> I am, you miserable pervert, send your assassins
> and your bullies. Target provided gratis and
> gladly. . . .

She stopped walking when the T'gurtt stopped. The
six girls came together a few steps off, by the mouth of
an unsavory alley. They milled about, gesturing and
whispering at each other. The boss t'gurtsa shut them
up, all except the dark-haired girl with the birthmarks on
her face. The two of them started going at it in hissing
whispers, throwing themselves vigorously into the argument despite how tired they had to be.

Tired. I wonder when they were to bed last. It wasn't much past noon . . . was it only yesterday? Seems like a year ago . . . when the boss girl was taking the thumb off that Connafallen freetrader. Old man said it, on Chissoku you don't sleep in the Spring; if you don't make your Winter stash then, you don't make it at all. Sar! Ginny the Creep is taking me on a tour of worlds I wouldn't be caught dead on otherwise. Dead . . . almost was . . . weren't for Kikun . . . right now I'd kill for a bed with clean sheets. Sheets! What am I saying! For a soft piece of floor. Poor old Lion, papa Goyo's pretty playtoy. You must be feeling top of the world right now. On your way. Wargun. He's keeping us quiet . . . doing the questioning himself . . . doesn't want other Goyo in on this . . . Kikun says . . . I suppose he knows . . . Ginny isn't someone you'd brag about knowing . . . even here . . . especially here . . . peer group is small, there's no hiding from them. . . .

##

The boss t'gurtsa made a chopping gesture with her right hand, cutting off the argument; shoulders swinging, elbows out, she strutted over to Shadith. ''Y' wait here. We got business.'' She sketched a yayyay, went bopping off down the alleyway, the others following her.

2

The dark silent little girls came out grinning ear to ear, with lumpy bags slung over their shoulders, other lumps distributed about their working jackets, loose garments that hung to their knees. The tall almost albino girl was half a step behind them, her lumps less obvious because they had more space to spread in; the three t'gurtsas paid no attention to Shadith, went off down the street, turned a corner, and were gone.

The t'gurtsa with the misshapen arms and the one with

the marked face came trotting out and vanished after the others.

Hmm. Stripping for action—or cutting me loose?

Shadith strolled into the alley. Noticeably thinner about the thighs, the boss t'gurtsa was slapping her belt round her waist; she gave Shadith a brief cold look, then went back to pulling the belt tongue through the buckle, radiating anxiety and a hostility whose target Shadith had no difficulty identifying. The t'gurtsa would be with her sisters-in-T'gur if Shadith hadn't stuck her nose in their business. As she waited for the girl to finish what she was doing, she felt a small sadness. Her own sisters had been that close, but they were dust twenty millennia ago.

The t'gurtsa yayyayed briskly, abruptly all business. "I am Pikka Machletta, the Chlet of Razor T'gurtt."

Shadith echoed the yayyay. " 'Roi Machlet."

"I . . ."

Kikun came out of the shadows at the back of the alley. Pikka Machletta snatched the razor from the snap-clamps, flipped it open and went at him.

"Sar!" Shadith brought a gull down to flap in the girl's face.

Pikka slapped it aside with only a tiny hesitation in her headlong attack.

"Chlet! No!" Shadith kept her voice low despite her anxiety; she wanted no spectators. "It's no trick, he's a friend!"

Kikun danced away from the girl, the idiot look on his face as he avoided the razor with no apparent effort. It was as if he knew her every move before she did, reading the moment ahead as easily as she read the point present.

Recognizing futility, Pikka Machletta put her back to the wall, stood panting and frightened—and raging—her face blank as a brick, her eyes flicking from him to Shadith and back.

Hands out, palms toward the t'gurtsa, Shadith backed against the other wall, took a step sideways, stopped when she saw the girl tensing. "Sorry about this," she said. "Meet

my companion Kikun. He's a dinhast from DunyaDzi, with
no tact and disastrous timing." She smiled.

There was no response from the t'gurtsa.

"Look, this is a cul-de-sac, isn't it? Right. What I'm
doing to do, I'll slide down this side till I'm past you.
I'm doing it now. Slow. You see my hands. No tricks.
Kikun, you back off, too. Right. I'm sliding along, you
can see that's all I'm . . . unh! No problem. Got poked
by a splinter, that's all. All right, I'm past you now. The
way's open. You can take off if you want. We won't follow. Or you can wait in the street and the three of us can
go talk over that deal."

Pikka Machletta's eyes shifted from Shadith to the
street, came back to Shadith. There was no change in her
expression. Abruptly she flipped the razor shut and darted
away.

Shadith sighed. "I suppose you had to," she told
Kikun.

"Best now," he said. "When she's alone. Be all
right." He scratched at the folds of skin draped along
his neck. "She bit and she's hooked."

Pikka Machletta was waiting at the mouth of the alley.
She didn't say anything, just started walking, staying a
half-step ahead of them.

2

Shadith and Kikun followed the t'gurtsa into another
alley, one that ran along the wall of an ancient warehouse, a squared-off mountain of stone several stories
high and a quarter of a kilometer long; the *Zatsudedi Oy*
was a pimple on its butt, the entrance just round the
corner from a long wharf lighted and noisy with the arrival and unloading of produce and fishing boats.

The *Oy* was stodging grimly between two clienteles;
too late for the night people and too early for the dayers.
There were small square tables scattered about the long

narrow room, abandoned glasses and dirty plates on some, a few scruffy holdovers sitting slumped over cloudy glasses at others. One man was stretched out on a settle pushed against the north wall, snoring and muttering, an arm over his face.

The floor was sawdust. A tired man, thin as the handle of the rake he was using, was working his way across the room, raking under spills and debris, smoothing out gouges and humps. He looked up when they came in; when he recognized Pikka Machletta, he stopped work, stood leaning on the rake handle, twiddling the end of one of the rattail mustaches dropping past his jawline. " 'Roa, Razoort. Rest not comin?''

" 'Roi, Iskikakku. They got business other places. Bring us a pot of tea . . . um . . . over there.'' She pointed at one of the booths that lined the south wall, started for it with Shadith and Kikun trailing along behind.

3

"I want a stand in the NightFair. Not a stall, a place where I can perform. Play my harp and sing.'' Shadith's mouth was dry, her stomach churning. She took a sip of tea, a bite of stale toast. "Doesn't have to be a good place, I expect there aren't any of those available. Some badluck spot maybe? I'll turn it sweet again.'' She saw the look on the t'gurtsa's face, moved her hand impatiently. "I know what I can do.''

Pikka Machletta sipped at her tea. She set a fingerpad in a drop of spilled liquid, pulled it in a line toward her, drew a second line across it. "Why talk to me? Go and do it.''

"Look, do I have to keep reminding you, I'm not one of those bonedomes you play your games on.'' Shadith shifted about till her shoulders rested in the corner between the booth divider and the wall. "Tseewaxlin told me a thing or three, like don't go tramping in there and get your head wiped.''

Pikka Machletta drew a diagonal through the cross. She said nothing.

"Listen, one hundred guims to get me to the Sirshaka and help me to acquire a renewable performance futak, plus two percent of each night's take, plus a weekly retainer of fifty guims to Razor T'gurtt, you acting as consultants, warning me when I'm about to step in wet shit. Especially where the Goyo are concerned."

Pikka Machletta drew a second diagonal across the first. "Five hundred. Five percent. Fifty each." She wiped out the star she'd created, printed the numbers on the wood. "And the reason why you're doing this."

"Two hundred. Three percent. Fifty flat. The reason's simple, stir the mix, study what happens."

Pikka Machletta examined her damp palm, wiped it on her one-sleeve tunic. "Don' believe that."

"It's the only answer you're going to get."

"We live here. Y' gone or dead when this shit hits, if it goin to hit."

"You play the game, you take your chances."

"You goin after the Star, an't y'. Won't be the first."

"The Star, what?"

"Don' y' try that spin on me, hoshyid. All of them like you come for the Star."

"Ah. You're talking about the Gem Museum. Well, you see me heading anywhere near Jazinedain Shimda, sell me to the Goyo." Shadith let her eyes drop closed a moment, then shook off her weariness and drank some more of the abominable tea. "That should cover you."

Pikka Machletta chewed on her lip. She was sweating, there were dark circles under her eyes and the lines of weariness were deepening in her narrow face. She looked haggish and absurdly young, barely more than a child. "Four hundred," she said finally. "Four percent. Fifty flat."

"I'll go with that—with one proviso, the arrangement's renegotiable every four weeks."

"Why?"

"My funds are limited. How long I can continue paying you depends on what I get at the Fair. And, to be blunt, on how useful you are.''

"I want a guarantee, then.''

"How much?''

"Nine weeks. Deposited with the Blurdslang, set up so we collect a week's fee every seven days.''

"Done.'' Shadith yawned. "I could use a little advance on that advice you're going to provide. A reasonably secure room my friend and I can catch some sleep in.''

Pikka Machletta started. She'd completely forgotten Kikun though he'd been sitting across the table from her. She scowled at him. "How. . . .''

Kikun smiled sleepily at her, his eyes orange slits.

Shadith sat up. "Useful Talent, isn't it. Well?''

"Ah ri', I know someone has a room she's wantin to rent. She minds her business an' expects her lodgers t' do the same. You gotta study somethin, forget her. Y' understand?''

"Good enough. I'll meet you at the Blurdslang Alley, when?''

"Any time after noon. Razor 'll be on line for futaks. You fight?''

"Some. If I can't avoid trouble.''

"No shooters.''

"I know. Tell you what, get hold of a hardwood stick yaaay long,'' she spread her hands about a meter apart. "And I'll bust what comes.''

"Two sticks,'' Kikun said.

Pikka Machletta started again. "Koyohk! Can't y' not DO that?''

Kikun folded his hands over his intricately knotted tunic and blinked amiably at her.

"Ah ri', two sticks and you meet us there after noon. Have the nineweeks and the introducin fee with you and at least a thousand more for the futak. You picked a bad time for bargainin. If you could wait till the worldship leaves. . . .''

"No.''

"Then we do what we can do.'' She dropped two dokies on the table and slid out of the booth. "Two more from each of you covers the tab. You wan' to go straight to Kuva Svila's?"

Shadith dropped the coins on the table, tapped Kikun's shoulder. "If that's the room, yeh. Let's go."

III. ACTIVITY OTHERWHERE
(Ginny's surrogates are busy)

TARGET: Huy na Kalos, CEO Botanicals
   Division, Cazar Company
   headquarters, JUODA CITY on K'TALI
   KAR-RA (Vendeg 3)
CAPTURE TEAM: Dyslaerin: Gyorsly the
                       Zadys, Macslyn,
                       Torvilyst, Tuzalys
            Tracer Op: Autumn Rose

1

Xuyalix the Caan smuggler threaded his silenced float through the wuerzzaur grove, took it in a quick hop over a prickly wall of pepperduffs, and set it down in the hollow center of that egg-shaped thicket.

"Nothing should bother you here," he told the team, "except maybe a few bugs." Translucent secondary lids slid down over his silver eyes, slid back; the sooty plush that covered his short wiry body drank the pallid light from a moon not yet clear of the horizon and left him as shadowy as ever. "I've used it as a stash more than once, never lost anything yet. Don't try going through the pepperduffs, if the thorns don't get you, the chiggers will. See that limb there . . ." he touched it a second with the beam of a pinlight, tapped the light off, "go along it till you get to the trunk, work your way round the trunk and up it about half a meter, there's another limb, a big 'un going more or less east. Walk along that till you reach the second meld point, change limbs, and keep on. The way the wuerzzaurs grow, you can cross the whole grove without touching ground—if you're careful and pick the right points. That's not hard. Just make sure they're old

128

melds, the nodes will have deep cracks and wrinkles in them, but no shoots growing out of them. You see anything green on a node, don't take that one.''

Gyorsly smoothed a hand over her coppery headfur. ''Right. Mac, get the shelter up, I'll help you in a minute. Torvi, you and Tuza unload the supplies. Rose, you been this way before?''

''I picked wuerz with my half brothers, this was one of the places we went.'' Autumn Rose looked around. ''It's way past its prime, this grove, due for grubbing out and replanting, someone's gone slack or it'd been done already.''

''I doubt we have to worry about that now. Well, let's get busy. Xuyalix, we'll have you cleared in a few minutes so you can get back to your ship. Anything else you want to say?''

The Caan scratched behind an earstalk. ''You just keep in mind you got four days, that's far as I can stretch it. The more you shave it down, the safer we'll all be. And you want to walk like your eggs are underfoot. Na Kalos, he's got traps everywhere, you never know when you might step in one and he sends his killer-machs at you.'' He made a chopping motion with his double-thumbed hand. ''He gets any of you, I'm gone.''

Autumn Rose snorted. ''He gets any of us, we're all gone.''

2

Autumn Rose rubbed her thumb on the soft crumbly bark, scowled through the night lenses at the city spreading like black moss over the stony slopes below Schloss Rock. Quiet. Too quiet. There should have been people in the streets, it wasn't that late, the moon had barely cleared the horizon. It was nearly full, a blue and cream balloon taking up a quarter of the sky; it was almost big enough to be a twin planet. She used to stand in the Schloss's watergarden and think she could touch it if only she could climb out onto the roof on one of the slender turrets rising from each of the corners of the curtain wall.

That was one of the few things she'd never tried, she knew even then that it was illusion and she didn't want to break the magic of it. The night was warm, lovely; the ertlilies were blooming, she could smell them whenever the wind puffed this way. There should be children chasing each other, shouting, laughing, while their parents were at the market. Neighbor should be chatting with neighbor, sitting out on the stoops, enjoying the sweet-smelling evening cool. The Platz should be thick with stalls and shoppers, the beerhalls around it booming with music loud enough to carry across the water to the tree she was standing in. It was what? only twenty years since she'd left, scooped up and taken along will-she nill-she when the grandfather who'd never acknowledged her or her mother was replaced by the current CEO. It couldn't have changed that much . . . no, there was another reason for that quiet, and she was very much afraid she knew what it was.

There was a faint rustle below her. Gyorsly swung into a crotch on the far side of the trunk. "What's the problem?"

"Memories . . . no, not really. Look and tell me what you see."

Gyorsly clicked on her lenses, scanned the street. "Nothing. Looks like they rolled up the sidewalks and went to bed."

"That's a Company Town on a Company World, Gyor. Daylight belongs to Cazar. The early evening's when you play and do your marketing."

"Oh."

"Right. He's expecting us. He's cleared the streets so he can use motion detects and his killer-machs. There. Look there, cutting across the Platz. Did you see it?"

"A ferret."

"Uh-huh. And where there's one you see. . . ."

"There's fifty you don't. P'rlash!" There was a soft brushing sound as Gyorsly rubbed her headfur the wrong way. "Someone sold us? Who? Xuyalix?"

"No. He owes Digby one huge favor and Voallts is paying him a fee that gives your Toerfeles a pain in the budget. Besides, he's been a trader from the egg and his word is his biggest asset.''

''Hmm. What about this? Seyirshi sent a warning to his prime clients: *Watch out for trouble from Voallts.*''

''As a guess, I like it. As something we have to deal with, I think it stinks.''

''Na Kalos ever come out of there?''

''You read the report. Not even to Board Meetings. Holo and fax.''

''We can't use your plan if we can't get to the Schloss. How do we do it?''

''Well, the one thing he can't do is shut down production. They'd yank him home so fast, he'd peel out of his skin. Unless things have changed radically, the supply barges will start coming in before sunup and the early morning shift will be on the way to work. He's got to pull the ferrets before then. Which gives us a half-hour of semi-dark to make it through the city. We can do it, it's not that big a place. If we can get to the blowhole on the east end of the Rock, we can lay up there till it's dark and take it as read after that. All right? Good. Let's get back. I could do with some tea, then a nap till it's time to go.''

They climbed down to the melding level and ran like ghosts along the broad oval limbs of the wuerzzaur trees. Gyorsly went first; like all Dyslaera her sense of direction/duration was close to infallible.

There was a faint light ahead, shining on the undersides of the topleaves. Gyorsly slowed cautiously, signaled Autumn Rose she was going to stop. She stood straddling a node, leaning forward tensely, her head turning, her ears shifting as she strained to hear. . . .

Nothing.

No random twitter of birds, no insect hum.

Just the rustle of leaves as the wind rose, then subsided.

She dropped into a crouch and tasted the wind. A faint bitter smell, no, a blend. Strangers, more than one, she couldn't tell how many.

Autumn Rose knelt behind her. "Hear anything?" she murmured.

"Hear, no. Smell. Strangers. More than one. Look, go on, but stop before you hit the last tree, I'm going to circle round," she paused, collected herself, produced a brief coughing hoot, then another, "when you hear that, I'm in place and ready to shoot."

3

Gyorsly stopped three trees away from the thicket, groped to the trunk, and climbed until she found a perch where she could look down into the camp.

The doorflap of the domeshelter was strapped open, the pressurelamp was just inside, enough light escaping to turn the darkness in the clear space to a pallid twilight. The light flickered occasionally as someone inside moved past it.

It was all quiet, peaceful. Normal.

She didn't believe it. Not for a minute. There was no way Mac would stay inside that shelter, not when she was hyper-hyper like she was an hour ago. More important, the air was thick with the musky, bitter scent of the strangers.

She dialed up the polarization of the nightglasses, refocused them, and pulled them on.

Whoever it was in there playing games was being by-gar careful not to show hide or hair. She increased magnification and inspected the ground about the dome. A few scuffs, otherwise neat as if someone'd swept it. Eyes slitted to minimize vertigo, she lifted her head and focused on the limb crossing the hollow, but waited a moment to gather herself before she inspected it, remembering all too clearly the reports she'd seen of the massacre on Kemarin 4, the cobben slaughter at Pillacarioda Pit. Rose might be used to this kind of thing, she wasn't.

She scanned slowly along the limb.

Nothing there. Blatantly nothing there. *Welcome home, little lambs. Damn, I can't see. . . .* She lowered herself onto her limb, straddling it, pressing her body into its gentle up-arc so she get could a better look at the higher levels of the wuerzzaurs on the far side of the thicket without exposing herself. Smell could give her clues, but it wouldn't locate the intruders, not with this light and variable a wind. Intervening trees were another problem, they limited how much she could see, but she wasn't about to move closer.

Nothing . . . nothing . . . ahhhh. . . . Moonlight filtering through the canopy touched something that was marginally more solid than a shadow, a hazy lump along an upper branch. *Yesss. . . .*

She located a second possibility in that wuerzzaur, shifted to another tree, then another, slow meticulous work that made her head ache and her eyes burn, but this was her sort of business, the patient observation of target beasts, locating them, learning their habits, their weak points, everything she needed to trap them without injury. That wasn't an object of this search, oh, no; this was going to be a culling, not a capture.

Five in ambush, waiting. At least one in the tent. Six. Probably more. She eased up the flap of the holster, slipped out the heavy duty stunner she'd planned to use on na Kalos and ratchetted beam strength to lethal. *All right, Rose. Here we go.* She licked her lips, concentrated.

As the last cough-hoot died, she touched the trigger sensor and swept the beam across the shadow she'd spotted first.

A blue-white halo outlined it. Shield cloak. Swearing under her breath, she kept the shadow pinned. Finally it flattened, an arm swung down. The pepperduffs below the tree rustled as something heavy dropped into them. A weapon of some kind.

Across the thicket Rose's stunner thrummed. One of the others Gyorsly had spotted was on his feet; for an instant the ambusher was haloed as his shield cloak deflected part of the beam. Gyorsly added her beam to the tracer op's. The dark figure crumpled, fell from its perch.

There was a short sharp whistle, other whistles answered it.

Several—five, maybe six—dark figures dropped to the meld level, vanished behind trunks, appeared again, bent low and running.

Gyorsly swept the beam toward them, one cloak flared, Rose's stunner hummed and he went down. Then two more went down as she and Rose hit them together. The others ducked and dodged. She shot again and missed. One dropped off, she shot at his hands as they clamped on the limb, they vanished, but she had a feeling it wasn't because she'd hit him. The others were in the dark somewhere on her side of the thicket. She swept the beam around, trying her luck, but that was just wasting energy, so she stopped, listened.

Nothing. They moved as silently as the shadows they seemed. They were as good as Dyslaera. Maybe better.

A cutter flared from the shelter, slashed into the foliage near Gyorsly, so near she could feel the heat as the leaves smoked and the sap burned. She scooted backward along the limb, the stench of the hot sap in her nostrils, the choking dust from the friable bark. When she came to the trunk, she climbed until she reached the highest crotch, then she crouched there waiting for the attackers to come at her.

The cutter sliced at the tree again, flaring as it hit the trunk, turning upward, groping for her.

Rose's stunner thrummed.

The beam faltered, vanished.

Gyorsly refused to think of her team; they were dead now if they hadn't been before, she'd stupidly shied from taking out the one in the shelter, there was just a chance . . they were dead, of course they were dead, but. . . .

A soft hiss, a tiny *chnk* by her hand. Darter. From below. An instant after the *chnk,* she fired down the trunk, swinging the beam in an arc to give her the maximum chance of a hit.

Cloak flare. She shot again. Again.

Something heavy thudded into the ground. *Gotcha!*

Across the way, one of the attackers slashed at Rose's tree, his cutter taking up what the shelter beam had started.

Gyorsly located the source, pinned it. Cloakflare. She shot again, Rose's beam melded with hers. *That's the way, rot there, cutthroat, damn your stinking soul.*

A faint rubbing sound. Smell of bark. Close. Too close. Burning in her leg. Hand on her ankle, pulling at her. Too close. Can't use the stunner. She extruded her claws, flung herself from the crotch, striking out as she fell . . . knife in her arm . . . she had him, her claws were in his face and shoulder, her weight was pulling him down, under her, they crashed into a meld limb, him under her, she jerked her claws loose, taking flesh with them, ripped his throat out with her tearing teeth.

She lay across him, washing in and out of awareness; he'd taken the brunt of the fall, but she'd cracked a rib or two and she was bleeding copiously from the places where his knife had got her; Misclaer be blessed he hadn't breached an artery or she'd be empty by now. She pulled herself off the attacker and crawled along the limb until she reached the crotch. With some difficulty she turned herself and sat straddling the limb with her back against the trunk.

With the claws on her right hand, she gouged out clumps of bark which she pressed into her leg wound. A tourniquet would have been better, but her left hand was nearly useless. The arm wound she couldn't do anything about, but the knife was still in it and it wasn't bleeding all that much. The stunner was gone, too bad, but she had her teeth and her claws—and that knife, she could hit targets blindfold, it was a game once. Not now. Let them come, she wasn't dead yet. . . .

There were sounds . . . a whistle . . . another . . . rustles . . . the thrumm of a stunner . . . a grunt . . . more rustles . . . on and on . . . and on . . . rusles, coming toward her . . . she stiffened, relaxed. Autumn Rose. The sour-sweet blood smell that was hers alone.

"Gyor."

Rose's voice. Rose's smell, riding the wind to her. Autumn Rose. What a strange name that was. Gyorsly coughed. "Rose?"

"Kakke! Gyor, we got 'em all, at least I think so, it's

a cobben, Gyor, nothing to do with na Kalos. They trailed us here. Somehow. I don't know. We have to have a look at security. . . .'' Rose's voice droned on as she eased along the limb, the Rose smell getting stronger, though she wouldn't know that. The Dyslaerin smiled wearily, they didn't know how easy it was to pick them out, these sense-dead cousins. Rose wanted to make sure she was known before she got close and didn't realize she'd announced herself before she spoke. "I called Xuyalix, Gyor. He'll be here in about twenty minutes." She reached the corpse. "Sheyss damn, you totaled this one." Some soft grunts and rubbing sounds as she muscled the body off the limb, then came warily closer. "How you doing?"

"Better'n him." Gyorsly giggled, but stopped when the sound went strange on her. "Got me with a knife. Leg. Arm. Think it had something on it. Bonus, huh?"

"Double kakke! I haven't a hope of carrying you. If I slap some patches on you, you think you can climb down?"

"Climb or fall."

"Hunh." Rose crouched on the limb, a little dark lump that kept fading out on gyorsly, fading out and going solid again. "Hang on, Gyor. You think you can stay awake enough to handle a cutter?"

"Why?"

"We're liable to have company before Xuyalix shows up. Na Kalos doesn't like noise in his back yard."

"Do m' bes' "

"Right. Give me your hand."

It was like lifting weights, but she got her arm up and managed to crook her fingers about the butt of the cutter. She rested the cylindrical accumulater on her uninjured thigh, let out the breath she was holding. "Let 'em come," she mumbled.

"Ri-ight, Gyor. You stay awake now. Won't be much longer." Autumn Rose got to her feet and went running off, her slight wiry body melting into the darkness though her scent stayed there with Gyorsly. It was a comforting thing, a friendly thing, overlaying the stink of the assassin below.

Gyorsly settled herself to wait, fighting off waves of fever and disorientation. A while more, just a breath or two, in breath out breath, keep on, just a while. . . .

4

Miralys stood a moment gazing down at the three bodies wrapped in cerecloth. She spat into her palm, drew her thumb through the spittle and touched each brow in turn. Then she left the coldroom, Autumn Rose trailing silently behind.

In her office, she dispensed hot tea and sutties, then settled into her tupple chair. "Gyorsly?"

Autumn Rose set her cup on the sidetable. "We dropped her off at University. The ottodoc stabilized her, but that's about all it could do. The wounds aren't bad, it's what was on the knife. Medschool doesn't know the agent, but the medic I talked to, he thinks they can figure it out, they've got her in stasis till then."

"Na Kalos?"

"Nervous and ready. We suspect Seyirshi or someone in his organization has notified the clients on his prime list that Voallts might be after them. Why I say someone in his organization, it was obvious na Kalos didn't know the cobben was there, or they would have had more backup. His flying killers didn't arrive till the fight was over and Xuyalix was come to collect us. We had a bit of a scrap getting away from them, but nothing like the trouble they could have made. Two hands, it seems to me, neither knowing what the other is doing."

"Nightcrawler cobben. That's the second time . . . you think they followed you?"

"Yes. We strongly suggest you update your security. We are already working on ours."

"The Singer Shadith recommended we approach Adelaris."

"Worth every florint. If you have an introduction, use it immediately."

Miralys sipped at her tea and contemplated the stone relief on the wall behind Autumn Rose. "It was courteous of you to bring out our dead."

"Not courteous, Toerfeles. I wouldn't leave a dead dog for Huy na Kalos and his lot."

"Nonetheless, Voallts owes you for it. Mm . . . we own a smallish estate in the Sarinim, you can stay there if you like while you're finishing your report, it's a pleasant wilderness, that. Peaceful." Her lips drew back in a feral grin that had nothing to do with humor. "With guards to keep it peaceful."

"If Digby agrees, I would like that."

"Digby has nothing to say about it. You'll be on Seyirshi's enemy list now, not a comfortable place to find yourself." She tapped her claws on the desk. "If the report's worrying you, I'll send Zimaryn to fetch it when it's done." She took up her cup, crossed her legs and let the chair curl round her. "Well, now. Digby says you were born on K'tali Kar-ra. A Company World. Not easy to escape. If you don't find my interest too intrusive, tell me how you managed that."

TARGET: Teslim Zachranny pirs Kali, the
         Chasekelits (Immortal Tigress
         and Godqueen) of Ekchua-
         TiHash (lmix 4)
CAPTURE TEAM: Dyslaeror: Ossoran the
               Zadant, Feyvorn,
               Veschant, Villam
               Tracer op: Samhol Bozh

1

The savannah stretched flat as a table into a golden
shimmer at the horizon, while heat vortices danced and
wavered over the striped tchu'qum grass. Qa'a'ims
(smoke trees) grew here and there, singly and in small
groves, blue-gray poufs attached to multiple trunks like
interlacing black threads.

Up close, the table wasn't all that flat. It was scored
and checked by washes and ravines; between these the
land erupted in close-set small humps like a measles rash.

Hidden among brush, fadecloth camouflage mocking
its stiff round leaves mottled maroon and green and spattered with orange flecks, peering out through tufts of
tchu'qum whose leaves were long and thin like epee
blades, with vertical stripes of olive and ocher, five men
lay at the lip of one of the wadis, their distance lenses
fixed on a Hunt a few kilometers off, the riders streaming
across the Plain heading vaguely in their direction.

##

First, the beast. The quarry. A mutated elk not much
smaller than an elephant, with an immense rack of ant-
lers, a shaggy brown coat, long, thin legs and a considerable turn of speed.

139

Then the hounds. The royal pack. Black and brindle shorthairs with floppy pointed ears and docked tails, standing high as the ribs on a not too small man. As they ran, they howled, a deep, resonant, oddly musical sound. A terrifying sound.

Last, the riders. The Chasekelits and her court. The courtiers wore brilliant primary colors elaborately slashed and dagged, with dags and ribbons fluttering in the wind. They rode mutated zebras, long legged, spirited beasts, black and white manes and tails flowing like the ribbons. They shouted and blew Hunt horns and beat Hunt drums while the slave singers who rode with them, bearing the Godqueen's banners, belted out Hunt songs.

The Chasekelits rode several strides ahead of the others, nearly treading on the bobtails of the hounds; her long black hair was braided with gold and silver streamers that snapped and rippled in her self-created wind. She wore black leather and silver braid and rode her muzebra as if she were part of him. Her arms were bare, her torso barely covered by a skimpy leather vest laced tightly across her full breasts. She was tanned and slim and might have been beautiful if her face weren't so contorted by the passions of the Hunt and ululating howls that rose high and clear above the noise.

##

Hands so tight on the longlenses that his muscles cramped, Samhol Bozh followed every twitch of Teslim pirs Kali's mobile face. The fadecloth began slipping off his shoulders as he wriggled about to keep her in view.

Ossoran nudged him. "Cool down, Op. Or you crawl right in her hands. Want that?"

Samhol Bozh eased himself flat, pushed his face into the short curlgrass growing under the tchu'qum while he fought to control the rage he'd suppressed for the past fifteen years, the loathing he felt for every member of that bloody, clutch-fisted, barbarous family. Parasites sucking the life out of everything they touched, nearly sucking the life out of him.

##

The hounds drove the beast into a Vee-fence, too high to jump and too massive to slam down.

The melk turned, lowered his head and bellowed. Two of the hounds darted at him, sprang away before he impaled them. Two more leaped in. He whirled to deal with them, but they were gone.

They worked him until he was staggering, then they were on him, teeth in his jugular, teeth tearing at his flanks, dragging him down. . . .

The Chasekelits was off her muzebra, knife in her hands. She plunged into the mess, used one of the melk's forelegs to lever him over and went down on him, opening up his thorax and ripping lose his heart.

Slapping a hound's muzzle aside, she sprang to her feet.

With a wild wordless yell she scrubbed the heart over her face and arms, across the bulging tops of her breasts, held it a moment over her head, an offering to her Totem Ghost, Tigress the Undying. Then she sliced a piece off and ate it, more blood spurting from between her teeth.

Servants moved among the courtiers, handing them crystal goblets filled with wine as red as the blood the Godqueen drank.

Still chewing, she tossed the rest of the heart to the hounds, swung into the saddle. Ignoring the courtiers milling about the kill, she spurred the muzebra into a gallop and came racing toward the wadi where the watchers lay concealed.

##

Samhol Bozh and the Dyslaerors heard her singing as she rode, loud and raunchy, like a sailor in a whorehouse after months at sea. They drew back under the brush, pulling the fadecloths more closely about them.

Clumps of grass and dirt sprayed onto the cloths, kicked up by the muzebra's hooves as he gathered him-

self, leaped the wadi and went thundering on toward a
large grove of smoke trees growing round a small spring.

The four huge Mutes that guarded the Chasekelits'
body followed more sedately, riding around the wadi and
circling back toward the grove and the bothy tucked away
there. Here in the Royal Preserve where the other claim-
ants to the Godseat couldn't reach Teslim pirs Kali, their
job was more or less a sinecure and they were half asleep,
bored by heat and blood and all that galloping, the same
thing every day for the past three months.

##

Back at the kill, the courtiers were straggling off, heading for the castle, leaving the hounds to finish cleaning
the bones.

2

"The Blood Kills arouse them," Samhol Bozh said,
"the Godqueens of Ekchua-TiHash." He wouldn't look
at Ossoran or the rest of the capture team, just stared
down at his hands as he fiddled with a pile of faxsheets.
"They keep a stable of . . . well, the politest word would
be consorts. Young men, ages between fifteen and eigh-
teen. Sometimes her Chamberlain locates likely youths
and has them brought to her. Sometimes, when a Chasekelits is on a Progress around the continent, she'll see
a boy who catches her fancy, she'll point him out and
her guards will fetch him along to the castle, put him
with the others she's collected. When she gets bored with
one . . . or his performance falls off . . . what she does
depends on how much he knows she doesn't want talked
about. Some she strangles with her own fair hands. Some
she sells offworld into contract labor." His fingers
twitched; the sheets rustled. He cleared his throat.
"Some she just turfs out, leaves to starve or beg a living
from the servants. Some she cuts the tongues out of and
turns into one of her Mutes. Her bodyguards." He
coughed again. "Point of this, it's the moment she'll be

most vulnerable—at the end of a Hunt, when she's hot and bloody and wanting. She has these little bothys scattered around the Preserve, available wherever a Hunt happens to end up. She'll have one of her consorts stashed there and go straight to him when the Kill is made.

"What we have to do is get into the Preserve—not as hard as it sounds—work out the pattern of the Hunts so we can lay up close to the right bothy. She'll be alone except for the Mutes and one or two consorts, the courtiers know better than to be anywhere in sight right then. The Mutes will stay outside, they usually spend their time gambling or sleeping, maybe some of both, depending on her appetite that day. A dart rifle will take care of them. Lethal loads, please. It's kinder. The death they'll get if they're found alive . . . well, you don't want to think about that. Then we go in." He separated a handful of sheets from the pile, gave them to Veschant. "Pass these around, Vescha. If you'll follow on the diagram, there's basically two rooms, a bedroom and a bathroom. . . .

3

Villam stepped over a Mute's body and tossed a gas grenade between the slats of an unglazed window. He put his back to the wall, dropped to a squat, and prepared to wait, hidden behind a thin line of brush, dart rifle across his knees. His twin brother Veschant was around back of the bothy, keeping low, guarding their retreat.

Ossoran kicked the door open and went charging in. He put a dart in the youth sprawled across the Chasekelits, then he stood by the door while Feyvorn and Samhol Bozh moved to the bed, lifted the dead boy aside and bent over the woman.

While Feyvorn buckled padded restraints about her wrists and ankles, Bohz seated distorters over her ears and pulled a darksac over her head, knotting the ties under her chin. Feyvorn cleared off the small table by the bed and set up the flake recorder there. He checked the accumulators, made sure there was a flake in the slot and the thing was ready to go the moment he touched the sensor.

Bohz opened his medapac and sprayed a stim shot into her arm to bring her out of the gas-induced stupor, then rechecked the restraints as she woke mad as a wet rat, cursing and struggling, promising a death of a hundred days to whoever was doing this to her.

He pushed the hood up a thumbwidth, sprayed a shot of babble juice into her jugular.

Her struggles grew feebler, less defined, her voice went mushy. Then she was limp, silent.

He touched a dagnos rod to her neck, inspected the reading. "She's under. This is going to be in Ektahash, the centers we're reaching don't know interlingue. I'll give you a running translation. If you want to ask her something, just let me know. All right?"

"Let's get at it." Ossoran dropped to a squat, balanced his rifle across his knees. "Where's the Auction going to be?"

4

". . . tchin chi okin kinsa. Tin ta' on'ine tchon ik."

"She says she doesn't know what I'm talking about. Nothing to do with her, what's the point of watching . . . uh . . . kh'hou' ki dhalokhch—that's hard to translate, it means something like insects-not-worth-stepping-on. Watching kh'hou ki dahlokhch kill other kh'hou'. Killing things is no fun if you don't get your own hands bloody. There's nothing like feeling the life going out of something into you."

"Gentle Lady. Dio!" Ossoran thought a moment. "Ask her about the last Chasekelits."

Samhol Bohz put the question and listened to the answer. "She says sure, she expects it's true. The old bitch lost it so long ago, she couldn't remember what it feels like, being alive, she means. There was a ton of money going somewhere, but she couldn't get a smell of it when she took the godseat. If she wasn't locked off from her emotions, she'd be steaming mad. She says there was a grand bonfire of the old Chasekelits' personal possessions before they let her into the castle. If she had anything like one of Ginny's Limited Editions, it went up with the rest. Dry hole, friends, that's all we got."

"Right." Ossoran stood. "Put her under and let's get out of here."

"You four might as well go on now. I've got things to do."

"Don't be stupid, Op. You want the woman dead, put a dart in her. I don't care how corrupt she is, I don't tolerate meatgames."

Samhol Bozh sighed, wiped at his face. "That's not it."

"What, then?"

Ossoran listened to his explanation, grinned, and nodded. "Feyv, get her ready. Look, Bohz, the five of us can handle it better than one. If nothing else, you need someone watching your back. We'll take care of that little thing and slide for home."

5

When morning dawned in A'au'ah'popeh'bin, the Godqueen's chief city, the folk there woke to find their Chasekelits hanging upside down and naked in the market. The tag on her dangling wrist said: TAINTED MEAT. FOR SALE CHEAP.

IV. BURROWING DEEPER, SETTING UP THE HIT (Ginny still sitting this out)

SINGER AND SLASHER APPEARING
SEPARATELY
KARINTEPE, CHISSOKU BOGMAK
63 Kirar Sorizakre, day 19, hour 21
Shadith and the Razor T'gurtt
at the NightFair

1

The night was warm, muggy, with a thick layer of clouds across the sky, blocking out light from the moons and the stars. There was no wind; the air was still, oppressive, sweat beaded on the skin and stayed there. Tempers were edgy, there was a feel hanging over the Square that anything could happen anytime.

Leaving the Halftwins to watch for Ingra and Fann, Pikka Machletta took Mem with her and went strolling round the Square to check the marks and read the mood of the crowd, to see how bad it really was.

Jinsbeks prowled about, looking for trouble, ready to start some if they didn't find it. Hoshyids—and Bogmakkers, too—were treating everyone as if they were thieves and cheats and bargaining was more like war than a game that both sides generally enjoyed.

It was a bad night for entertainers, people were hard to please; their pockets might have been sewed shut for all the coin they tossed.

It was a bad night for everyone.

Pikka and Mem saw a pair of jinsbeks hassling a merchant's git as he tried to go into the *Filigree Hole;* he had a round baby face and they were threatening to take his pants down to make sure he had a man's hair at the bottom of his belly.

They saw two youngers from Liondog Torkkus caught with their hands in the wrong pockets; the hoshyids yelled and kicked at them until a triad of jinsbeks came roaring up and did some kicking of their own, booting torksos and hoshyids without caring which was what.

They saw a jinsbek slap a girl from Hummingbird T'gurtt, force her to disgorge everything she'd got so far, slap her again when he saw how meager her take was.

"A bad night," Pikka muttered. "A stinkin night."

Mem made a face. "It's as well we're not working."

"Ay-yeh. We better get back."

2

Ingra came grinning through the Sun Gate, collected her futak, and pinned it on. "Fann be along 'n a minute."

The Halftwins jigged with excitement, whispering: "She comin? She really comin?"

Pikka fingered her razor's handle and said nothing. She envied the hoshyid. That was all right. That was natural. She liked her. A lot. If the girl stayed around long enough, she'd maybe end up liking her more even than Fann who was her best friend forever. It was confusing. Hoshyid were marks. Prey. You don't make friends with something you're going to eat. She admired the hoshyid, that was confusing, too. The girl was sharper than a razor's edge, she'd handled the Sirshaka as if she were a slumming Goyo doing him a favor and she'd made him like it, smiles and subtle flatterings, nothing said, everything implied. She looked too young to be that good . . . which meant she wasn't what she seemed. . . . That wasn't the worst. When she came away from that meeting, the hoshyid looked drawn . . . anxious. . . . Trouble. . . .

Pikka wavered whenever she thought about what the hoshyid was really here for. Something bad . . . bad for her . . . bad for Razor. But the money . . . the money

was better, surer, coming faster already than anything
Razor could make on their own . . . and they hadn't
started collecting their percentage. . . .

Mem was quiet, her eyes fixed on the Gate, her hands
moving up and down the sides of her working jacket.

Pikka ached for her. Despite the hard truths the hoshyid had given Mem, it was obvious the girl smelled like
hope to her, a way back—somehow—to the safety and
. . . and . . . Pikka couldn't think of a word to describe
what she knew of Mem's first life, that was part of the
problem with Mem, none of them knew the right
words. . . .

Ingra giggled and bent close to Kynsil's ear. "Sure,"
she whispered, "she comin with bells on, din't Fann 'n
me follow her 'n the Liz cross the bridge? Wait till you
see her. Whooo-eee."

Kynsil scowled at the Gate. "You here. Why in't she?"

"Why?" Hari, Kynsil's echo.

"Cause she 'n the Liz, they stop for tea at *Amod' Aachana's.* Letting the crowd thicken up, I s'pose. What
Fann said anyway."

A fluting whistle came through the noise, a bit of dance-
joy singsong, liquid and lovely. There was no one could
whistle like Fann.

"Ah ri'," Pikka said. "Ing, y' better get goin. If y'
smell trouble anywhere round the spot, don' y' go nosin
for more, y' get back to us fast, y' hear?"

"Ay-yeh, you said it twenty times already, Pikk."

"And I goin to say it twenty more, make sure y' hear
me. A stinkin night, Ing, jinsbeks jumpin anyone who
look at 'em. So y' keep your horns in, huh?"

"I hear, I hear. . . ." Ingra went dancing off, trailing
little bursts of giggles as she moved.

"That Ing! That Ing!" Pikka Machletta sighed, shook
her head. "Mem. Kyn. Hari. Say it."

Mem looked at Kynsil, then back to Pikka. "We troll
the middle, we stay a couple meters ahead and out to
both sides, watching for trouble coming at you and the
hoshyid. We stay away from Goyo and jinsbeks and pres-

sers and Torkkusses and T'gurtts and drunks and all that lot.''

''Ri'. Go.'' Pikka Machletta watched them vanish into the surly crowd, sighed again. What happened, happened. Nothing she could do to stop it. *Luck stay sweet,* she breathed and made an *O-U* sign, *five guims each to the first ten beggars I see tomorrow.*

3

The hoshyid came quietly through the Sun Gate. She wore a loose black velvet robe over a filmy gray gown. There was a circlet on her head with points that curved outward. Over this coronet she'd thrown a gray veil embroidered gray-on-gray about the edges; it hung in graceful folds to mid-thigh in front and to her knees in back. She moved with a slight sway, the suggestion of a reed bending in the wind, a stillness pulled around her that snagged the eye somehow and got people staring at her.

Pikka couldn't see how she did it, she wasn't tall like the Goyo and she wasn't showing any figure. She didn't have much to show anyway. That stillness thing, that wasn't . . . but Pikka kept looking back at her, looking away and looking back again; she couldn't seem to stop it. She could see other people doing the same thing. Another Talent? Or the Liz. . . .

He was following two steps behind her. He wore a heavy black robe, its cowl pulled forward, the edge stiffened and weighted to keep his face in shadow without blinding or strangling him. He had the harpcase strapped to his back and he carried a three-legged black stool in his gloved hands.

Fann came wriggling through the crowd and stopped beside Pikka Machletta. ''In't she somethin? She said she goin to make a bad place good. I think she goin to do it.''

4

The place Shadow had acquired was a backwater close to the North Wall and near the western edge of the Temple court. There was no light except what the mirror columns caught and reflected and nothing around but a few furtive drug dealers and their customers. Stall keepers and entertainers didn't want to come back here, being that close to the Temple made them nervous; besides, the people flow was less than a trickle and the trade wasn't worth the price of a place.

She pointed.

The Liz set the stool down and swung the case around. He took out the harp and gave it to her when she'd got herself settled and the folds of her clothing arranged to her satisfaction, then he moved round behind her, sank into a squat and effectively vanished.

She sat quietly looking around. At least, her head was turning. Pikka couldn't see what her eyes were doing.

A few hoshyids and a Bogmakker pair had been intrigued enough to follow her. They were waiting without much patience for something to happen. Mem was sitting beside one of the mirrored columns, the Halftwins with her. Ingra was prowling about behind some drugged out goomoos too far gone to know anything was happening outside their skins.

Shadow began to make her music.

At first it seemed pleasant enough, but nothing special; the harp notes sank into the noise around them with less effect than a stone thrown in roiled water. Shadow crooned wordless sounds, her voice rich and flowing. Cool. Caressing. Magical. Like Spring rain falling from clouds so high the drops seemed to come from the sun. Joined with the harp it was pleasing. . . .

No, more than that. . . .

What? What?

Something was happening. . . .

Pikka shook her head, not in denial, in confusion—there was something happening in her she couldn't quite. . . .

It wasn't that she heard the music more clearly, it was more as if it had moved inside her skin.

It wasn't just her this was happening to.

People were coming from all round. Hoshyids and Bogmakkers from the Fair.

Monks from the Temple—Goyo Monks. Lurking like landsharks among the mirrored columns.

Pikka could feel them there, watching. They made her skin itch.

She forgot them.

The mirrors on the columns, the ones that could move, they were turning to focus on the singer. The others shimmered, the lights in them dancing with the lilt of the song.

There were faces in the mirrors, forms dancing to the music, spinning other forms out of themselves.

Her mother gazed out at her, smiling, loving; when she was alive, especially toward the end, she seldom had time or strength to look like that, like she had when Pikka was a baby. Her mother bent toward her, drifting like smoke from the mirror. Her mother's arms were out, not quite touching her. Her mother sang in Shadow's voice, sang a hushaby song Pikka could just remember.

Pikka wept without knowing what she did. Tears dripped down her face and fell onto her tunic.

The song changed.

Her mother faded, she saw shapes . . . and things . . . veiled forms. . . . Disturbing, wondrous things she had no words for. They passed through her head like dreams, churning her emotions until she was close to bursting. . . .

The Singer's voice rose to a triumphant note, cut off. She swept a final chord from the harp, then stilled the strings and sat with her head bent as the Liz came to his feet and took a collecting basket through the crowd that had gathered, drawn by that extraordinary song—or whatever it was. "Bless O sister, bless O brother," he intoned as coins rained into the basket. "Bless O sister, bless O brother."

Pikka shook herself loose from her trance, scrubbed

impatiently at her face. She felt invaded . . . happy . . .
she was angry at the hoshyid for doing this to her . . .
and she wanted her to sing again, now . . . not later
. . . now. . . .

The Liz carried the brimming basket back to the
Singer. "Shadow sings again in one half hour," he de-
claimed in a surprisingly robust voice (Pikka started,
turned to stare). "Come again, despoies."

63 Kirar Sorizakre, day 20, hour 12
Rohant and the Rij and others
at the Arena on Yugoyyum Shimda

1

Rohant followed the Rij Tatta Ry and his assistant from the dark, dank tunnel into the blue twilight of the Arena. It was a long oval under a barrel dome like half of a blue glass bottle, sand-floored, with a slick-tiled black wall shutting the fighters away from the plank seats on the south rising steeply till they met the dome, and on the north, from private boxes (one with an elaborate cartouche beneath it), ranks of padded chairs, and a section shut behind copper walls with a carved wooden screen across the front.

By Tatta Ry's design they'd come out at the east end of the oval; he limped wordlessly along the major axis, one hand on his cane, the other clamped around the Tindarij's arm. When he finally reached the center, he stopped in front of the box with the cartouche and turned to face Rohant.

"You see," he said. He waved his cane along the curve of the north wall. "They sit there. The Goyo. You needn't bother with those others, the rabble on the south. Forget them. Remember, it's the Goyo who make you or destroy you. If they take against you, it won't matter how many fights you win, you're useless and I'll dump you. You see that?" His wavering cane jabbed at the cartouche. "That's the Kralodate's box. You go down on your knees here, Unmate. He probably will not be there for your first fight, but you make your yayyay to the box and make it with serious intent to honor. Doesn't matter what you

153

think other times other wheres. When you pay honor to the Kralodate, the man or the symbol, you mean it or I'll have you spread and caned till you understand what I'm saying. You find too many things amusing, Dyslaeror, it makes enemies for you. Hear me. I want no hint of that while you are on the sand. Kirar can sniff out disaffection before it surfaces. And he cuts it down faster than a medic lances a boil.''

Rohant nodded. He got the message. The Kralodate was a paranoid mokha with a habit of disappearing anyone he took a hate to.

The Rij dug the tip of his cane into the sand and stared over Rohant's shoulder at nothing in particular. "Note well the screened area. Do not disdain the Hidden Ones. They have more influence than they deserve." He ran his eyes over Rohant, the lines deepening on his face. "They will drool over you, no doubt about it. If you have a chance to display to them, take it. Hmp. You'll be getting notes, if you know what's good for you, burn 'em. If you work out like I think, it'll be presents later. Those you can keep." He moved his head in a slow arc, looking along the North side, looking back at Rohant. "I am slotting you only into death duels, Dyslaeror, you have no grace to you, nothing to recommend you to the Goyo except your ability to slaughter quickly and bloodily. The thinking beast. Hmp. In the beginning your one necessity is to make your kill. Make it where and how you have to. Here, if possible. Display yourself when it does not interfere with the engagement, but don't waste opportunity or take a chance on missing your strike. Flourishes come later, when your reputation is established. Perhaps I should say if. No matter. K'ch'en, escort our recruit through the locker area then back to the Tay. His first slot was confirmed late last night. He'll go tomorrow. Third Round. Against Kuyhan Sil of Karuhamar Tay. Give him all you know of Sil, what he should expect and what will be expected of him. Have you any questions?''

The Tinda-rij K'ch'en yayyayed. "None, Rij-Seffyo. Do you wish me to call an escort?''

The Rij produced a small tight smile. ''I think that is a question, K'ch'en. No matter. No, I am not yet reduced to the litter and the chair. Go. I'll stay here a while and remember.''

63 Kirar Sorizakre, day 21, hour 3
Shadith and Kikun
in their room in Karintepe-on-Maine

1

Shadith looked up as the door opened and Kikun came in. She closed the notebook on the stylus and set it on the table beside the chair. "Well?"

He slid out of his sandals, sat down on the bed. "Anything worth listening to?"

She made a face at him. "Worm. Want some tea? I think there's some left, probably ready to crawl out the pot by now."

He shuddered. "If I want to tan my tongue, I'll go lie on the beach." He pulled his legs up, twisted them into a knot, patted his knees, rested his forearms on them, and contemplated her.

"Gods, Kikun, that gives me a pain just looking at it."

He blinked at her, smiled his slow sweet smile, his orange eyes molten in the lamplight.

"All right, all right. How's Ro? What did he have to say?"

Kikun stopped smiling, looked away from her. "He has his first go tomorrow night. Death match. The Rij told him that was all he was going to get. Death matches."

"Tsoukbaraim."

"He was low, Shadow, sick. When I said what's wrong? he said nothing's wrong. Then he said S'ragis and started crying. His granddaughter, Shadow. Lissorn's baby. She was killed by the bomb Ginny got into the compound. Miralys didn't tell him till after we were gone."

156

"Gods, Lissorn's hardly more than a boy, she couldn't have been. . . ."

"Not quite two. Lissorn was wild to get after Foltsorn, Rohant said. Miralys had to put him down for a while, she didn't want him wasting time and resources on a slime like that. The Unmating would cancel Foltsorn out soon enough. When Lissorn heard what you said, Shadow, he was hot to come with us, but Rohant talked him out of it, told him: *Wait till we find out where Ginny is, then you can come.* He was on Pache at the conference, that's why he didn't say much."

Shadith closed her eyes. "Kikun, we have to tell him, we have to get him out of there. We have to. . . ."

"Lissorn saved my life, Shadow. He could have died doing it, he knew that and got me out anyway. What I do, I do for him. I am going to find Ginny for him and I will let nothing prevent that. Rohant protects us where he is. If he runs, he alerts Wargun. Remember, the Fevkindadam thinks that we're in Jinssi Hole and that his mercs have gone offworld the way he planned it. He thinks Rohant is all he has to worry about. I will not tell the Ciocan anything. Not until we have what we came for."

"I see. Go on."

Kikun laced his hands together, gazed down at them. "After he washed his face, I said what do you want to do? He said keep on. He's seen Wargun, too. Different circumstances. The Fevkindadam is married to the Rij's youngest daughter. He came to the gym."

"Go on."

"I said all right, we'll be there if you need us. At the Games, I meant. He said NO. I said why. He wouldn't answer."

"This business isn't good for him, Kikun. Look, he's Lissorn's father, doesn't that apply? There are other ways we can do this." She sighed as Kikun shook his head.

He straightened his back, sat with his hands resting lightly on his knees, staring cross-eyed at things invisible to anyone but him. "He will survive . . . he will . . . thrive."

"Will we? Thrive, I mean. When you betray a friend . . . what else can you call it? . . . what are you left with?" Shadith got to her feet, went to the window and stood gazing out at the night. It was late, quiet, dark. She could see a faint yellowish glow above the Old Town buildings on Araubin Shimda and a thin scatter of stars. Both moons were down; it'd be dawn in a few hours. "Since you're in a mood to prophesy, tell me what good all this singing is doing us. Tell me why I have the feeling we're getting nowhere." She rubbed at the crease between her eyes. "Seems to me I'm in as bad a trap as Rohant." She swung round, hitched a hip on the windowsill. "Birdy in a gilded cage, right? Sing for my supper and a snatch at safety that might be more imagination than real. Sar! I wonder if Pikka Machletta knows anything? Better not bring it up. She hates Goyo, but she'd sell me in a minute if she thought I was going after them. I suppose I could use Babblespec on her, come to that. No. Don't know enough yet, can't throw Razor away until I'm sure. . . . Kikun?"

He was staring at nothing, eyes crossed, an idiot blankness on his thin, wrinkled face. If he had answers, he wasn't saying.

She made a soft, exasperated sound. "All right. What about this? I don't care what Ro wants, I'm going to watch him fight. I couldn't stand it if he got killed and I wasn't at least trying to stop it."

That woke him up.

He blinked, frowned, then a tentative smile pushed aside soft gray-green folds of skin. "Gaagi says are you so ignorant of need or don't you care for more than flesh? You won't have to help him stay alive, Gaagi says. Leave him to sorrow in solitude, his shame a thing private to himself. When the fighting is over, then you may birth the man from the beast. Gaagi says."

Shadith frowned. "Gaagi?"

"Raven."

"What?"

He laughed, dropped his legs over the edge of the bed, slid his feet into his sandals. ''Doesn't matter now, not now.'' He stood and went out, pulling the door shut with the faintest of clicks.

''Now? Raven? Sar! I hate it when he does that.''

63 Kirar Sorizakre, day 21, hour 21
Rohant in the Arena
Opponent: Kuyhan Sil of Karuhamar Tay

1

Kuyhan Sil was a hard rubber ball of a man who bounced when he ran, a squat heavyworlder with thick gray skin and a crop of hair like coiled steel shavings. Straps wound round his torso, his arms, his legs, knives all up and down those straps, little knives with leaf shaped blades, throwing knives glittering in their leather loops. His only other articles of clothing were little square boots with scratched and stained steel toes. *Watch out for his jumps,* K'ch'en said, *he can go straight up two meters from a standing start, not a twitch to show you what's about to happen. And kick your head in before you have a chance to move. He's fair with the knives, but they're more a distraction than a real danger. It's his feet that get you.*

Eyes like matte black plums peered at Rohant from deep beneath massive brow ridges; with no discernible change of expression, he turned his stare on the hawk perched motionless on Rohant's wrist.

The *A'unsa Vermak* came stalking from his station beneath the Cartouche, a scarred and ancient Goyo so heavily loaded with copper ornaments he clanked like a perambulating junkyard. He inspected the two fighters, satisfied himself they were standing a proper five meters apart. With a brisk, approving nod, he swung round, tapped the sensor on his belt, waited until the reverberations of the great gong died away, tapped his throat pickup alive.

"On the east, fighting with knives and body, Kuyhan Sil representing Karuhamar Tay."

Sil dropped to his knees with a soft grunt, yayyayed with adequate reverence, bounded to his feet and stood preening at the whistles and shouts of appreciation from his claque among the Goyo.

"On the west, fighting with claw and hawk, the Unmate Rozash representing Taiikambar Tay."

Murmuring inaudible reassurances to Sassa, Rohant went to his knees, did the yayyay with one hand, a ritual he'd practiced under K'ch'en's exacting eye; the Tindarij kept him at it until all hint of behind-thought was wiped away.

As soon as he was on his feet again, he sent Sassa up, stifling a smile of satisfaction as he heard a growing murmur from the watching Goyo and copper-on-copper clanking like hail as they laid new odds into their personal boards.

The *A'unsa Vermak* frowned until he saw that Sassa was gliding through slow figure-eights out beyond the Dyslaeror, not encroaching on the area between the two fighters. He nodded again and went creakily back to his station. He faced them. "To the Death," he intoned. "B'hi. N'ki. Sai'si. MABASH'K!"

"Ha'haiiii!" Sil came bounding at Rohant, his short legs working so fast they were a blur, his hands blurring as he snatched throwing knives from their loops and rained them like hail at the Dyslaeror.

Rohant threw himself to the right, batting the knives aside with his gauntleted arm, whipped backward as Sil bounced into a high wheeling leap, his steel toes skimming past Rohant's head, the miss so close Rohant could smell the boot polish. He raked Sil's leg with his right-hand claws, deep enough to draw blood, roared with pain as Sil lashed out even as he fell and got in a glancing blow at Rohant's thigh.

Sil landed awkwardly, but didn't seem to notice that, he was up an instant later, rebounding from the sand like the ball he resembled, flicking two more knives at Rohant, running at him, driving him back toward the wall.

One of the knives sliced across the outside of Rohant's thigh, cutting a gash less than a centimeter deep. He swore, flicked another knife aside and flashed in a wide circle around the heavyworlder, a feint while he tested how well his leg worked. He was faster than Sil, with double his reach, but he was already tiring while the little gray man hadn't even worked up a sweat. He slowed, looking for a way he could get past those knives, those feet, a way he could move in close enough for his claws to do some damage.

Sil came at him again, leaping, feet together, his hard heavy body a projectile aimed at Rohant's chest, coming fast, ah fast, a bullet, a blur.

Rohant dived under him, whipped over, hit the sand with his shoulders, swept his feet up and caught Sil just above the kidneys with his footclaws; he raked the claws as hard as he could along Sil's back, then straightened his legs with all the power he could muster, sending the heavyworlder into a sluggish sprawl a short distance off. A push with his shoulders and Rohant was on his feet again, thinking, *Dio! He weighs a ton.*

No change of expression as Sil untangled himself and stood, but he was angry now, Rohant could smell it on him. He bared his teeth in a threat grin that had a lot of satisfaction in it, but he kept his distance from the heavyworlder; that much mass meant too much strength for him to handle straight on. K'ch'en had warned him, but he hadn't really absorbed the lesson until now. He alerted Sassa and watched Sil come toward him.

A flicker of Sil's hands and he held a knife in each. Knives with longer blades than the throwers. He came stumping stolidly at Rohant, all finesse forgotten; he was going to walk the Dyslaeror down and stick those knives in him and nothing was going to stop him.

Rohant darted to the right, whipped through a tight arc, trying to stay behind Sil long enough to get his claws into the man's throat. He came too close and nearly lost a hand. Bad judgment. Underestimating Sil's strike speed.

He cut round to the left. Same thing happened.

With no change of expression, no evidence of disappointment, Sil trudged steadily toward Rohant, a smallish gray tank of a man.

The Dyslaeror retreated again. He was sweating, starting to feel pain in his hip where the knife wound was, breathing through his mouth, gulping down drafts of air that did him no good.

Sil smiled and kept coming. Blood was drying on his arm and dripping from his back, but he showed no sign he was getting tired.

Rohant retreated, feinting to one side, then the other, staying well away from Sil. When he was ready, he called Sassa.

The hawk circled away, picked up speed, stooped, struck at the back of Sil's head, getting one ear, gouging a ragged cut in the side of his neck, was away again an instant ahead of the sweep of Sil's right-hand knife.

When the stoop began, Rohant ran full out at Sil; at the last moment he leaped aside, using his reach advantage, slashing his claws across the inside of the heavy-worlder's elbow, ripping open an artery, loosing a fountain of blood.

Sassa swooped again, striking from the side, ripping Sil's eye half out of his head, breaking free, back again, hitting his neck again, gone. . . .

Rohant tore Sil's throat out. More blood.

The spectators went wild, stamping, whistling, shouting.

He ignored them.

He whistled Sassa to his wrist, stood soothing the bird while he watched Kuyhan Sil die. His first kill for money. "Ru ru, my dar, ru ru, my dal, I know, oh yes, I know this is evil, but I'll pay, not you, ru ru, my dal, not you . . . not. . . ."

When Sil shuddered finally, stopped groping about with his undamaged hand, Rohant swung around, yayyayed perfunctorily toward the Kralodate's box and stalked off, a great angry beast, concealing the sick emptiness in his middle, ignoring Goyo and non-Goyo cheers, showing his contempt for all of them in every line of his body.

It might have gotten him killed. He didn't care.

It didn't.

He walked out on a standing ovation and emptied his stomach in the toilet.

K'ch'en was furious and worried.

Tatta Ry was angrier than he'd been in years; he was ready to throw Rohant in the mines for the rest of his life, however long that was.

But it worked.

When the ratings came out, the Taiikambar Tay had climbed two full points, tieing with the Tayuzin Tay for primacy. Karuhamar Tay dropped to fifth.

Tatta Ry read the notes of praise and congratulations, shook his head, and passed word to Rohant to keep on as he had begun.

63 Kirar Sorizakre-days 22-25
Shadith at the NightFair
Facing down the Monks

1

day 22, hour 24

Shadow sat collapsed in her robes and veil, shoulders rounded, head down; she looked exhausted.

Pikka Machletta had no difficulty believing in that exhaustion. It seemed like half the fairgoers had come steaming over to stand about and groan and snort and sniff while they listened to the singing. She'd noticed before that the bigger the crowd, the more the song squeezed out of the singer.

She prowled angrily back and forth in front of the slowly dispersing mob, snarled at a set of weird-looking offworlders who thought they wanted to gush at the Singer and wouldn't take a hint and clear off. She snatched her razor loose, whipped it open. "Cumma cumma, ruymi-kumi, y' wan' trouble, cumma see. Hah! Hah!"

The furry spiders recoiled, went scurrying off.

A chuckle.

Pikka glared around, located the laughter, a short dark man with long hair pulled through a silver clasp. "You wan' summa this, huh?" She swung the razor.

He laughed again, strolled on, followed by another hoshyid, a dark cat of a man with pointed ears that moved restlessly, restless eyes; Pikka met those eyes, shivered.

Every time Shadow sang, the hashshar got pushier.

It's going to get worse before it gets better, Pikka told herself. Unless I do something. She folded the razor shut, shoved it back into the clamps, glared at a triad of tiny hoshyid, who blinked at her and sheared off. As she watched them trot away, a flicker of red caught her eye. She swung round. Mordo ducked behind a stall. Koyohk! Dragons. She glanced over her shoulder. Fann and the rest of the T'gurtt were in the shadows behind the Singer, helping the Liz sack the take and stow it in the harpcase. Trust Kidork to sniff out piles of it.

When the area had cleared out a little, Pikka Machletta signaled Fann to join her and moved into the murk next to the wall where she squatted and waited.

Fann drifted back, leaned against the stone. "What?" she murmured.

"We goin to get tromped we don' do something, huh?"

"Ay-yeh."

"Dragons." Pikka flicked a finger toward the stall where Mordo had gone to ground.

"Ay-yeh. And I spotted Kalkosh and the Liondogs, Mersheh and the Humminbirds. And there's always more 'n y' see."

"Sheeeh. Sharks. Mm. 'Member Pepri sayin she goin to put the boot to Dobb?"

"Ay-yeh. Did, too. Saw her stickin the notice up this mornin." Fann rubbed at her nose. "You thinkin. . . ."

"By Fairend that case goin to be stuffed. Half the torksos 'n t'gurtsas in Old Town already sniffin after us, huh? Y' go find Pepri, get that room for us, huh?"

"Costish. What 'bout key-money? Pepri don' do nothin without cash in hand and she goin to want a thousand guims min."

"We an't payin, she is." Pikka pointed with her chin at the Singer's back. "More'n a thousand in that case ri' now, huh? Bring the Liz back here, I talka it outta him. I want that key soon's y' can pry it loose."

2

"Ing, y' know some jinsbeks who stay bought?"

Ingra made a face. " 'Pends what they bought with." She slapped Pikka's hand away before she got pinched. "Na-neh, Pikk, I'll be serious. Hmm. Ay-yeh. Costish."

"Tell you like I told Fann, we not payin, Singer is. We

goin to get run ov-ah next time, 'thout some muscle out front, huh? Liz says don' toss it round, but spend what we need. Get three if y' can, but we settle for two. Y' got a half hour, Ing. Shift it.''

3

"Mem, y' got a good eye for size. Go over to Iba Chayt's stall, look out some secondhand clothes for Shadow and the Liz so they can get outta that stuff into somethin real before they go back 'cross the bridge. If we can keep 'em from gettin killed, the way she haulin it in, we got our Winter Stash made.''

Mem nodded. "Then I'd better get cloaks, too.''

"Ay-yeh. Stop by the Liz, he give you the cash.''

"Um, Pikk. The monks keep getting thicker.''

"I see 'em. Not much we can do 'bout it. Shift it, Mem, y' be back before she do it again or y' never get through.''

4

The Singer stood, stretched, walked back to the wall. "Busy busy.''

"Makin up for lazy heads.''

"Bad planning, you mean. I must admit I hadn't expected this much this soon.''

"Goin to be craaa-zee till worldship leave.'' Pikka fingered her razor. "Calm down some then. Maybe.''

"Mm. No Goyo yet.''

"Y' don' want to get mess up with Goyo.''

The Singer hesitated, impossible to see her face through that veil, so Pikka had no idea what she was thinking. "I might need to get messed up with Goyo.''

"Why?''

"Investigation. Why I'm here.''

Pikka Machletta looked past her at the shadows among the mirrored columns. "Y' goin to get what y' want, but y' an't goin to like it.''

"What?''

"Temple. Take a look in there, all them, they monks. Goyo monks. Holy holy holy, y' get? Ol' Sh'dok'n, seem like he got a letch for y'."

"Shudokan . . . mm. That's the head man in there, him than which there is no higher?"

"Y' got it."

"How bad is that? How much power do the Monks actually have?"

"They got relatives." Pikka snapped thumb against finger. "Ooh ye-ah, they do." Her voice as deep as she could force it, she said, "Drop that suck-kah down tha mine." The next words were shrill falsetto. "Oh yeh-aah, oh yeh-aah, holy holy." She grinned. "Y' got fannypat from Luck. Sh'dok'n, he was eldest uncle to Atsui tha Souse, Kralodate 'fore Kirar, he got to watch where he step or Kirar disappear him down the Jinssi Hole. He only hangin on 'cause Goyo," she spat, "they don' like change."

"Hmm. Is all this poking around because I'm using the mirrors?"

"You know 'bout that?"

"Pikka," her voice went up and down, breaking the name in half with a choke of laughter, "it's my business to know. Oh. I see." She ribbed at her back. "Sar! Almost time to do it again. No, Pikka Machletta, I don't have the faintest notion what you're getting from the songs, I don't read minds or anything like that. I have my own ghosts. Everybody's visions are different. It's all very private, no secrets leak out. The Shudokan, O Chlet, what's he up to?"

Pikka shrugged. "Goyo don' talka me."

"Guess."

"Y' somethin new, somethin wild, turns out there an't no danger in y', maybe so maybe no he thinkin he goin to use y' to crawl up next to Kirar."

"Hmm. Sounds reasonable. I can work with that."

"An't goin near Goyo, none of us."

"I hear you. What's. . . ." She lifted her head, swung around. Ingra was back with the jinsbeks, three grinning meat mountains, laughing and joking with her.

Ingra waved. " 'Roa, Shadow. These Sougoury, Vlees, and Slanin. Gonna cool down the goomoos."

5

day 25, hour 4

The monks came swarming out of the Mirror Court less than ten minutes after the Closure Gong boomed and the futaks went dull and rough.

The Singer sat hunched over on the stool, too tired to move, almost too tired to breathe. Five times she'd sung, and the last time half the Fair had come to listen.

The Liz and the Halftwins and Mem were sacking the take and stowing the sacks in the wicker trunk with the shoulder poles they'd bought the day before when it was obvious they needed something bigger than the harpcase to hold the offerings the audience almost flung at them in its eagerness to hear more and yet more. Ingra was joking with Sougoury, the youngest of the jinsbeks; it looked like she'd be off with him the rest of the night. Fann and Pikka Machletta were standing together a short distance in front of the Singer, shielding her from lingering fair-goers.

Fann saw the monks coming, pinched Pikka's arm.

"I see 'em. Go on, Fann. Get Razor outta here and the Liz if he'll go and Sougoury and Slanin. Tell Vlees to stick with the Singer."

"What 'bout you, Pikk? An't you comin with us?"

"Change m' mind. Shift it, huh?"

"Y' not goin to stick your head in that noose?"

"Fann!"

"Ah ri' ah ri'. 'M goin."

6

Fann hustled Razor and the two jinsbeks off with the night's harvest half a minute before the monks closed the circle around the Singer.

Watching the ring of Goyo thicken around her, Pikka thought how much they were like the horde of vermin the

Singer fetched not so long ago. *I liked the vermin better.*
She couldn't understand what she was doing here, why
she'd changed her mind about slipping away and letting
the hoshyids take care of themselves, she was shivering
. . . sick . . . Goyo Goyo Goyo . . . they were all around
her now, standing there . . . almost touching her . . .
drooling yellowface jiccamels . . . *Luck stay sweet, I'll
make it ten quims . . .*

"Singer."

*Ai yi, it's the hot-iron man hisself, Mommajogga
Emkakkaei! Ai ai aaaah, what am I doing . . . diving
headfirst down a mine?*

"I am the Emkakkaei Rossoldur, Servant of Guintayo
the Light and of Dirin Mashudokana Hido'imuth dan
Sorizakredam. The Shudokan desires to speak with you.
I am come to take you to the audience chamber."

The Singer got slowly to her feet. She was tiny before
the Goyo's three meters plus, but she stood with a regal
assurance that made nonsense of that difference in size.
She bowed her head a thumb's width as a matter of cour-
tesy, but she said nothing.

"Send them away."

"No."

Vlees the jinsbek moved up beside the Singer, un-
clipped his holster flap and rested a meaty hand on the
grip of his pellet gun, a casual reminder that he belonged
to the Sirshak-kai whose love for Goyo monks was somewhat less than microscopic. "We stay."

Singer and monk stared at each for several tense moments, then the Emkakkaei muttered a shidduah he didn't
mean and turned away. Over his shoulder, he said,
"Come, then. All of you."

7

Dirin Mashudokana glittered and glimmered in silk and
velvet, diamonds in a sunburst pectoral (gold), diamonds
on gold armbands clasped over heavy white silk sleeves,
diamonds in heavy gold rings on every finger and both
thumbs, diamonds in a gold headband holding in place a

velvet cloth embroidered with gold thread, gold sandals
with diamonds on the straps. He shimmered with every
breath he took. Unfortunately, in the middle of all that
sheen and show was his long wrinkled yellow Goyo face,
juiceless and charmless as a squeezed out lemon. He
crouched up on his dais in his gold chair with its white
silk cushions and peered down at the Singer and her com-
panions, visibly annoyed she wasn't alone. His eyes flickered to the jinsbek, skittered away, came back to the
Singer. He scowled at the veil. "Take it off," he said.

She lifted the gray gauze, turned it back over the silver
coronet so it fell in heavy folds that framed her face, still
covering all but a narrow strip of eyes, nose, mouth. A
grudging obedience that Pikka Machletta applauded silently.

"Sit down. The bench there. Rest of you stand where
you are. Keep your mouths shut. You weren't asked. What
are you doing here?"

Pikka flared her nostrils. *Typical. Goo says don' talk
and then he ask y' what y' doin here.*

Shadow bowed her head, smiled sweetly; she was
modest and deferential and Pikka wriggled inside her
boots, biting her lip to keep from grinning. This was how
the Singer played the game when she conned the Sirshaka
who wasn't any genius except when you compared him
to this stinkworm. "They came with me because I wished
it, Mashudokana Seffyo," the Singer said. It was as if
she sang the words rather than spoke them; her soft, clear
voice filled the vast chamber and came whispering back
as echoes. She spread her skirts and sank onto the bench,
sat with her hands folded, waiting with delicately exag-
gerated patience for the Shudokan to explain himself.

He missed that, saw only the deference. He sat back,
relaxed, the wrinkles loosening in his lemon face.

The Emkakkaei moved closer, cleared his throat, whispered in the Shudokan's ear.

"Aaankh." The Shudokan straightened up, sat tapping
his fingers on the arms of his chair. "Who are you?"

"I am Shadow, Mashudokana Seffyo."

"What does that mean?"

"It is my name, Mashudokana Seffyo."

He tutted irritably, but moved on. "Where do you come from and how did you get here?"

"I came on wings of light, I come from nowhere, my people are ghosts, my world is ash, Mashudokana Seffyo. I am an orphan cast upon your mercy."

"What?"

She smiled sweetly, dark eyes wide, her young face soulful, expectant.

Pikka squirmed; she hadn't expected to enjoy this half so much. Actually, she hadn't expected to enjoy it at all. Swallowing her giggles was giving her gas. She didn't mind. Gas she could put up with to see the Goyo mocked so expertly. And the Goomoos hadn't a clue what was happening. *Tayo damn, even braindead Kidork would get it first time she open her mouth. Goyo Goyo mommajogga jiccamels, nose in the air and foot in a piddypat.*

The Shudokan consulted briefly with the Emkakkaei, then let that one go also. "What is your reason for doing what you do?"

The Singer spread her hands, folded them again. "I am getting my living, Mashudokana Seffyo. I do not wish to be a burden on the charity of others." She was gravely serious, her eyes lowered, a hint of a lilt in her voice that made music of the words.

Pikka made a fist of her right hand and pressed it against her stomach. Oooh-eee, what a pain.

"Ankh. Quite right. Quite right. How do you produce those effects? Do you use mechanical means?"

"There is my harp. . . ." She turned, took the case from the Liz, who'd been doing his not-there thing again.

Pikka started when he moved, swore under her breath, then decided it wasn't such a bad thing after all to have someone around who could pop out of nowhere when they needed him.

The Singer opened the case, lifted out the harp. It sat on her lap, its dark wood glowing, light from the chandeliers running like water along its delicate inlays. She touched the strings but did not try to play them. "It is, I suppose," she said, "a machine of sorts."

The Emkakkaei cleared his throat, spent the next few minutes whispering with the Shudokan. Finally the Shudoka said, "Yes yes, let it be done."

The Emkakkaei pulled a sensor plate out of his sleeve, played with it and put it back, then everybody waited. Old Shudokan dropped into a doze; his eyes were open, but he was gone. Pikka shifted her weight. One of her boots scraped against the stone floor and the Emkakkaei glared at her; she ignored him.

A pair of non-Goyo service monks in the bulky brown robes of the slavery rank came hurrying in, carrying between them a heavy wooden case. The one on the right patted Pikka's arm and eased her aside so they'd have room to work on the Singer. Pikka didn't know him, but that wasn't odd; she didn't know techs, only messengers and the beggar monks, all of them non-Goyo. Like old Kaoyurz. *Worth all you hashshar put together and the Kralodate on top.*

One of the monks opened the box, took out a pair of delousers. He handed one to his companion and they began waving the black-glass rods around Shadow and her harp.

Pikka coveted the delousers for a minute, but that was useless. She clasped her hands behind her, flared her nostrils as she saw the Goyo monks looking pained as if there was a bad smell down at the foot of the stairs. *Rat butts, all of you. Do you good to get your bony fingers dirty once or twice.*

The little monk yayyayed and waited.

Whore's git dumped on the Temple, Pikka thought, off some spacer on Starstreet; no Mix in him. He learn his lessons ah ri', sucked them in. Slaves, ay-yeh, both of them. Slavey slaves. How they can! I'd never do it.

The Emkakkaei frowned. "Well?"

The monk yayyayed again. "The harp is wood and wire, nothing more. The clothing is silk gauze and silk velvet, nothing more. Beneath the clothing the woman is as she was born, nothing more. Shall we also test the jinsbek, the t'gurtsa, and the other?"

"Get to it."

Pikka held out her arms to let the monk sweep her. *Glad you not here, Kaoy, sick-making to see you like this pair of milkworms.* What she liked about him, the shit-licking smarm the Goyo had tried to beat into him just sort of beaded up and ran off, didn't change him a hair.

The monk finished with her, trotted around the bench and tested Kikun while the other one was timidly waving the rod at a scowling jinsbek.

"Well?"

The monks yayyayed in unison. "They are not enhanced in any way, Seffyo," they chorused.

Goomoo tripled. *Go away,* Pikka thought, *get out of my sight before I toss my biscuits.*

8

When they were gone, the Emkakkaei stepped back beside the Chair. He glanced at the Shudokan, cleared his throat with a crash like thunderclaps.

The old man woke with practiced slyness, blinked twice; the fact that the service monks had gone and the Singer was still sitting there was enough to clue him in as to where they'd got. "So, Orphan, how do you do it?"

She bowed her head again, let her long thick lashes veil her eyes, the image of a timid, gentle creature.

Pikka wasn't so amused this time. She was getting tired of all this and wanted it to end. You could pull a Goyo's tail only so long, until it finally sunk in what you were doing, then you were washing matrix and eating slop with no hope either thing would end.

"Spirits seem to like me, Mashudokana Seffyo," the Singer said. "I play my harp and croon my croon and they come to dance for me. I don't see them, but everyone tells me they're there. And people seem to like that. They pay me so I'll do it again. They feed me and they take me places when I ask them to. That's all I know."

"And if I asked you to play for me?"

"I am very tired, Mashudokana Seffyo. But I will try if you desire it."

"Perhaps a sample now, with more to come another time."

"This is a holy place, Mashudokana Seffyo, perhaps the spirits will not wish to enter, perhaps dangerous ones will come meaning to do harm. I do not control them, Mashudokana Seffyo, I only sing and play my harp."

The Shudokan paled and his fingers twitched. For a minute Pikka thought the Singer had scared him enough to change his mind. Then his mouth squeezed into a lemon-rust sphincter. He moved his hand in a chopping gesture.

The Emkakkaei scowled, shifted impatiently. He didn't believe a word of it, but he had his orders. "Play, girl. No more fooling around. Stop the minute I tell you to."

Pikka Machletta eased a step backward, moving slowly so she wouldn't catch any jicamel eyes. The hoshyid was worried, there was sweat on her face; so was Pikka, when she thought about it. Some of the things she'd seen in the mirrors, wooo-eee. Fake it, she thought at the Singer, you've made your excuses, don't take a chance on scaring them. A scared Goyo is mean to the bone. Come on, come on. Do it and let's get out of here.

9

Shadow settled the harp against her shoulder and began.

It was a simple, primitive instrument with a limited range, but it had a wonderful tone and it sang when she played it.

It was a bad room for a concert with all that stone and the whispering echoes, but she fought it into order, until she was using those echoes to enrich the sound, rather like she'd used the mirrors to enhance the effect of her dream songs.

It was only then that she sang, the wordless croon weaving in and out of the harp notes.

Guintayo came and danced for them, golden goddess with many arms, her hair a burning sunburst. . . .

"STOP!"

She broke a croon in half, flattened her hands on the strings, stilling them. Her face was drawn with weariness and streaked with tears. After a minute of tense silence, she passed her tongue across dry lips. "What is it, Seffyo? What did you see?"

"You don't know?" For the first time the Emkakkaei sounded uncertain.

Ordinarily Pikka would have reveled in that, but she'd seen Tayo the Light and suspected he had, too, and she was holding her breath. They teetered on a thread thinner than a catwhisker and not half so strong. If he shouted blasphemy. . . . She tensed, ready to run.

"I see my six dead sisters, Seffyo. If you have a tru-threader, I will say that before him. I have been told that others see other beings, but I have never done so. I explained that before I began, Seffyo."

"Na-Nay, Rossoldur, send the girl home." The Shu-dokan pushed himself creakily erect. "Of course she wouldn't see The Light, she is half mad and wholly unworthy. Orphan . . . what's your name?"

"Shadow, Mashudokana Seffyo."

"Appropriate, yes, most appropriate. Yes . . ." he frowned, fumbling for words that had momentarily escaped him. "Ankh. Yes. You will not speak of this." He waited.

"Yes, Mashudokana Seffyo. I will say nothing at all. I swear it on the souls of my sisters."

"Ankh-hm. Very good. You have our permission to continue your performances."

Pikka Machletta glanced at Vlees, pinched his arm to warn him to keep his mouth shut. The monks had nothing to say about who did what at the NightFair, that was the Sirshaka's business, but they could make life hard if they worked at it. He mightn't like the encroachment, but there it was.

The Singer bowed her head. "You are generous, Mashudokana Seffyo."

"Yes yes. They do disturb our meditations, you understand. You must reduce their number. No more than two a night. You hear?"

"I hear and obey, Mashudokana Seffyo."

Pikka Machletta chewed her lip and clenched her hands
into fists. Cut the take in half with a word! Got no business interfering. No business. She trembled with rage, it
took every ounce of will she had not to shout at them,
curse them, cut them. . . .

"Ankh-hm. Escort Orphan . . . aaa . . . Shadow to the
Sun Gate, Rossoldur, then come to my chambers. I have
some things I wish to discuss with you."

10

day 23, hour 5

"Gods!" Shadow looked over her shoulder at the re-
treating monks, shuddered. "I need a bath." She
groaned, reached up under the veil and scrubbed at her
eyes. "All that sugar. I'll draw flies for a month."

Vlees grinned. "You talka talk good as you sing, Sha-
dowgirl."

"Ah, Vlees." Shadow giggled, a child suddenly, layers and layers of portent and power scraped off her; it
was as if she'd exploded after all those hours of control.

Pikka Machletta walked along a half-step behind them,
glooming about the troubles she saw coming down on
her and Razor. Every time the Singer notched another
win, Pikka got antsier; Shadow was after something else
besides all this mooha from the crowd and the gelt she
was hauling in, that was clear from the beginning and it
got clearer with every night that passed. And tonight she'd
gotten closer to it. At least, she thought she had. Pikka
could feel that. Shadow might complain, but she was riding bubbles right now.

They turned into a grimy sidestreet. Pikka dropped
back another step, her razor out and ready. If there was
going to be trouble, it'd be here, just before they reached
Pepri's room. For several minutes now, she'd been hearing stray creaks and an occasional clink of metal against
metal, a bad sign this time of night.

##

Unfastening his holster flap, Vlees ran ahead of the Singer, his eyes sweeping across the narrow way, scanning the mucky ceiling above them for dropholes.

"What's happening?" The Singer moved back beside him, caught hold of him, resisted his attempts to shake her off. "Don't be a fool, tell me."

"Busy busy overhead. Heard a squint go open. Trouble, I think."

"Wait there. Let me . . . no! Be still." The gray veil fluttering about her she ran ahead a few steps, then stopped, her head lifted. It looked like she was staring up at the floor running across the street, making a ceiling for it.

There was a pattering like rain on a roof, though rain never reached down here.

A scream thick with horror.

Feet running. More screams, fading, muffled.

Shouts, muffled curses, bumps thuds clangs.

More feet, going away, clatter dying to silence.

Soft laughter behind them, the Liz amused at something or other.

Pikka started, almost cut herself. She folded the razor, slipped it back in the clamps. "Don't DO that, Liz."

Vlees shifted his stare from one to another. "What's going on? What happened?"

Pikka flipped a hand at the Singer. "Ask her."

Shadow sniffed. "Two-legged rats tend to not like the four-legged kind."

"What?"

Pikka sighed. Vlees was starting to get temperish. Well, he WAS a jinsbek, no matter how cozy he was getting with the Singer. She'd turned him sweet, which was good, best not to waste the work. "She got a witch thing she do with whatever beasts are handy." She shook her head at the Singer who looked like she was about to protest. "Tolls 'em out and sics 'em on tricksy torksos. How long you had 'em herded up this time, Shadow?"

"I started collecting just past the Sun Gate, sent them

ahead of us through the walls.'' Shadow shook her head,
started walking fast, her bootheels clicking on the paving
stones. "There was a miscellany up there, felt like half
the t'gurtsas and torkksos in Old Town. Only one Dragon.
There should have been more. I don't like it he was
alone. . . .''

Vlees trotted past her, slowed when he was where he
wanted to be. His pistol was out and ready. That's what
he trusted to keep him alive, not a herd of licey rats.

"Dragons," Shadow went on. "This was the night they
were going for us, they stunk of it. Their bad luck." She
stopped at a signal from Vlees, waited for him to wake
the concierge so she'd let them in. "The one upstairs was
the blondy called Prettybutt."

"Ooo-eee, no wonder he scream like that. He got a
thing 'bout rats.''

Pepri's daughter opened the hatch. She looked tired
and cranky, snorted when she saw Vlees. "More trouble.''

"Ay-yeh, if you don't go to open tha door." He stepped
back, waved Pikka Machletta and the Singer into the re-
cessed doorway, twitched when the Liz came trotting
past, but remembered who he was in time to keep the
pistol pointing at the street. "What trouble?''

"Torkkus. Tried to break in upstairs.'' Pepri's daughter
pulled her head in, slammed the shutter down. Chains
rattled through staples, the high-lo bars thunked into their
standhooks and Pepri's daughter pushed open the battered front door. "Three dead, two wounded. Them.
Noisy. None a yours hurt. Not bad anyway.'' She waited
until Vlees was in, then shouldered the door to and swung
the bars across. "Had city police bangin on tha door and
wantin in, but one a yours,'' she jerked her chin at Pikka
Machletta, "she dropped a fist a guims on 'em and they
went away. The dead uns, your mates chuck 'em down
cinerator, Vlees. Wounded went off on their own. Happen again, we be wanting danger pay.''

Vlees ignored that and went charging up the stairs,
passing Shadow and the Liz.

Pikka Machletta stayed behind a moment. "Lezzet,

put the word round. Why we late, Sh'dok'n had her in to play for him. Next thing y' know, it'll be Kralodate. Best not mess with her.''

Lezzet lifted a chain, watched it swing. ''Trouble. Nothin but trouble.''

''An't it the truth.''

64 Kirar Sorizakre, day 3, hour 20
Rohant in the Arena
Opponent: Frar arrau Kreastikke of
Zekkaytin Tay

1

Rohant stepped onto the sand and started for the middle.

On both sides the stands were packed and the crowds there roared their approval.

He ignored them.

He was walking rage.

Five men's blood on him, he meant to make it six before the hour was out. No more uncertainties, no hesitation, no images of Miralys or his children, no wondering when or how he could close the distance between him and Wargun. When he was on the sand, he forgot why he was there, narrowed himself to the one thing, the man coming at him.

The Arena Board of Governors had given him the East this time, the power side.

That was one sign of his rise in favor. There were others.

The Kralodate was in his box, his current favorites from among his thousand concubines fluttering around him, his bodyguards in a line behind him with two at the front corners of the box, glistening steel blue and brushed silver in their polished armor, assault rifles primed and ready.

From behind the copper screen where the Hidden Ones sat came a loud clacking, hail on a tin roof, Goyo femmes rapping their folded fans against their copper wristbands.

And a new fashion was spreading among the younger Goyo, more apparent each night he fought. They twisted their long black hair into dreadlocks and stiffened these

with gel into Dyslaeror manes. And they added a jet chain
to their copper ones and attached the mid claw of a Hyospar to it each time Rohant made a kill. They hissed their
approval, whistled, stamped their feet, and went crazy
when he dispatched his opponent.

Frar had his adherents, too, holding copper tridents
polished mirror smooth, pounding the floor with the
shafts.

Rohant recognized Frar the moment he saw him.

The Soncher from the first day.

A trident to keep him off, a net to snare him if he got
too close. Or Sassa. If Frar still had it when Sassa
stooped.

Big man. Fast.

Almost as fast as you, K'Ch'en said. *As quick with his
feet as he is on them. Watch out for sand in the eyes or
a boot in the groin. His trident hand, that's the left one,
it's a shade slower than his net hand. Not enough to worry
him. He can't switch hands, that's a weakness, but no
one's figured out how to exploit it, not yet. You can't trick
the net from him, he's had every ploy there is tried against
him. The points on his trident are razors, if he hits you
anything but a glancer, he'll bore it through you before
you can grab the pole. Even you, Unmate. And if you
don't want to see your bird skewered, you'd better keep
it off. He'll be waiting for it. My advice? It's the combination that kills you. Get the net away from him without
him killing you while you're doing it. How? You'll have
to figure that out yourself, I've never seen it done.*

##

"On the east, fighting with claw and hawk, the Unmate
Rozash representing Taiikambar Tay.

##

"On the west, fighting with net and trident, Frar arrau
Kreastikke of Zekkaytin Tay.

##

"To the death! B'hi. N'ki. Sai'si. MABASH'KI!"

##

Frar came at a fast trot, the net bunched into a thick rope which he flicked at Rohant's legs over and over, targeting knees, calves, ankles. Held lightly in his left hand, responsive as a butterfly wing, the trident darted in to sting at the Dyslaeror, twitched away as Rohant slapped at it with his gauntleted hand, came back at him again. And again, agile and elusive. Missing by a hair, skimming sweat-clotted fur, twice getting close enough to draw a trickle of blood. . . .

Rohant zagged and stuttered, always shifting, back and back, away, always away.

He couldn't get close.

Frar pressed him harder.

The Soncher was grinning now, confident. He had his rhythm. Jab. Flick. Jab. Jab. Flick. Arm. Knee. Hip, arm. Ankle. . . .

Rohant alerted Sassa, then tangled a trident point in the leather weave of his gauntlet, the interlining of metal mesh keeping it away from his flesh. He slammed his fist around, hit the tine, tore the shaft from the Soncher's grip; at the same time he flung himself down, caught the claws of his free hand in the net and jerked.

Sassa stooped as Rohant attacked, hit Frar the instant the trident tore from his grip, ripped through an eye and an ear, swooped away as the Soncher screamed.

Rohant was on him, scrambling up the net, clawing up the Soncher's long body, tearing out his throat. Blood spraying over him, he shook the man, mauling the corpse as rage whined in his throat. . . .

He flung the body away, controlled himself enough to make the required yayyay toward the Kralodate's box, then stalked off—ignoring as always the roars from the

stands, the Goyo on their feet in a kind of wardance, the
non-Goyo whooping and howling—concentrating on
keeping down the contents of his stomach until he was
in the dressing room allotted to him.

1

Shadith dug in the pocket of her toweling wraprobe for
the key to her door, blinked as it opened before she got
the key out.

Kikun touched his finger to his lips, stepped back.

Pulling the towel off her head, shaking out her wet
hair, she walked in.

Rohant was sitting on the bed. He looked up, went
back to staring at the floor; the rage stink was on him,
filling the room despite the open window. Sassa was
perched on the sill, chattering his beak, turning his head,
his feathers ruffled.

Shadith shut the door, locked it, moved across the room
to the armchair. "What's this?" She sat, pulled the robe
around to cover her knees. "I thought we weren't supposed to meet."

"He wasn't followed here." Kikun dropped to a squat
beside her. "I made sure."

"Why take the chance?"

"Frustration," he said. "Better this way."

"You tell him about the invitation?"

"Not yet. Waiting for you."

She crossed her legs, readjusted the robe. "Ah."

Rohant stirred. "Tell me what?"

"Trouble."

Kikun nodded. "Don't know where it takes us."

"Round and round," Rohant said impatiently. "What
is it?"

Shadith lifted a hand, let it fall. "We had a visitor

185

tonight, after the last performance. Envoy from the Kralodate's chamberlain. We're summoned to Joggorezel
Shimda for a command performance. Some kind of celebration. He called it the *Jusa Nonz*. Seems both moons
are up and full tomorrow night and they make a big deal
of it.'' She slid her fingertips slowly up and down the
rolled lapel of the robe as she watched Rohant's dreadlocks move, his mouth work. "Tomorrow night," she
said. "Trouble all round. The Sirshaka in charge of the
NightFair changes then, too, means I've got to renego-
tiate the futak and the Roush if I want to go on singing.
Everything's up in the air, everybody elbowing for a new
deal. Like I said. Trouble.''

"Saaaa!" Rohant's claws came out, his lips drew back.
"Seven men. Seven fights. I own half the Goyo each
Game. And nothing happens. Nobody tells me anything.
Not a damn thing!"

"This kind of something we can do without. Pikka
Machletta says Goyo notice you, you dead." She hesitated, guilt a sour taste on her tongue. She and Kikun
were worse than the Goyo, they weren't telling him things
and they were his friends. Kikun dropped a hand on her
foot, a wordless plea to keep that silence. She sighed and
went on. "At least you've seen the target."

He used his right thumb to massage the back of his left
hand until he relaxed it enough to retract his claws, then
switched hands. "Seen him. Oh, yes, I've seen him."
He growled the words. "Six, seven times he came to the
practice hall, he watched us work out a few minutes and
left. The first time . . . I thought . . . when I start winning, you'll come to ME. It's not going to happen. He's
not interested in us, I don't know why he keeps coming.
Favor to Tatta Ry, maybe. I don't . . . I know how whores
must feel . . . no . . . not feel . . . can't feel and go on
doing it . . . doing it for money . . . that's the thing . . .
Shadow, I . . . these games, they're abomination! I don't
know how much longer. . . .''

Sassa began treading at the sill, his steel-sheathed tal-
ons gouging ruts in the wood.

Shadith closed her eyes, tried to pull the shutters round

her mind. It was hard. Hard because his hurt was so strong. Hard because she had a powerful fondness for him. He was suffering, she could read how deeply his sense of himself had been eroded.

"No one knows when the break's going to come, Ro," she said finally. "We just have to keep worming along. Kikun?" There. Now the dinhast could do what he wanted.

Kikun took his hand away. "Any voice there is, is drowned by the beat beat beat of Ginny's heart. He is awake and angry. He moves toward us. Time slips away from us, slips, slips away. . . ."

"Don't!" Shadith scowled down at Kikun. "You're pushing it."

He blinked and slid away into *nevernever;* his body was pressing against her leg, but he was gone.

"Well." She combed her fingers through her hair, dried them on the robe. "You get anything from the other fighters, Ro?"

It was a full minute before he answered.

"We're no band of brothers, Shadow." He scowled at his hands, set them on his thighs, worked them up and down. "There's one or two I can talk to, low down the line. Hangers on. I'm not taking applause from them or prize money, so I can buy them with a mug of beer and a handful of guims. Asking about Wargun, no, I didn't, I'm not such a fool, I asked about them all, the Goyo who hang around and watch us, like I wanted to know who to approach and what I could get out of them. No one knows why he comes there, they think maybe it's an excuse for something else. He shows, you never know when, he hangs about a while, frozen face, pretends he's watching someone work out, he isn't; they've tried him, displayed, wagged their tails, you know, nothing, forget him, they told me. He's nothing. Walking dead."

"But he does keep coming?"

There was a flare of rage in him that ran like acid along her nerves. He fought it down, but she began to be frightened for him—and a little of him. When he had his fist on it, he said, "Once, sometimes twice a week."

"Does he come in the daytime, evening, night? Which?"

"Evening. Usually."

"Of course you thought about following him."

"He can come and go as he wants, I can't. Like tonight. I said I was going for a woman and I didn't want their tame bitches, I wanted to find one on my own. Took a quarter of an hour to argue my way out." He used his thumb claw to scratch at a leathery palm. The soft *whtt-whtt* was like a shout in the tense silence. "Want to tell me what you're on at?"

"Remember my Talent? Who'd suspect a gull or a redbird? We need a beeper of some kind so you can let me know when he's there. Plenty of secondhand junk at the NightFair . . . no, on the Raba Katir, better stay clear of the Fair. I'll get one of the Razors to buy me some twinned tin, Kikun can bring you your half. They know I'm up to something, but they're willing to go along with it as long as I keep the money flowing."

"You trust them?" He was gradually cooling out as the hope of doing something real came alive for him. She was happier, too. It might even work.

"No. I can't. I'm playing the odds. They've no reason to be loyal to me, I'm their employer, not their friend, but they're smart and they're survivors and they loathe the Goyo and they sock away coin as long Kikun and I keep working. It gets iffy if we stop. Which I'll have to do if I'm going to be available to track Wargun. I'll probably have to go down sick for an excuse to stop performing, so I'll have to figure out another way of holding them. Well, what do you think?"

"I can't take any kind of tin into the Tay. The place is wired too tight. Other than that, sounds a lot better than what we been doing."

"True. Can you leave Sassa outside without too many questions?"

"I don't take him in. Not any more. He doesn't like it in there. You want me to plant the tin on him, call him to my window when Wargun shows up, give you a beep so you can start watching. That what you're thinking?"

"Yes. Can you do it?"

"Yes."

"Good. Ro?"

"What?"

"Stretch out," she said. "On your face, Rohant the Ciocan."

"Why?"

"Do it, do it. Don't argue."

She crawled on his back, began working at rockhard shoulder muscles. "Razor says a worldship came in last night." She moved her hands up his neck; the soft silky fur was slippery as water. Easing her fingers onto his scalp, she pressed down and pushed, loosening the hot hard skin, moving it in small circles. "The *Pilaryoll*. Razor gets nervous with so many Goyo in the audience, they're looking forward to a dilution of the solution." She laughed at the muffled snort that came from the huddled quilts. "Funny, I should probably split the take with the Temple, the Shudokan limited me to two performance and saved my neck."

A sleepy rumble vibrated through his body into her.

"No. It's true. The Fairfolk were starting to get hostile. Kikun noticed it. And Pikka, though she didn't give a damn. I was pulling too much custom, didn't leave time for buying." She smoothed his dreadlocks down, smoothed them and smoothed them, as if she were stroking a cat. They were as soft as his fur and springy, bouncing against her palms, tickling her. This business was turning her on like crazy, but she hoped he wasn't picking up those vibes, he was disastrously perceptive sometimes. And sometimes he wouldn't notice a slowworm crawling up his nose. "With our singsongs shut down to two, I'm a draw. When I turn 'em loose, they spend like there's no tomorrow and the Fairfolk love me." She manipulated his shoulder muscles some more, then slid down so she could pummel his back. "It's true, it's true. They do, they do."

##

By the time she finished with his feet, he was snoring.
Kikun was gone. And Sassa.

She stripped the robe off, tossed it on the stool, went
rummaging among her belongings for a shirt.

Rohant was too heavy, she couldn't get the quilts from
under him, so she crawled into the little space he left
next to the wall, managed to free enough of one quilt to
cover her, then she nestled up against him, sighed with
pleasure at the warmth he radiated—and was asleep in
seconds.

V. ACTIVITY OTHERWHERE
(Ginny takes control, begins moving)

TA'HAI TOLLA (Patan 3)
  A desolate world out the back of beyond
  with a dim ancient sun population: three
    Ginbiryol Seyirshi
    Pukanouk Pousli
    Ajeri Kilavez

1

Ginbiryol Seyirshi came from his lab, locked the door behind him. The editing was done, the duplicates finished and slotted into their sealtights, the teasers were done, sealtighted and piled up for Ajeri to pack in the message rats she was addressing at this moment; tomorrow she'd run them out to the Limit and dispatch them to his chosen bidders. All he had to do was organize the presentation, insplit to *Bernie's Hole,* and get the place polished up for his clients.

It was good, one of his best Editions, despite the stubborn perverseness from that trio of idiots he'd chosen to play his Avatars. It could even be that the resentment they showed and all their efforts to fight him helped create the production's intensity. The scene where the girl made the gods walk was astonishing, the worship, the awe, the fear . . . all of it . . . marvelous. It was a shame he couldn't stay to witness the death of the world and had to fudge that part with a final play of light and heat and a blend of amplified emotion quarried from earlier agonies, but all in all it was an exquisite creation.

He was a small man, meager, with thinning gray-brown

hair and a nothing face, the kind of man who'd be lost in a crowd of two. Impossible to understand he had destroyed or participated in the destruction of at least twenty worlds so he could record and sell their death agonies.

He stood blinking like an owl at daylight. After months of intense and extended labor in his lab, he couldn't adjust quickly to having nothing more to do. He came farther into the room, touched the back of a tupple chair, felt it move against his palm as it responded to the faint weight of his hand. He shook his head, he didn't want to settle yet, he was restless, there was a vague itch floating around inside him but he didn't know what it was he wanted, not yet.

He drifted across to the window and touched a sensor that cleared the opacity from the glass.

The room was like a slice of melon with the seeds scooped out, the inner curve filled with cases and curios and even some ancient books; rubbed and foxed, faded and stained, they had a constipated look as if their covers were glued shut by age and disuse. The outer curve was all window, seamless, with the faint bluish tinge of polarizing glass even at its most clear.

The room was near the top of a tower built from local stone, a broad squat immensity whose size disguised its height, a Xanadu with enclosed pleasure gardens whose domes clustered like soap bubbles about the southwestern sector of the tower, lush green gardens filled with the sound of running water and the scent of blooms chosen less for their colors than their perfumes.

He chose to look out toward the east where the land fell away in ragged chunks and wind sculpted stones stood rust-red and blue-gray, brown and ocher, subdued ghostly tints melting into each other so that nothing seemed distinct or asserted any dominance over the broken, eroded landscape. He was fond of the view, he liked the understated subtlety of the coloring, the agonized contortions of the rock. It was early morning and the sulphurous sun was still squashed against the horizon, the shadows were long and stark. There were no clouds in the sky, there almost never were. Rain came at most once or twice a year. The water for his gardens he recycled thriftily and when he needed more, he made it from the wind. The atmosphere was quite breathable, if one ignored the extreme cold, so that endlessly keening wind kept him supplied with most everything his garden needed. It also turned his generators, filled his accumulators; he seldom used his backup piles.

He stood watching the shadows shrink, his true hand picking at the fauxskin on his prosthetic. The shadows were the only things that moved out there, erosion was too slow a crawl for mortal eyes to catch.

His knees grew tired.

He left the window and crossed to his desk, moving stiffly, annoyed with his body for reminding him he was due for his ananile shots. He had to go to the gray market for them and under those circumstances, who could be sure they were all they should be? Perhaps it was time to investigate the Directors and look for a means of gaining access to the quality crystal they used on themselves. Perhaps. . . .

He eased himself into the tupple chair behind the desk, sighed with pleasure at the gentle massaging. With her usual efficiency, Ajeri had printed out precis of his messages and left them on his desk with the earliest on top. She knew he liked an overview before he began detail work with the kephalos.

*Tzayl 7 . . . good . . . Pillacarioda . . . very good . . . Shagglefoot . . . yes . . . Trumpet Vine . . . Sangria . . . Spotch Helspar . . . aaaahhhh!

He reread the report on the bombing at Voallts Korlatch Compound, noted the fuss Spotchals Business Bureau was making about spill-over damage to adjacent properties and persons. That suggested a line of attack more subtle than outright destruction, but not less devastating.

Hmm . . . rumor . . . blacken their name with their neighbors . . . make the Spotchallix so unhappy with the Dyslaera they were driven offworld . . . yes . . . splendid!

*Digby the tracer, after ME. I shall have to punish him for that, but he is nothing, a flea.

*What is this? Cobben Nerlkyss slaughtered on K'tali Kar-ra? What were they doing on . . . ah, following Dyslaerins and a female tracer op. Three Dyslaerin dead, one moribund. Satisfactory. The op away alive, bad. . . .

*Report from Betalli. Kiskai was regrettably intact, it was the next world out that went. No explanation for that.

And none needed, Ginbiryol thought. The Hunter managed it somehow with that Vryhh ship of hers.

*The Ciocan Rohant was home, the girl and the lizardman were on their way to University. No information at present as to what they intended to do there.

Ginbiryol stared at the sheet for a long minute, then he tore it in half and continued tearing it until the pieces were too small to hold. He gripped the arms of the tupple chair and let it massage his fury to manageable size, a fury all the sharper because for the first time in decades he was afraid. It was that girl. That miserable girl. Her Luck was too strong. She should be dead a hundred times over. Each time she walked away. Each time. . . .

He disciplined himself and went back to his plodding progress through the pile of sheets.

*Cobben Boitkoerrin, refused commission, cobben Sarokneh, refused commission, coryfe cobben Fennsouoit, grudging explanation, no cobben will sign with Seyirshi agents again, reason, lack of support leading to the extermination of cobben Nerlkyss. That is annoying.

*Note from Huy na Kalos, thanking me for the warning, irritated with presence of a cobben so close to him. Warning? What warning?

*Note from the Matriarch syndicate, thanking me for the warning, ha! and suggesting I do my own housecleaning.

He tapped the Notepad alive. "Ajeri, remove the Matriarch syndicate from the approved list, substitute the

Omphalos Institute with the notation that the invitation is for this time only. They are too dangerous to deal with on an extended basis. Note—this is important: Arrange for their representative to rendezvous with Betalli, instruct him to bring the Omphalite under blindfold conditions to the Auction site.''

He thought a moment, called up a second page on the Pad. ''Ajeri, this immediately: Unseal the teasers, rename the Auction Site. No more *Bernie's Hole*. Same place but . . . hmm . . . call it *Koulsnakko's Hole*. As a matter of precaution. It will not be possible for interested parties to trace a Hole which does not exist. Include a rendezvous point . . .'' he paused, searched memory, ''a rendezvous at Anaso Satellite *Laybogby's Star*, tell the clients they will be given a pilot flake to take them to the Hole. Embed a recognition signal in the teaser and warn them to have the teaser flashing before they surface and approach the star, otherwise one or more of the mines planted about the rendezvous ship will blow them to dust.''

He contemplated the message with pleasure, tapped the sensor to send it into the lab where Ajeri was working, then went back to reading his mail.

*Report from Betalli(1) . . . access to information inside the Korlatch compound shut off . . . Voallts Korlatch hired Adelaris Security Systems . . . also, no more voice com with Capture Ships . . . only sources left are those in Spotchallix Buroc . . . not helpful . . . am looking for leverage into crews, but not hopeful . . . suggest indirect attack, rumors, framing, blacking . . . await instructions.

Ginbiryol set that sheet aside for further thinking and worked his way methodically through the pile of sheets, six months of unanswered communications.

*Four hundred and seventy-two notes, amused, irritated, waspily sarcastic, supercilious, obsequious . . . each in his or her own fashion asking obliquely what is Ginny doing that requires such warning, each in his or her own fashion offended at Seyirshi's presumption and half-ready to drop him from the list of those known and spoken to.

Who? Was that even a question? No. Only three people had access to his list of prime customers and Ajeri had neither the ambition nor the stupidity to try something like that. No. Puk.

Though he needed no confirmation, Ginbiryol queried the kephalos. Five days after their return, three days after Ajeri released him from the tranx web, Pukanuk Pousli accessed the list, copied it and made a clumsy attempt to hide what he'd done. He raided the store of message rats, took three. He tried to obscure their destinations, but the kephalos recorded these also. *Betalli. Anghrad's Daughter. Luottar.* Covering note: *See the enclosed delivered indirect mail.* Signed: *Ginbiryol Seyirshi.*

Puk was in his Xanadu on the far side of the world. No doubt he thought he was safe.

"Unreliable," Ginbiryol said aloud. "Too bad."

He was going to be hard to replace. He was loyal and it was a loyalty of the kind that couldn't be bought. This was another blow Ginny owed to those Three. "I will have my hands on them," he said. "I will have them."

He straightened the sheets and pushed them to one side. Tears gathered in his eyes and flowed over. He mourned the loss of a friend, follower, and gifted assassin. Fifty-seven years they had traveled together. Puk and he and Ajeri. More than half a century. And sentiment aside, looking for a replacement meant losing time and wasting energy. Half a dozen times in the last decade, as Puk grew more erratic, more explosive, Ginbiryol had thought of finding another enforcer, then changed his mind; it was a complicated undertaking, the new third would need to fit with him and Ajeri, would have to treasure the Praisesong sessions as they did, would have to learn Puk's loyalty, would need at least a moiety of Puk's murderous efficiency. It was difficult, certainly, but he no longer had a choice, not after this.

He summoned a serviteur with a damp cloth, wiped his face and hands, dried them.

A last sigh, then he spoke the WORD.

On the far side of the world a relay opened.

Three seconds later Pukanuk's Xanadu was a hole in the ground and dust in the wind and Pukanuk Pousli was dust in that dust.

Ginbiryol Seyirshi folded his hands over his little pot belly and spoke to the kephalos. "Work up for me a profile and assessment of every merc we have had dealings with in the past, then any individuals in memory who approximate the profile of Pukanuk Pousli. While you are doing that, print out the original text of all messages and include any collateral data in memory."

He left the chair and went to stand again at the window, looking out over the softening landscape. The stark shadows of morning were being swallowed into the grays and browns and a yellow haze that crawled along the ground. That was sand blowing, it meant the wind had shifted to the south. "Are you out there, child? Are you searching for me? I can feel you there, groping. We have to do something about that, don't we. Yes, indeed."

1

"Go on."

"Pedder Mashouk. Peddar 4. Team withdrawn. Target Qitchka gone elsewhere, no one knows where, at least no one the team could reach. Residence successfully penetrated, without result. All references to Seyirshi expunged. Conclusions: One. Qitchka is certainly one of Seyirshi's customers, the fact that he was warned about us is sufficient proof of that. Two. Waste of time and effort to chase after him. Team is proceeding to next on list, the Olom Myndigget."

Miralys stretched, folded her arms behind her head and wriggled deeper into the tupple chair. "Go on."

"Lommertoerke. Zunja 5. Report from smuggler. Team captured, tracer op sold into contract labor, the Dyslaerors vanished. Smuggler Lastik doesn't think they're dead; it's possible, but the Lommertai are compulsively thrifty (that's putting it politely, she says) and not likely to waste good muscle. She says give the situation time to settle, then we can probably get them out, either by taking them, or if that fails, by buying them free."

"The op?"

"Digby says he'll take care of that and we'll get his bill."

"Dio!"

"Yes. I suggest we think seriously about accessing Seyirshi's funds when we get to him."

Miralys dropped her arms. "When. Have you read Lyrsallyn's report?"

Zimaryn shook her head. "It's on my desk, but I haven't had a moment free."

"We're a delivery or two from running on unsecured credit, Zim. Unless something happens soon, I'll have to go home and see if I can arrange to use clan funds for collateral. You know what that means for Voallts Korlatch."

"Cousin Tuernor." Zimaryn flattened her ears. "Dio indeed." She turned a page. "That's the last of the team reports, Mira. Digby sent over what he's got so far from the ops working the merc market. They've tracked down several of those who've hired on with Seyirshi once or twice; from those . . . um . . . interviews, they've compiled a list of past Auction sites. He uses a different location each time. That's bad. Something useful, though. A consistency in the type of site that might be helpful if we can get at least a hint as to the sector from future team reports. The Auctions are always in Clandestine Pits." She looked up. "Confirms what that girl said. Interesting child." She ran her foreclaw down the page, found her place. "Digby has sent over a list of those he knows about. He says it's probably less than ten percent of them, just look at the merc list, at least half of those he'd never heard of. He's asked the merc team to see what they can find out."

"Sounds like we could nose about for a century and still miss him."

"True. You want to hear the rest of what they learned?"

"Yes yes. Go on."

"Mm. When Seyirshi has a Limited Edition ready, he generally holds from ten to twenty regional auctions, selling about a hundred copies at each; the first one is the most important, he's certain to be there himself, along with about three to five hundred invited bidders. Later auctions bring in less money and sometimes he calls in outsiders to hold them and collect for him, a man called Betalli for one. He's at least as illusive as Seyirshi. Digby's working on him, but doesn't offer much hope of success and there are associations with that name that trouble him. The Vair Horde.'' She turned the page over. ''We've run across traces of the Horde ourselves. Um . . . Halvayes the Zadys, for one, in the Di-lamia Cluster, two worlds reduced to rubble, Vair Quarries they call them, a third with the population decimated, knocked back to stone tools from an early industrial civilization. There are several other such, I've got them listed here if you want to go into that further.'' She set the pages aside. ''And there is a faint smell of Omphalos Institute. Digby says he has only one source for this and that not reliable, but he believes it.'' Zimaryn looked up, a twinkle in her hazel eyes. ''He says the hair's standing up on the back of his neck and he's never known his neck hair to be wrong.''

''Nor I. Not all the time I've known him.'' Miralys sighed. ''Anything from Rohant?''

''Nothing.''

''Hmm. Zim, I want a council. Day after tomorrow. I want Lyrsallyn to make a verbal report on Korlatch finances, be ready to answer questions from the Board. See that her report is distributed to everyone concerned. Agenda will include that, ideas about increasing income inflow, ideas about future direction of attack against Seyirshi and any—and I mean any—ideas about how we're going to survive this, I don't care how ludicrous they sound. Anything you want to add?''

''Only this, Lyrsallyn is coming into season, she'd better attend by holo.''

''Arrange it. Um . . . you might check Belityn, see if she's on the brink, I seem to . . . ah! It's been so long since I thought of anything normal, I can barely remember my name.'' She got to her feet, stretched. ''I am so tired, Zim.'' She shook her head. ''Ah, well, we do what we have to and I have to go to a dinner meeting with Entroost Kuerbel who will spend the whole time bitching at me which means I'll come home with enough gas to light an urnep tree. Ah, I suppose I don't need to say it, but get to me the moment anything at all comes from Rohant, I don't care where I am or what I'm doing.''

VI. CLOSING IN (Ginny in the field but not felt yet)

HUNTING WARGUN

CHISSOKU BOGMAK
64 Kirar Sorizakre, day 7
day 7, hour 18

Meeting, Svanilery Tenement,
Karintepe-on-Main
Shadith and Pikka Machletta

1

"You'll come with us?"

"Na-nay!" Pikka Machletta flew around so violently the weights on the end of her hair thongs looped out then swung hard against her neck. She ignored that. "Bad 'nough I went into Temple. Joggorezel? Never! Y' wan me dead, huh?"

"Explain."

"Goyo notice y', y' dead."

"I see."

"Somethin y' better think on, Singer, huh?"

Shadith pulled her feet up on the bed, rearranged her robe. "I won't be here long enough for that to matter," she said finally.

Pikka Machletta hitched a hip on the windowsill. "How long?"

"I'm not sure."

"Y' close to gettin what y' want?"

"You've never believed I was a scholar, have you?"

"Y' never try makin me believe it, huh?"

"I suppose not."

"Tell me what t'is." Pikka leaned forward, tense, anxious. "Y' can get out, we here t'morrow and t'morrow, till we dead. Trouble y' make, we pay for."

"I . . . know." Shadith shifted her legs, pulled the quilt up around her. "I have some ideas about that. I'm not ready to talk about them yet." She watched the t'gurtsa relax; despite the skepticism beaten into her, Pikka wanted to believe what she heard. She was so young, so needy. . . . "Give me a few days more, hmm?"

Pikka Machletta slid off the sill, swaggered to the door. Her hand on the latch, she looked back. "Soon, huh?"

"Ay-yeh. Before I do anything drastic. My word on it."

day 8, hour 12
Meeting at the Zatsudedi Oy
Shadith and Arel

1

Arel shuddered as he watched Shadith swallow a mouthful of the local tea. "You'll rot your plumbing."

"It's not that bad. Gives me a kick where I need it. How's the enterprise?"

"Very nice, thank you. That why you set this up?"

"No. I wanted to let you know you should be ready to jump any day now. Things are getting a bit out of hand over here."

"Just how out of hand? I remember on Avosing. . . ."

"Nothing like that. I'm summoned to Joggorezel to entertain at some sort of party. The t'gurtsas tell me Goyo notice you, you dead."

"There's precedent." The lines deepened in his face; it looked heavier without the sardonic amusement that usually lay under everything he said and did. "You take care, Shadow. No games this time. Pull their hyvos like you've been doing and you could set the zasrats off, then. . . ." He shrugged. "Your t'gurtsas are right."

"I'll say it like young Kynsil, I'm not stoo-pid."

"No, too much the other way, I think." He frowned at her. "Don't discount paranoia, luv . . . speaking of which, I went to hear you sing."

She giggled. "My singing brings paranoia to mind?"

"Don't be difficult, Shadow."

"You want me easy?"

"Just want you. I heard you sing, then I put myself through my ship's ottodoc. I'm clean and randy and non-fertile. Believe me?"

Shadith gulped at the tea. The astringent fluid helped her steady her breathing. There was a part of her that floated aloof and watched with amusement her reversion to teenage virgin, but that didn't help her deal with this body whose tumultuous emotions were beginning to overwhelm any remnant of sense in her head. ''Yes,'' she said and was relieved when the monosyllable came out sounding calm and slightly amused.

''Come Upper with me now.''

''Now?''

''Yes, sweet echo. Now.''

She looked around, wrinkled her nose. ''Not much romance in this place.''

''Leave that to me.''

''Oh.'' She stretched the word into three syllables, managed a wobbly grin. ''He doesn't think much of himself, does he.''

''You've been there, luv.''

''Thing is, this body hasn't. I'd rather hoped. . . .''

''Trust me.''

''All right.''

2

The room was as stale and sordid as she'd expected; she felt a little sick when she saw it. She closed her eyes and told herself it didn't matter. But it did.

Arel put his hands on her shoulders. He was exactly her height, his mouth on a level with hers. She focused on that mouth, not daring to meet his eyes. He was laughing now, enjoying her reactions with a relish that made her hate him right then. She pulled away. ''I don't think . . .''

''Give me a minute, luv. Now. Go sit down over there and let me get busy.''

Whistling softly, he tossed the bedding into a closet, brought out clean sheets. ''Bribed the tender,'' he said. He made the bed with an expertise that had her smiling; he caught her at it and his whole body laughed at—no, with her. For a minute she couldn't breathe.

"Practice," he said. "Nothing like it."

He took an incense burner from his shoulderbag, filled and lit it. The scent of pines drifted to her, cool and clean. She smiled again. He nodded. "Thought you'd like that. And there's more from the magic bag." He brought out a pair of thick green candles on wooden candlestands, lit them, and turned off the light.

A standard seduction scene with all the props, it could have been absurd if he weren't enjoying himself so much—and inviting her to share his pleasure. And she did.

The room was filled with flickering shadow, the candlelight touched it with magic, a magic the incense underlined. It was a different place, almost a different universe. The outside world with its threats and dangers, its complicated questions that never had clear answers, that world was banished for the moment. She knew it was only for the moment, but she let herself forget.

And he wasn't finished, he set a small flake player on the table, turned it on. Music. Her music, harp and voice. . . .

"Come here," he said.

She got to her feet, walked slowly to him.

day 8, hour 22
Going to Joggorezel
Shadith, Kikun
Assorted Goyo and a Helmsman

1

The wind blew in erratic gusts, the night was velvety
dark, even the city lights seemed subdued. A heavy layer
of clouds hung low overhead. Though she was going to
help celebrate the Double Full, Shadith could see neither
Myara nor Mompri, only the bobbing lights from the lan-
terns swaying at bow and stern of the galley approaching
the Ferry Landing.

Despite the chop, the helmsman brought the slim black
boat silently, smoothly alongside the Landing. He was a
squat non-Goyo dressed in black from head to toe, standing on a platform at the back of the galley peering through
inadequate eyeholes in a headman's cowl as he worked
an antique tiller with a skill Shadith found both impres-
sive and depressing.

The rowers were dressed in black also, Goyo monks
from the Temple doing their service to the Kralodate.

Two of them stood, unfolded a walkway, then held onto
straps attached to the pier, steadying the boat while Shadith, Kikun, and their escort came on board.

Shadith let the young Goyo guards ease her onto the
cushioned seat in the three-sided passenger hutch. They
tucked pillows around and behind her, spread a lap robe
over her knees. She was very glad of those cushions and
the poufy down pillows; Arel had left her glowing, but
stiff and sore.

From the moment they'd met her at the Ferry Landing,
the Goyo guards had treated her with a tentative awe she
found amusing, but exasperating because they were de-

termined she would do nothing for herself that they could do for her. It was like being wrapped in cotton candy. All but the pillows she would happily have done without.

She heard Kikun's throat-catches as he settled beside her; he was laughing at her. Little Worm. She pinched his arm, gave it a good nip despite the interfering folds of cloth; he was muffled in his black robe, but had his *no-see-me* tuned down, probably so the boat wouldn't go off without him.

"Naughty-naughty," he breathed. In Dyslaer, she noted.

"Don't like them," she breathed. In Dyslaer also. "Don't like kings, don't like privilege, don't like ritual, don't like any of this."

"Gaagi says, mind your manners or fall on your face and let your friends perish."

"Sheesh, Kikun, it was only a pinch."

More of Kikun's chuckles, then silence except for the steady rhythmic sound of the oars, the cries of nightbirds drifting unseen overhead and the distant brush of the bay water against the stony sides of the islands around them.

When the galley rounded the blunt nose of Araubin Shimda and passed under the narrow suspension bridge that connected this island with Joggorezel, Shadith saw the reason for the boat trip. The last section of the bridge was swinging ponderously around; when it completed the motion, it would stand parallel to the shore, leaving a large gap, denying access to or escape from Joggorezel. She made a small annoyed sound, subsided into worried silence as Kikun dropped a warning hand on her arm.

2

The boat nosed into a narrow inlet, drew up to a small pier. Kikun winked at Shadith. "Servant's entrance," he murmured.

She snorted. "Bunch of damn snobs."

"That, too."

The young guards hustled them out of the boat into a curving tunnel cut through the curtain wall. It was clean

enough and dry, well-lit. A handsome hole, if you liked
such things. She didn't. She could feel tonnes of stone
hanging over her head, just waiting to fall and crush her.
Kikun walked beside her, his hand on her arm; she had
to look at him now and again to remember who it was
touching her. His *no-see-me* was working harder than
she'd ever known it to. This was Goyo homeground and
he wanted none of them noticing him.

The Wall was sixty, seventy meters thick. Formidable
if you were a Great White Hyospar, laughable if you had
access to a lightcannon. Or even a miniflit. Or in a pinch,
a long rope with a grapple on the end.

They left the tunnel, went down a short covered walkway and plunged into a warren of narrow dimly lit corridors.

Hordes of little scurrying servants moved about them,
darting into side holes as they came near.

The servants were generally less than a meter and a
half tall, all of them uncousins, radically so, furries and
sauroids, pteroids and arachnoids, some oids so different
Shadith couldn't put a name to them, contract labor with
no contact outside Joggorezel Shimda. In effect, they were
slaves. If she and Kikun got into trouble, they'd be no
help—no, a danger instead as they scrambled to protect
themselves. There were so many of them and they were
everywhere . . . she could smell their fear . . . they were
like small wild things, frightened by anything unknown
passing near them. . . .

Eyes . . . shining from the dimness of the shadowy
holes . . . pairs, triads, cluster of eyes . . . hundreds of
eyes . . . they flittered over the Goyo, rested on Shadith,
skipped over Kikun. . . .

The Goyo ignored them, but she couldn't. Despite her
struggle to hold her shields up, their fear battered at her,
burned her.

It was going to be a bad night. The way she was feeling, she wouldn't know half of what she was projecting.
She could get herself killed. . . .

day 8, hour 23
Waiting room, Great Hall,
Joggorezel Shimda
Shadith, Kikun

1

The Goyo guards left her in a small bare room that opened into the grand ballroom. Wait, they told her. You'll be called when it's your time.

Black walls, unpainted stone. Black stone bench with woven reed mats piled on it. More mats on the floor. A lightbowl pasted to the ceiling, white alabaster with concentric circles of acid-opaqued glass.

"Lovely," Shadith said, twitched as Kikun chuckled. "Can't you turn that off for a minute? You'll give me a stroke."

"Oh, sad." Gentle mockery, but he was more present after that.

"Thanks." She tried the door they'd come through. "Locked. It's forward or nowhere."

Kikun slipped the strap off his shoulder, set the harpcase on the bench and began working on the catches. Shadith moved to the arch at the front of the room, stood there looking out.

Sounds came to her, male voices and music. A flute, she thought, guitar of some kind, keyboard, strings. Not a lot of energy in any of it.

Some party. I don't think. No wonder they wanted me. They need SOMETHING to save it from an early death . . . you don't know, Shadow, maybe they like being stiff-nosed duftas . . . I doubt that, what about those bloodgames? I suppose if it really gets dull, the Kralodate will call in his headsman

210

*and cut a throat or three . . . sheesh! Shadow,
you're nervous enough, going on like this will have
you whimpering like a sick puppy.*

To the right and to the left, the black wall had more
holes in it, arches into similar rooms, no doubt. If there
was anyone in those rooms, she couldn't hear them. Or
feel them. Unless her Talent was taking a recess, she was
IT for tonight. THE entertainment. The Singular Article.

A few steps away a three-meter-high screen stood between her and the rest of the room, bone sliced paper-
thin, carved and fitted together in elaborate patterns. She
crossed the narrow walkway, folded the veil back over
the coronet, and stood close enough to the screen to see
through it.

She was looking the length of an immense chamber.
There were the obligatory tall narrow windows along the
north wall, the power side, with their stained glass he-
roics, images of posturing Goyo males with cartouches
naming the Goyo Families; the windows were dark now,
more texture than color. On the south, the wall was an
elaborate screen of gold and crystal, the Goyo femmes
behind there watching the men and holding their own
celebrations. The screen glimmered in the wavery light
from nine immense elaborate chandeliers. These confec-
tions of natural crystal and gemstones and loops of gilded
chain should have been hideous, but the lighting was soft
and they were high enough to be partially lost in shadow
and shimmer.

Reluctantly she pulled her eyes down and scanned the
room, shivered as she realized just how many Goyo
hommes were gathered there. So many. . . .

*Pikka has got to me and old Tseewaxlin. Hate-the-
Goyo week, huh? More like Scare-the-Singer. They
don't know you. Except maybe Wargun. Is he here?
I don't see him. Dafta, you. Why should you care
if he does see you, he hasn't spotted you before this,
all the time you were singing at the Fair. Makes me
sick to see them . . . Goyo, Goyo everywhere and*

never a smile among them . . . Goyo, Goyo every-
where and . . . oh, gods, I wish I'd had an excuse
to get out of this. . . .

There were hundreds of them, representatives from all
the Great Families. . . .

You knew they were going to be here, the monk told
you who all was coming when he lectured you on
how you should behave . . . gods, behave or get
stomped. . . .

They were so heavy with copper chains and charms,
brooches, armlets, ankle rings they looked like to her
like the collections of kitchenware she'd seen piled on
tinkers' mules.

She thought about scruffy scurfy mules with their long
faces and malignant stares. Thought about them, looked
at the Goyo, and grinned.

Their crimson togas were fineweave with a touch of
starch, so they hung in disciplined folds; their hair was
moussed and wired and braided into constructions as
elaborate as the chandeliers, with almost as many gemstones clipped and wired into the loops. And in the middle of all this glamour, there were those long, yellow,
mule faces.

Some stood about in groups, talking, drinking from
crystal horns. Others lounged on longchairs, propped up
on white velvet pillows, low tables beside them with bits
of fruit on skewers and piles and piles of finger food.

Out in the middle where there was a cleared area several young Goyo males had discarded their togas and were
dancing together to the music from the group of non-
Goyo musicians huddled at the base of the broad dais
where the Kralodate was. Except that their swords were
sheathed and their energy levels low, they might have
been replaying the duel she'd witnessed on the Landing
Field.

The Kralodate sat in a plain black chair, wearing a
plain black bodysuit. He was too far away for her to be

sure, but she had the feeling he was bored to his back-teeth.

A touch on her arm.

She flinched, relaxed when she realized it was Kikun. "I don't see him, she murmured.

"He's there. Behind the dancers. He's there. Put the veil down, Shadow, and come away."

2

She edged herself down on the reed mats, winced as the cold struck up through the several layers of clothing she wore, exacerbating her soreness. There was no way she was going to be comfortable, she might as well accept that and ignore her body while she played. She slid carefully back until she could rest her shoulders against the wall, then sagged into a easy slump.

And drifted into dream remembering. . . .

The textures of Arel's hair, his skin, his hard eager body. . . .

The fleshy softness of his mouth, his agile tongue. . . .

The way he smelled . . . tasted. . . .

She flushed under the veil . . . shivered. . . .

She wanted him here, now . . . not to make love again, just to have him with her, where she could touch him, brush up against him, look at him. . . .

One minute she was happier than she'd been in millennia, glowing with it. The next, she was close to weeping because he wasn't there. . . .

No time to think until now. . . .

Now was a stupid time to indulge herself like this. . . .

Why not now? . . . so busy getting ready . . . no time to . . . to realize . . . in love with the man . . . giddy with it . . . out of control. . . .

The watcher in her head was amused, the part of her that was old, worn out by the cascade of millennia since she was born, the part of her that had nothing left for this . . . this confusion . . . this raving clamor that rioted

through body and mind. Amused and wearied by it.
Afraid. . . .

She started as Kikun slapped her lightly on the arm.

"It's time," he said. He took her hand and helped her
onto her feet.

3

day 8, hour 25

Shadith went onto one knee, danced her hands through
a graceful yayyay she'd practiced over and over in front
of a mirror. "O Johinmaleffa, may one speak?"

The Chamberlain scowled; she wasn't supposed to
speak unless spoken to. He started to scold her, but the
Kralodate waved him to silence. A spark of interest in
his dour face, Kirar leaned forward. "Say."

She raised her head, stayed kneeling. "O Johinmaleffa,
I am Shadow the summoner of shades. I say to you, Great
and Gracious Kralodate, the shade that comes to you
when I sing is yours alone. I see only my six dead sisters
dancing, but I am told that each who hears me sees other
spirits, come to them out of memory, ancestry, or dream.
There will not be two among you who sees exactly the
same images. I am Shadow and nothing, forget me and
enjoy." She spread her arms to make black velvet wings,
fluttered her pale fingers, touched her head to the floor,
exaggerating the yayyay to the point of caricature. Arel
had warned her about pulling Goyo whatevers, but she
couldn't resist this one touch, this declaration of an intent
to mock. It was something she found necessary. A private thing. The Kralodate smiled on her and graciously
acknowledged her obeisance. No problem there.

Then she was on her feet, taking the harp from Kikun,
settling herself on the three-legged stool he'd placed for
her.

She began with a simple tune put through variations
until she'd read the sound characteristics of the room; the
chandeliers were going to be a problem, already there
was a sympathetic stirring among the crystals. And the
Goyo, they were restless; she could feel a growing irri-

tation. A little gray lump out there in the middle of the floor, that wasn't entertainment.

Wargun was there, close to the dais. Important man. Though looking through the veil was like trying to see through thin fog, she recognized him. And she saw him freeze when she started speaking, felt a surge of rage and fear, mostly fear. He knew her. Oh, yes, he knew.

She'd gone over and over her decision to reassure the Goyo before she sang. She knew if Wargun was there he might recognize her speaking voice quicker than her singing, but she didn't want the Kralodate deciding to put her away as a threat to state secrets. That seemed the more dangerous risk.

More muttering among the Goyo. They didn't quite dare start stomping and whistling, but they were making their displeasure known.

> Let them wait, they came for me, I didn't ask for this putative honor, putrid, purgative, purulent nonhonor, ninny noddy, noodle, nugatory non-nor.

She returned to the first tune as she felt the wave growing in her, simplicity was her need now. Kikun was her ground, he crouched behind her giving, not counting cost, giving. . . .

It seized hold of him and fed him to itself, that building surging wave. It wasn't something she willed, nor was it something she could stop. . . .

She didn't want to stop it.

She sang.

Wordless sounds filled with joy, pain, desire, fear, the feelings that had been flooding her since the afternoon. . . .

They came now, they poured out of her. . . .

In a half dream, deeply relaxed, she sang to her sisters, her six dead sisters, the Weavers of Shayalin. . . .

> They rose from the mirrortiles, slender and angular, black and silver similitudes of Naya, Zayalla, Annethi, Itsaya, Tallitt and Sullan, spinning threads from themselves to shape the images of Goyo dreams. . . .

She sang the ancient croon that mated with that dance and filled the spaces this alien voice she'd claimed could not reach with the pure flowing tones of the harp. . . .

Her sisters danced HER joy, celebrating her love with her, commiserating with her on its ephemeral nature, helping her rejoice in what it was and refrain from unreal expectations. . . .

She sang laughter as she saw Itsaya wink at her, saw Naya smile and clap her slender hands, saw Zaya shake her hips and grin over her shoulder, as she saw each of her dead sisters show their pleasure in their own way. . . .

She rode that surging wild wave, a hair away from disaster always, out of control . . . rode it with a mastery she'd never reached before and might not again. . . .

The watcher-behind was there, appalled, faded like the ghost of a ghost, frightened—impotent, exhausted. Body/mind were eager and passionate, driving for a perfection she'd only dreamed of.

The song ended.

She flattened her hands on the strings, stilling them, closed her eyes and rested against the harp to catch the last small vibrations. . . .

The Goyo sat in stunned silence, then exploded.

She heard them as if from a great distance, meaningless sounds, unimportant.

Looked at objectively, it was stupid to indulge herself like she had.

No matter. She wasn't sorry. To have denied herself THAT would have been self-murder

4

Kirar Makralodatta tolerated the noise for several minutes, then got to his feet and touched off a gong. When the reverberations died, he had the silence he wanted.

Shadith lifted her head, took a quick look at the longchair where Wargun had been. He was gone.

Her HIGH drained away, changed to total exhaustion. The Kralodate was talking, she knew she should be listening, but it was too much effort. She closed her eyes.

Thinking was hard labor, so she didn't bother with that either. She sat like a lump waiting for someone to tell her to do something.

"On your feet, Singer." The Chamberlain. Screaming at her. "The Makralodatta Kirar addresses you."

She didn't move.

Chitinous pincers caught roughly at her shoulders, jerked her up. She looked dazedly around, saw a flash of blue-based iridescence. Two of the coleopteroid guards were bracing her between them. Her hands worked. The harp . . . where was the harp?

A third coleopteroid was a few paces off, holding it, his motile pincers cutting into the wood.

She tried to break free. "Put it down, magdoub! PUT IT DOWN NOW!"

"Let the Singer go." The Kralodate.

The guards let go and stepped smartly away from Shadith. She stumbled forward a few steps, caught hold of the harp. "Let go. You're hurting it."

"Give her the instrument." The Kralodate again.

The sudden weight in her arms sent Shadith banging to her knees.

She ignored the jarring and stayed on her knees, examining the wood to see how badly the pincers had marked it. There were some crushed fibers and scratches, that was all. She plucked the strings, tested the tone, sighed with relief as the wood sang to her and through her.

"It is harmed?" The Kralodate.

She blinked. She'd forgotten for the moment where she was. She bowed through the Bogmakker yayyay, straightened her spine, weariness flooding back into her. She sang the shidduah, her voice a little ragged, "Bless O Johinmaleffa Makralodatta." Then spoke. "No harm."

"Good. I see you are a visitor. The bracelet."

She'd fetched it from the room in the ottotel and worked it back on; she'd gotten away with leaving it off when the monks had her, she didn't want to take a chance on Kirar, not with all she'd been hearing about him. "Yes, Johin-

malefa Makralodatta. I am here until my shades call me on.''
    "You have a patron?''
    "No O Johinmaleffa.

Oh, gods, I have a feeling

    She licked her lips, glad of the veil. "I live by my own efforts and owe nothing to anyone.'' She knew she was stumbling along a step behind events, too far behind to counter what she saw coming, but she didn't know how to change that.

Noooo, don't

    "You need discipline, Singer, I'll see that you get it.''

Luck, you bitch you. . . .

    The Kralodate touched the sensor again, again the gong boomed out.
    His amplified voice filled the room and the corridors beyond.
    "Be it known here and abroad, henceforth the Singer called Shadow is counted among the chattels and appurtenances of the Kralodachy of Chissoku Bogmak. Let no Goyo or other approach the Singer called Shadow save by the express permission of Kirar Makralodatta dan Sorizakredam or his appointed respresentatives.''

Chattel! I won't. No. I will not. . . .

    He tapped the speaker off, looked down at Shadith. "Yes. You are an astonishing little creature. Don't be afraid, we'll protect you. You needn't worry about anything the rest of your life.'' He snapped his fingers, smiled as the coleopteroids clattered through a yayyay. "Get the rest of her belongings and take her to the women.''

5

day 8, hour 26

Too angry to speak and too experienced to struggle, Shadith let the coleopteran guards lead her away.

One of them had her harpcase. She saw it and remembered Kikun.

He was gone. Not just Not-There, he was physically departed. He must have slipped off the minute the song was done.

> *Gaagi got to him. Thanks a lot, raven . . . you couldn't 've mentioned something to me? Take me to the Women? Dump me in a harem and call me slavery. Funny, just a few hours ago I was telling myself it'd never happen, I'd never let it happen . . . Gods!*

The veil was a nuisance, but she left it on. Bad enough Wargun knew her when he saw her. Behind her she could hear the quartet beginning to play a tune like the one the young Goyo were dancing to earlier. The guards were taking her through the Goyo and around the side of the dais. It wasn't a comfortable walk; the Goyo were watching her intently even when they pretended to be looking past her. They lusted at her—not honest lust for her body, they wanted the power she represented, that was so strong she could smell it.

The guards took her into a corridor at the end of the Wall Screen, marched her past two right turns and stopped before a pierced steel door.

The coleopteroid on her right tapped a sensor and a screen came alive, on it a smaller coleopteroid with a different conformation and red-based iridescence. His mandibles clicked and his face-plates moved, then he stilled, leaning forward a little, eyes and antennas directed straight out of the screen.

The blue bugman did some clicking and twitching of his own.

When the door opened, he slid the strap of the harpcase onto her shoulder, nudged her ahead of him into a passage only wide enough for one person at a time and gave her a slight push to start her moving forward.

He stood in the opening watching until she moved out of sight around the curve.

She emerged into a room as large as the one she'd left, decorated with rather better taste. No chandeliers, only alabaster globes with copper edged florettes, dropping on copper chains in clusters like white gooseberries. Tiled floors and ceilings with a delicate tracery of black line on a white base with an occasional accent of copper. A fountain in the center of the room, water leaping and running down a glass and alabaster semi-abstraction of a tree into a broad black basin, its gentle plish-plash a pleasant background for the women's voices.

There were Goyo femmes everywhere, some stretched out on longchairs drawn up together, talking and laughing, some on couches in among piles of bright cushions, playing boardgames and cardgames. Some were walking about, parading themselves and their jewels, their clothing, some were playing small tronkeyboards, making a muted kind of minor music, some were over by the ever-present stained glass windows (these had female figures in them, dancing, embroidering, playing long-necked instruments), some were standing close to the screen, looking through the openings into the room beyond. Small bright pteroids barely over a meter tall trotted about carrying trays, serving and fetching, massaging hands and feet, applying perfumed napkins to aching heads, tending the women like small gardeners nursing exotic plants to optimum bloom . . . and kneeling humbly when they were abused or scolded. With their fanciful plumage and delicate bodies they were almost as much ornament as they were servants.

Shadith stood in the arched opening hugging the harp with the case hanging behind her. No one noticed her for the longest time and she hadn't a clue what she was supposed to do about that. The harp got heavy and she put it down by her feet. She felt stupid and insignificant, less than the Shadow her friends called her. If she didn't get some sleep soon. . . .

The bending movement attracted the attention of one of the little pteroids; she came fluttering up, eyed Shadith for a moment, then went rushing off, her crest rising and falling rising and falling in excitement.

A moment later several of the pteroids came twittering up, their eyes blank and incurious. Hot little hands with loose wrinkled skin closed on her arms; they tugged her with them, taking her toward the fountain and the group of Goyo femmes reclining on longchairs beside it.

##

The Kralodicha had gray-streaked black hair braided into an elaborate knot, a simple copper circlet set with firestars around it. She was a long lean woman with a stern face more handsome than beautiful. A woman accustomed to rule, with a will as adamantine as the walls that shut her in. The women around her—all but one—were faded copies, senior wives of family Heads.

The Kralodicha pointed to a cushion on the floor by the foot of her longchair. "Kneel there, Singer."

Shadith knelt. Under her veil she clasped her hands tightly together, worked them against each other, using the pain and the effort to keep herself reasonably alert.

She could feel the youngest woman watching her. She shivered, looked at her, then away.

That particular femme was half the age of the others and beautiful. Her hair was a lustrous blue-black mass, piled in a high soft knot with wispy tendrils coaxed into a halo along her hairline with spiraling curls dropping past her ears. Her skin was cream satin, glowing with health, her eyes were a pale gray, almost colorless—odd silver eyes that should have been cold, but were instead as hot and feral as the eyes of a hungry tigress. She wore a body-skimming sheath of heavy black silk with a plunging neckline. There was a fine silver chain about her neck with an oval black opal resting on the gentle slope of her bosom. Opal teardrops hung from her ears, her bride bracelet was silver with only a thread of copper outlining the joined sigils of the two merged families. She was like a block of polished black marble in a field of gravel. The other women knew it and they didn't like it or her, that was projected so strongly it was like a stench around her. She had to be the premier wife of someone important or this lot wouldn't have tolerated her. And she was very interested in Shadith, something Shadith could have done without. She had enough problems.

The Kralodicha continued to contemplate her for several minutes. No one else spoke.

Shadith knelt and tried to keep hold of her temper. She was so very tired, reamed out, empty. Nothing was worth this. Another two minutes and she was going to get to her feet and leave.

The Kralodicha lifted a crystal stemglass, sipped at a straw-colored drink. "Take the veil off," she said. "All the way off. We play other games in here."

Moving stiffly, reluctantly, Shadith pulled the veil off and dropped it beside her. She felt a surge of fear and anger, it was like a hot wind driving at her. It came from the exotic femme.

You're Wargun's wife, aren't you. The youngest daughter to Tatta Ry. You wouldn't know me otherwise. No wonder they tolerate you when they'd like to tie you to a stake and set your feet on fire. Interesting. I wouldn't think he'd tell his family about his little tastes. Well, at least my brain is still working . . . pay attention, Shadow, the bosslady's talking at you.

"You're a child."

Shadith closed her eyes, forced them open when her head started to swim. "I'm older than I seem."

"What's that mark on your face?"

Weary, cranky to the point of recklessness, Shadith stared mutinously at the woman. "A family matter."

"Explain."

"I prefer not to." She was tired of making up lies and trying to keep them straight.

"Prefer not to?" The Kralodicha was more amused than angry, but it wouldn't take much to tip the balance. "You have no preferences, chattel, you do what you're told, you seem to be intelligent enough to understand that without painful reeducation. Explain." She held up a hand as Shadith started to speak. "One more thing. Address me as Saniya Meiyess. If another wife speaks to you, address her as Sani. Do you understand me?"

"Loud and clear, Saniya Meiyess. I ask you to please understand this, I am very very tired. The mark. . . ." She scrubbed the heel of her hand across her eyes. "You wear your copper, I wear the brand. Same thing. My bride mark."

"You're wed?" The Kralodicha sounded startled.

"Yes, Saniya Meiyess."

"Your man, where is he?"

"Dead, Saniya Meiyess."

"In what circumstances?"

"He was killed in a raid, I was wounded and nearly died, Saniya Meiyess."

"I see. Interesting. Collect your memories, child . . . but we'll talk about that later. How do you do that thing, what did you say it was? call spirits from the mind?"

"I don't know, Saniya Meiyess. I sing and they come to dance for whoever hears me."

"I don't think I believe you."

"I can't do anything about that, Saniya Meiyess."

"You can tell the truth."

"What is truth?"

"A question to avoid an answer. You disappoint me, Singer, I thought you had some intelligence."

"Look there, Saniya Meiyess." Shadith pointed at one of the globe clusters. "You touch a sensor, the light comes on. Can you explain to me what happens? So it is with me. I awoke an orphan, a widow, and wounded. I sang the dirge for my man and my family and as I sang, my dead sisters came and danced the death watch with me. I don't know why or how, I only know it happens.

When I sing, they come. And when I sing for others, other shades come for them, I don't know how or why."

"Sing for us. Us alone."

"You say you want the truth, Saniya Meiyess, I'll give it to you. I cannot. I must sleep before I sing again. I could not even lift the harp, I am so tired."

The Kralodicha frowned thoughtfully at her, then nodded. "Yes, after that performance you certainly should be tired. In any case, it is about time this celebration dissolved. Your harp, where is it?"

"I left it by the door, Saniya Meiyess."

"I'll have it fetched to you." The Kralodicha touched a sensor. "The servants will take you to a room where you can . . ." Her eyes swept over Shadith. "Have a bath and get the rest you need. We will be keeping you busy, Singer, you may be sure of that."

6

day 9 hour 1

Feeling considerably more alive, Shadith came from the bathroom into the small sleeping chamber, rubbing at her hair, enjoying her well-scrubbed weariness.

"I might have known that soft fool would botch the business. I suppose he went off and left you to buy yourself free. Mercs, you can't trust them to do what you should do yourself." Wargun's wife stood in the doorway watching her.

Sar, what next? Watch it with this one, Shadow. Or she'll eat you raw.

"You babble, Sani. I don't understand a word of it." She pulled the towel off her head, stood holding one corner, swinging the rest in slow circles.

"Oh, yes you do, and you'll be the one babbling tomorrow when Dedegar questions you. I can't let that happen. No." She snapped one lovely hand and a garotte of Menaviddan monofilament uncoiled, the end toggle swinging free. "Struggle, little fish, do. I'll enjoy that."

She was whispering, her pale eyes shining in the half-light. She was so beautiful and so wild and so stupid. . . .

Shadith snapped the towel in her face, dived across the bed, found her boots and came up with the hideout knife.

Before she was off her knees, there was another person in the room, a tall woman standing in the doorway. "Alousan, cousin, it's time you went home." The Kralodicha. No mistaking that deep, almost baritone, voice and that stately delivery. "You are not thinking correctly, my dear. I will not permit a scandal in these quarters. You will come see me tomorrow and we will discuss your difficulty."

"Dede. . . ."

"No. Not now. Tomorrow. Go home, Alousan."

The wild grace drained from the younger woman. She went out, her shoulders rounded, her feet dragging.

The Kralodicha stood for more a minute gazing after her. Then she turned back to Shadith. "Interesting, child. I wonder how many lies you told tonight. All of it? We'll see come the morning. You'd best get the sleep you claim to need; I must say, it's the one claim I do believe. To make sure you are not disturbed or tempted to do something foolish, I'm locking and barring this door. Sleep well, Singer."

7

day 9, hour 5

Someone was shaking her. Whispering in her ear. "Shadow. Shadow."

She was still tired. Her body ached.

The shaking kept on and on.

She started to groan. A hand dropped onto her mouth, warm, dry, smothering the sound. "Shadow, wake up, we've got to get out of here now."

Out . . . yes!

She pried her eyes open, nodded against Kikun's hand. "Have to get dressed," she murmured. Her head started throbbing worse than before, every muscle protested when she turned over and pushed the quilts down. "You wouldn't happen to have an aspirin, would you?"

She heard a pair of throat-catches and a soft snort, then he took her hand, wrapped it around the stem of a cold glass. "Other hand," he breathed. He found it, closed her fingers on a pair of tablets. "Gaagi said bring these."

"And a splendid thought it was."

It was a small room and the whispers filled it. She forced her body out of bed, pulled on her clothes, and felt about for the harpcase.

"I've got it, Shadow, let's go."

"Wait, wait. You're moving too fast, Kikun. Come here, sit down and tell me how you got in here. I need to know what to expect or I could sink us both."

"Time's limited, Shadow. You can't hear it in here, the walls are too thick, but there's one huge storm outside, lightning, thunder, tornados. The generators are out, the techs are under the impression they were struck by lightning. I've stunned the guards, the gate opened automatically when the electricity went off. They'll have the damage repaired any minute now, we've got to be out before then."

"I hear, let's go. They're under the *impression* the gens were struck by lightning?"

She felt rather than heard him chuckle as he led the way along the corridor. "I did some rearranging on the input terminals. Quiet now, we're going into the fountain room."

The room was blackbag dark, illuminated now and then by flares of grayish light as lightning walked around the Gotasaray. Kikun led her over to the screen and they felt their way along it toward the massive wall where the exit tunnel was.

There was a sudden intensification of the storm; even through the mass of stone she could feel its power.

More lightning.

A funnel touched down just beyond the windows.

"Get down." Kikun jerked on Shadith's arm, went flat behind a longchair.

Shadith hit the tiles an instant behind him.

The windows shattered, glass crashing inward, spraying fragments across the room.

The wind roared in, a thrumming base note that vibrated in the bone. She clutched at Kikun and tipped the longchair toward them, clawing the thick velvet cushions between them and the storm.

Howling louder and louder, until the NOISE was as numbing as a stunner beam, the wind slammed chairs and tables and anything movable at, over, around them, it was an enormous beast stomping about the room, destroying everything it touched, tearing open the screen between the two halves of the audience chamber; it hammered at Shadith and Kikun, driving them, against the stone at the base of the screen, tried to lift them and throw them through the twisted bone and metal strands.

It seemed to go on forever, but only lasted seconds, then the funnel moved on, the force of the wind dropped sharply. Rain hammered in, debris came through the broken window, skittered across the room.

Kikun wriggled free. He slapped lightly at Shadith's arm. "Come, we'll go out here." He got to his feet and went running toward the windows, a curious stuttering run forced on him by the glass and other debris littering the floor, lightning like a strobe increasing the jagged quality of his movement.

Shivering with cold, Shadith picked through the debris after him.

Kikun caught up a tree branch, knocked out the last fragments of glass in one of the windows, climbed through it.

Shadith pulled the velvet robe more tightly about her and climbed through after him.

The wind snatched at her skirts, threatened to whip her off the narrow, heavily-carved ledge. The stone around her had an eerie luminosity, faint, but enough to give her the outlines of the building, the walls and towers—and, to her dismay, show her that the ground was at least five meters down where what must have been a lovely garden on nicer days, trees and fountains and flowerbeds, was rapidly converting to a garbage pit under the pounding of the rain and the tearing of the wind.

Kikun whistled urgently. He was near the edge of the windows, clinging to some decorative stonework; he waited for another flare of lighting, pointed to a large tree near him being savaged by the wind. He launched himself into that tree, belly flopped across a limb, and pulled himself out of sight among the foliage.

Shadith groaned, cursed her tangling skirts, and began edging along the ledge; the rain came at her in near horizontal stings, stinging her face, half blinding her, saturating her clothing so her dress and the heavy robe clung to her legs and threatened to trip her. A nightmare, trying to stay on those weatherworn carvings.

She reached the end, clutched at the stone, and waited for lightning; the tree was jerking desperately about, creaking, groaning, breaking apart; a section of branch tore loose, came flying by her and slammed into the next over window; it caromed off some still intact muntins and went clattering away along the wall.

A flash.

She measured the sway and distance, jumped.

Like Kikun, she landed sprawled across the flattish limb, clutched at it as it bucked under her, threatened to throw her off. She steadied herself and eased into the rhythm of the tree's movements, then crawled cautiously inward, cursing some more as her robe and her dress snagged repeatedly on broken limbs; she tore free each time and struggled on.

When she reached the trunk, she hugged it and yelled, "I'm here. Where now?"

"Up. Till you reach me."

"I hear you." She got slowly and carefully to her feet, her body pressed as close as possible to the trunk, her fingers jammed into cracks in the bark. Her boots were composite-soled and gripped well enough, but it was awkward climbing in them, they were old and comfortable, the edges worn off the heels.

A touch on her head.

She looked up.

Kikun was a dark lump crouched on a branch just above her.

She could just see his hand as he slapped the trunk, then pointed along a branch that was whipping about, bending like a bowstave under the pressure of the wind. Lightning on cue. Wall, the top of it passing under the wildly waving end. "You're joking," she shouted up at him.

"Get going," he shouted back. "Go on."

Grumbling under her breath, she edged around the trunk and got herself straddling the branch. It leaped and bucked under her, thudded against her legs, her groin. That hurt. She felt a warm wetness creep down her thigh and knew she'd torn herself open again. Swearing in half a dozen langues, she clamped her hands on the wood and pulled herself along; the farther out she got, the more precarious her hold was, the more danger there was her weight would be the thing that finally tore that branch loose.

The wall was black stone and would have been impossible to locate in the murk except for that luminescence. She could see the balustrade and stones as she worked her way laboriously along the limb. She could also see that her weight was going to depress the branch below the top of the wall, maybe too far below for her to climb onto it.

She reached the wall and found herself more than a meter below the top. Even at a stretch she couldn't get a grip on the stone.

Washk! Triple washk! How . . . oh, gods, I'm not ready for this. . . .

She got a good grip on the branch, then rolled off it and hung bouncing next to the stone, banging into it as the wind snatched at her.

Carefully she increased the period of the bounce, then started her body swinging in a swooping arc. When she thought she was ready, she pulled herself around in a giant circle, ignoring the tearing of her palms, came up the second time, released her hold, went up and over the balustrade, twisted in air, came down head tucked in, falling forward. She rolled, unfolding as she flipped up, landed solidly on her feet, feeling like a full-body bruise.

Kikun came over a second later, ran past her, the harp-case bouncing against his back, its weight apparently no problem for the little dinhast. His strength had surprised her more than once, he was doing it again. He looked over his shoulder, beckoned impatiently. "Come on, come come."

"Aaaaah!" She ran after him, half blinded by the rain.

He led her along that wall, up a flight of stone stairs and out on the great curtain wall that circled the whole island. The battlements cut down the sweep of the wind and if she stayed close enough to them, sheltered her from a good deal of the rain. She caught up with Kikun, walked beside him.

"Where we going?"

"Bridge. With a little luck there'll be transport."

"I hate to umm throw cold water . . . more cold water on you, Kikun, but the Goyo disconnected that bridge. We both saw it happening when we went under."

"If we can't contrive something, we'll just have to swim."

"Oh, glorious; something wonderful to finish off the night.'

He clicked his tongue. "You think Goyo won't have a back door? That they'd prison themselves on this island? Na-nay, Shadow, no way. There'll be something."

8

The lights came on as they reached the twin towers of the main Gate.

Kikun stopped. "Shadow, how many in there?"

Shadith leaned against the battlement, closed her eyes and gathered the rags of her strength. She *reached* into the stone monster, swept down from the turret into the great round rooms at the base. She straightened up, sighed.

"Two in the turret with a cat. Cat's curled up on a bench, didn't want to wake up, but I poked her into looking around. Windows are shuttered. While the lights were out, the men had a candle going, cat didn't like the smell of it. They were playing cards. When the lights came on again, they blew out the candle and just kept on with their game. They won't be much of a problem unless we get really noisy about this. Um . . . four more on this level. Sleeping, all of them, didn't let the storm bother them; with those walls they didn't have much to worry about. Off duty, I suppose. No insomniacs or wanderers. So, where do we go from here?''

"In and out. Through and down."

"That easy, huh?"

"Why not?"

"Gaagi say?"

"Kikun say." He wiped rain off his face, bent into the wind, and trotted the last few steps to the tower door. He lifted the latch, pushed, and the door opened. He grinned over his shoulder and went in, keeping hold of the latch so the door wouldn't bang against the stone.

Shadith waited while he closed it again, looked around.

The tower was a sham as far as defense was concerned. There were no baffles in the broad corridor that cut through the middle of the mass, not even any doors or gates to open.

Nice to have inside info . . . sheesh! Gaagi . . . I don't believe a scintilla of that, not a . . . a . . . nanobit!

She followed Kikun through an open archway, down spiraling stone stairs and out into a link-fenced parking area with several monojits that had been tossed about by the storm. A section of the fence was twisted and torn apart, leaving a hole wide enough to drive a dozen emjits through.

She laughed, the sound lost in the howling of the wind that nearly swept her off her feet when she left the shelter of the tower. "When you're right, you're right," she yelled at Kikun.

"Who's ever tried this place?" Kikun yelled back at

her. "Lazy is as lazy does and guards get lazy if they're never pushed."

"Right, right, right." She helped Kikun turn one of the emjits onto its buffers, laughed again when it hummed alive after a few preliminary hiccups and hesitations. The headlights didn't work, but that seemed a minor problem. Once they were on the bridge, there was no place to go but straight ahead. "Right, right, right. You want to drive this thing?"

"No."

"Get in, then. And hold on."

9

day 9, hour 6

Kikun slapped her arm. "Stop now!" he yelled, urgency turning his voice shrill.

Shadith stamped on the brake, fought the emjit to a shuddering, slewing halt. She started to ask why, then lightning showed the drop-off less than a meter beyond.

No lights, no warning barriers, not so much as a chain or a rope, nothing to keep her from driving straight off into the water.

She started shaking, dropped her head on the steering wheel. After everything else that had happened, this was the straw too much. She was dimly aware of movement beside her, but she paid no attention to it; her mind and her body were both quivering mush, she couldn't think and she couldn't move.

"There's something. . . ." Kikun's voice in her ear. "I'm going to have a look. . . ." It was sometime after he left before the meaning of his words came clear; even then, she was too sunk in lethargy to do anything about them.

10

Kikun shook her. "Come on, Shadow. You can fall apart later."

Shadith looked round blearily, then made an effort and

straightened her back. "Sar! I couldn't swat a mosquito. If you're thinking about me swimming, Kikun, you might as well forget it."

"No no, nothing like that. Take my hand."

He steadied her as she climbed down from the emjit, led her to the massive buttress on the north side of the bridge. He slid open a door and urged her inside.

She inspected the control panel, the wide screen. "Two things, no, three, Kikun. I haven't a clue as to the codes and no time to play with this. It's tied direct to the Gotasaray and the Goyo would be on us before we blinked twice. And even if I could get the section to swing, you saw how slow it moves."

"You finished?"

"What?"

"I'm not interested in that, come over here." He spoke sharply; his usual patience seemed to have evaporated.

She glanced at him. In the dim light, he looked drawn, ancient and weary beyond description. For the someteenth time she wondered why he bothered with them, why he was here at all.

He stopped before a cabinet door, tall and narrow, Goyo sized, set a lockpick humming at the lock.

That explains a few things. You're not quite as mystic as you like to play, huh li'l Liz.

She leaned against the controlboard and watched as the pick labored to shift layers of grease and dust, the grime of centuries solidified into a substance close to stone. She could almost hear the pick whimpering as Kikun flogged it on.

Poor baby. . . .

It blinked and he pulled it off, tucked it under his tunic and dragged the door open, the hinges squealing and shrieking.

"When I was poking around in here, I came across a spec manual, it's in that drawer by your elbow, if you want to have a look at it. Oh, and I left the harp by the door, better get it." He felt around inside, found a sensor and a dim yellowish light came on in the cavity beyond. "This should be an emergency exit. Complete with inflatable raft and a slidepole. I hope." He leaned into the opening, then pulled out again, looked around with a half smile. "Pole's intact, got the original shine. Little dust, that's all. The raft, I don't know. It's there, seals intact, how long it's been there, I don't know. You heard the hinges."

She moved across to him, looked over his shoulder.

The raft was a cube about a handspan on each side. He took it off the shelf, shoved it against a membrane next to the pole, nodded with satisfaction as it broke through and went whooshing away.

"Now we see. Either it opens or we swim. Bring the harp and climb in, Shadow. You go first."

11

The end of the pole curved, she went shooting out through the catch membrane onto a small circular platform with a pipe railing about it, five rings, shoulder high. She bounced off the railing, knocked the wind out of herself, had just sense enough to get out of the way when she heard a faint whistle. Kikun came shooting through the membrane and slammed into the railing where she'd been a moment before.

He coughed and rubbed at his ribs. "This could have been better planned." He worked his way around the platform until he reached a gate Shadith hadn't noticed. "Good. It deployed. Come on, Shadow, your boat awaits you."

"Wonderful. Wait a minute." She worked the locator bracelet off her hand, flung it into the bay.

Kikun curled his fingers around her wrist. "Dead and drowned, dead and drowned. Gone is the Lady, dead and drowned." He winked at her.

"Let's hope." She shifted the strap and settled the case more comfortably, then she followed him down the steel ladder to the raft bobbing in a small hollow in the buttress, a tiny waterjet like a pimple on its rear.

VII. ACTIVITY OTHERWHERE
(Ginny on the move,
longdistance stringpulling)

TARGET: BETALLI, Onero Berrekker's
                  Hole (clandestine pit), the
                  Asteroids of Symel
CAPTURE TEAM: Dyslaeror: Ossoran the
                                Zadant, Feyvorn,
                                Veschant, Villam
                        Tracer op: Samhol Bozh

1

Symel was an undistinguished sun, cool yellow with a greenish tinge; it had a single planet, a gas giant, and an asteroid belt rich in metals—before Ou-maa-dajin Company finished with it.

The eponymous Berrekker came by after the Company moved on and stopped to nest in the holes the miners left behind. Who he was, WHAT he was, why he was there, why he chose to stay, no one knew and no one cared much.

He lived there for several centuries and left behind a lumpy collection of living spaces; it passed through many hands after he withered to dust, added to by each of its controllers until the Hole was a planet in size if not in density.

Its defenses were formidable and highly illegal at their sources if not in their present deployment, legality in the Hole being what the current Berrekker said it was.

2

Samhol Bozh spread his notes on the table, scratched thoughtfully at his wrist as he looked at them. "That's where we're going," he said. "It won't be all that hard to get into, it's getting out again that's the problem." He fidgeted with his thumbs, pushing skin down at the base of the nails. "In the organized Clandestines like Berrekker's, the bosses don't ask questions; if you pay their price, you can come and go as you please, do what deals you want."

Feyvorn leaned back, frowning. "Harder to get into Voallts Compound, and we're legit. Doesn't sound right, Bohz. You sure?"

Bozh shook his head, began working on the other fingernails. "They don't have to ask questions. They have Security EYEs everywhere. And the EYEs are tied in to stunners and shockers." He curled his forefinger up, wiggled it. "One tap and that's all she wrote. They don't bother apologizing for mistakes, just send the housebots to clean up the mess." He scratched at his nose. "Berrekker's is the tightest we know of. And the nastiest to tackle. We've picked up rumors of strings to Omphalos, talk that the Institute collects one out of ten of those who go there. They disappear down somebody's gullet, anyway, and for all you hear of them after that they might as well not have been born. No proof, only talk. Someone knew someone who. That kind of thing. It's Betalli's home base. A snitch we have says he's there now." He tugged at an earlobe, looked past them at the wall. "Still there."

Ossoran frowned at the pages in front of him. "What about mutes or full spectrum blocks?"

"Personal blocks, mutes, what have you, they're all confiscated on entry. No chance getting them past the scanners." He reached into his tunic, scratched at an armpit. "You can rent equipment from the Berrekker's stores, the fields are supposed to be impermeable, but there's no chance that's anything but a polite fiction." He examined his nails, wiped them against the side seam of his trousers.

Villam watched Bohz scratched and fidget until his nerves twanged with the op. "So what's the point?" His voice was a snarl, tangled with tension. Veschant closed his hand about his twin's arm and he quieted. "I mean, if there's no way to get at him. . . ."

"I didn't say that." Bohz drummed his fingers on the table.

"That's what I heard, Vescha, isn't that what you heard?"

"Yeh, we jump 'im, we get squashed."

Bohz smiled, a quick tight compression of his lips. "If we jump him."

"If we don't, why stick our head in that brangle-braht?"

"Shut up, Villi. If you listen, you might learn something." Ossoran leaned back. "Oblique approach, right?"

"Very oblique. We don't go anywhere near him. More about that in a minute." He went back to drumming his fingers, heard himself and thrust his hands in his pockets. "If you're not an army or threatening to blow the place to dust, it's not hopeless. You can get components in if they look like something else, say samples. And sidearms. Anything rated a nuisance, cherry bombs, sneeze gas, they don't bother scanning for that kind of thing." He coughed. "There's something else I have to say. The well's been poisoned on us. What I mean, two ops went in at the beginning of this. Security or someone got them. We know that because they had deadmans under the skin. Their dying triggered message rats from their ship." He smiled again, a grimace.

"The Hole's that dangerous they went with dm's?"

"Yes." Bohz tapped his head behind the right ear. "Mine. Ottodoc is set up for implants. Up to you what you do."

"Hmm. Does Security there know who the ops were after?"

"I wouldn't bet against it." He leafed through the papers on the table, squared them, set them down again.

"Could be an advantage."

"What I thought. So." He folded his arms, leaned on them looking intense. "We don't go anywhere near Betalli himself. We go for his pilot. Betalli has a weakness. He doesn't advertise it. Digby got it by chance and by cost, those ops, one of them got a com-man drunk and telling Betalli stories; he'd worked a stretch as com-second on Betalli's ship. He stuck the recording in his rat and went back in. Never came out." A muscle twitched at the corner of his mouth. "He's a starclass phobic, Betalli is. He's scared shitless of infections and wears a fully body filter when he's around people, fumigates any room he goes into. He won't deal with a kephalos, stays away from terminals, he thinks they're all plotting against him; he works with paper and pencil, if you can believe that. He thinks the Insplit is getting at his brain so he spends split-time in a stasis pod. Which means his pilot has to know things most pilots wouldn't. The Auction's getting close, so that probably includes the coordinates we want."

Ossoran frowned. "Seems to me he'd be as protected as Betalli is. Why isn't he?"

Bohz smiled again, another quick compression and release. "*He* isn't exactly the right word. The pilot's a neuter from some hole-in-the-wall species no one's ever heard of. According to our snitch and what was in those death-rats, Betalli doesn't waste security on the hired help, even someone so important as the Pilot. It has other ways of protecting itself." He straightened up, closed his hands so hard on the edge of the table, his knuckles whitened. "Oh, yes. Among other things, I suspect the Pilot's been conditioned to die under probe, but if we can get it out and clear and still alive, we can keep it in stasis and haul it to University. Digby has connections there that can get through any conditioning known." He sighed. "I have to tell you, I'm about to pee my pants just thinking about going in there. But it's not impossible and I'm willing to try."

3

Villam and Veschant kicked along the narrow metal
walkway, making the skirts of the robes they wore swing
wide. The heavy cloth fell back slowly, the gravity in
here was barely a fourth of norm.

Their cowls were pulled forward to obscure their faces
and their hands were hidden in the long loose sleeves;
the cherrybombs they'd smuggled in were pushed into the
wide hems and made enough of a weight to set the sleeve
ends swinging.

These metal catwalks twisted through the complex like
the strands of a spider's web spun inside a bunch of
grapes. There were ankle- and waist-high lights at inter-
vals but the rest was obscurity, the silence turgid with
unspoken things.

Villam giggled, poked his elbow into Veschant's side,
ducked the swing that came at him and ran backward a
few steps, jumped onto the rail and dived off, drifting to
a second webway where he stood and jeered at his twin.
Veschant yelled and plunged after him. They chased each
other about the nexus for several minutes more, then Villam spread his hands, the black cloth of the robe dropping in folds over them. "Hey, Vesh, truce?"

Veschant slapped at one of the hands, slapped again.
"Truce, Villi." He fumbled the sleeve back and checked
his ringchron. "Almost time, let's get there, huh?"

They'd come in together on an old ore hauler, humping
cargo for the Master, hot cargo heading for Fences' Row,
and smuggling in everything they could think of they
could use to make nuisances of themselves and create the
maximum of confusion without pulling the roof in on
them.

They were the distraction. The smoke screen to draw
attention while the rest of the team scooped up the pilot
and got it away.

They came out of the dark nodes into Playground, stood
blinking in the glare and shivering at the noise.

It was Starstreet cubed, with holofacades and drifting
holoas shilling the pleasures of the taverns and the clubs,

the arenas and the duel/kill stages, the bordellos and casinos, the flake palaces and sensi dromes, the chassures
with live prey, every taste catered to, every nuance tickled.

They were supposed to start a riot, but now they were
here, they didn't quite know how to proceed. They stood
a moment on the edge of the light, looking around at the
jumbled garish hollow.

Veschant turned to Villam. "Tic-tac blow," he said;
he pushed his sleeves back, bared his fists, set one against
the other. "Call."

Villam pushed his sleeves back, bared his fists, set one
against the other. He knocked his fists against his brother's. "One. Two. Three. Go!" They knocked fists again,
again, again. . . .

Veschant jerked his hands apart, two fingers flipping
out of each.

Villam was a second behind, his thumbs up and out.

Veschant said, "Four."

Villam said, "Ten."

Veschant said, "Fourteen up, east west."

They knocked fists again again again. . . .

And continued the game until they had the coordinates
laid out, then they linked arms and went strolling into
the confusion, hunting for the place that Chance had
pinned for them.

They stopped in front of the *Bannerman's*.

It wasn't much, a grimy box simmering in self-created
murk, a flickering facadeholo (a line of shapeless forms
that might once perhaps have been cousin hommes, doing something that might once perhaps have been dancing), a thick smell of sweaty feet, grease, and beer.

Villam looked at Veschant, shrugged and pushed
through the door.

It was dark inside, cavities like ratholes lit by purple
lusotorches, heavy tables in them with dark shapeless figures hunched about them.

Villam stopped, hit by a wave of hostility that was hard enough to stop his breathing for a moment.

Veschant bumped into him, knocking him a few steps farther.

There was a hiss, it got louder, the forms at the tables, they all turned to face the two in the doorway.

If this place had catered to cousins some time in the past, the clientele had obviously changed.

Ophidians. Lots of ophidians. And they didn't want company.

To the young Dyslaerors the stink was loud as a shout and it announced an ancient enemy. Their dreadlocks bushed out, anger musk poured off them.

The hissing increased, and the stench. The hate was mutual.

Villam wrinkled his nose, spat. "Stinks in here," he said; his voice carried to the far corners of that convoluted space. "Snakehouse in the zoo. Whoo-ee, gonna stomp me some snakes." He dug into his sleeve, fetched out a cherrybomb, scraped his thumb across the igniter and flung it into the middle of the room. As it went off, he hauled out his pellet gun and began plinking lusotorches, spattering the customers with hot components.

With his heater set at singe, Veschant was sweeping the beam about the room, starting smolders in the robes and raising blisters on ophidi skin.

As the hissing rose to shrieks of rage, Villam poked Veschant and dived for the door.

Cutter beams flared behind them, left smoking holes in the floor, missing them by the seven centimeter shunt programmed into their robes.

They ran into the webways with a horde of raging ophidians after them, howling for their hides.

Villam got a handful of the cherrys, scratched and threw them over his shoulder, slued round into a crosswalk, ran along it till he came to a change node. He hauled himself up on the handrail, took a quick scan of the murk, and jumped. He hit his target, waited for Veschant to land beside him, jumped again, landed, took off down a dim hole.

He scampered through another few turns and switch-backs, stopped to listen.

Nothing. If there were EYEs around, they weren't activated.

"Vescha?"

"Lost 'em." Veschant pulled his cowl back up, settled his rope cincture. "Let's go get us another mob."

4

Alone in a small meeting room, Samhol Bohz sat before a terminal and watched the minutes flick past, waiting for the set time when the Twins were scheduled to begin creating as much trouble as they could manage. He smiled when he thought of them, he liked that scratchy irreverent pair and felt a flare of satisfaction when he thought of the grief they were going to give the Berrekker and his lot.

Ossoran and Feyvorn were posted in the corridors around the area, standing guard. They didn't try to hide what they were doing, that would have been ludicrous, but the few beings that passed them paid no attention to them. In any Clandestine and this more than most, nervous dealers were common fare.

He checked his chron. *Time is*.

He opened his shieldcase, began clicking components together into one of Digby's prize patent pries, the mighty mini-wonder. When he had the blackbox ready, he tapped on the terminal and accessed the directory.

Onero Betalli wasn't listed.

He nodded. What he'd expected, not much there but businesses and the snitchcode and a few services.

He attached the mini-wonder to the terminal and set it to digging.

1sec . . . 2sec . . . 3 . . .

The coordinates of Betalli's Nidus came up, an instant later the Pilot's present locus, a sensi-dome close to the Nidus.

The min-won printed this out. At the same time it

seeded a virus into the system, then destroyed itself and, Bozh hoped, all traces of its activity.

Bohz snatched up the printout and ran out.

With the Dyslaerors following close behind, he raced to the nearest nexus, snatched at handpellers and went jetting through the web.

The Hole was in an uproar.

Distance muted the noise, but the ways were filling with enforcers and disturbed visitors, all of them looking for the cause and panting to obliterate it.

Bohz swallowed and swallowed again. His gut was burning; if he came out of this without a recurrence of his stomach ulcers he was going to go back and apologize to his god-queen. It seemed to him he'd been terrified from the moment he was born with a few brief days of bliss thrust into his life just to make the rest more miserable. That pair, that goddamn brace of devilborn imps, they were supposed to set up a distraction, not bring the goddam Hole down around their ears.

As they moved deeper into the Hole, the noise and confusion faded; anyone who wanted to move from where he was had already done it. By the time they reached the sensi-dome where the pilot was dreaming the hours away, they were alone, moving through a stately calm.

They shot their way into the Dome.

There was no time for subtlety.

They strangled the attendant a little, Ossoran extruded his claws and threatened the little being's sex organs.

Without further persuasion the attendant led them to the Pilot's cubicle.

They shot the door open, went charging in and dropped—

and dropped and dropped and dropped—down a long dark slide.

Down the gullet. . . .

A flare of light, a sense of bursting through a membrane, then—

nothing.

5

Veschant glanced at his ringchron, slapped his brother's arm. "Cut-out time, Villi. Let's get."

Villam nodded.

The two Dyslaerors slipped off their robes, pulled the ripcords and watched the dark cloth flare to ash.

They sprayed themselves with a can of altron, blanking gen-traces, tossed the can.

They raced through several turns, jumped the web at one node, then another, then slowed to a walk and went sauntering along, heading for the shuttle port. They walked around a corner—

and dropped and dropped and dropped, down a long dark gullet. . . .

CONVERSATION

FIRST PARTY: Ginbiryol Seyirshi, on his ship
enroute to the newly renamed
Koulsnakko's Hole, the *Anaso
Sink* region
SECOND PARTY: Onero Betalli, *Berrekker's
Hole*

1

Betalli was a lean bony man with soft thin skin, very white,
a lot of pink showing through, especially at the tip of his
long, thin nose. His hair was rough and spiky, a dull ash
brown, his eyes a shiny faded blue. All his edges were
tucked in, clamped down, this impression intensified by
the transparent mask he wore whenever he was in the
presence of another being, even if that presence was
merely symbolic, a holo or an image on a com screen.

He wore a shipsuit constructed from impermacloth with
a muted gray sheen, rather like moire silk. His hands had
a gray sheen also because he was never without his spider-
silk gloves, though he seldom touched anything or anyone.

He reclined on a longchair in his Nidus at Berrekker's
Hole contemplating the damage the search team had done
and how close they'd gotten to him and assessing the
chances a third team would come after him.

2

Ginbiryol Seyirshi sat in the Captain's Chair on the
bridge of his ship and stroked the soft round head of the
simi he kept as a pet.

"Ajeri tizteh, are we in position yet to speak with Berrekker's?

"Just about, Ginny. We've come round the fringes of

the Zangaree and we'll have a direct line in a few more minutes. There'll be some breakup, not enough to worry.''

"Put a call through to Betalli, if he is still there."

"If he isn't?"

"Then you must see if you can get through to his ship. Leave a message with the Pilot asking him to call me when he surfaces."

"Right. I'll ring you when the call's through, Ginny."

3

Betalli touched his gloved fingertips together, gazed down at Seyirshi from the screen's center cell, his glassy blue eyes floating in pale hollows. In a wire of a voice, he said, "We've had an intrusion here. Dyslaerors and a tracer op. I had been expecting something like that, two tracers came after me several months ago. They suicided before I could question them, but they were deadmanned so I had no doubt there would be others."

"Have you questioned these?"

"They are in no state to be questioned. It was necessary to act with some precipitation. However, I know what brought them. They did not come after me, they went for my Pilot. This fits with other information I've acquired. The Dyslaera are trying in every way possible to locate you, Ginny. They want the site of the Prime Auction and once they have it, they'll be coming for you."

"Yes. I had reached that conclusion myself and have done what I could to counter it. As you are aware." He paused, frowned. "Have you by chance come across news of a team of three, one Dyslaeror, one young girl, one sauroid from an unlisted species?"

"These are the three your Lieutenant sent the warning about?"

"My former lieutenant."

"I hear. Chissoku Bogmak. My agent in Karintepe said nothing about the sauroid, but the girl and the Dyslaeror are most definitely there. Going after the Fevkindadam, no doubt.''

Ginbiryol Seyirshi closed his hands hard on his chair arms and fought down the rage that sought to consume him. The Pet ran back and forth along the top of the chair chittering its distress, Ajeri and Betalli stared at him. He drew in a long breath, let it trickle out, drew in another. ''Yes,'' he said finally. ''Yes. I want you to go there, Betalli. I want you to kill her. The Dyslaeror also if you have the opportunity. The girl is the one, though. Kill her.''

''What about the bidder from Omphalos? I had begun arrangements to meet him.''

''Let your Second handle him. Dealing with the girl is more important and more difficult.''

''Difficult? She is only a child, what? fourteen, fifteen?''

''She rides a wave of Luck like none you have ever seen, Onero Betalli. We have tried repeatedly to remove her and have failed. You will need every wit you possess to survive her and destroy her.''

''I will arrange things as you wish and leave within the hour. Remember, Ginny, it's a good month's travel between here and Chissoku. Perhaps it would be best to send my agent against her; if he fails, I can take over when I get there.''

''Be wary, my friend. You have always been good value, I would hate to lose you.''

''Yes, yes,'' Betalli said. ''Shall I report when it is done, or come directly to the Hole?''

''Come. This is nothing to discuss long distance.''

Ginbiryol Seyirshi ended the call. For several minutes he sat frowning at his terminal, then he called up the kephalos and began a minute examination of the security of the Hole. He couldn't do anything about Betalli's skepticism, so he wrote the man off and concentrated on protecting himself.

VIII. THE LAST DAYS
(Everybody on the move)

EVERYBODY'S IT IN THIS HIDE-AND-GO-
SEEK, BUT SOME ARE MORE IT THAN
OTHERS
CHISSOKU BOGMAK
64 Kirar Sorizakre, days 8,9
Karintepe here and there
day 8, hour 22
Razor in flux

1

Pikka Machletta squatted under the eaves of the fer-
ryhouse and watched the galley leave. "What y' think,
Fann?"

Fann was stretched out beside her, lying along the next
beam over. "Three things, Pik. She does the thing with
Guintayo and gets sliced for Blasphemy. . . ."

"You don' believe her, then, that she don' know what
we see."

"Some. Mostly not. Y' want to hear the rest?"

"Not really. Ah ri', go ahead, blue me down low,
huh?"

"Think 'bout this: something she sings set Goyo at
each other, they not too tight-wrapped anytime, be worse
tha night, half-boxed or all the way, party party. She get
caught in the middle and sliced. Or she do it too good
and Kralodate say hoo boo-ee, I want that, that's mine,
and he sticks her with his Women and she there rest a
her life. Or she run which she pro'bly will, which's
worse. Whatever happens, we get chopped."

"Huh." Pikka wriggled around and began climbing
down the side of the building. She dropped to the stones

of the Ferry Plaza, waited for Fann, then went strolling along the G'sok Kuraweg heading for Eastbridge.

They bopped along talking in spurts, wary as always but not riding their nerves. Since Razor's association with the Singer and the taste that Torkusses and others had got of her Talents, even the Dragons had left them alone.

On Bridge Street they trotted up behind a flat going home empty, scrambled aboard, and sat swinging their legs over the end of the bed.

2

Pikka Machletta glanced at the clouds, shivered at a gust of wind heavy with damp. "Goin t' be a bad one."

"Ay-yeh."

The flat trundled up the slope onto the bridge, shuddered and shied as the windgusts turned into wet blasts out of the south. Pikka and Fann swung around and laid down flat so the short side racks would cut the worst of the pressure.

Pikka rested her chin on her folded arms. "Think we sh'd move?"

"Old Town?"

"Na-nay. That's a trap. Go to ground."

"Don' know. That's for Razor, an't it? Sh'd wait for Ing to get back. And the Halftwins."

"Ay-yeh." Pikka gave up and lowered her head till the side of her face was resting on her arms. She stopped worrying for the moment, closed her eyes, and let the rumble of the flat drone her into a doze.

Ingra was off with the jinsbek Sougoury, she'd be home when she showed her nose, no use wondering when that'd be.

Kynsil and Hari were at the Mussonga Hall watching the show, up high in the cheap seats with half a dozen t'gurtsas their age, be after midnight before they got back.

No point in fidgeting herself. None at all.

Even Mem was safe. She stayed in, drawing. She was obsessed by the Singer and the Liz. Since that first day, she'd spent hours trying to get them down, drawing them over and over, working from memory because she was afraid the Singer would stop her if she knew.

3

The first flurries of rain came as the flat went swaying off the bridge. It slowed to turn into the axroad along the waterfront. Pikka Machletta and Fann dropped off and moved quickly through the tenement section to the crumbling monster they called home.

The concierge grumbled as she always did, but undid the bars and chains and let them in.

Pikka flipped her a dokie. "Anything doin', Auntee Kik'ney?"

Deft as a frog snaring a gnat, the old woman plucked the coin from the air, dropped it in a tin cup. "Till you got back, Sh'ka, peaceful as the grave."

Pikka grinned, sassed a yayyay, and went inside.

4

day 9, hour 1

The Halftwins banged at the door, then came in, filled with excitement left over from the show. "Y' sh'd a come, Pik, y' sh'd a come, Fann, there was this clown, he got up like Goyo, but he only soooo high . . . oooh, Pik, he eee-villl, he. . . ."

The door slammed open behind them, knocking Hari into a sprawl. Two mercs came in, stunners threatening.

"Don't even think it." The bigger uglier one was the speaker; his voice was tiny, thin, almost a girl's voice, but Pikka Machletta didn't feel like laughing. She dropped her hand from her razor, moving very slowly. This wasn't the moment to act, it'd just get her dropped, maybe killed. She bit down on her temper and waited.

A third merc beside him, Wargun Muk'hasta dan Fevkindadam walked in, ducking down to get through a door not sized for Goyo. He looked temperish, bitter. "If you're sensible, vermin, you'll survive this business." His slow deep voice was devoid of anything but a profound weariness. "I want nothing from you, you're nothing, less than nothing, it's the Singer I want. She has a fondness for filth, I think, so you will be hostages for a while; if she responds properly, you'll be back on the streets stealing anything not riveted down. If you cause trouble, these men will strangle you and drop you down the nearest cinerator. Do you understand me? Good." He turned to the mercs. "Line them up, the youngest first. Kill that one," he pointed at Hari, "if the older ones even look like they mean to act up."

5

day nine, hour 1, fifteen minutes later

Ingra came ambling down the G'sok K'narma, a little drunk and filled with the afterglow of hard loving. The rain had let up for a while and she was wrapped in her second-best cloak, so the wind wasn't worrying her. Nothing was worrying her. Sougoury wanted to come back with her, see she got home all right, but she wouldn't let him. She liked him for the thought, but she was careful to keep the two parts of her life separate. It made everything simpler.

She turned into G'sok K'zuprunn. Almost home, she thought, smiled as she looked along the narrow way to the tenement in the middle on the east side—and ducked into a doorway, her contentment abruptly shattered.

A merc was standing outside their tenement, his back to a large closed jit, the kind only Goyo were allowed to own.

Another merc came out, then the Halftwins, then Mem, then Fann, then Pikka, then another merc, then a Goyo muffled in his toga so she couldn't see who it was. It didn't matter. It was a Goyo and that was awful. The Singer, she thought, something she did. . . .

Her sisters-in-T'gur were pushed into the back of the jit, the mercs got in with them, all but one, he got in the front beside the Goyo and drove off.

Ingra sobbed and ran after them, keeping to the shadows as much as she could.

The jit turned the corner, another, gradually picking up speed as it worked through the narrow streets of the tenement area. She fell farther and farther behind, just caught a flicker of it as it turned onto the access highway along the bayshore and sped away toward the north.

She leaned on a corner timber, gasping for breath, tears burning her eyes, dripping down her face. Out of town, they were going out of town. She couldn't follow them there. Even if she had transport. No Karinteper was permitted in the countryside, they'd land on her before she got two marils beyond the Limit.

A raindrop splatted beside her, another hit her face, the cold shocking her from the daze and into grief . . . terrible tearing grief . . . she reached up, touched the razor . . . Razor was her family . . . Razor was gone . . . was dead . . . No! She shoved against the timber, stood straight, the rain beating into her face. "Maybe not," she said aloud and tasted the salt from the tears washed into her mouth. "Why take 'em away to kill 'em? Goyo don' bother theyselves, they just leave 'em lay. The Singer. It's somethin to do with the Singer. I got to. . . ."

She pushed away from the wall, swayed as a windgust hit her. Pulling up the cowl to her cloak, hunching her shoulders, she faced into the wind and trudged toward Eastbridge.

6

day 9, hour 3

The storm blew down on the Islands, the Ferry Building shuddered in the wind, the waves beat up and over the breaks, hammered at the landings, lightning walked, hit one of the moored ferries, danced from rod to rod on the ridgepoles of the warehouses.

Wrapped in her sodden cloak, Ingra lay along a beam up under the eaves of the Ferry Building and waited for the Singer to come back. She was cold and weary and frantic, but there was nothing she could do about any of those. If the Singer agreed to help, that was all right, Ingra was convinced she could do anything she wanted.

Razor would be saved. If she refused, Ingra would kill her, then herself. There was nothing else.

7

day 9, hour 7

Ingra almost missed the Singer and the Liz. They brought a rubber raft past the breaks into the scarcely calmer water around the landings, managed after considerable difficulty to circle to the leeside of the outermost landing and moor it there.

Shadow climbed onto the landing. She was alone. Ingra wiped the water from her eyes, struggled to see through the murk. The hoshyid just stood there, looking out beyond the breaks.

A minute later Ingra saw what she was watching. The raft, it was heading out by itself, empty, its waterjet going full, Ingra saw that when the huge waves lifted the raft and nearly flipped it before it passed out of sight.

When she turned back to the landing, Shadow was helping the Liz over the rail. They started walking away.

Ingra climbed down recklessly, nearly falling several times, tearing her hands, she didn't care, she couldn't lose them, she couldn't. . . .

They went quickly along the rain-hammered streets. There was no one else about, anyone with any sense was inside and asleep. Her eyes aching, her body aching, coughs building in her throat, nearly strangling her as she stopped them, her body shuddering with fever and chills, Ingra followed them. She didn't hope to fool the Singer, she knew the hoshyid's Talent too well for that, but she didn't want to catch up to them until they were deep enough among the warehouses to make sure there was no one to see her meet them.

It seemed to take forever. She was floating, drowning with fatigue and pain; in the end she forgot what she was doing, she just kept on pushing herself after them because that was the job she'd set herself.

Hands caught her, jerked her to a stop. Small slender hands, a little rough but very soft. The Liz, she thought dimly. She blinked at the Singer who loomed in front of her, frowning, angry and maybe afraid.

Shadow pushed the cowl back. "Ingra. Why were you following us?"

Ingra licked dry and cracking lips. When she tried to speak, all she could do was cough; she bent over, holding herself, coughing and coughing until she couldn't breathe. . . .

The Singer swore, caught hold of her. "Let's get her inside, Kikun. I don't like our faces hanging out like this."

8

"Drink this."

Ingra's hands shook so, she spilled half the tea down her front.

Shadow shoved a hip on the chair arm, supported Ingra with one arm, took the cup from her and held it to her lips. "Drink. Slowly now, get it all down, then you can tell us what's wrong. . . ." Ingra's teeth chattered against the porcelain, she moved her head precipitously, knocking the cup away, spilling the rest of the tea. "Sar! you're a fool, Shadow, what timing. Kikun toss me that towel, then fill this up again. Calmly now, Ing. You just waste time if you get too excited." She wiped away the spilled tea, her hands as gentle as Mem's. When the Liz brought another cup filled with tea, she fed it to Ingra a sip at a time.

"There now. You should have yourself a hot bath and a sleep. I'm going to give you a shot to keep off pneumonia, I don't want you dying on me. No, be still. You can talk first. Tell us what's wrong."

"Tonight. . . ." Ingra coughed again, a hacking that shook her whole body. "Tonight, in the first hour after midnight, I was comin home from . . . I was comin home and I saw mercs and a Goyo takin Razor away. They come outta tha tenny, put Pikka and Fann and Mem and Kynsil and Hari in a closed jit and went 'way with 'em. I run after it, they turn on the axroad and go north. They take 'em outta tha city. It's 'cause of you, I know it, you gotta do somethin, Singer, you GOT to.''

"Yes, you're right. We have to do something and we will. But not right now, there's no way. We have to think first, rest."

"No no no . . ." Ingra struggled against the Singer's hands; she was weak, so weak. "No! Now. He kill 'em. Now!"

"That's the fever talking. Let's get you on your feet. Kikun, my bag, take it in the bedroom. Quiet now, Ing." The Singer helped Ingra stand, led her stumbling down a short hall. "Don't get yourself in a twist like that. Through here." She led Ingra into an elaborate bedroom. "This place is a giggle, isn't it. Sit down a minute, we'll get those wet things off you and slide you into bed, then we can talk. Moving too fast, you know, without any planning, it'll get us all killed. Razor, too. You're not thinking. If they're not dead now, they won't be killed until Wargun makes his offer."

Ingra grabbed her arms, her fingers biting into the girl's flesh. "Wargun. Y' know who. . . ."

"We don't know for sure, but the odds are it's him. He already tried to kill me. Hold her, Kikun." Shadow set a rod against Ingra's arm, touched a sensor. Ingra felt a faint prickle, then nothing. "That'll take hold in a few minutes and you'll feel a lot better. He thought I was dead until tonight when he recognized my voice, my speaking voice, I mean. I imagine he means to trade Razor for me."

She worked busily, stripping the sodden clothing off Ingra, drying her with a huge soft towel, pulling a shift of some kind over her head.

"I'm not going to play that game, Ing. I'm definitely not suicidal. We'll get Razor, I'll figure a way. I promise you that. Come on, it's into bed with you. We need to get you warmed up. Gods, I'm tired. I'm going to have to get some sleep. We can't go rushing in like fools, Ing. Just get us all killed."

When Ingra was tucked between silk sheets and poufs soft as the down on a hakkug's belly, the Singer left her a moment, came back with a towel round her own head, her wet clothes changed for a soft velvety wraprobe. The Liz was with her, he had a bedtray with tea and sandwiches on it; he set it on the bed beside Ingra then went to squat with his back to the wall. She forgot him as soon as he was gone.

Shadow pulled a chair over, settled herself with her legs tucked under her. She filled two cups, took a sandwich, and finished it before she said anything else.

"Wargun. What do you know about him, Ing? Anything you can tell us will help."

Ingra scowled at her, suspicious. For reasons she couldn't have named she was suddenly sure the answer to that question was why the hoshyids had come to Chissoku. Why should she give away information like that? It went against everything she'd learned since she was able to think. "Why sh'd I tell you anythin? Your fault he took Razor, y' HAVE to get them out."

Shadow shifted her legs, resettled the robe. "Obligation. With that and a dokie you can get a cup of tea. It makes people nervous, that's all, doesn't get you anything."

"Y' said y' would." Ingra bit into a sandwich, refused to look at the Singer. "That don' mean anythin?"

Shadith sighed. She pulled the towel off her hair, dropped it beside the chair. "Do you know where he took your sisters-in-T'gur?"

"Na-nay."

"Then we have to ask him, don't we?"

"Oh." Ingra gazed at the sandwich remnant she was holding, shook her head fretfully, dropped the crust on the tray. "Pik tell y', y' go 'way, leave us up to our ears in Goyo shit. What's it do, y' get them loose, y' cut out, leave us?"

"All right, I concede the point. And I've thought about it. I can get you offworld, to University, if that's what you want."

"The Goyo won' know? Won' stop us at the Field?"

"I have a way . . . um . . . around that." She grinned. "What works for me will work for you."

"Ah ri'." Ingra lay back, closed her eyes. "I know this, Goyo do anythin he damn well want, well, y' know that, but Wargun don' go after kids. Some of 'em do, some of 'em like real young kids. He don'. He won' bother 'em that way."

"How do you know?"

"Pik tol' us one time she got real drunk. She a whore, y' know. After her mema die. She was in this House, y' know, assig shop. The Chupey take her in where Wargun was, thinkin she be a special treat. He gets madder'n spit, say he don' jigga-jog wit' babies, he don' even like to think 'bout it, if she ever do that to him again, he goin to drop her 'live in Jinssi Hole."

"I see."

The Liz stood up, came over to them. "Why does he go to the Taiikambar Tay when he's not really interested in the fighters there?"

Ingra blinked when she saw him, startled he was still in the room. "Oh, ev'body know that." She blew her nose into her fingers, looked around for something to wipe them on; the Singer threw her the damp towel. "Wargun, he own the assig House next door t' Taiikambar." She giggled. "He kinked. He so kinked, he be lookin up his own ass if he bend over."

"I know that. He like hurting people and looking at people being hurt. So?"

"Na-nay, an't like that, 's other way round. He differnt from tha other Goyo. Weird. Really weird. He like being beat on and peed on and treated like dogshit, he get off on it. Tha other Goyo w'd howl if they know. We know 'cause his whipmama's the Chupey who run Pikka back when, like I told you. He play like he int'rested in tha fighters, when all he want is go nex' door and have his ass whipped and all."

"Then we get in there, we have him."

Ingra yawned. The shot was working on her, mixing with the warmth and her fatigue; she could barely keep her eyes open.

The Singer swung her feet down. "That does it, Ing. That's all we needed to know. Um. He'll be in touch with us sometime tomorrow, he knows how, he'll let us know what he wants in exchange for Razor. And maybe he'll go to the House after that. If he does, we have him. If he doesn't we bargain, stall as long as we can. I'll look for Razor myself when I'm rested up some, but I don't have much hope from that.'' She stood. ''You might as well give in and sleep, Ing. When you wake up, you'll feel a lot better and we'll probably know more. All right?''

''Ah ri'.''

TARGET: Wargun Muk'hasta dan
     Fevkindadam
CAPTURE TEAM: Rohant Vohv Voallts,
     Ciocan of Family Voallts, Gazgaort of
     Company Voallts Korlatch of Spotch
     Helspar.
   Naiyol Hanee the Ta'anikay, called Kikun
     in freespeech, Incarnation of the
     clowndancer god of the dinhastoi of
     DunyaDzi
   Shadith Twiceborn called Shadow

Chissoku Bogmak
64 Kirar Sorizakre, day 9

1

day 9, hour 8
Shadith, Kikun

Shadith loosed the gull, pushed herself up, blinking rapidly from the disorientation of the sudden transfer of viewpoint. "Not a hope, Kikun, I could spend a year looking and still find nothing. We have to do this the hard way." She sat hunched over, sick with worry about the girls; there were many things she didn't understand about Wargun, but she hadn't a doubt he'd kill them if she didn't come when he called her.

Kikun bent over her, stroked fingertips up the side of her face. "Rest, Shadow. We'll get them."

"Gaagi says?"

"Kikun says." He moved away. Over his shoulder, he said, "You have a way offworld?"

She smiled. "You mean you don't know about that?"

"Would I ask?"

"Would you? No no, it's a simple thing. My own little bit of double-knotting. Remember the smuggler on Kiskai, the one I used to get a message out to my friend?"

"You were very quiet about him then, too."

"You know the saying, a secret shared. . . ."

"Is a secret bared. It was a good thought, a good knot."

"Which reminds me, I'd better let him know he might have six more passengers . . . what time is it?"

"Third quarter of the eighth hour."

"I wonder if they've missed me yet?" She stared at him, demanding an answer from his Talent.

His eyes crossed, his mouth sagged open, he seemed to wilt . . . for just a second . . . then he was bright and alive again, like putting water on a dessicated plant. "No."

"The sun's just up. And the streets are more or less empty, the servants have got to their jobs so they're inside, Old Town's asleep still, visitors—not many stirring yet. . . ."

Kikun leaned against the doorjamb and smiled his slow sweet smile. "In other words, you're talking yourself into going out. There's a public com at the Ferry Building. No doubt the flow in and out is monitored; if you're careful, that shouldn't matter. Fix your face."

"Yes, O guru." She giggled, sobered. "Does it bother you, Kikun, us using you like some sort of chunk-your-money-in-get-your-answer oracle?"

"You use me, they use me, I'm used to it. You're nicer."

"They?"

"They."

"Right. Well, let me go put my face on. I'm going to use you again, Kuna. I need to be sure I'm not followed back here."

"I know."

"I suppose you do."

2

day 9, hour 13
Rohant

Rohant was in the gym against his will, sullenly following the instructions of the Tinda-rij who was drilling him in elementary moves that the Dyslaeror had botched in his last two fights; it was K'ch'en's declared opinion that Rohant was getting sloppy through too much success and needed the edges smoothed off. Over and over and over again while the sweat dripped down him and his fur matted and ruffed, he went through those moves, one two three four, one two three four . . . over and over until the rage that filled him was near to blowing him apart.

Coktchee came padding onto the mat. He grinned spitefully at Rohant and touched the Tinda-rij's arm. The boy loathed the Dyslaeror, had never forgiven Rohant for his looks that first day or the scold he'd gotten for impudence to a visitor.

K'ch'en bent down, listened to him, scowled. In the end, he nodded and sent the boy off. "You have a visitor, Unmate. Go clean up, wait in the locker room, I'll send him to you."

Rohant drew an arm across his face, smearing the sweat more than wiping it off. "Who?"

K'ch'en tightened his mouth, but he finally decided to answer. "The Fevkindadam. You mind your manners, you hear?"

Rohant grunted, not trusting himself to talk. He strolled out, taking his time with a deliberate insolence that helped him keep a precarious control of himself.

Kikun had come by earlier, after Shadith had completed arrangements with Arel the smuggler. Sitting quietly in a corner of Rohant's room, the dinhast told him everything.

If Kikun had moved in any way, if he'd said one word after he finished his tale, if he hadn't sat there quiet and mild, he'd be dead.

Rohant wept, devastated by the betrayal.

He shivered with fever and chills, the fur on his hands and upper body ruffed into peaks.

Kikun moved finally, held him, soothed him, helped him realize it didn't matter, the thing was finally over. He wouldn't have to fight again, he'd be going after Ginny, wiping him out, wiping out the stains on his honor. And he'd be going home.

Now he stripped, showered, taking his time.

He rubbed himself carefully dry, dressed in the drab travel clothes he'd worn at home and at work and went as calmly as he could to meet the Target and listen to the threats he expected to hear.

##

His mouth clamped shut, his eyes on the floor, Rohant followed the Goyo into the Eating House. He was walking on the dirty remnants of his pride and had to keep reciting the litany that had sustained him this far: Miralys, Lissorn, S'ragis, the children, the beasts, Miralys, Lissorn. . . .

##

Wargun led him to a private room, ignored him as he ordered the meal, then settled back in the longchair and began talking about Rohant's last fight.

##

When the servers had cleared the remnants of the meal and left, Wargun filled a crystal stemglass from the stone winebottle, pushed it across to Rohant, filled another for himself. He held the glass cupped between his hands, looked across it at Rohant.

"Listen to me, clawman. No. Keep your mouth shut. I have words I want passed on. I can't touch you right now. There's no point pretending I can threaten you. I'm sure you're also aware how ephemeral that protection can be, so I suggest you court my favor and work to keep it.

I have a long memory and no living enemies, at least, none capable of threatening me.

"Two things I want, Dyslaeror, your silence and your cooperation in passing this to your friend, that Singer. I hold the Razor T'gurtt. Your friend can ransom them by coming to a place I designate when I'm ready to receive her. I will guarantee her life and I will keep her out of the Gotasaray. You can be sure of that last. I don't want her anywhere near Goyo." A bitter smile. "I give away nothing by saying that, you know it as well as I do. I have men hunting her, the Kralodate has men hunting her. There's a reward posted, so everyone's hunting her. Karintepe is a limited space and there's no way she can leave it without betraying herself. Unless she speaks to me, she is dead."

Rohant dropped his hands below the table, worked his claws as he struggled to focus on the Goyo's words rather than his throat. "And dead if she does," he growled finally.

Wargun sipped at the wine, set the glass gently before him. "Possibly but not necessarily. There are several ways in which we can reach a mutually satisfactory disengagement. But we must meet. You're not the beast your fans like to think you, Ciocan. You understand the situation. If we don't meet, nothing will happen. And the T'gurtt will die in exquisite pain. And I will be waiting for you to slip from your pedestal, clawman. And when you do, you die. I'll see to that." He got to his feet. "I will return to the Tay this evening. Have my answer then."

3

day 9, hour 15
Shadith, Kikun, Ingra

"That's the setup," Kikun said. "Rohant is going to negotiate a meeting place as if he's serious about it, set the time for tomorrow night, saying he couldn't arrange anything sooner. He thinks Wargun will go directly to his mistress after that and it is so, it is so. Yes.'' He blinked, dropped into a brooding silence.

Ingra scrubbed at her eyes. ''Tonight?'' You'll get them out tonight?''

''Tonight or never, Ing.'' Shadith rubbed at her back. ''We can't use the bridges. Can you get us a boat? We have to get from here to Dysinnia Shimda, then wherever Wargun's got Razor, then across the Bay to Starstreet.''

''I know a man . . . he'll want to be paid.''

''Then pay him, you know how much it should be.''

Ingra scowled. ''It's your business.''

''They're your sisters.''

''Ah ri'. Where you want him? And when?'' Her misshapen hands were knotted, her polyjointed arms wrapped about her plump breasts; she was angry and confused; she was the child of impulse, depending on Pikka and Fann to do the plotting and keep her safe. Now she was alone, dependent on people she didn't—couldn't—trust and she hated it.

Shadith watched these things pass across her round pretty face and was unhappy with what she was doing to the child, but she had no choice; if she used the credit bracelet, she was shouting come get me. And Ingra had to realize the real danger out there. It was sick-making to take her laughter away from her, she'd suffered enough since she was born, poor baby, but if she was going to get away from here alive, she had to settle down.

It's going to be a hell, shut up on Arel's ship all the way to University with these . . . uh-oh, I nearly forgot. . . .

''Um . . . that reminds me, there's something you should do, Ing. Unless you mean to abandon your stash, you'd better collect it this afternoon. When we go, we won't look back. Um . . . get the guims translated to Helvetian gelders . . . you'll lose some value doing it through Setzumero instead of waiting till you get to University, but better lose a little than all of it. A credit bracelet, see this one. . . .'' she held out her wrist, "when it's tuned to you, no one can steal it and it's good just about wherever you go. Obviously I can't come with you, but I'll give you a note authorizing you to use my contact on Helvetia, that should help the exchange." She got to her feet, moved across to the writing table, took a sheet of paper and wrote. "Favor for favor, Ing. Razor gave me Setzumero here to handle my take."

Ingra took the paper, got to her feet.

Shadith could feel her uncertainty, her fear; the t'gurtsa understood at last what was happening, that she was leaving everything she'd known, leaving it behind forever.

"There's nothing we can do till tonight," she said. "Be careful, Ing. I don't think you've got a problem, but I can't read Wargun's mind. I don't know what he knows. Just be careful."

Ingra stared at her; the t'gurtsa's face was drawn, pale, her tough cheerfulness was drained out of her. She nodded and left.

Shadith grimaced. "Gods!" she said.

"She'll be fine, Shadow. Given time."

"Time." Shadith shook her head, crossed to the longchair and stretched out on it. "Arel was not pleased," she said. "He'll do it, but he's going to paitsch all the way to University." She plucked fretfully at the worn silk upholstery. "Six hours to kill, maybe more. Sar! Kikun. . . ."

"Sleep, Shadow. You need the rest. I'll wake you when it's time."

"How can I sleep?"

He came and knelt beside her, took her hand and began smoothing his dry soft fingertips across and across her palm. "You can sleep, yes oh yes, you are exhausted, Shadow, let it go, let go . . . sleep. . . ."

4

day 9, hour 21

Rohant met them behind the House. "He's in?"

"Went straight here after he left you."

"Where's the t'gurtsa?"

"On the boat watching the owner, making sure he doesn't get ideas."

"Couldn't have been easy shedding her."

"She's not liking me much, trusting me less. Wasn't hard."

He looked at the back of the building. It was flat stone from street to eaves, no windows, no airslits, nothing but a metal-capped garbage chute and a heavy door at the top of a narrow flight of stone steps.

Kikun was at the door, bent over the lock. He straightened, stepped away. "Yours, Shadow. Two bars, here . . ." he reached up trapped the wood, bent, tapped it beside his knee, "and here. No electronics, but there's a guard, sitting. He's dozing. Too much noise and he wakes up and we've had it."

"I see." She climbed the stairs, leaned against the door and *reached: man, bored, drowsy, but not quite asleep*. She probed about the lower regions, found a rat colony, brought them swarming up from the basement and sent them leaping at the guard. Apparently he had a morbid fear of rats. He went running off as if fifty smoking devils were on his tail.

Shadith took the braincrystal knife carefully from its sheath, inserted the blade into the crack between door and jamb. She held her breath, pressed down, stopped her hand. The top bar was severed. Keeping the blade carefully turned away, Kikun's small hands steadying her, she knelt. When she was braced, she slid the knife into the crack, pushed down, stopped her hand. The bottom bar was gone. She eased the knife back into her boot, got to her feet, and pulled the door open.

The hall inside was narrow and filled with ancient building smells, moss and must, with a flavoring of garbage and old farts. Shadith twisted her face into a comic grimace. "Makes wearing these things worth it," she murmured. She inserted the gas filters in her nostrils, pulled the clear hood over her head.

Farther inside the guard was still screaming and half a dozen other people were yelling at him, trying to get him quiet.

"Sar! What a hoo-ha. Go get 'em, Kikun."

As soon as Rohant was in, she touched a gluepip to
the severed bars, pressed the pieces together. In the dim
light there was little sign of tampering. When she turned
round, the noise had stopped and Kikun was coming back
"Let's go," she whispered.

##

They went up the narrow stairs at the back of the
House, Shadith first, her senses *reaching* before her to
warn them of servants or anyone else there. Twice she
touched Kikun's arm and he tossed a gas grenade ahead
of them, taking out a handmaid and an insomniac wan-
derer.

##

Goyo don't like change, Ingra said. I'd bet my life he'll
have the same room. She grinned rather nastily, then said,
well, make that your life. The big room, second floor
front, north side. There are peepholes, she said, and a
runway along the back of the rooms. Sometimes the Chupey lets clients go in there and watch. Mostly it's for
times when the clients get too rough and need to be
cooled down. There'll be runners in there, off and on,
usually young girls or boys, ones the Chupey has in training. Pikka did that a lot, the first year she was there.
There's a latch at the top of the back stairs, mechanical
latch, not electronic, it lets you in. The runners won't
fuss when they hear you, but take them out before they
see you, you don't look like clients.

##

Second floor. Into the runway. One child, a runner.
Gassed. Check the peepholes. Nothing . . . nothing. . . .

Wargun, bound and naked with four women working
over him.

Shadith wasn't really surprised when she saw that the woman in charge was the Hindor who met her at the ottotel.

Kikun and Rohant went prowling, making sure the runway was clear. It was no time for interruptions.

It was very quiet in there, none of the noise in the streets. Very quiet in the room, except for the voices of the women. Shadith wrinkled her nose. The things they were saying . . . twenty thousand years, she'd seen a lot, she still couldn't understand why people needed that kind of thing. Ah, well, at least he didn't fool with children. And he was doing this to himself, not some slavey. In the context that made him almost heroic. And confusing. Everything said he simply wasn't the sort of man to enjoy Ginny's productions. He couldn't kill her, couldn't even watch her being killed. Odd, odder, oddest . . . if he didn't know so much about Seyirshi, if he wasn't so intent on protecting himself, she'd have been convinced it was all a mistake.

Kikun touched her arm. "Clear," he murmured.

"Get the panel ready to open." She tossed a gas grenade through the peep, slid it shut.

Rohant and Kikun lifted the women, laid them to one side, tossed a coverlet over them and came back to Shadith who was running a clipper over Wargun's head, taking off his long long hair, coarse and black, with gray streaks that shone like brushed pewter. It was loose now, combed out, the crimps softened by sweat and scented oils. She handled the strands with distaste, throwing them aside as they came off.

Rohant stood back. He didn't trust himself, he'd told Shadith that, Kikun agreed. He couldn't touch the Goyo without loosing the rage in him and doing something bloody to the man who'd become the focus of that rage. Wargun hadn't killed his grandchild or attacked his family, but Ginny was an abstraction, out in an endless nowhere, Wargun was there. Under his nose.

Kikun took off the token shackles, replaced them with padded ropes, spreading the Goyo out on the floor, tieing his legs to the bed posts, his arms to brackets on the walls—there were a lot of brackets all over the walls, ready for any combination or permutation that occurred to the client or the mistress.

Shadith spread a depilatory cream on the Goyo's head, wiped it off. Then she marked the set points on his naked scalp, squeezed on the goo and set the crown of the probe in place, sealing it down with plastape. She activated the keybox, began making the minute adjustments necessary for a true reading.

Kikun wiped antiseptic across the interior of the Goyo's elbow, set the popper against the skin. "Ready?"

"One minute." She finished with the box, set it down, got to her feet, bent, stretched, shook herself all over. "Rohant, come over here. I want him to see us looking down at him, I want him to know how helpless he really is. It's one thing to play at bondage, it's another to lose control completely. Hit him, Kikun."

##

Wargun came awake quickly, his eyes darted from them to the ropes that held him; he shook his head, trying to dislodge the crown. She'd set it on too solidly, it didn't shift. He threw his body against the ropes. They held. He lay looking up at them, no, her, mostly her, not hating them, not hating her, no emotion at all that Shadith could see or read, just a blue-steel determination. He'd surprised her again.

She turned to Kikun "Whenever I try the probe, he's going to throw himself into convulsions."

The dinhast nodded. "Yes. The lock."

"Yes. I wanted to avoid possible complications, but I see that's not feasible. Pop him."

Wargun's eyes flickered; he didn't like being discussed as if he were a senseless slab of meat. Despite his control anger flared in him.

She smiled "Now."

Kikun stepped on the Goyo's arm, pinned it down, bent over and pressed the popper against the inside of Wargun's elbow. He touched the sensor. The Goyo's body jerked, went limp. "Done," Kikun said. he straightened and came to stand beside Shadith. "Shall we begin?"

##

"Ginbiryol Seyirshi is holding an Auction for his new Limited Edition. When?"

The question surprised Wargun, weakened his initial resistance; the probe whispered and flickered, the triggerlight flowed with opalescence, then went green. Shadith touched on the recorder, then set her finger on the trigger.

Eyes glaring, mouth working as he fought to obscure as much as he could what his brain was forcing him to say, Wargun gave the date, using Chissoku equivalents since they came most readily to mind. "67 Kirar, day 13." The words were clear enough despite his efforts.

"Ginbiryol Seyirshi is holding an Auction for his new Limited Edition. Where?"

"*Koulsnakko's Hole* . . . edge of *Anaso Sink* . . . between Anso and Zangaree."

"Coordinates?"

"Don't know."

"Explain."

"Proceed to Anaso Satellite *Laybogby's Star,* cat. drs. 193845, pilot flake waiting.

Shadith slapped her thigh. "Tsoukbaraim! Trust Ginny to complicate things. What signal for the flakes?'

"Don't know."

"Explain."

"Ginny sent teaser for the Edition. Signal buried on that flake, read-protected."

"Where is your teaser?"

He fought again, a new desperation in him that nearly overwhelmed the mechanical exactitudes of the probe; he chewed his lips bloody, tried to bite off his tongue. Kikun got a hardrubber rod between the Goyo's teeth, then squatted beside him, watching anxiously as the probe wore the man down.

Wargun mouthed something.

Kikun withdrew the rod.

"Again," Shadith said. "Repeat."

"Alousan." He was crying suddenly, his face contorted, the tears mixing with sweat and blood, flowing down over the tape that held the crown to his naked scalp. "They're for her, not me. She has the teaser. She is the buyer. Don't tell. I beg, don't tell. They'd put her down. Her own father would put her down if he knew. Tatta Ry who taught her pain. Don't tell. Please. Don't tell."

Shadith shuddered under the impact of the terror rolling off the man. Terror for the woman, not himself. "We are not interested in that." She forced the words out, repeated them when he didn't seem to hear. "We have nothing to say to Goyo. Only to Ginbiryol Seyirshi. When we know all you have about him, we'll leave Chissoku. You can do what you want."

He took that in and in his relief, babbled endlessly. He adored his wife, was obsessed by her, he raved about her beauty, her passion, how he would do anything to please her, to keep her complaisant to his needs. She had her little flaws, they were part of her infinite charm for him. He never watched the Editions, though he paid for them. He looked at a part of the first one and loathed it. Though he shuddered from inflicting pain and death himself, he'd do anything to protect her to the point of destroying himself and the world with him.

"Kill him."

Shadith looked up. Rohant was standing behind her, staring down at the Goyo. "No. Ro, move away. Listen to me. We still have to find out where Razor is. Do you want to be responsible for their lives?"

Kikun moved to the Dyslaeror, stroked the soft fur on his arm. "Come Ciocan, you don't mean that. It's the blood speaking. Come away, come. . . ." He eased Rohant away from the Goyo, took him back to the door and stood beside him, hand on his arm.

Shadith sighed. Old Lion was closer to a breakdown

then she'd suspected. Kikun was right, it was the blood speaking, all the men he'd been driven to kill, all the pride he'd had stripped from him. Ginny had a lot to answer for. And he never would. Dying wasn't enough. But it was all they had. There were limits. . . . She turned back to Wargun who was still babbling. He was relaxed now, repeating himself. "Wargun!"

"I . . . hear."

"You took Razor T'gurtt. Where are they?"

"Razor?" He sounded confused. He wasn't fighting her, but the t'gurtsas meant so little to him, he couldn't remember for the moment who they were.

"The girls, the ones you took yesterday."

"Them. Dungeon playroom. Here."

That surprised a laugh out of her. "Well! Luck blows us a kiss instead of a kick. Let's close this out. Kikun."

Kikun popped him with a soporific; it would keep him unconscious for the next twelve hours. He stripped the coverlet off the women, used the popper on them.

Shadith squatted beside the Goyo, frowning. "Not much help. Considering what we've gone through to get it. We need that teaser . . ."

Kikun tossed her the popper. "No. There's a faster way."

"What?"

He tapped his nose. "We go to Laybogby's Star, wait in the insplit, someone shows up, gets his flake, dives again, I sniff out his trail and off we go."

Shadith rubbed at her eyes. "I remember . . . you said something about that before." She combed a hand through her hair. "Kikun to the rescue. Again. You sure?"

"I've played with it before now. Enough to know I can do it, not enough to know how long or how precisely. The trail has to be fresh and I'll need to keep close to them, but not quite near enough to show on their screens."

"Only three months till the Auction and this world's too hot for us to hang around anyway. It's about all we can do, so I suppose we'll have to see if it works." Shadith got to her feet, stretched, yawned. "Ro, you all right?"

The Dyslaeror managed a tooth-covered smile. "Temporary sanity, Shadow."

"Good. Grab his feet and help me get him on the bed."

"Women, too?"

"Right. All comfy together. We don't want to spook the locals before we're long gone from the scene."

##

Rohant looked at the bed, shuddered. "Let's get out of here."

"Yeh. Dungeon playroom. Ingra said that's up under the eaves. Shall we go collect us some prisoners?"

IX. CONVERGENCE

CONVERSATION 1

First party: Onero Betalli
    at the Transfer Station, Spotchals
Second party: Ginbiryol Seyirshi
    at *Koulsnakko's Hole, Anaso Sink*
    region

1

Ajeri Kilavez opened the door to the Blackroom and
walked carefully through the murk to Ginbiryol Seyirshi.
She waited until he finished his decade, touched his arm.
"Betalli, sir. He says it's important. He says the girl got
away."

Seyirshi sat very still. "Go," he said. "I will be there
in two minutes."

2

He came onto the Bridge with the Pet in his arms.
"Where is he calling from?"

"Spotchals. Transfer Station."

"Ah." He snapped the Pet's leash chain onto the sta-
ple, set the simi on the back of the chair and settled
himself in it. He composed himself, nodded to Ajeri.
"Put him through."

Betalli looked paler and wearier than before. "I salute
you, Ginbiryol, and apologize. I have failed. I mistrusted
your evaluation of the female's Luck and must acknowl-
edge my error."

"Report."

"After our previous conversation, I activated my Agent
on Chissoku immediately. The girl wasn't difficult to locate. She was performing as a singer at Karintepe's

274

NightFair and attracting considerable attention. At first, my agent attempted to arrange an assassination. It was difficult. The Goyo do not permit the import of energy weapons except for the Kralodachy guard, even the Families are restricted as to how they can arm their own guards. And the girl had bought protection. None of the local talent was willing to work without the blessings of the Sirshak-kai which they couldn't get. Besides, they were afraid of her. She has odd Talents and a reputation for being dangerous to meddle with. He decided to do the work himself, but before he could complete arrangements the situation fell apart. The girl vanished. Young Goyo looking to make a reputation, guards with an eye to the reward the Kralodate offered, and some independent entrepreneurs started turning the city over, looking under every rock.''

"They did not find her."

"No. She managed to keep out of sight all that first day and apparently got to the Fevkindadam in spite of the uproar; I say this because sometime during the night following her disappearance, Wargun dan Fevkindadam strangled his wife and killed himself. My agent reports whispers that Wargun's head was shaved; that would be a great scandal. It is my opinion the girl removed his hair so she could use a probe on him. You understand the implications. Best have a stingship at the rendezvous; perhaps you can get her there.''

"She has left Chissoku Bogmak?"

"It is my opinion she has done so. My agent has discovered traces of a smuggler called Arel. It was difficult to pin the times down, but it seems likely he arrived shortly before she did. And he was gone the day after the confusion began. I think there is no question she went with him. The Dyslaeror also. As to the third, no one seems to know anything about him, though she did have a cowled figure with her when she sang. If that was he, he went also.''

"Arel." Seyirshi turned to Ajeri. "This is twice that man has inserted himself into my affairs. I want a trace on him. I want him dead." He thought a moment. "Be sure his death is recorded. We can use it as a minor production." He turned back to Betalli. "Why are you at Spotchals?"

"I have my agents on planet assembled about the Voallts Compound. The Ciocan will certainly attempt to contact his Toerfeles, a smuggler's ship is insufficient for an attack on a Hole. In any case, it is most unlikely that the smuggler will be willing to risk himself or his ship in such a dubious undertaking. Because of the work Adelaris Security did, it is impossible to get EYEs within the Compound, but I have five flits moving constantly back and forth over it, sending me detailed views of the exteriors and listening for any incoming calls. The Toerfeles has complained of this to the Traffic Bureau and action will be taken in a few hours, but it is possible the skipcom contact will be made within that limit. Possible though not wholly likely. The smuggler has been insplitting for less than a week and may not be in a position to use his com. There are some disturbed conditions between here and Chissoku. We had considerable breakup when my Pilot bespoke my Chissoku agent. I have a ratsnatcher deployed, but it's likely that Spotchals Security will take it out any minute. There are too many businesses here with incoming rats they want protected. I welcome any suggestions as to how I can tighten the net about Voallts."

Seyirshi frowned, tapped his fingers on the arms of his chair. "You have done all that is possible given the circumstances." He continued to tap as if he counted the beats of silence before he spoke again. "Break off your surveillance. If you keep your people in place much longer, Spotchals Authority will become involved in this business and that will complicate matters considerably; you could be barred from Spotchals sovereign space. The gain is not worth the pain." Another long pause. "Let them come as they surely will, we will be waiting."

MORE CONVERSATIONS

Rohant vohv Voallts, Ciocan
Miralys vey Voallts tol Daravazhalts, Toerfeles

Miralys touched the screen with the tip of her foreclaw.
"You look well."

Rohant echoed the move, set clawtip against clawtip.
"Well enough. And you look tired. Has it been hard?"

"Dancing on a highrope on fire at both ends. You have
an answer?"

"Yes. The Auction will be held at a Clandestine Pit
called *Koulsnakko's Hole*, eighty-seven days from today.
Anyone else call it in?"

Miralys' ears twitched, her nose wiggled, her eyes
laughed at him. "So so, my Ciocan. No, you're the first
with the name. Digby's people found out it was going to
be a Clandestine, but no one knew which or where.
Nothing except that Clandestines are never down a gravity well, so it will be asteroids or hulks. Which confirms
your Singer friend's prediction. Nice for her. Where is
Koulsnakko's?"

"That we don't know exactly; it's in between the Anaso and Zangaree Sinks, about two months travel from
Spotchals, less from University, that's where we're heading. Seyirshi has been doing more of what Shadow calls
double-knotting. He's arranged a cut-out. A rendezvous
where the Bidders pick up a pilot flake. Does Digby have
data on the Clandestines? Maybe he already knows the
coordinates."

Miralys leafed through some fax sheets, took up one, glanced down it. "He has some fifty listed now. Koulsnakko's isn't one of them."

"Dio Misclaer!" He combed his thumbclaw through his mustache. "They never make it easy. We'll just have to wait till someone hits the rendezvous and follow him."

"How? Unless you can plant lice on him, I thought following through the insplit is impossible without crowding so close you spook your target."

"We have a chance, better not talk about it, who knows what ears are cocked our way. Mira, we need Lissorn now and his *Cillasheg*. Have him head for University huphup."

"He's already at University, waiting for you. He figured you'd go there first and he was too restless to hang around here doing nothing much."

"Good. Time is cramping down on us. Not much room for mistakes or maneuvering. Listen, the rendezvous is at *Laybogby's Star*. The *Karidion Worlds* are around three days away from there. Send any teams you can get hold of to *Hetohongya*, that's at *Gamma Karidion*, along with any ops who chose to come. We'll meet them there."

"Talking about ears. Until yesterday we had a mob around us, with overflights every five minutes. Today, nothing. What's going on?"

Rohant looked away, listened a moment, turned back. "Shadow thinks Ginny called them off. He's going to have everything he can assemble at the Hole, waiting for us."

"It isn't fair, Ciocan. It is not fair. I have to sit here and wait. I wish I were with you."

"Me too, my Mystka Drygg. One way or another, though, it won't be long now. . . ."

2

Outside the *Spi'itibay* of the Olom Myndigget
Tasylyn the Zadys
Tracer op Ayyakaabi

Tasylyn gloomed at the intricate swirling spires of the

Spi'itibay. No one went in, no one came out, she couldn't
even decide where the doors were.

"Tzt." Ayyakaabi slid round the rock like a small
plush shadow, flattened herself beside the Dyslaerin.
"You maya f'get sa," she said, fluttering webbed fingers
at the complex structure filling most of the valley below
them. "Dig'b an t' Miral's, they saya Ci'o, he got it. We
go."

3

Hank the Fang's Place, the *Herka Bidj*
Zarovan the Zadant
Tracer op Woensdag Addams
   The target was half boxed and ready to go banga-bang
if anyone looked at him cross-eyed. Wetting him into a
proper pliancy was taking longer as well as being a heel-
luvo lot harder than Zarovan had planned on when he
oozed up to him and started bargaining as if he meant it
when he said he needed a working man to help him kid-
nap a vip from Frangipan. He was patient, though, it was
his business to be, use the beast's habits to build the trap,
he was good at that. Two-legged didn't seem so different
from four-legged, or six or eight.
   Woensdag came in, looking harried, his drag starting
to unravel.
   What the wet hell. . . .
   The op got a look at Zarovan's glare and he sheered
off, settled in a booth and began to repair his plastice and
plak and resettle the wig of long blond hair.
   Grunting his displeasure, the Dyslaeror inspected his
burnt-out stib and thumbed a sensor. The waiter was a
rusty bucket of a barbot, its wheels squeaked and it had
a stutter in twenty langues, but Hank didn't care as long
as it counted the money right and tossed out drunks and
any clients too stiffed to keep buying.
   "Hit him again and bring me 'nother stib." He
dropped a gelder down the barbot's readyslot, wincing at
the thought of Miralys going over his expense sheet.
   When his target was deep enough in his renewed plea-

sures, Zarovan sneaked a look at Woensdag. The op was signaling *door, now.*

What the wet hell? He knows better . . . something wrong?

He ran an eye over his target. Maybe a bit green yet, but at least he could still walk, he wouldn't have to carry him. He slapped a hand on the table. "Time," he said thickly. "C'mon, ol' girl, we collect you pretties and hit the port. All that loovely lolly, think on it and move you feet."

The merc blinked at him, gulped the rest of the smoky fluid in the shotglass and set it down exactly on its former ring, a delicate precision that belied the woozy wandering of his droop-lidded eyes. "Ga pee."

"'M' ship gotta head." He went stiff with righteous indignation. "What you thinkin, I run a barbobuck't?" He giggled. "Talkin head. . . ." He waved Woensdag over. The op was together again and in the smoky haze was looking deceptively delectable. "'S m' Second, she give head like you woon't . . ." he belched, blinked, surged onto his feet. "'M going, do what y' wan."

He went rolling out with Woensdag hanging on his arm and processed down the street like the tank he resembled in his worn armor.

The merc sniffed, got to his feet, and stumbled after him.

Two turns and a patch of dark and he was laid out on the mud, Talsren and Sugnorn standing over him.

Zarovan shook himself, struggled to throw off the fumes of the geezert; that was the trouble with this ploy, you ended up nearly as buzzed as your prey. "What's with you, Woen? You nearly blew it, coming in too soon and looking like you'd been tossed by a barbarian horde."

"Message from Digby, came through half hour ago. We're to break off and head for the Karidion Worlds, fast as we can slog it. The Ciocan has the location nailed."

"Huh. Well, I'm not going to argue waste with Miralys. We'll go, but we'll take this 'un with us, got to do something while we're insplitting, might's well work him over, suck him clean. Right? Right."

4

And so it went.

On *Strazha Uho* (Kalebas 4) and *Perezos* (Sandric 2) in the Bug Arm Region, teams broke off surveillance and retreated as soon as they were able to move without bringing Security down on them.

On *Ghaltar* (Louat 4) the call came in the middle of a firefight and the survivors only learned about it when they struggled to the rendezvous and were picked up by Ilta the smuggler. Two of the team were cold, the op was only breathing because Hannys the Zadys had improvised a breather from an oxypac. Hannys had a hole in her leg, a head crease that took off a piece of her ear and cut a shallow groove in the bone, a wide burn on her left arm, the fur singed off, the skin barely broken, an insignificant wound that hurt worse than all the rest of them; Belligys, her Capture specialist, was equally battered and singed, but between them they managed to bring off the dead and the moribund and get them aboard Ilta's ship

##

In the Insplit:

The op Rizga was in the ottodoc on maintenance.

Hannys leaned against the cot and watched Ilta bandaging Belligys; she was feverish and exhausted and hurting.

Ilta looked up. "Both of you should have your heads examined. You ought to let me take you to Spotchals with Rizga."

Hannys flattened her ears against her head, but she was too tired to stay angry, besides Ilta was making sense. Just happened that good sense wasn't applicable to this mess. "No. You drop us off at *Hetohongya*, then get Rizga home." Her mouth twitched. "They'll patch us up so we can go get killed.

UNIVERSITY (Convergence continued)
Dropping back to organize the strike

1

Shadith and Arel
Aboard the *Matassa Ray* on route to University

Shadith looked up as Arel came into the cabin. Her smile went stiff, fell away. He was pale, the humor gone out of him.

"What is it? Something's wrong?"

"Nothing's wrong." He toed up a chair, dropped into it, sat staring past her shoulder.

Shadith shut the notebook on her stylo. "You look like your puppy died."

"We'll reach University tomorrow, 14 hundred ship, noon local." He went silent again.

"And you'll have your ship back, clear of pesty guests. Finally." She stretched across, touched the back of his hand. "This hasn't been an easy trip."

There was a flicker of laughter in his eyes. "Next time you ask me to ferry the infantry, I'll know to say no."

"What is it? Something's bothering you. Tell me."

"When we dump the kids, if you want, I'll go with you."

"What?"

Another flicker. "Hard enough to say once, Shadow."

"Sar! What bit you?"

He ran a long slender forefinger down the crease from his nose to his mouth. "Ego, I suppose. I want to look good in your eyes, luv." He dropped his hand onto his

282

thigh, rested it there, thumb moving across and across his fingertips. He looked supremely uncomfortable. "Hero, galloping to the rescue. You know."

She started to say *I've never found stupidity particu100larly sexy*, then realized what that would sound like to him—*I don't WANT you; I don't think you're man enough to make it in a flatout battle*—and bit down on her tongue before the first word got out. The problem was . . . the offer was generous, but it WAS stupid . . . she couldn't possibly say that to him . . . he was clever and fierce when he had to be, lethal, twisty as a magna-coil, honorable in his way . . . and she loved every slip-pery atom of the man . . . she'd never feel that way about someone like Rohant, she liked old Lion and got turned on by his fur and his strength, but love him? no . . . and she didn't want Arel anywhere near this fight . . . he'd get himself killed and maybe other people, too, trying to do what he wasn't suited to do.

He knew it, too. He wouldn't look at her and he was so tense if she pinched him, he'd bang his head on the ceiling.

Gods, what *do* I say?

"If you really want to . . . what the hell, it's your play, Ara . . . but I wish you wouldn't. I'll go into this a lot happier if I know you're out here, out of reach, back-up just in case . . . you and Lee. Ginny . . . you know what he is, Ara. He has to be stopped and there's no one else I'd trust."

"All right. Back-up it is, we'll save the hero for an-other day."

She watched him amble out, the tension gone.

If the rest of this could be that easy . . . if there was just some way we could do this thing without spending so much time getting there . . . winds the nerves up till you want to scream . . . a month to get here, another month to get over to the Karidion Worlds, gods know how long to Kouls-nakko's. . . .

She shook her head, opened the book, and went back to worrying over a line she was relatively sure she was going to junk in a few more revisions.

2

Pikka Machletta and the Razor T'gurtt
Aboard the *Matassa Ray*
Watching the world come closer

Pikka Machletta ignored Joran's cold glare and flicked on the screen in the aux control. She settled back in the chair and watched the world come swimming toward them, glancing occasionally at the rest of Razor.

As the world swelled to fill the screen, the enormity of what they'd done hit her; her stomach lurched and churned. She felt like throwing up, but she kept her face still and did what she could to swagger sitting down; it made her feel like she had a grip on things.

Fann was beside her, the side away from Joran. She and the catman got along like a hashshar and a kedsnake. She was cool, cool, real cool, she had her droop-eyed look that said *y' can't com ov-ah me.*

Mem was standing, too excited to swing one of the chairs around and sit. She vibrated with terror and delight; she'd gotten older in some indescribable way during this trip, older and exquisite, what had been a promise was now a bloom.

Kynsil and Hari sat on the floor, settled into small dark silences.

"Don' look all that different from Chissoku," Fann said. "Same colors."

Mem danced up behind Fann, set her hand on the back of the chair. "There are lots of differences, not nearly so much water, different shapes, different textures even. It really does look older, all its edges rounded off, remember what Shadow said, the hills worn down like a grasseater's teeth? I wonder what it smells like, what it sounds like? That'll be different, too. I can't wait, I wish we were already there."

"One good thing. . . ." Pikka smiled, her own fears pushed back by Mem's enthusiasm. "An't no Goyo."

3

University
Landing Field, a bright summer day
Waiting by the Field Stream for transport

Pikka Machletta stood on the stream bank understanding for the first time what the Singer had been trying to tell her.

This place was different. Strange. She didn't know anything here.

She felt helpless, uncertain, worse almost than the day her mother died and she was nine, alone in a small room at the sufferance of the concierge, the rent two weeks past due, nothing to eat, no one to take care of her.

The Field was a busy place, two more shuttles had landed and three had left within the few moments since Arel had decanted them from his. There were a lot more scattered about, being on and off loaded by ant trails of men and bots. There were no fences, only trees and shrubs and beyond them grassy rolling hills. She could see the roofs of a few structures, low rambling buildings fitting comfortably into the landscape, a profusion of plants, trees, flowers. And she was standing beside a stream with landscaped banks that actually cut across the field itself, a humpy wooden bridge a few steps off, looked like it belonged in someone's garden, not here. And beyond that, there was a glittering tower, an elegantly spiraling flitport.

There was a sense of leisure and spaciousness. A sense of time unfolding at a pace slower and richer than in other places. Different from the sort of individual leisure flaunted by the Goyo on Chissoku, very very different from the desperate search of the rest of the Bogmakkers as they tried to provide for the Winter years. She got the feeling that everyone was less driven here.

She looked at Mem. Her sister-in-T'gur was radiating delight. The world had a lighter pull to it, not much lighter, but enough to give Pikka a sense of floating and Mem's long legs seemed spelled to dance. Seven league legs for sure.

Fann touched her arm. "Someone's coming." She pointed.

Two jits were coming across the field from the flitport, one a half length behind the other. They were doing an odd sort of dance with invisible partners, turning, turning again, swinging wide in one direction, then wide in the opposite, going round places where shuttles were landing, round places where shuttles were about to land or would land five minutes later.

The jits pulled up beside the stream, there was a touch of white noise, then an announcement. "Return delayed twenty minutes."

##

A tall strong-featured woman whose clothes looked like they'd been thrown at her and stuck where they landed came laughing to the grassy streambank where they waited, her hands out, her long streaky hair blowing in the wind. "Shadow, look who I've brought."

A small white-haired sprite came waddling round her, waved at the Singer, then rolled on toward Razor. "Hallooo, I thought I knew you when they told me the name. Pikka, right? And, yes, Fann. And Ingra, I think. I don't know the others."

Bogmakker. For the first time since she left Karintepe. Bogmakker with a strong Old Town accent. Pikka's ears seemed to relax and there was a loosening of her whole head, no, of her whole body. Razor had to use trade Interlingue the whole of that interminable trip through nothing and she was weary to death of straining to listen.

Now when the Old Man spoke to her in her birth tongue, she almost cried.

"Well, now," he said. "I've fixed up housin for y'. Come along, come along. While we're waiting, I want to hear all about Karintepe, Aslan hints it's one whizzding of a story."

Pikka giggled, took his arm. "Soolee soola the story-teller say, spring was on the world and. . . ."

4

University
Landing Field
Still waiting

Shadith watched Pikka go bopping along, talking up a storm, exploding out of her leaden fear, watched as she climbed into the second jit and got her sisters-in-T'gurr settled around her. "I never thought about bringing Tsee-waxlin. Aslan, you're a genius."

"Of course. Didn't you know?" Aslan tugged Shadith to the other jit, stopped beside it and looked toward the Dyslaerors a few paces off.

Lissorn had piled out of the jit before it stopped and run to his father. He was a golden Dyslaeror, a dark gold, and in the bright summer sunlight, he shimmered and shone like a god. Rohant was Vulcan to his Apollo, harsher, rougher, the dourness of his days of killing still on him.

Rohant hugged his son and wept his joy at seeing him whole and well.

"Mother took one look at Lissorn and started salivating. Not that it did her any good."

"Adelaar's here?"

"I'd forgot you'd met her. Saved her life, she tells me." Aslan flushed, embarrassed. "Um . . . you do know about Mother, don't you? She's a good friend, but. . . ."

Shadith smiled. "But she'd ferret a profit through two meters of battle steel. She saw the pods?"

"Yes. Rohant," she called. "Lissorn. If you don't want to walk, get over here, we're going. Three minutes."

Shadith watched the Dyslaerors part and come toward them. "Does she know what they do?"

"No. Nobody can figure it out, even the crafters. They tell me they've tested the circuits and they work just fine, but what they'll do when they're powered, they haven't the least notion."

"Good."

"Cruel, Shadow, too too cruel." Aslan stepped into the jit, inspected the readouts. "Get in, the delay's almost over and we've got to catch the moment or wait god knows how long."

Shadith swung up beside her, shifted over so Kikun could fit himself in next to the slidedoor.

Aslan saw him, blinked. And remembered him from before. She shook her head. "I still don't believe it, dinhast. You do it in front of my own eyes and I don't believe it."

The jit rocked slightly as the Dyslaerors climbed into the back seat.

It was an old machine, lovingly maintained. The seats were a tightly woven canvas, the weaving an elaborate pattern, the worn places rewoven invisibly when they got too thin. The paint was handrubbed until it glowed. In places the metal was beginning to show through, but even those patches had a polished look. Things were built to last here and honor came from keeping them in service. This was a crafter's world as well as a magpie collection of knowledge, a world oriented to preservation, rather than consumption.

The delay over, the machine hummed up onto its effect-cushion and started its swervy dance across the Field.

Aslan shifted around so she could see Shadith's face. "How long will you be here this time?"

Shadith shook her head. "Don't know exactly. I'll have to see if the . . ." she grinned at Aslan, "the pods work the way they're supposed to. And Ro has to check his supplies, pick up any news from Spotchals. We go asap, I suppose. Maybe two weeks, maybe a month."

"Well, Lissorn's living on his ship, he said he'd take care of Rohant. I've arranged a guest suite for you. Forgot about Kikun. Your fault, dinhast. Does no one ever remember you except when they're looking straight at you?"

He chuckled, three throat-catches and a hiss. "No."

"Well, I'd hate to have your sex life, luv. Anyway, I'll

see what I can come up with, for now you'll stay with
Shadow, or I suppose Lissorn will take you in.''

Shadith dropped her hand on Kikun's arm. "Don't fuss,
Lan, he's certainly welcome to stay with me. If he wants
more privacy, he'll find a way. He always does. Tell me
about Adelaar, what's she after?''

"She saw the pods and, I'm afraid, managed a look at
your sketches. Mother's an artist in her way, she knows
her tech. And she doesn't need a detailed survey to tell
her she's seeing something new. Fair means or foul,
Shadow, she's going to know what you've got. I suppose
I should say I'm sorry. . . .''

"I know. You don't like what she's doing, but she's
your mother and you have this little touch of subversive
pride that says *go mama*. It'll work out all right, Lan.
What with this and that, I'm just about cleaned out. If
she likes what she sees, she can cover my expenses and
do us both a favor.''

"You going to tell me what those things are?''

"No. But you can come along and watch if you want.''

"If I want!''

5

University
Crafter's Loft, *Hoban and Sons*
Shadith, Hoban

The next week Shadith spent most of her days going
over the ten pods laid out in a row in the long assembly
shed. They were a dead black with a skin of crysarmor,
tougher than most metals but much lighter, grown from
seeds planted on honeycomb struts. They were elongated
eggs, two meters along the minor axis, nine meters along
the major; despite their size and the complexity of the
interior, they were light enough that two men could carry
them from place to place.

She went over them with test meters she'd built for
herself from components the crafters provided, making
minute adjustments in the electronics, growing more excited with each one she finished. It was hard to wait,

hard to do that finicking, exacting work when all the while she was remembering riding the lightwinds, remembering the wonder of it and having to choke off a growing need to say *forget this, it's good enough, let's fly, let's fly. . . .*

##

She finished the tenth and stood back, grinning like a fool.

Crafter Hoban stood beside her looking baffled. "Are you going to tell us what we've been building, Shadow? Or are you going to make us choke on our curiosity and maybe die of it?"

"Give me two more days, friend, and I won't tell you, I'll show you."

"What more's to do?"

She opened up the last of the pods, touched the smooth flooring of the interior. "I need a pad one side shaped to fit in here, the other shaped to my body, front and sides, exact fit but with some give to it, some elasticity, bodies alter every day. I'll leave materials up to you." She crossed to the work bench, dug into her shoulderbag and brought out the pages she'd worked over one last time last night. "These will have to be printed into the pad with surface sensors in intimate contact with the body of the flier."

"Ah. Flier."

She laughed. "You got it. Call it a Moth. Sun Moth. You'll see why. We can take a mold this afternoon, the sooner the better."

"Moth. I'll be thinking on that."

She slipped the strap over her shoulder, started walking for the door. "I'm sure you will. Bright winged moth spiraling to the sun, huh?"

6

Star 579-31-743, Versachio-Terria Catalog
Aboard Lissorn's *Cillasheg* for the first trial of the Sun
    Moth
Shadith, Rohant, Kikun
Lissorn and the Dyslaerors of his Capture Crew
Autumn Rose
Aslan and Adelaar
Hoban

''I call her *Farashonay* the Sun Moth. Hoban has a
glimmer of what that means and the rest of you will know
when you see her deployed.'' Shadith gazed the length
of the table, smiled at each in turn.

Lissorn at the head (it was, after all, his ship). His
father beside him on his right. Nezrakan, his Capture
Specialist, sitting at his left. Kinefray and Azram,
Nezrakan's apprentices, looking so alike she couldn't tell
them apart. Tolmant from Logistics, the oldest of the lot
with a frosting of gray in his mane, one of the dark Dyslaera, his bodyfur a deep brown-black. His apprentice
Tejnor, the youngest Dyslaeror present, little more than
a cub, but fiercely determined to be in this. Autumn Rose,
they said she was one of the tracer ops, a small woman,
wiry, radiating a barely suppressed anger. Aslan and
Adelaar sitting side by side, Adelaar seething under her
steely front. And Hoban.

''You've been patient with me, especially you, Rohant,
and you, Lissorn. I appreciate your trust.'' She sucked
in a breath and exploded it out. ''The waiting's done. At
least it will be, after today's test.''

She clasped her hands behind her. ''Rohant and Kikun
know what I'm talking about, the rest of you, listen hard
and believe what I say.

''Ginbiryol Seyirshi is waiting for us. He knows we'll
come. He set up his cut-outs, but he expects us to negate
them. He will have defenses and alarm systems about that
Hole, layer on layer of them. I doubt even you could get
through them, Adelaar. You should praise whatever gods
you own that you don't have to try. There is NO way we

can get near the Hole using conventional means. Nothing clever we can try. No disguises, no sleight of hand. The only people who will be allowed alive inside Teegah's Limit will be ships broadcasting the signature embedded in the pilot flakes they receive at the rendezvous. And getting one of those is almost as impossible as crossing the Limit.

"But . . ." She smiled. "Yes. I think—and may I emphasize *think*—I know how to get round all this. Due to circumstances I have no intention of detailing, I have access to a technology radically different from any available at present. I spent hours going through Library Files, trying to find anything remotely similar and could not. Our Luck, Ginny's loss. I believe in two things and only two. Luck and Chance. The rest is folly. Well, or hard work. And your intelligent application of what you know. With Luck that's enough, by Chance you win or lose. Win or lose. Ginny's a genius level double-knotter; he thinks round corners other people can't even see, but even he can't guard against something he doesn't know exists." Her audience was getting restive. Too many generalities, not enough detail.

Ah, well, the detail comes in the doing and you'd better get started doing, Shadow.

"Right. Lissorn, once the pod is deployed, use direct visuals, not the kepha-analogs, see what kind of detail you can get and for how long."

Lissorn leaned forward frowning. "Direct? You can't get any detail with direct. Nobody uses. . . ."

"Ginny just might. You can't tell with him, so I don't want to take unnecessary chances. And . . . ahhh . . . try me with every sort of probe you have, everything you can think of, get all the readings you can. I expect . . . well, hope might be a better word, you'll get zilch. I'm going to tack toward the sun, riding the lightwinds. Ah, yes, I see you begin to understand, wait till you see her with her wings spread, a full AU from tip to tip. We're beyond the Limit out here, but if she works properly it should only take about fifteen hours to reach the sun and less than that coming back. She gains speed faster than a dream, my darling, though I'll not feel it, that's part of her charm.''

Rohant combed his thumbclaw through his mustache. ''Thirty hours. That's a long ride flat on your face.''

''I've done this before, Old Lion. There's the time compression close to one light, remember. Besides, you lose all touch with time in there, it's like . . . it's an orgasm hours long, rising and falling in intensity, but . . . well, I'm not worried about being bored.''

''Dio!'' His face went red, but he refrained from comment. ''Should we be worried, then?''

''If I don't show up on visuals on schedule, yep.''

''There's no com in there.''

''No. I have an emergency beacon, sealed so it won't show up on searches, but nothing else. We're going to sneak up on them, remember?''

''On wings of fire an AU wide?''

''Absurd, isn't it.'' She grinned at him. ''It doesn't matter what shows if no one's out there looking.'' She turned to the others. ''Questions?''

Hoban tapped the table in front of him. ''The power source. The accumulators are so small. . . .''

''She feeds on what she rides; the accumulators are for spreading her wings, after that she maintains herself. She's never in a gravity well, you understand, and she's tiny, the sun's pull on her is more than balanced by the outward pressure of the lightwinds. She's a racer, a luxury, she has no purpose but flight.''

Adelaar tapped the table. ''Guidance systems?''

''That's . . . um . . . complicated to explain, but easy to do. User friendly. No harder than driving a groundcar without a program. And babies can do that, you know.''

''When we get back. . . .''

''Yes. We'll talk.''

Lissorn tapped the table. ''User friendly, you say. You had ten built. You mean to teach nine of us to fly them?''

''I had ten built to provide redundancy. If we can make nine fliers besides me, we will be ten. If there are fewer

who can do it, we'll take fewer. The physical requirements are very loose, the psychic requirements a bit more
stringent. The dark out there is huge and crushing and
you're trapped in a tiny space, with only a thin shell to
keep it out, with only a few chips and circuits and your
faltering brain to keep you from frying in the heart of a
sun or freezing to a corpsicle out between the stars. Some
thrive, some go catatonic, most are merely competent.
It's no shame if you can't fly a Sun Moth; we have different gifts, all of us. This is important. Be honest with
yourselves and with us, otherwise you'll put us all in
danger.''

"I see.''

"If there's nothing else, I'd like to get started.''

Lissorn looked around, then got to his feet. "Right.
Rose, take Aslan, Adelaar, Hoban, settle them in the
auxiliary com room. Apa, the Bridge is yours. The rest
of you sort yourselves out, you know where.''

7

Star 579-31-743, Versachio-Terria Catalog
The first trial of the lightsailer
Shadith, Kikun

The pod was on the launcher, a shadowy black seed
with a hole in its side.

Kikun had the checklist and was leaning into the flightspace, making sure everything she'd need was in there,
along with emergency supplies and a spare recycler. His
voice came to her in a pleasant drone as she stripped and
stowed her clothing in a flightbag. ". . . can of sealant,
emergency suit, water bottles, catheter saddle, waste
pacs, stimtab feeder, extra tab pac, hipropaste, extra
tubes.'' He pulled his head out. "All there, patched
down, ready to hand.''

She tossed him the flightbag. "Patch this down, then
help me get settled.''

After he tucked the bag into the flightspace, he climbed
down, drew his hand along the smooth black surface.
"On wings of light,'' he murmured, "dance well,

Shadow." He gave his throat-catch chuckle. "A wish from the depths of my being and purely selfish. I want to dance this dance and soon."

She barely heard him and didn't take in the sense of his words until much later, when she had time to remember. She crawled into the flightspace, stretched out on the pad and eased herself into its hollows, fitting her skin against the sensors, settling herself about the saddle. "I'm in. Check me, will you?"

His dry, soft fingers touched here, there, the length of her body, then he pulled the sensiweb over her and clicked it down. He tapped her shoulder. "Luck ride with you, Shadow." He closed the hatch, closed her into a darkness thick and soft and waiting.

A moment later, an eternity later, she felt the hard sharp kick of the launcher and she was out.

7

Star 579-31-743, Versachio-Terria Catalog
Flying *Farashonay*
Her vision cleared. She could see the *Cillasheg* floating half a kilometer away, could see all round herself. The system had no planets, only a Belt with gravel-sized pellets of stone and ice, a few scattered rocks big enough to qualify as asteroids. She shifted her vision out and out until she could see the gravel, frost in the darkness, white and black glitter in the light of the dim, distant sun, shifted down again until her vision was confined to an area the width of her wings at full deployment.

Cautiously she moved her fingers and spread her wings—only a little, enough to give her some way—then she began testing her memory and the machine.

She dipped and turned, yawed and rolled until she had the feel of the Sun Moth printed in her body.

It seemed heavier, somewhat less responsive than she remembered, but memory was like that, gilding pleasures, making them more than they ever were.

All right, Shadow, let's go for it.

She snapped the wings out full, gossamer fields like shadows in glass. The lightwinds filled them, pushed her outward. She let it happen, gathering speed for the turn, feeling *Farashonay* come alive under her as she drank the winds and rode them out and out. They were one, she and *Farashonay*, the wings were her arms, her hands, enormously enlarged, enormously sensitive, her finger-tips reading the lightwinds, her body the balance, the rudder. She laughed and groaned, making love to the winds, laughed again and swung round, tilting her wings, slipping the winds, tacking right, tacking left, sweeping toward the sun, on and on, faster and faster, time com-pressing to nothing, she was huge as the universe, her blood was wine, her body sang, on and on until the sun's heat began to intrude. . . .

She whipped round the sun, went racing back, faster and faster. . . .

The *Cillasheg* was a dark seed caught in her wings, she remembered and reluctantly brought *Farashonay* curving round, using the wind pressure to slow her, fold-ing her wings, the old skills back as if no time at all had passed, as if she wore her first body and was racing her first race.

She brought *Farashonay* to a gentle stop, nudging against *Cillasheg's* flank.

Tractor beams touched her carefully, brought her into the cargo lock, deposited her on the launcher.

She drifted in utter darkness, pleasantly depleted. As she'd told Rohant, it was like hour on hour of great sex, and when you were finished, though she hadn't told him this, you were a rag.

There was a tapping on the shell.

She blinked, tripped the inner lock so Kikun could open the hatch.

He unclicked the web and eased her free, helped her out of the pod.

Her legs were rubber, no strength in them.

"That good, was it?"

"I'm still a little drunk with it."

"Stretch out here, Shadow. They can wait." He helped

her down onto a pad, brought a bucket of warm soapy water and a sponge, washed her with the affectionate detachment of a man tending a prized racehorse. "It truly went well?"

"More than well. I'd forgotten the glory of it. I thought I remembered, but I hadn't."

"A wonderful way to begin a fight, with legs like damp noodles." He fetched the flightbag, helped her to her feet.

"Into each life some rain." She stretched, shook herself, then began pulling on her trousers. "It won't be this bad—well, good—when we go for the Hole. Half the distance and a different mindset."

"When do we begin training?"

"You really do want this, don't you."

"Very very much, Shadow."

"Right now it's back to University, we have to fit the pads to the pilots and the pods and test for claustrophobia and the rest of that. You're not claustrophobic, are you? Good." She smoothed her hands down the sides of her tunic, wiggled her feet in her boots. "Let's go see what the readings say."

FINAL PREPARATIONS
University

1

Shadith, Adelaar

"I can't deal with this, not now."

"Why not? You're here until your pupils are ready to solo. Why should we lose this opportunity?"

Shadith laughed, though she was too tired to be much amused. "Can't suborn the crafters, huh?"

"Haven't tried. Not ethics, practicality. Alien tech is a slippery thing."

"If you want the truth, Adelaar, I'm not up to dealing with you. My mind's on Ginny and coping with him. Tell you what. I won't talk now, but after this is over, we'll get together and see what terms we can agree on."

"If you come back."

Shadith closed her eyes. "There is that. Right. Why not. Listen. You pay my expenses on this and I'll leave a release with *Hoban and Sons;* if I'm not back in five years, they're to give you all my notes and their schematics. And I'll escrow an explanation of field structure and the principles behind the tech, the mathematics, everything, with instructions to hand over to you at the end of the same period unless I collect the material myself. My terms for this last. You'll control forty percent, the remaining sixty will be divided like this, twenty-five to Aleytys of Wolff, twenty-five to Swardheld Quale of Telffer, ten to Vejtar Arel y Kleftis, based out of the ship *Matassa Ray.* ONLY if I don't survive this mess. If I do, we can go round a few times, work out something." She grinned at Adelaar. "If I still have something to sell. Tech's slippery in a lot of ways. You'll be busier than . . . what cliché do I want, huh? . . . than a four-armed paper hanger, trying to duplicate what you saw done. Right?"

"Right." Adelaar relaxed, radiated contentment. She was so satisfied with the deal it made Shadith very nervous. "When do you want to draw up the papers?"

"Tomorrow morning. Before we leave for 579 again."

Adelaar raised her brows. "I want the Arbiter to see what you're escrowing, so perhaps we should wait till you're ready?"

"I have the material completed, I passed the time on the trip from Chissoku getting it ready. No no, I didn't know you were here, Adelaar, I was going to leave the papers for Aleytys."

"Tomorrow, then, nine by the clock, at the Arbiter's Office in the Library."

"Right."

2

Shadith, Kikun
Guestroom

Something was after her. She was sweating. Terror shook her, she was sick with it. Ginny was sitting, looking at her, saying something, she couldn't hear the words, his voice was bland and flat, his mouth moving endlessly. She looked down at herself. She was flaking away, her clothing, her flesh, hair, everything was peeling off the bone in small brown flakes. She saw the whiteness of the bone, she felt herself peeling loose with her flesh, she saw herself snuffed out, nothing left, nothing there, nothing . . . there, nothing . . . nothing. . . .

She woke sweating, sick, every part of her shaking, she thought even her cells were vibrating. This was the third night she'd dreamed, each time she came back from a training trip. Flying the Sun Moth she was fine; back here, haunted. She knew why.

It had shaken her considerably, authorizing that escrow. It was an admission she could die in this business.

She'd told Arel to see she was avenged if she didn't come back, but she didn't really believe that would happen, she just wanted to keep him out of trouble.

When she imprinted that document and registered it, she looked death in the face and was terrified.

Twenty thousand years. She'd thought she was tired of living and uncertain about how hard she'd fight to continue her existence, but life had suddenly become terribly dear and so so fragile.

She sat with the covers huddled about her, her knees drawn up, her arms hugged across her breasts. She was trembling, gasping for breath.

Light flashed across her, the door, opening. Kikun came in. "Shadow, what's wrong?"

She tried to say something, but she couldn't; her teeth were chattering, her throat so tight she couldn't get a croak out.

He stood in the doorway, a spindly black form that could have been something from her nightmares, but wasn't, there was too much warmth and affection radiating from him. "Ahhhh," he breathed. "I see. You imprinted escrow and your body has realized at last that it could cease. . . ."

He came onto the bed and sat beside her, drew her against him, held her, caressed her and made love to her spirit, though not to her body. He wasn't interested in her body, didn't care what it felt or needed; it took a complex of smells and textures she couldn't provide to awaken those sensitivities in him. Yet love her he did, in his way. And he brought her back from the terror that had nearly kicked her loose from this body.

##

She withdrew the trays from the delivery slot, carried them into the garden and set them on the table. She patted a huge, aching yawn and collapsed in the wicker chair. "I owe you a big one, Kikun."

He filled a cup with tea, passed it across to her. "Take me sailing, that'll more than pay any debt. Not that there is one. No debts between friends."

She sipped at the tea, sighed with pleasure. "Friends. Oh, yes." She listened to the birds sing, a curious assortment from half a dozen worlds flittering about the trees and shrubs in the common green at the back of the guest houses, trees and shrubs that also came from a hundred different ecologies, melding into an odd harmony on this eclectic world. The shadow of the nightmare still hung over her; it touched everything about her, even infected the air. Colors were darker, richer, like they were when clouds still hung heavy after a rainstorm, the air had an electricty as it touched her skin. She watched Kikun sipping at his tea and smiled; an aura like heatshimmer clung to his outline. She wondered if he saw one vibrating about her. They were both very very alive and rejoicing in it. She reached out, closed her hand over his, squeezed. "I went to see Hoban after I left Adelaar, ordered a new Sun Moth. For after this. It's yours." She lifted her cup in tribute. "For the best sundiver there ever was or will be."

The Dyslaera were very good sundivers, their intuitive grasp of distance/duration the key—and not a single one had any difficulty with the dark; they were predators in those pods, fiercely competitive.

Kikun wasn't good. Kikun was perfection. He was born to sail the Sun Moths. His peculiar connections with otherness were part of it, his quickness and sensitivity. It was more than skill, it was a calling. Clowndancer god reborn to flesh, with his fingers twined in the fabric of the universe.

He closed his eyes. She could feel him tremble, his joy exploded in her and for a moment neither moved.

Then Kikun coughed and took a bite of toast. "We can polish Kinefray and Azram this trip if we both work. Tolman and Tejnor the one after. And leave for the Karidion Worlds before the end of next week."

Shadith combed her hands through her hair, winced at

the tangles. "Well, maybe. Azram needs a kick in the ass. He keeps thinking he knows it all."

"Set us in a race."

"Hah!" She crunched down on a slice of bacon as if she bit into the young Dyslaeror. "Don't humiliate him too badly, Kuna, just a little."

"Just a little."

"By the way, how's your meadow coming?"

"Thriving. Come see. The grass is a cm longer and the juniper perfumes the hold."

"You talk to it, don't you."

"Of course. The hold is a cold and alien place for plants, I have to make them comfortable there."

"Hmm." She sipped at the lukewarm tea, grimaced, pushed her cup over for a refill. "You ready for your run?"

"Oh, yes. And you?"

"I don't know. I think we'd better practice in place . . . if it won't hurt the meadow."

"Be good for it, set the song into the earth and the grass and the juniper. Help me later when I run for real."

"Let's do it this afternoon, on the way over to 579. If a ship happens to be leaving around the same time, you can track it a while." She patted a yawn and reached for another piece of toast. "Three weeks and it's over, one way or another."

"I can't read that road, Shadow." He was answering the question she was afraid to ask. "Gaagi won't play this time."

"That bad?"

"Oh, no. Sometimes he doesn't feel like talking. Means nothing."

She shivered. "I hope."

ACTIVITY ON THE OTHER SIDE
Koulsnakko's Hole
Ginbiryol Seyirshi
Onero Betalli

1

A tall, stooped figure in a fullbody filter, heavy robes and gloves, Onero Betalli stood in the shadow at the edge of the room, watching a horde of droids and bots laboring to create the glow of rich but subdued elegance the bidders were most comfortable with. The suites were already finished and the individuals on the Prime List were starting to arrive.

Ginbiryol Seyirshi sat in a heavy swivel chair in a pulput at the front of the room, raised high above the action, there to make sure the effect was what he wanted.

Betalli stirred finally, made his way to the pulput, rode the lift up to the pit at the top.

Seyirshi swung round to face him. "Well?"

"A report from University. The girl Shadith hired the crafters *Hoban and Sons* to build something. My agent can't discover more about it, he was warned off by crafter security when he pressed too hard. He did manage to get a look at the finished product. Black pods, two meters wide by nine long, light enough to be lifted by two men. Ten of them. The last note in the report said one of the pods was being loaded into a Dyslaer Capture ship, the *Cillasheg*, the Captain and Capture Chief, one Lyssorn, eldest scion of the Toerfeles and Ciocan of Voallts Korlatch. Destination unknown as of now."

"Ten pods. Ten infiltrators." Seyirshi sat with his hands clasped, brooding. "Those are for the attack on

303

the Hole. How, Betalli, how is she going to trace a ship through the insplit without warning us?''

"Not possible.''

"I know it is not possible. But she will do it. Somehow she will. . . .'' He tapped open his com. "Ajeri, rat this to Harmau. Sweep each ship that comes through for lice, make sure there are no tracerbugs attached anywhere, inside or out.''

Ajeri's voice came to Betalli as an insect whine, barely audible above the noise of construction. "Better be ready to soothe the clients when they get here. You know them, they won't like the delay.''

"They can soothe themselves or go home. I want the message off within the half hour.''

"You got it, Ginny.''

Seyirshi contemplated the dark plate a moment, turned to Betalli. "That is the only possible entry I can think of unless the name change has got out. Have you heard anything about that?''

"No. Not a smell. I heard Koulsnakko's repeated several places, no one questioning the name.''

"Hmm.'' He tapped an irritable rhythm on the chair arms. "She will find a way. Oh, yes, she will find a way. We must be ready to receive her.''

Betalli bowed his head, unwilling to comment on Seyirshi's obsession. All this was nonsense, but saying so was unpolitic. "I had better check with the Pilot. Perhaps more information has come in.''

Seyirshi stared full at him for a moment, that deep-cutting look he got sometimes—then he went back to inspecting the work going on below.

Betalli felt sweat popping out on his face, felt the faint vibration as the body filter labored to absorb the moisture. Afraid suddenly and furious at himself and Seyirshi because of that fear, he stepped onto the lift and let it take him back to the floor.

2

The Pilot looked up as Betalli came onto the Bridge. "Two more rats have come in. Just."

"Have you opened them?"

"They're being peeled right now. The contents will be in the safe . . ." a gesture at the readouts at the station, "within a minute, fumed and ready in another minute. Shall I bring them through here or in your quarters?"

"My quarters. I'm going to bathe and change. I think it would be wise to place the kephalos on alert and go into defense mode. Seyirshi is developing suspicions of us."

"Any reason?"

"None that I can see. It has to be instinct; the man has a remarkable nose for trouble. Fortunately he's so obsessed with that girl he isn't paying full attention to his twitches. Otherwise I could be dead by now."

"Will you be going back there?"

"I have to. You know that. Besides, I don't think Seyirshi will act on his feelings until after the Auction is done. And that will be too late."

3

He pulled a pair of flimsys onto his hands, took up the reports, and began to read.

From University:

. . . *Cillasheg* back in parking orbit . . . air of extreme excitement about the crew and passengers . . . Adelaar aici Arash of Adelaris Securities was on board . . . no more information about he pods, except that they seem to be the source of the excitement . . . *Cillasheg* left again . . . gone three days . . . pattern, ship in for one day, two at most, out three . . . continued for three weeks . . . aici Arash on first two flights . . . went with the girl you're interested in to the Arbiter's Office and registered a contract . . . contract under seal for five years . . . no chance of getting a look at it or the material sealed with it . . . aici Arash departed after that, presumably for ho-

meworld, Droom in the Hegger Combine . . . *Cillasheg*
gone again yesterday . . . all pods loaded aboard . . .
gave up parking slot, paid bill . . . destination unknown. . . .

From Louat 4:

. . . on *Myndig*, *Herka Bidj*, *Strazha Uho* and here,
the Voallts teams have broken off surveillance or attack
and have left the scene . . . destination unknown . . .
have checked with University and Spotchals, none of
these teams or others have surfaced there, no contact in-
sofar as can be determined. . . .

From Spotchals:

. . . compound sealed, no contact Capture ships or
search teams. . . .

Betalli read through the reports once again, scowling.
"If I were as obsessed as Seyirshi," he said aloud, "I
would suspect they know how to find us and were coming
for us." He thumbed the com sensor; the pilot's etiolated
face filled the screen. "I'm faxing copies of the reports
to the Bridge; read them yourself, have them droid-
delivered directly to Seyirshi, he should still be in the
Auction Room."

"Bad news?"

"It could be interpreted as such. Wait half an hour
before you send the droid. Seyirshi might call here, tell
him I am meditating over the meaning of the reports and
will speak to him later."

4

Bernie's Hole (renamed for the occasion *Koulsnakko's*)
was a collection of hulks connected by flexible tubes in
shrouds woven from Menaviddan monofilament; the heart
of the collection was an ancient gutted worldship with its
engines gone but its gravity webs intact and operating at
full capacity, powered by collector arrays aimed at the
sun. Onero Betalli stepped into the repairways between
the worldship's inner and outer skins, moved quickly
along the catwalks until he reached the section where the

guest suites were. He counted the back panels, found the suite he wanted and touched a tronkey to the access plate.

The man waiting for him was tall and broad, dressed in a robe with a heavy cowl that hid his face, his only ornament a spiral of silver wire on an onyx ground. ''The suite is sealed to us,'' he said. His voice was deep, the slight vibration on the sibilants the only clue to the degree of distortion programmed into the privacy shield.

''Very good. I've brought copies of the reports, I thought you'd like to see them. It seems there is a possibility of a very interesting capture. . . .''

FINAL PREPARATIONS 2
The Karidion Cluster

1

Karidion was a small compact star cluster, six stars less than a light-year apart, same age, same size, as if products of some primeval stellar mitosis. Among them they had a score of planets with seven at least marginally habitable.

One of these had a name: *Hetohongya.*

It was a world with sweeping winds and purple storms, saturated browns and oranges, strong dark colors, tree analogs were low and twisty with maroon and purple foliage, the grass analog was succulent and bladed, with vertical stripes of crimson and ocher. Herds of six-legged ruminants grazed on the crimson grass; bird analogs like feathered gasbladders drifted about them.

The only settlements were mining towns in mountain ranges like rotten teeth; the largest of these, called *Teyohdiac*, was thrown up on the edge of an alluvial plain, a landing field beside it.

On the day the *Cillasheg* arrived there were twelve landers grouped in a small cluster in the center of the field.

2

It was a proscenium stage with dusty worn curtains framing the front, curtains that looked like they'd been compressed from the dust outside and smelled worse.

Shadith stood half behind the folds on the left side inspecting the audience gathered in the hard wooden seats.

"Fifteen, sixteen," she murmured, "Twenty, twenty-three, twenty-nine, thirty-four Dyslaera. One, two, five, seven, ten, no, eleven ops. Tough looking lot, huh, Kikun?" She shivered. "It stinks of rage in here."

"Leave them to Rohant, they're mostly his people; he knows how to handle them."

"He is looking better, isn't he?"

"Much better. Now that he has a legitimate target for his claws."

##

Rohant carried a chair to the center of the stage, plunked it down and sat on it, leaning forward, his hands on his knees. "We've got the name of the Hole where the Auction will be. *Koulsnakko's.* Anyone know that one? Zarovan, you were working on the merc line."

"New one on me, Roha. We were 'ticing a merc when we got the call to break off; didn't want to waste him so we brought him along." Zarovan swiveled round. "Sugnorn, go put the question to the little man, come back soon's you got some kind of answer." He produced a ferociously amiable grin at his crewman's snort.

"Anyone else? No? Right. What we figure, Seyirshi got wind of us looking for him, set up a cut-out. There's a rendezvous three days from here, Laybogby's Star. The bidders are showing up there and getting pilot flakes to take them on to Koulsnakko's. If Zarovan's merc doesn't come up with coordinates, Cillasheg is going to sit out there well beyond the Limit, waiting for a bidder to show up. When he's got his flake and drops into the insplit again, we drop behind him and track him to the Hole.

Siddown and stop smirking, Tasylyn. I know it's supposed to be impossible, I know if we get close enough to read him, he reads us and drops a mine on us or goes evasive and leaves us nose to nothing. But the folks who say all that have never met a dinhast called Kikun. Here's what we want from you. We need crews for the Cillasheg Landers once we reach the Hole area. I'll let Lissorn handle that, it's his ship. Questions?"

Zarovan cleared his throat. "Why?"

"Because him and half his Capture Crew are on the hit team, so they won't be around."

There was an instant mutiny, angry questions thrown at him from all sides.

He roared them to silence. When they were simmering but relatively calm, he said, "Any of you would-be volunteers know how to fly a Sun Moth?"

Hannys got to her feet. "What the hell's a Sun Moth and what's it got to do with hitting Ginny?"

"Get to that in a minute. Any of you gamebirds know how to get at a defended Hole without losing your tailfeathers or a lot more? If you think you do, give us a shot at it. He waited. There was some muttering, then silence. "Right. Shadow, get out here."

Shadith grimaced but left the shelter of the curtains and went to stand beside Rohant.

"A few things I want straight. I know what she looks like. Forget that. She's got more Talents in her left toe than most of you got in your whole body. She's tough and she's tricky, I owe her my life so many times over I stopped counting. And she's given us the way in. The Sun Moths. Transport that's so close to undetectable it might as well be smoke. They're something else, Dio! We tested them and you just can't see the things except on visuals and even then you blink and they're gone. Ten of us. Me, Lissorn and his crewpeople, Autumn Rose, she's a tracer op, Shadith and Kikun, ten of us. We go in and drop Ginny or get dropped ourselves. Nothing fancy."

Zarovan unfolded and stood beside Hannys. "Seems like you've got this thing sewn up, so what are we doing here?"

"You all want a chance to get yourself killed, I'm going to give it to you. Once we've got into the Hole, things are going to get smelly. We have to find Ginny before we can rip his throat out. We need time. Any of you want to volunteer, you can buy us that time by roaring in as if you were bent on attacking the Hole. Watch out for mines, try not to get killed, don't go all that far, just get their attention for an hour or so.''

Hannys gave a shout of laughter, socked her fists onto her hips. ''Juicy bit you saved for us, Roha. And here we were complaining you shut us out.''

''Dio, Hannys, when I thought distraction, I thought of you.''

Tasylyn crossed her legs at the ankles, clasped her hands behind her head. The ottodoc had healed her ear, but the tip was gone, replaced by a knot of keloid. ''Say some of us manage to survive this distraction, how long you want us to hang about?''

''Hmm. Give us twenty-four hours, if we haven't got out by then, you're on your own, do what you can.'' He got to his feet. ''Any more questions?''

AMBUSH
Laybogby's Star
The Cillasheg and the Capture Fleet

1

Twelve ships and the *Cillasheg* hovered on the edge of the *Anaso Sink*, in clear space but protected from discovery by the fringes of the Sink chaos wavering between them and *Laybogby's Star*. A ship cobben waiting. . . .

2

The dance meadow was a drum of grass and brush in the center of the hold, illuminated by plant lights like spots pinning the site, developing it out of the metallic darkness of the hold; the black seeds of the Sun Moths that were stacked in ranks about it were touched by the fringes of that light, a curve here, a blunt end there.

Shadith sat beside a potted juniper bush, a drum with slanted sides between her loosely crossed legs; she was surrounded by the smell of the juniper, damp earth, crushed grass, leaf mold, forest smells laid over the metal and grease and acrid electrical stench of the ship.

Kikun sat on the grass, facing her. His head was down, his eyes on his knees, his shoulders rounded. He was breathing slowly, not really there, wandering in *never-never* as he waited for his call.

Their support crew was gathered about them with the stim shots and water tubes liquid food they'd need once the tracking began.

They were all waiting.

An hour passed. Another.

Rohant's voice boomed through the hold. "Ship surfacing. We're moving out a little to get a better view."

The *Cillasheg* stirred, shifted, the sublight drone filled the hold.

Another hour. Shadith felt the tension in the hold like a membrane tightening about her body.

Rohant came on again: "Ship breaking from tie with stingship, going for the Limit. This is a real one. Four hours to drop."

3

"He's dropped. We're dropping . . . now. Over to you, Kikun."

##

Kikun lifted his head. "Start the beat, Shadow."

She smiled stiffly, her dark brown eyes like holes in her head; she was afraid again, but handling it. He wanted to reach out and take her hand, but this wasn't the time for that. She drew her fingers across the drum head, pulling a whisper from it, did it again, tapped it: whisper whisper, toom toom whisper whisper toom toom ta toom too toom. . . .

It sang in his blood. He felt her *reaching* for him, lifting him; he'd been ground for her when she sang, she was ground for him today, giving without thought of cost. He received her gift, loving her as sister, loving her as other, the third in the dinhast triad, loving her as herself. That, too, sang in his blood.

He sucked in a long breath, breathing the forest that was there in sign though not in size, gathered himself and let his spirit run free, spirit hound hunting the traces of the ship that had gone, howling as he ran, a resonant belling that filled his head.

He visualized a compass rose like a moving shadow sliding with him as he ran, his spirit paws touching down on the white smoke trail spewing from the ship ahead. It

smelled acrid, dark, smoky, like electrical insulation
burning. A good strong smell. He liked it.

The rose rocked and yawed, then steadied.

He put his nose down, sniffed at it. The numbers came
into him as hound and out again, threads of white smoke
streaming behind him until they reached into the hold
and Kikun-there breathed them in and spat them out for
the recorders of those who listened . . . then he was running again, his ghost body stretching, glorying in the
play of muscle, the sense that he was bounding through
eternity, biting off a century with each stride . . . or
something like that.

The drum was the beat of his feet, the pulse of his
heart.

Shadow steadied him, warmed him, poured strength
into him.

He ran and ran, the ship always ahead of him, never
pulling away. . . .

Time passed. Hours uncounted.

Kikun-there's mouth went dry, his body flagged.

The tending crew popped a stimtab into a vein, sprayed
water over his body, gave him sips from the water tube,
the food tube, fruit juice to take the taste away, more
water.

The beat changed, slowed for several minutes, then
picked up again. It was the agreed-on signal. The first
day was gone.

The second day was like the first.

Keep me going, he'd told them. *And Shadow. Without
the drum I'm lost. Whatever it takes, however long you
have to keep on, do it. Don't worry about distracting me,
you won't. If I break off, I'm done, I can't pick up the
trail again. I don't know how long I can hold together,
but what will can do, I WILL do.*

The tending crew popped more stimtabs into him,
sprayed water over him, gave him sips from the water

tube, the food tube, fruit juice to take the taste away,
more water.

##

The third hour of the third day the ship ahead dogleg-
ged to the right; Kikun-hound howled a warning, summoned the rose, and ran.

He put his nose down, sniffed at the rose. The numbers
came into him as hound and out again, threads of white
smoke streaming behind him until they reached into the
hold and Kikun-there breathed them in and spat them out
for the recorders for those who listened . . . then he was
running again, his ghost body stretching, glorying in the
play of muscle . . . howling with pleasure and triumph
as her felt the *Cillasheg* shift and follow.

The drum was the beat of his feet, the pulse of his
heart.

Shadow steadied him, warmed him, poured strength
into him.

He ran and ran, the ship always ahead of him, never
pulling away. . . .

Time passed. Hours uncounted.

Kikun-there's mouth went dry, his body flagged.

The tending crew popped a stimtab into him, sprayed
water over his body, gave him water, food, fruit juice to
take the taste away, more water.

The beat changed, slowed for several minutes, then
picked up again. The third day was gone.

##

The fourth hour of the fourth day, the ship ahead dog-
legged to the right again; Kikun-hound howled a warning, summoned the rose a third time.

He put his nose down, sniffed at the rose. The numbers
came into him as hound and out again, threads of white
smoke streaming behind him until they reached into the
hold and Kikun-there breathed them in and spat them out
for the recorders of those who listened . . . then he was

running again his ghost body stretching, glorying in the play of muscle . . . howling with pleasure and triumph as he felt the *Cillasheg* shift and follow.

##

The fifth hour of the fifth day the ship ahead began slowing.

The hound slowed until he was walking, slowed again, fighting against the drive of the drum, for the first time fighting against the drum. He lifted his muzzle and howled his distress.

Slowing getting ready to surface stop stop stop. . . .

The words were threads of white smoke streaming behind him until they reached into the hold and Kikun-there breathed them in and spat them out for the recorders of those who listened. . . .

Shadow slowed slowed slowed the beat. . . .

Pulling him back, spirit hound dissolving, spirit into body . . . .

##

Autumn Rose held the water tube for him, sponged off his face, arms, hands, gave him a glass of fruit juice.

Young Tejnor took the drum from Shadith and began working on her hands; they were cramped and bruised, the skin almost completely abraded from her fingertips. He spread soothing lotion on them, worked the lotion in, pulled knitted silk gloves over them, then he held her cuddled against him, her head resting on his shoulder, helped her drink a glass of fruit juice, then gave her the water tube to suck on.

Rohant's voice filled the hold: "We did it, Kikun, Shadow. All of you we did it. There's a star out there and the ship is heading for a collection of hulks about one AU out from it. *Koulsnakko's Hole.* Ugly sucker. Come see. Come on, take a look at the end."

GOING AFTER GINNY

1

At the Limit

The Pilot Gyfallan looked around. "Visuals active."

Anyagyn the Szajes tapped a sensor and her voice sounded throughout her ship. "Anyone who wants a sight of the Sun Moths leaving, get to a screen now. Visitors are welcome on the Bridge. Five minutes."

Ship crew (everyone who could leave her post), Hannys and her Capture Crew, the ops aboard—they crowded onto the Bridge and stood in a ragged arc along the back wall, their eyes fixed on the screen.

##

Tiny black seeds came swimming away from the *Cillasheg*.

There was a soft flicker of light along the first pod's sides, then the wings sprang full, gossamer shimmers against the black of space. It swept outward, past the watching transports, lightwinds filling wings, waking them to glory; faster and faster the Moth fled the Sun, then it curved round and went swooping inward.

The second followed. The third. Five minutes apart the Moths sped inward, ten phantasms of shimmering glimmering light.

Five minutes. Ten. They were all gone, beyond the range of the visuals.

"Dio Misclaer!" Hannys slapped her hand against the

wall. "We get out of this, I want one of those. I don't care what it costs."

Anyagyn started breathing again with an explosive pop. "Yeh, damn. Whatever, it's worth it."

##

Thirteen ships hung beyond the Limit and everyone in them, Capture Crews and Ship Crews and Tracer Ops, yearned to be out there, racing through the dark.

The vision of the Moth Winged with Light struck beyond thought and feeling. Species didn't matter, or culture, or ways of thinking; the flight touched something fundamental in each of them, set them aching with desire.

When the Sun Moths had left the screens, they swore or were silent, then they got on with the grim business of war.

2

At the Hole

Shadith followed Kikun's Moth into the snarl of transport tubes joining a surreal assemblage of hulks to the worldship/mothership floating in the center of it all, a monstrous amalgam of metal and stone, roughly spherical, dead and dull.

Rohant came after her, then Lissorn and the others, black seeds with wings folded down to a faint fringe, moving slowly, so slowly through the interstices of the tangle.

Her pod touched down on rock, bounced, settled

I'm good, I am, theeee greatest. Except for Kikun and who's like him anyway?

Shadith shut the field down completely and slid the cover off the coldlight cells; for a moment even their dim bluish-white light made her eyes water and it was hard to focus now that she was deprived of the pod's augmentation. Moving with care she freed herself from the flight-pad and the catheter saddle. She'd never regretted being female, but there was no denying men had an advantage in situations like these. She tore open a packet of handi-wipers, cleaned and dried herself. As she wriggled into her tunic, trousers and boots, it became quickly and painfully evident that the human body had too many hinges, all of them bending the wrong way, but she managed despite the cramped quarters.

Airsuit next.

Tool belt. Crystal blade in its special sheath, steel knife, gluegun, belt pouch with the plastic sheeting, heavy-duty stunpistol, emergency kit, cherrybombs, smokers. . . .

Ready as you'll ever be, Shadow. Time is.

She lay still a moment, gathering herself. It hurt to abandon the Moth and it was harder than she'd expected to do what had to be done, but she couldn't leave *Farashonay* for this lot of crud to pick over and pull apart. She hit the delayed destruct, started the airbleed and when the light went green, she popped the hatch and crawled out.

3

At the Limit

The Voallts ships were transports, set up to haul all shapes, sizes and temperaments of exotic beasts, conservative in their fuel-use, but faster than most commercial vessels despite this. They were not warships. They had no armament. None. No missiles. No long-range beams; nothing that reached farther than a few ship-lengths. They could clear out a parking orbit with tractors and pressers, they could destroy intrusive dustclouds, but their only effective way to take out an attacker was ram the sucker.

Which was suicide unless the mass difference was overwhelmingly to their advantage.

Rohant their Ciocan expected them to hit and survive. They meant to do just that.

These were Capture Crews—and Tracer Ops—with long experience of surviving against odds on hostile worlds.

They were improvisers, fast on their feet. Born guerillas, the tendency stamped deeper by hot experience.

They knew at the gut level that plans fall apart under the impact of reality.

They knew that glitches would arrive just when they were least able to handle problems.

They knew problems could be flipped into opportunities if they were clever and quick enough.

They were confident they'd be quick enough.

They waited.

4

At the Hole

Azram was the last to land; he came down hard, bounced and rolled into a crack that blocked the hatch on his pod. Kinefray and Tejnar bounded over to him, worked the pod loose and got it properly settled.

He emerged, embarrassed, holding himself like a kitten who'd just knocked a lamp off a table in the next room and was pretending it hadn't happened.

Shadith chuckled, shook her head. She waved at the nearest tube, started toward it, moving with extra care because there was almost no gravity beyond a worldship's skin, the web focused the weight inside.

The tube came up and over, plunging in a nearly vertical line into the stone.

She took and incautious step, bumped into it, rebounded and nearly went flying off. Rohant snagged her as she tumbled in slow motion past him, put her on her feet again.

Sheeh! Wonder if klutziness is catching, maybe somebody ought to innoculate Azram before he infects us all.

Eerie silence. Been a while since she'd been out like this and she'd forgotten how still it was.

Well, Shadow, let's get this plot moving.

She snapped loose the lockstrap, eased the Jaje brain-crystal blade from its sheath, swore vehemently as Azram came bounding up, wanting to see it closer. Braincrystal was rarer than brains in his head, or so it seemed.

Hastily she turned her shoulder to him, holding the knife away from her, trying to fend him off with her body. The idiot! Didn't he know what that edge would do to her or him if it just barely brushed them?

He didn't seem to have a pause-button; what he thought of, he did.

Nezrakan snagged his apprentice as he went unsteadily past, jerked him up and back before he blundered into Shadith, then spent the next several minutes helmet to helmet with him, putting the blight on the young Dysla-eror's enthusiasm.

Shadith started breathing again. She tapped Rohant's arm, pointed to the tube, flattened her free hand, jerked it up.

He nodded, jammed his boot toes into cracks, got himself set and lifted her, setting her feet on his thighs, holding her steady, his big hands round her waist.

She reached as high as he could, set the edge against a strand of monofilament and applied a faint pressure. The knife skimmed down, cutting away the weave as if it were cobweb instead of one of the toughest known natural substances.

When the cut was as low as she could reach, she stopped the blade, waited.

Rohant eased her feet to the ground, squatted with her so she could finish. When she got all the way down, she changed direction and sliced away the web along the lower edge of the tube, leaning recklessly out, trusting him to keep her solid.

##

When she finished the cutting, she'd cleared a section
a meter wide and two high.

She tried the knife on the tube itself, breathed a sigh
of relief as the edge sank slowly into the dense plastic.

*Good. Takes muscle and time, but there's no noise.
Nothing to joggle a sensor and say there's rats in
the walls.*

Moving with care she sheathed the knife, slapped Rohant on the arm, touched the worklamp on his belt.

He set her down, then he and Lissorn turned their
worklamps on the tube, two overlapping circles of yellow-
white added to the faint blue-white light coming from
inside.

Shadith frowned. Unless the Holeboss was being extra
sneaky, all the transmitter fibers were gathered in a wide
belt running along one section of the tube, just beyond
the edge of the workspace she'd finished clearing.

Avoid that bit for sure. Right. Here, I think. Yes.

She slapped self-sticking brackets for Rohant's hands
and feet about the line she'd chosen, then she felt along
her tool belt until she found the pouch, tore its flap free
from the clingstrip, brought out the plastic film she'd
scrounged after she'd got a look at the monster they were
about to attack. Emergency mending film, tough, resil-
ient, probably close kin to the tube stuff. Voallts Capture
ships carried large supplies of this infinitely versatile material.

She looked around, beckoned to Autumn Rose and
Kikun.

While they were unfolding the sheet, passing it over
Rohant and Lissorn and the rest, she took the gluegun
and began squeezing a double line of time-set glue about
three sides of the clear space.

When she was finished, she and Autumn Rose began

pressing the edges of the plastic square against the glue,
pleating them to fit them in, going round and round,
pushing the plastic down when it threatened to come
loose, holding it in place until the time ran out and the
glue set with a faint shudder that shook the film under
their fingers.

Shadith tapped Autumn Rose's arm. The op nodded
and went to herd the others into place as Kikun and young
Tejnar began tugging the free edge toward the tube.

It was an awkward business in the trace gravity, Dyslaerors toppling over, bumping into each other, elbows
in faceplates, feet where heads should be, Rohant and
Lissorn falling away, almost losing their lights, the circles of the beams dancing like fireflies here, there, all
over the crumpled plastic sheet. All of it in silence, an
eerie, surreal scene which Shadith watched with growing
exasperation.

Kikun and his helper got the edge to her before the
time ran out on the new section of glue, helped her pleat
and press it down and complete the bubble.

She went round the ragged circumference one last time,
laid down more glue to make sure the seal was continu-
ous, then clipped the gun to her belt and waited until she
saw the shudder that meant the glue was set, the bubble
was made and tight.

Watch your ass, Ginny, we're coming for you.

Rohant squeezed her shoulder, pushed his feet into one
set of brackets, arched his body and closed his gloved
hands about the others.

With Tolmant and Nezrakan to steady him, Lissorn settled onto his knees and shone his light past his father's
body at the section of tube where Shadith would be working.

Azram and Kinefray cracked spare oxypacs they'd
brought from their pods and began bleeding air into the
bubble.

Sweating in her airsuit, Shadith crawled into the cradle
the Dyslaeror had made for her, wrapped her legs about

one of his, grabbed at his arm with her free hand; he was
rock-solid, his mass comforting. Using his body to steady
her, she took the crystal knife from its sheath and set its
edge against the tube.

The blade began a slow slow bite into the slick greasy
plastic. She started breathing again, then increased the
pressure infinitesimally. The knife sank in and in, up to
the hilt.

She loosed the hilt, worked her fingers, did some
breathing exercises, rested against Rohant for a moment,
taking strength from him. His mind was a rock, too; his
determination bled into her. She gathered herself, began
pushing the treacherous cranky blade up and away from
them, aware always of Rohant's hands and arms up there,
in danger if she lost her concentration and let the knife
get away from her.

When she was finished with the cuts, she had a slot 80
centimeters long by 30 wide.

A letter drop of sorts—and the mail to go through it
was them.

Account Due letters addressed to Ginny Seyirshi, with
collection agents included.

5

Autumn Rose wriggled through, forced her feet down
until they touched the clingstrip. Her mocs sticking and
ripping clear with a sound like tearing paper, she moved
aside and shucked the backpack that had made life difficult from the moment she left the pad. It was her idea all
right, but she didn't think it was fair making her carry
all the robes; Lissorn had laughed at her, Shadow
shrugged and Kikun giggled. Nice they were all having
such a great time. She undid her toolbelt, peeled off the
airsuit, tossed it aside, clicked the belt back on.

Azram was wriggling through the slot; the other Dyslaera were standing around, stripping off the airsuits and

tossing them back into the bubble, slapping their tool-belts on again. She looked down at her suit. "Hey, Lissorn, toss this for me." She kicked it into a slow-motion arc, then knelt on the clingstrip and ripped open the packflap. It was good to talk again.

Her own disguise was the one on top. She left the others and got to her feet, pulled the robe over her head.

##

University, three weeks past

Getting Dyslaeror unrecognized through the corridors of a Clandestine was a problem they'd kicked around and around while they waited for the training to end. Then Autumn Rose had a notion.

"Look," she said. "Digby picked up rumors Betalli has a tie to the Omphalos Institute. Rumors. Passed around. So lots of people have heard them. If a clot of initiates turns up where he is, who's to know they aren't real? It isn't as if we'd be trying to fool HIM; just get at him. Any of you ever seen an initiate?"

Aslan nodded, surprising her. "I knew one once, he's dead now. Very strange man. So?"

"You remember his robe and that cowl?"

"We were prisoners at the time. No robe, no cowl, just an ordinary shirt and trousers."

"You're a big help. Anyway, USUALLY when they're out and around, the initiates wear this heavy black robe lined with barrier cloth, gloves to hide their hands and a cowl with a privacy shield. What I mean, if we prance around the place in those cowls and the robes and the gloves—wallah! no Dyslaerors, just a bunch of lowly scrubs from Omphalos out to see the sights."

##

At the Hole

Shadow glued a strip of plastic over the slot; it wasn't an invisible mend, but it was a lot less conspicuous than a gaping hole would be to anyone passing along the tube. She frowned at the gluegun, shrugged and clipped it back to her belt, then let the Ciocan help her on with her robe and cowl.

Autumn Rose inspected the dark forms with emptiness where their faces should have been. ''We're an ugly lot of nerks, enough to scare the shit out of any one who comes cross us not expecting the boogeyman in his face.''

Shadow sighed. ''Let's hope they all think that and leave us alone. Turn on your field, Rose. Time's passing.'' She pushed a glove down, checked her chron. ''We've got about twenty minutes before our pods and our friends do their thing and we'd better be well in before then.''

6

Kikun touched the lock sensor and the barrier slid open without a hesitation, no sound, no nothing, not even a question about who they were.

Shadow put her hand on his arm, then signed something. Autumn Rose couldn't read it, but she didn't really have to.

No alarm. That's alarming. She groaned within at the feeble pun.

The little dinhast raised his hand, forefinger touched thumb, a universal all-go sign, at least among those beings with multiple digits.

Definitely alarming. Why none?

Kikun shook his head, the cowl exaggerating the motion, then he went striding in, head held as high as it got.

They say he knows what he's doing. I hope they've got it straight, good ol' they.

7

At the Limit
     At the appointed time, thirteen transports hit the Limit
as nearly simultaneously as Dyslaer reflexes would allow.
     Hit and vanished too quickly for the mines to react and
blow.
     The fifteen Capture Landers they left behind scattered,
each going for its target mine; they were armored by their
size (too small to trigger the mines) and ten of the fifteen
were augmented by the sneakiest and widest ranging detects the tracer ops had been able to talk Digby into pro-
viding.
     The tiny Landers scooted up to the mines, snagged
them in monofilament capture nets and slung them in
tight circles, releasing them at just the right moment to
sent them flying inward, picking up momentum and speed
as they went, sliding toward the Hole. Mechanical davids
using goliath's own weapons against him.
     Within moments they'd cleared a wide section of the
minefield and were nosing about to see what other traps
Ginny Seyirshi and the Holeboss had laid for them.
     The thirteen transports surfaced again and surged for-
ward, crowding into that gap, heading inward.
     A stingship broke from its patrol-orbit and came dart-
ing toward them, spitting its stings at them, missiles like
shot the size of a man's fist.
     The transports withdrew.
     The Landers scattered—and blew and blew and blew
as the tiny stings scythed through them.

8

At the Hole
     They stepped into gravity as they left the lock, .8
Norm. Much more comfortable. And the corridor beyond
was a considerable surprise.
     Tubes of colored light danced down the walls, bright
and joyful, a giggle at the dark encrusted metal they were
fixed to; the floor was lit from beneath. Translucent but

not glass, it gave comfortably underfoot. Bad luck or good, Autumn Rose couldn't tell, but it was obvious they'd hit a major in-out.

And we'd better get off it soonest or before that.

As if he'd read her mind, Kikun turned down a dim little sideway, turned again into a dusty lounge.

Curiosity, get your head down. No talking, not with Ears and EYES here there and everywhere. I suppose it's time for Shadow to do her trick.

Kikun beckoned to Rose.

Right. Guide dog prez-ANT and EEE-gah.

Rohant took Shadow's left arm and Rose held the right one. She felt the girl tremble, then grow tense, then relax and sigh.

"Go," Shadow said, her voice converted to a hollow tenor by the privacy shield. She pushed against them, heading for a wall.

With Rohant's help, Rose turned her toward the door. She resisted a moment, then let them move her. It was awkward, trying to keep step with her, not knowing how she was going to turn next, but behind the shield her eyes were closed and she was listening—or whatever it was she did—so intently she wouldn't know where she was going; she needed them. Guide dogs was right

She took them straight back to the giggle hall.

Autumn Rose wasn't happy with that, nor Rohant, she could tell that by the mutters that came from under his cowl, but what the hell, Shadow was the only one who could find the man, and they went where she took them, like it or not.

9

At the Limit

Lofordys screamed when the Lander beside her flashed and dispersed as dust, her brother dying with it. She ran her claw tips over the sensor pad, adjusting the drives so her Lander hovered in place. Beside her the Op Laaka Vam narrowed the focus of her detects, flashed a schematic on the forescreen showing the flight patterns of the stings.

Another spray of stings came at them, clearly visible as points of light.

"Laaka, get that setting to the other ops." Lofordys worked some more on the board, manipulated two of the tractorbeams into swiveling sweeps, one to each hand, using them as a stickfighter uses his staff though their effect was more limited. "Balyt, help me with this."

With her second in the co seat operating the other two beams, she managed to sweep the missiles aside, brushing them into each other; what one missed the other picked up, Dyslaer reflexes doing the impossible again with the help of Digby's tech.

Lafordys laughed aloud as the stings blew around them but never came close to touching them.

She was still laughing when the cutter beam sliced across the tiny bridge, going through the armor as if it were no stronger than paper tissue.

10

At the Hole

Shadith leaned on the arms holding her and *reached* for Ginny. She couldn't look through his eyes as she could through an animal's, but she knew his FEEL so well, oh yes, knew it so well it nauseated her thinking about it, and touching him was. . . .

She found him, went stiff with loathing, forced herself to relax. Direction was strong. No problem there. She started for him. . . .

They stopped her, tried to turn her. She resisted at first, the pull was strong, so strong. They held her. . . .

What? Oh. Can't walk through walls.

She let them lead her from the room, then took over again, going toward him. He wasn't far . . . less than a kilometer . . . it wasn't long now . . . not long. . . .

Turn. Turn again. Pulled away from the direct line

again and again . . . always back, always going at him
. . . getting closer by the breath . . . closer. . . .

She grunted. Shook to her nerves. Burst of hot hot rage
like lava erupting.

*What? Ah . . . I know. I know what that is. The
ships. They're attacking and he's having connip-
tions . . . go, Hannys, go, Zarovan, all of you,
you're getting to him. . . .*

She pulled herself together and started on.

11

At the Limit
    Helyorst and Vitorias went after one last mine; they
whirled it round and slung it at the Hole and when they
finished found themselves separated from the others and
watching their cousins die.
    They wept for their dead, but worked at the problem
without giving time to their grief. They had no op with
them to augment their detects so there was no chance
they could maneuver in that killing field; it was a limit they had to include in their calculations. Helyorst
rubbed at the pale copper fur on her forearm and frowned
thoughtfully at the stingship.
    Vitorias nodded. "Weakpoint."
    "Lot of clutter around the ship." Helyorst grimaced.
That clutter was mostly the remnants of their kin.
    "Yes. And we're already half behind him."
    "Ram?"
    "That, too. Overload the drive. Hot it up till it blows.
Think we can hold it together?"
    "Can't know till we try."
    "We can go to lifepods. Suicide's not my thing."
    "Sure. Take a darter each, just in case."
    Vitorias clasped wrists with her cousin. "Yes. Just in
case." She broke away. "Let's do it."

##

Preoccupied by the efforts of the Dyslaera in front of it to sweep aside its missiles, picking them off one by one with its cutters, the stingship missed the tiny craft that was drifting behind it, moving slowly slowly, with just a thread of pressure, nearly invisible in the chaos of destruction and death.

##

Leaving the ship on otto-p and their survival to Luck, the two Dyslaerin labored over the drive and the control pad at the coseat, removing safety stops, setting up the timing.

The drive cut out completely as the otto-p reached the stop command.

Helyorst put her tools down, contemplated what she'd done. "It's good as I can make it," she called to her cousin. "You ready?"

"Ready."

They met in the belly of the Lander, clasped wrists again.

Helyorst laughed nervously. "Any last words?"

Vitorias shook her head. "Everything I can think of sounds stupid. Let's just go."

##

The Lander turned in a slow circle, locked onto the stingship.

Relays tripped.

The drive woke and went screaming into overload, slamming the Lander into the podsection an instant before it went nova.

A sudden spreading whiteness ate at emptiness, ate and died.

Helyorst and Vitorias floated tired and contented in their lifepods, watching all this on small grainy screens.

When it was over, they triggered their rescue beacons and waited for someone to notice them.

12

At the hole

Noise behind them. The whine of glide effect, voices.

No crossways at that point, no time to find one, get out of the way.

Rohant pulled Shadith aside, stood against the wall with her.

Reluctantly she dropped her *reach* and blinked her way back to awareness of what was around her. She and the rest of the pseudo-omphalites were lined up against the tubelights as three glidechairs hummed past, the richly dressed clients in them protesting vociferously and blasphemously about being interrupted in the middle of their pleasures; the guards straddling the broomstas murmured soothing responses but kept herding the clients along. Several of them glanced curiously at the dark figures as they rode past, but went on without interfering with them.

Shadith smiled behind the privacy shield. "You were right," she told Autumn Rose. "They didn't bother us."

"More than that, explains why there was no fuss at the lock, all those babies out playing."

Rohant stirred impatiently. "Let's go. How much longer, Shadow?"

"Not long."

13

At the Limit

Anyagyn sighed with relief as she saw the few Landers that survived move away from the battle area and head back toward the Limit. It was time and more than time to get the hell out. The Ciocan had his distraction.

A second stingship came driving out from the Hole.

She threat-grinned at it. "We got one just like you, Tref. Watch your tail. . . ."

Another thread of motion caught her eye. One of the

landers was heading in, not out. She read the tag. Hannys. It would be Hannys. that crossgrained hardheaded. . . . "Gyfallan, get her for me. Hannys, what do you think you're. . . ."

"I think we ought pick up the pair that blew the ship for us, hmm?" Hannys sounded euphoric, riding the kind of high no one was going to haul her down from. "I have them pointed, won't take long."

"Damn! Hannys, there's another stinger heading for us. If you get yourself killed, you. . . ."

No answer.

"Damn that Fefash to Mertaine's lowest rungs. Gyfallan, get after her, we'll have to snatch all three of 'em. Think you can do it before the stinger gets here?"

Gyfallan was too busy to answer for several moments, her clawtips dancing over the pad, her mind working furiously as she balanced the demand for speed with the need for mating with the Lander. Passing control to the kephalos, she sat back, shut her eyes. "Be close, but we'll do it," she said. "We'll just make the Limit ahead of them, they'll singe our tailfeathers some, but we'll drop before they can do more than that."

14

At the Hole

With Shadith going blindly forward, once again locked onto Ginny Seyirshi, the raiders moved in a quiet block through the complex interior of the worldship, circling in and in, getting closer and closer to the Auction Room.

A guard came from a half-lit room, saw them, held up his hand. "Who you? What you doin' here?"

Rohant said nothing, just stood there radiating menace.

The guard got red in the face. "You zulls, you don' ansa me, you. . . ."

Nezrakan came silently behind him, used one thick voluminous sleeve to smother his mouth and killed him with the skinning knife he wore strapped beneath his other sleeve.

"Move it," Kikun said. "Quick. This one was on his own; we're still clear, but. . . ."

Nezrakan nodded. He and his apprentices took the dead man away and left him in a small side chamber with a neglected look that promised no interfering nosybodies, caught up with the rest a moment later and moved placidly along with them.

In and in they went, pulling Shadith repeatedly off the direct path as they took the smaller sideways, but always always winning closer to their Target. Occasionally they attracted curious stares as they moved past clumps of locals—no clients out here, these were dead-eyed mercs and chiggerheads with no place else to go.

The deeper they got, the busier the ways were, people moving in and out of holes in the walls, no one bothering them, no one much interested in who or what they were. Because everyone there—mercs and thieves, smugglers, arms dealers, drug sellers, pseudo-chems, assassins, hangers-on, the sane, the partially sane, the wholly crazy, shapes and shadows—they all had their secrets, their vulnerabilities that they protected, often violently.

When this was a working worldship, there were boutiques in this area, now there were murky secret *places* that sold anything or any service money could buy or the mind could conceive.

The air was thick enough to chew, sweat and pheramone, drugs and body fluids, layer on layer of stench laid down over decades of self-destruction, conspiracy and murder.

15

At the Limit

Helyorst and Vitorias came grinning onto the Bridge, Hannys and Belligys behind them, metaphoric cream dripping from metaphoric whiskers.

Anyagyn inspected them, sniffed. "Your mama raised crazy kits," she said. She looked around. Nodded. The Bridge exploded with whistles and clatter, she came down from the Chair and hugged all four of them and joined the celebration while the ship raced outward, drawing slowly, oh so slowly away from the stinger.

They passed the Limit and dropped into the Insplit.

Safe.

16

At the Hole

In and in they went until they reached a Galleria with rings of railed galleries overlooking what had once been a hanging garden and now was a dank, dark hole. Kikun stopped them before they turned onto the gallery at their level.

"Trouble soon," he murmured to Rohant. "Gaagi says." He used Dyslaer quickspeech. "Shadow. Which way?"

She shook herself loose from Ginny. "What?" When he repeated what he'd said, she sucked in a breath, blew it out. "To the left," she murmured, Dyslaer quickspeech also, let Rohant have his thrill and it might work out, there wouldn't be time for translation if they got this thing rolling right. "And not far." She looked back along the corridor. "About the distance from here to that curve there."

"Guards. How far in, how many, how alert?"

"One minute," She *reached*. "Six. Twenty meters in from the gallery. Maybe. Less than thirty, anyway. On the job. Worst kind. Relaxed and alert. You know how it is, Bossman's eye on you. I don't know the ground, nothing there with eyes I can look through. Ginny's about twenty meters past them." She blinked. "Hang on a minute, I'm picking up something. . . ." She slumped against Rohant, *searched* with all the strength in her. "More . . . not guards, not exactly . . . watchers . . . could be manning screens, something . . . most likely part of Security. How many . . . I don't know . . . I can *read* four separate . . . call it smells . . . but there are more, farther off, can't differentiate . . . can't get at them either. Um . . . others, concentration . . . get the feel of men . . . um . . . working. Cool. Doing something that satisfies them. They're no problem, not right away.'' She straightened. ''That's it, all I can give you.''

Rohant pulled off his gloves. He did it slowly, carefully, making a kind of ritual of it. ''We'll take it straight and slow. Walk like we know what we're doing and got a right to be there.'' He pulled his arm inside the robe, brought out his stunner, clicked it up to lethal. ''Kikun, Shadow, watch them. Let us know when they're about to move. Before they know it themselves, if you can. Nothing fancy, just yell.''

Shadith nodded. ''Yes. I'll do that.''

''Right. We go through them and in. Hard and fast. That's the only way it works with Ginny. Hard and fast.''

They started on again.

17

At the Limit

The thirteen ships turned and went back, surfacing a safe distance outside the Limit.

The stingship waited just inside, buzzing back and forth like an angry wasp.

They waited, watching it, watching the Hole, wondering if they'd done enough, wondering what was happening in there, if the Ciocan and his raiders had reached Ginny Seyirshi yet.

18

At the Hole

Ten dark forms walked along the broad corridor toward the Auction Room.

No one spoke.

Autumn Rose smelled the anger musk rolling off the Dyslaera around her and worried; it was a powerful stink and overwhelmed the perfumes the Holeboss had sprayed about to damp down the primal stench of his lair, catering to the delicate senses of his special clients. The musk reaction was involuntary and a dead giveaway if Ginny had known about the trait and included sniffoons in his defense mix.

When she thought about it some more, she stopped worrying. They'd have been blown away by now if he had. *Sense dead cousins.* Gyorsly said that before they got her into the ottodoc. *Silly Rose, talking and talking and talking to let me know it was her coming when she was tagged before she spoke.* She said that, too. We're eye and ear people, Autumn Rose thought, nose just there to decorate the middle of the face. Ginny, too, bless his li'l blind spot.

They marched round a curve into newly painted antechamber with woven grass mats on the floor and metal benches scattered about, heaped with bright pillows of silk velvet and avrishum.

The guard were there, six of them, relaxed and alert, lounging about an ogeed opening leading into the Auction Room. *Shadow called it right. Tough lot, not liking us much, but not ready to shoot, not quite yet, we might might might be clients. Here comes the lotboss. All right all right, every step we get from now on is a bonus. . . .*

Stunrifle held with deceptive casualness under his right arm (where he could get it up and working in half a breath), the merc strolled toward them. "Now, friends, you know better. The room's not ready yet, just turn yourselves around and come back tomorrow."

Shadow yelled and shot him.

The others went down before he hit the floor.

An alarm started yelping.

The instant Shadow yelled, Azram got his arms around one of the metal benches and charged the opening, getting there before the metal doors could slide shut. He dropped the bench on the slide tracks and went plunging through as the doors kept trying to shut, whining and slamming repeatedly at the bench.

Shadow jumped the dead and went running after him.

Lissorn went screaming past her, tearing off his cowl, clawing out of the robe. He'd forgotten everything but Ginny.

Autumn Rose swore and ran after him, went down as

she tripped over a dead guard, stayed down as the Dys-laerors stampeded over her.

Rohant roared his own rage as he got stuck temporarily in the gradually narrowing space between the doors as they beat at and crushed the bench between them. He freed himself and plunged inside.

Rose rolled onto her knees.

A hand grabbed her ankle.

She twisted around, shot along her leg, swore again as she hit her own foot as well as the guard.

She pushed onto her feet, went limping to the door. She crawled over the bench, swung herself inside, her leg dead from the knee down.

Lissorn was racing toward Ginny, stunner forgotten, claws out. He was only a few steps away, but the little man wasn't moving; he stood watching unperturbed near the front rank of the pulochairs. It seemed to Autumn Rose he was more interested in the degree of his attack-er's rage than in any danger to himself. Directing his own death? Ginny Seyirshi's last and best?

No.

He raised a hand.

Four cutters flashed from overlooks, hit Lissorn in mid-stride.

For an instant the Dyslaeor was a black core in the furnace where the beams met, then they winked out ant there was nothing left, not even dust.

Rohant roared, his great voice filling that room. He lifted his stunpistol.

The other Dyslaerors spread in a broad arc converging on Ginny.

Shadow stood at the edge of the bidfloor, staring at Ginny.

He turned, nodded at her, started to lift his hand. . . .

Autumn Rose shivered, touched her head. . . .

A hand closed on her arm, small, warm. . . .

Pulled at her . . . no . . . she couldn't move. . . .

Oppression . . . her head, her head. . . .

Hard to breathe . . .

Things moving slow . . . ly . . . slooow . . . ly . . .
slooow. . . .

Blackness. . . .

Nothing. . . .

19

At the Limit

A bidder's ship left the parking orbit, fled around the
sun. Another went, another and another. Then no more.
The Hole hung in the darkness, silent, enigmatic.

The watchers wondered. Who was in those ships? Why
were they leaving? What happened to the Ciocan?

More time passed.

Nothing happened . . . nothing . . . nothing. . . .

The Hole went Nova.

Shadith woke in the hold of a ship.

She was lying on a pallet, canvas, something like that. Naked. Half frozen.

Sometime before . . . while she was out . . . she'd been beaten . . . and . . . yes, raped . . . brutally . . . she was torn, septic, she could feel the heat of the infections, the blood oozing from the wounds.

She lay in filth and stench, she hadn't been catheterized, just left where they threw her.

She'd been fed, watered, there were tubes taped to her face, running into her nose.

They wanted her alive, but broken.

They. Who?

Ginny?

She shifted position slightly, felt feces squishing under her. When she had her stomach in order, she looked around.

Stasis pods, dozens of them, all around her.

She *reached*.

The lifesparks in those pods were dim; most of them she couldn't recognize, but Rohant was there, nearest her. Azram. Tolmant. Nezrakam. Kinefray. Tejnar. Ginny.

Ginny?

She looked more closely at the strangers, picked up a faintly familiar "smell," connected it to one of those clients she'd watched glide past her when she was in that corridor.

Ginny and his clients. Prisoners?

What's happening here?

Prisoners or passengers?

Ginny wouldn't tolerate stasistime. I know him. This isn't his ship. He wouldn't take any other. I know him.

Prisoner. It has to be prisoner.

Who?

Never mind. Time for that later.

Her hands were fettered, but she had a little play in the filament that joined the cuffs.

Her feet were free.

She rolled off the pallet, used her feet to push it aside, then drew herself up so her hands were close to her nose.

She pulled the tubes free.

It was painful, sickening, but she got them out.

She used the water tube to wash herself.

It took a long time, but she managed to get her body reasonably clean.

She was cold, half frozen, the chill from the metal she lay on struck up through her flesh into her bones, but she was clean.

Using her feet, she got the pallet turned over, the bottom side was filthy and stained, but hospital hygienic compared to the mess she'd been lying in.

She clamped her teeth on the water tube, used her feet and knees to find the food drip and maneuver it into her mouth, then she slid the pallet over and stretched out on it. It was warmer and softer than the floor, not much, but enough. She sucked on the food tube and began to feel almost human.

Kikun she thought suddenly. I didn't *touch* him. Or Rose. Dead? Or what?

She went painstakingly around the hold once more, *touching* each of the lifesparks. They were all there, except Lissorn who was dead. Ginny was there. His clients. And this time she located Ajeri the Pilot. All there but Kikun. And Autumn Rose.

He slipped them.

Clever little Lizard. Took Rose with him. I hope. Unless she's dead as Lissorn.

He'll come after us, I know it. Yes.

All right.

They mean to break me any way they can.

Let them try.

DAW

DAW Presents the Fantastic Realms of

JO CLAYTON

DAW

Exciting Visions of the Future!

W. Michael Gear

DAW

Another Part of the Universe

J. BRIAN CLARKE
☐ THE EXPEDITER   (UE2409—$3.95)
For humans, first contact was the fulfillment of a dream—to the
alien Phuili, it betrayed all the laws of the cosmos. For the
Phuili refused to admit there could be more than one sentient
race in the universe. Yet a shaky alliance was forced on the
two races when they encountered the Silvers, a dread beserker
race sworn to destroy all other life forms. . . .

FRANK A. JAVOR
☐ SCOR-STING   (UE2421—$3.95)
His name is Pike, and he is a free-lance photojournalist in
an age when media communication is strictly controlled. Called
upon for aid by comrades from his military past, Pike finds
himself on a planet hostile to human life, where the most
important discovery to the future of the human race *may* lie
hidden among storm-swept desert dunes. Is it real—or is it just
a scam? Either way, it could be worth Pike's life to find out. . . .

IAN WALLACE
☐ MEGALOMANIA   (UE2351—$3.75)
A galactic jet of destruction was the force Dino Trigg chose to
take revenge on his mentor, Croyd, the leader of Sol Galaxy,
after failing to overthrow him by political means. Trigg swore
he'd have his revenge, not only upon Croyd but upon all the
civilized worlds. And, unless Croyd found a way to stop him, he
would fashion a doomsday weapon from the Magellanic Clouds
that would not only form a new galaxy for him to rule, but would
release a deadly stream of energy aimed right for the heart of
Sol Galaxy!